Love, Liana...

SINCERELY, KADE

Allie Doherty

First published in the United States of America April 2022 by Lake Country Press & Reviews

Cataloging-in-Publication Data is on file with the Library of Congress.

Publisher website: https://www.lakecountrypress.com

Proofreading: Samantha Costanilla

Cover: We've Got You Covered Book Designs

Formatting: Dawn Lucous of Yours Truly Book Services

For all those who believe in the magic of Rom-coms. Never settle for less than the movie-love you deserve.
Also...
Look, Mam! I wrote a book. Eek! *waves*

AUTHOR'S NOTE

Hi my lovely readers! Thank you so much for picking up my book. I appreciate you and I hope you're having the amazing day you deserve. To keep your day going great, I want to have a little chat before you jump into the love story of Liana and Kade. This book will take you on a romantic, hilarious, ecstatic, and (sometimes) sad, journey. To ensure you have a pleasurable reading experience that is good for your heart, and your head, I would like to make you aware of some potentially triggering themes in this book. This way, you can make an informed decision if this book is safe for you to enjoy.

(May contain spoilers)

This novel contains:

- Alcohol use.
- Explicit sexual scenes.
- Mentions domestic abuse of a side character.
  (Though never shown, it does contain depictions of resulting injuries.)
- Mentions loss of a parent.

- Explicit language. Mainly, use of the 'F' word.
- Mental health journey of a main character.

Chapter 1

Liana

Oh, not again! My eyes collided with the clock standing on my frosted glass desk reading 8 a.m. and I discovered, for the third time this week, I'd been up all night. I lifted my head from my work and saw the sun peeking out over the steely clouds of the Manhattan sky, a stream of light mocking me through the crack in the sheer white curtains of my Upper West Side apartment.

My body ached in an all-too-familiar way; the sweet twinge that came with being hunched over a keyboard for ten hours. With a soft groan, I stretched like a cat in my desk chair, the bones in my back cracking and screaming at the first sign of movement.

Across the room, past the plush white sofa, I saw the door to my bedroom standing ajar; showing the edge of my fully made bed, taunting me with its ruffles and throw pillows like a painted whore. *If only I had time...*

My hand moved to my mouse and double-clicked on the email that had kept me up for the better part of three days. Rereading it for the ninetieth time, it continued to stump me. Never, in all my time as a romance-advice-blogger, had I encountered such an... *ass*. Though I admit, he was an

1

intriguing ass. A man named Kade with a fascinating complex: an egotism he felt inferior about. And, to top it all off, he didn't believe in love. *How cliché of a bachelor to say*? To me, it sounded like an excuse to sleep with every woman he could from Manhattan to Jersey, and back again.

Dear Liana,

I'm a busy man approaching my thirties and find myself tired of endless one-night-stands—brief interludes of two-hour sessions twice a week with women I meet at a bar near my office...'

He considered two hours brief interludes. I didn't know whether to scoff or be impressed. In the end, I went with skeptical. In my experience, no way sex *could* last that long. Bile lurched up my esophagus at the thought of my two-pump ex, Ronnie, and I once again questioned the lapse in judgement that led me to him. He wasn't a bad guy, but a selfish son of a bitch in bed, who only ever took.

I shivered and continued reading.

'The women are like me: high-pressured, fast-paced, workaholic-types looking to let off steam. But I've found myself in more than one sticky situation where they couldn't let me go.

Not that I blame them. I'm a pretty impressive guy.'

There's that confidence. Not for the first time, I rolled my eyes at his words.

'But letting them down easy isn't as 'easy' as I'd like, and though I don't like hurting people, I'd be lying if I said I was nice about it. My best friend, Stephanie, calls me cold-hearted, but I'm not sure I am. I think I'm... different.

Different—synonymous with asshole, apparently.

Lately, I'm surprised to find I've been pondering the mechanics of relationships. Once or twice, I've caught myself daydreaming about how I'd be as a boyfriend, a husband, and even as a father. I don't think I'd be good at any of it, but that hasn't stopped me looking at the women in the bar with more interest—searching for qualities in them that might work well with me long-term.

Unfortunately, every woman I've come across as of late has been so boring, I've considered, on over one occasion, diluting my whiskey with a shot of arsenic.'

I loved that part. The snort that ripped from my nose was an inhuman mix of a bear and a moose. I'd been there. Every date since Ronnie had been mediocre—forgettable, really. A blur of thirty guys who all looked the same, spouted the same cheesy lines, liked the same six TV shows, and bragged about how they understood women, *but didn't.*

'My problem: I hear sonnets about fireworks and butterflies, songs about hearts racing and kisses that make knees quiver, but I've never understood, nor experienced, such a kiss. I've never had flutters in my stomach or felt fireworks from a touch. I'm not sure I understand what love is, or how a person could fall into feeling it. I've never loved anyone or anything. Even Stephanie—I'm not sure I love her, rather I've become accustomed to having her around.

Maybe there's something wrong with me. My last therapist muttered something about impulse control issues and 'prescribed' meditative breathing exercises, as if I don't know how to fucking breathe after twenty-nine years of doing it daily.

I quit therapy there and then, leaving me to seek out answers in unlikely places.

And so, I turn to you, Liana, and ask: If love exists, is it something that can be taught?

(P.S. Do you have any tips on impulse control exercises that

*don't involve sitting cross-legged with my eyes closed and humming
like a damn bird?)*

I await your answer with anticipation.
Sincerely, Kade.'

I, too, awaited my answer with anticipation. Despite being able to recite his email from memory, I had nada when it came to being able to help him. I wasn't even sure I wanted to. He seemed like any other bachelor having a mid-life crisis at the thought of growing old alone after pissing away his time in the clutches of sex. He didn't need love advice; he needed a car shaped like a penis and a beach house in Malibu.

The door behind me swung open, and I jumped, remembering I had a roommate. Kit giggled, seeing me there—my hair piled atop my head like Cindy Lou from *The Grinch*—and rolled her eyes.

"Up all night?" she teased, narrowing her dark brown eyes with a perfectly manicured hand on her hip. The white line of where an engagement ring used to be stuck out like a sore thumb against her semi-tan skin. "Why are you such a vampire?"

I ignored her remark. "My readers are up early today."

Her shoulders shrugged. "So? Give 'em something to read."

She didn't get it. It wasn't as easy as throwing out any advice. I had a reputation to uphold. Grumbling a response, I slammed my laptop shut—the noise sent a shockwave through my brain that made me wince.

"Tapped out?" Kit moved through our open plan apartment to the wall-mounted mirror in the hallway and flattened her sleek black hair with one hand as she applied her lipstick with the other.

I nodded. "Completely, and I'm yet to respond to the email I got Friday night." I half-whispered the last part, hoping she wouldn't hear me. Her eyes widened and the heat of shame rose on my cheeks. Even on my worst days, riddled with writer's block and menstrual cramps, never had it taken me so long.

"*The Kade guy*?" Kit, already in her pantsuit and ready to take on the world, whirled on me. "What about your one-day guarantee? That can be deemed false advertising."

I groaned, not in the mood to hear the ins and outs of PR and advertising again. "Kit, can you not be ad girl right now, and just be my sister? I'm freaking out as it is without stressing about the guarantee. Two days of trying to think of something to say to him, and all I've got is a migraine."

Kit sprayed her wrists and neck with her favorite designer perfume. My nose wrinkled, inhaling the smell of hyacinth, eucalyptus, and a faint tinge of dollar bills. Sometimes it was easy to forget I was the eldest sister. It wasn't that Kit *looked* older than me; it was that she possessed a more mature vibe. One that told the world *she* would never be caught in her pajamas at three o'clock on a Wednesday, eating Nutella out of the jar with a spoon…

She made her way over to our modern black and white kitchen and performed the magic of coffee-making with an annoying amount of perk. I hoped making the coffee would distract her from asking the dreaded question I knew was on the tip of her tongue. "You have the bookstore thing today, right?"

No such luck.

My chest inflated and concaved as I heaved out a sigh. "Yes, I am dipping my toes in the ocean of public speaking, even though the thought makes me want to hurl."

"You know, it's not as bad as you think it is. I *loved* my time as an actress in high school." Kit beamed, pouring black liquid into two cups, and adding creamer to mine. "I brought a depth to Sandy that Olivia Newton-John herself would call a miracle. If I wasn't so good at my job, I would be famous by now."

As she mentioned her job, my eyes collided with the ID

card swinging from around Kit's neck—the one that told the world she was a big deal—and the familiar surge of sickening failure and doubt creeped in, the same way they did every day since I quit my job.

"What if I made a mistake going out on my own? There's not a huge market for freelance romantic advice columnists. At least at *Liberty* I had a following... and a wage."

Kit's eyes softened. "Lee, that sinking ship of a magazine was beneath you. You weren't happy there. Your boss was a pig, and the whole environment was so overrun with testosterone, it was a pubic hair away from being a giant testicle."

"I know, but—"

Kit held up her hand, cutting me off. "You deserve better than that. I mean, sure, your office was really, *really* nice, the perks were *great*, and oh my god, *the money*... Wait, what was I saying?"

"I deserve better?"

"And don't you forget it." Kit grinned, putting her perfectly straight teeth on show. "Lee, nobody knows more about love than you."

Ironic, considering I was one set of granny panties away from becoming Bridget Jones, but she was right. The undergraduate degree I held in psychology and my staunch belief in love made me uniquely qualified to offer advice on romance and relationships. I was damn good at it, too! But going out on my own had a price that I wasn't earning enough to cover.

"I'm not getting enough traffic on the site to pay my half of the rent," I said as Kit slid my favorite elephant mug onto my desk, brimming with caffeine. "It's not fair of me to rely on you."

"I have a solution for that, but you may not like it," she said, with a sly upturn of her lips.

My eyebrow lifted. "What is it?" I asked, bringing the rim of my coffee mug to my lips, and inhaling the deep scent of burnt, bean-roasted energy.

Kit squirmed under my stare and my nerves jolted, putting me on edge. I squinted my eyes. "*Kit*?"

The upturn of her mouth strained, forced into a smile against its will. "Don't worry about it. Go get ready for your appearance, and by the time you get home tonight, I will reveal all. And who knows? With any luck, you'll be gaining fans as fast as I gained new purses in Italy last year."

I pouted, recalling the memories of succulent carbs and gelato, garlic, and pesto... and the fun I had, carefree in *le strade di Roma* once a year for the last decade. But not this year. I sighed. "I should've gone to Italy one more time while I could afford it."

Mug in hand, I stood from my desk chair for the first time in almost ten hours. My legs wobbled under me, but I managed to stay upright long enough to walk off the pins and needles without them giving out.

I opted to use Kit's bathroom, knowing using mine would require the strength to bypass my bed without crawling in it. I headed in the direction of her bedroom and through her open door; stopping for a moment to feel the squidge of her fluffy, white carpet between my toes, and marvel at how organized she was—*and wasn't*—at the same time.

A neat freak by nature, Kit's room was always spotless with nary a dust particle in the air. The white wooden surfaces of her desk and wardrobes were gleaming, the books on her shelf were arranged by color, and every item of clothing she owned —despite being housed in built-in wardrobes—lived in its own crease-free bag like private apartments. Her desktop, rarely used, was polished so much the screen shined, and the gray-painted walls were regularly washed down with a cloth and water spurted from the rose pink glass spray bottle that sat on her desk like a pretty ornament.

Nothing was out of place, which made it all the weirder how she left her comforter heaped in the middle of her unmade bed.

My spine tingled as I fidgeted on the spot, clamoring to make it. I almost did, stopped only by the realization of my hypocrisy. My room was a perpetual bombsite. Books collected dust in every nook and on every wooden shelf, paper notes, crinkled into tiny basketballs, were dunked in places even I couldn't find, and heaps of makeup products were scattered on my vanity—despite having ample number of cases to pack it all into. And, to put the cherry on top of the sloppy cake, all shoes, sneakers, and hell, even my extremely-comfortable-despite-being-ugly-as-shit Crocs, were piled up in one messy mountain in the corner. I was as opposite of neat as a person could be, but Kit's habit of kicking the sheets to one side and leaving them —*shudder*.

Forcing myself to move past it, I pushed the door to her bathroom open and flicked the light switch. The six spotlights beamed down on me, too bright for my delicate, sleepless eyes. I hissed, looking at the ground until they adapted. It took a few seconds before I could look up, and when I did, my mouth gaped, seeing the renovations Kit had made to the bathroom since moving in. Before Kit, the bathroom was plain and uninteresting. Now, the moss green tiles decorating the walls sparkled at me with subtle specks of glitter. The dark stone floors, partially covered with two plush bathmats were somehow warm as I made my way across them, and... *her bathtub!* I gasped.

The beautiful, freestanding ceramic tub with built-in jets stood proud in the middle of the room, flaunting its magnificence over the less attractive amenities. I was awash with jealousy, picturing my bathroom's basic plastic tub. I itched to slide down into the ceramic haven and let the jets massage the kinks out of my back, but I didn't have time. Instead, I headed for the shower, hoping a minute under ice-cold water would jolt my body awake.

Fiddling with the nozzles, I found the perfect pressure and braced myself. The tumbling water hit the base of her shower like hailstone hits the ground, so hard I expected the floor to dent. Before I could talk myself out of it, I stripped off and stepped under the cascade and suppressed a scream as the water stung my skin like mosquito bites, leaving welts of red in its wake.

As quick as I stepped in, I stepped out. My heart pounded and my adrenaline soared—spurred on by the sub-zero temperature of the water, but the thought of addressing a crowd made my body feel heavy and exhausted again. I sighed, grabbing a towel from the heated rack on the right, and moved in front of the mirror. On the left side of her double sink, Kit's hair section: a shelf of products and styling tools all wrapped up so neatly, it was like an episode of *The Home Edit* swept through the place. I grasped a can of dry shampoo and popped the lid. Getting to work, I unleashed my hair from the tangled updo it had been in for two days. The tightness in my head relieved as my hair ran all the way down my body, tickling my skin, and landed an inch above my navel. It was long-overdue for a cut, but the thought of yet another thing in my life changing made me want to cling to every strand on my head.

Pressing down on the can, I sprayed until my hair looked almost freshly washed, and brushed it through, wincing at every knot—and there were a *lot* of them. I scraped my hands through my thick locks and held my hair in one hand, wrapping the hair tie on my opposite wrist around it three times. When I was sure it was tight enough, I sprang back upright and reveled in the dizzy feeling that accompanied the movement. The long ponytail was frizzy and messy, with finger-raked bumps in the front, but somehow, it looked better than it did when I took great care to make it perfect. *I tamed the great Aslan.*

I breathed out and stared at myself in the mirror. I frowned. The cold water did nothing to banish the bags underlining my eyes. With no other option, I got to work covering them with concealer and heavy amounts of gold and brown eyeshadow to take the focus off. Honestly, I wasn't convinced any amount of make-up would help me. My skin took the form of an aggressive tomato, my eyebrows were overgrown crops on my face, and a bout of stress-acne claimed my chin as home. *If only it paid rent.*

"Crackheads look more alert than I do," I muttered to my reflection.

I dropped my towel and looked down at my body. It wasn't a model body, by Instagram's standards, but it was pretty great if you asked me. In fact, it was pure luck I looked as good as I did with a diet of coffee, carbs, and nothing green. And a workout plan that said, "not today, but *maybe* tomorrow." (I even owned a T-shirt with those words to live by printed on it.) My stomach, semi-flat on the good days, couldn't be called toned but nor would I want to be. I loved that my legs and butt jiggled when I moved, my thighs kissed when I walked, and my breasts—*chef's kiss.*

My one insecurity: A love-hate relationship with the length of my legs—they looked amazing in skirts, shorts, and dresses, but in certain high-waisted jeans, I could cosplay as a trendy praying mantis.

I finished up with a touch of cherry lip gloss, careful not to smudge, and tinted my eyelashes with the black wax until they reached so high, they'd be sure to smear on my glasses.

Finished, I poked my head out of her bedroom door, surprised to find Kit still home. In the kitchen with her eyes glued to her phone screen, she took a deep breath and huffed. *Why was she hanging around?* She was usually the first in the office.

I'd have to be stealthy. Kit would have a bitch-fit if she saw my fully-made face. Using her bathroom was one thing but daring to touch her makeup... *a death wish.* Clear to run, I left her room and rushed to my own before she could chew my ass for using her products. I almost lost my balance on my way, but by the grace of God, stayed vertical long enough to make it into my room and shut my door before I landed with a slap on my hands and knees.

I pulled myself up on my bed, grazing the sheets as I went. *So soft. So tempting.*

Letting out a whimper, I headed for my closet—which was relatively bare since most of my everyday clothing lived on what I liked to call my *floordrobe.* Only the 'need to impress' outfits stayed on the hanger. I rifled through the selection, emerging with a black, knee-length tulle skirt, and a white, silk T-shirt. Elegant, but trendy.

Dropping the towel, I fished out some of my prettier under-garments—for the extra confidence boost—and got dressed. I tucked the shirt into my skirt and finished the look with a pastel pink blazer, and a pair of black, calf-high boots that laced up in the front. Very Carrie Bradshaw.

"*Whoa!*" Kit exclaimed as I emerged from my room. "You're speaking to a few people in a bookstore, not walking the red carpet at Fashion Week."

"Is it too much?" I fidgeted in the clothes. They were itching against my skin, almost as if they knew they didn't belong on me anymore. "The shirt was on sale."

"I can't tell. Do you *feel* overdressed?"

I thought about it. "No. These people are coming to see me. I think I at least owe it to them to make an effort, right?" I left out the part about how my outfit would most likely be the most impressive thing about the speech I was yet to write.

"Then you're good to go." Kit gave me the thumbs up. "I'll get you a car..." She pulled up an app on her phone and pressed a couple of buttons. "Six minutes out."

Time was ticking on. By the time my car arrived, it would already be nine-thirty, leaving me only ten minutes to get to Minnie's bookstore on 79th and 5th, which in rush hour was cutting it fine.

Anxiety chomped at me as I envisioned being late to my first public appearance. I squirmed on the spot, unable to stay still, nausea swelling in my stomach. I was freaking out, which seemed as perfect a time as any for Kit to drop a bomb.

"Dad called while you were in the shower."

My eyes widened. I stopped moving, my head whipping in her direction. "What does *he* want now?"

"*Us.*" She scoffed, sucking her teeth. "He's determined to be the Kris Jenner of the talent agency world and, apparently, having two prominent daughters who won't speak to him is bad for that image... He offered me a job."

I snorted. "Of course, he did." I'd had three offers in a month, not including a snide bid to buy my blog, which I could only guess was my father's attempt at derision, said with a condescending smirk. But no matter how desperate I got; Eric Dawson wasn't even on the list of last resorts. *I'd rather sell feet pics online.* (*Perhaps I should invest in a pedicure, just in case.*) "Was it at least good?"

"I got a full verse of lots of money and my own department with a chorus of, '*at least forsaking your fiancé would be worth something,*' which he's not wrong about. Mark dumped me because I chose my job over him. I don't regret it, but I'm busting my ass every day and I'm in the same position I was two years ago." Kit licked at her bottom lip, a nervous habit. "Lee, I —" Her phone chimed in her hand. "Your car is here."

Eek. I grabbed my over-the-shoulder bag from the hook by the door and headed out, giving Kit one quick smile as I went. "We can laugh about Dad's delusion of us working for him ever again when I get home. Wish me luck!"

I was late by a couple minutes—not a good start to the morning.

From outside, the store looked quaint. A tiny hole in the wall I wouldn't have noticed if my old assistant turned social media advisor, Jana, hadn't sent me a photo of the entrance when she'd arrived. The door was down three little steps and looked more like a hobbit hole than a door. I opened it and it gave a loud ding that didn't stop until I passed the threshold and let it close.

Once I got inside, the store's Tardis-like charm surprised me. There wasn't an enormous amount of space, but a *lot* more than I thought at first glance, and every inch was purposeful. The bookcases stood as high as the ceiling, pushed back to the walls, which created an open space for the shoppers to peruse and have a coffee at the café bar in the middle of the room. Between the cases, deep alcoves with comfortable beanbags and overhead lights, acting as multiple reading nooks. And, to the back of the store, a small stage where I assumed I would stand to give my talk. In front of it, an abundance of people muttering my name.

Gulp.

A small-ish, old woman with a stern look on her face stepped up to me and sighed. "You're late. I don't take kindly to having my day delayed. Follow me."

Taken aback at her brash tone, I blinked twice before obeying her command and had to catch up with her bobbing head as her little legs moved faster than I expected. Minnie, I assumed, led me behind the till counter, through a black wooden door, and into what looked to be a stock room. Books were everywhere, stacked up in boxes, most of them unopened. My interest piqued at the thought of new releases, awaiting prying eyes. I tingled with the desire to rip into them and move into a nook full-time, but Minnie's sour face as she caught me ogling told me to not bother asking. Continuing, she led me to the other end of the stock room where another door stood slightly ajar.

Minnie stopped, ushering me in front of her. I stopped, too, unsure what she wanted me to do.

"The door sticks," she said, as though it should have been obvious. "Unless you wish to see a frail old lady break a wrist tugging it open? Are you sadistic, dear?"

My eyes widened. "I— no," I said, and moved to pull it open. It squeaked against the floor. "Sorry."

Minnie rolled her eyes and huffed. "Stay here until I announce you out front."

Satisfied I'd arrived at my destination, she turned on her heel and moved back through the stock room, leaving me in the makeshift waiting area behind the stage.

The room had cream walls, a concrete floor, and stood completely bare; aside from a couple chairs and an espresso machine that had seen better days. I moved past it, holding my breath. Not one to pass up free coffee, it shocked me to find the smell made me sick. But then again, that could've been the noise of the crowd whooping as Minnie started her introduction speech making my stomach twirl. I swallowed hard and tried to keep the nausea at bay.

I was so lost in my nerves; I didn't see Jana until her hand on my arm made me jump.

"Oh good, you're here," she said, relieved. "I thought you'd bailed, and I wasn't sure Minnie would let me out alive if you had." Her tone suggested she was joking, but the chips in her long, matte-black nails told me she'd been chomping at them with nerves.

I didn't blame her for questioning me. I would have bailed if not for Jana. The effort she'd put into arranging the meet-

and-greet made it impossible to leave her hanging. She'd used hashtags, geotags, Instagram Stories, Twitter ads, and she'd even capitalized on the irrational fear of missing out a lot of people seemed to have. The result: crowds of people... all there to see me.

Oh God.

"Ready?" Jana asked, her high cheekbones protruding through her skin as a smile widened on her blemish-free face. She brushed another finger through her pink side bang and straightened her glasses. Behind them, her crystal clear blue eyes shone with excitement. Lifting her phone camera, she pointed it at my face. "I'm going to scan the crowd first. When the applause dies down, you flash them your dazzling smile and start your welcome speech, moving swiftly into the Q and A. Keep it brief, ten questions max before snapping a few pictures with fans. Then, we get the hell out of dodge before the mean-mouse, Minnie, kills us both. Got it?"

Not giving me a chance to argue, Jana ushered me up three steps, through a black curtain, and pushed me out onto the stage. I froze, my legs refusing to move me to the podium. It took Jana ramming my body in front of the crowd for me to get where I needed to be.

I forced a smile as the crowd went wild, and Jana gave her a countdown with her fingers. *Three. Two. One.*

Action.

CHAPTER 2

KADE

"I saw your date of the day as she ran past me in the hallway." My roommate, Stephanie, stood by my bedroom door massaging rose-scented moisturizer into her flawless dark skin. Her hair was magenta this month, tied on the top of her head in a tight braided knot. I always wondered how she didn't suffer from headaches with her hair that high and tight. She smirked. "I think she thought I was your girlfriend about to catch you in the act. She had that deer in headlights look."

"They all think you're my girlfriend, Steph." I laughed. Shaking my fresh-from-the-shower-and-soaking-wet head, I stood from my bed and pulled my favorite blue jeans over my legs. Stephanie threw me a fresh towel from the hallway closet that I caught with one hand. I rubbed at my hair until it dried to an unruly mess of brown, two shades darker than the tan skin I inherited from the man my mother had a torrid affair with on a vacation to Maui in her twenties. "She was pretty though, right?"

She narrowed her emerald eyes into a squint. "Are you asking if *I* thought she was pretty? Or did you drink so much whiskey you genuinely need to know?"

"Ha. Funny. Is that for me?" I pointed to the bottle of water tucked under her arm. "I have serious cotton mouth."

Stephanie nodded, tossing it carelessly at me. It took my hungover reflexes a few seconds to kick-in and the bottle bounced off my chest before landing in my hand.

"*Well*?" I persisted.

"She was beautiful," Steph admitted. "Are you going to call this one back?"

"Why would I do that?" I scoffed in disbelief as though she'd asked me to slap a nun in church on Sunday, and then spank the priest on my way out for added measure. "It was a one-time thing. But I have her number if you want to take a shot?"

"Oh, gee, thanks." She snorted. "Not only do I not want your leftovers, buddy, but I'm with Cleo. You know that."

My spine turned rigid. I shrugged, not wanting to get into another argument over Cleo Kilmer—or as I liked to call her, the lovechild of a Banshee and a Mongolian Death Worm, with the attitude of a high school mean girl.

"Get ready, we're late for work," I said, pulling a white dress shirt from where it hung in my wardrobe. Slipping it over my arms, I buttoned it up, sure to leave a little gap at the top for my own vanity. I had my eye on a girl in the coffee store around the corner from my office and hoped a little flash of the chest would get me a bed buddy cute enough to keep the nightmares away.

Steph's lips tilted up and her arms crossed. "You own the place. I think as your best friend and assistant, I'm allowed a few late days."

I almost snorted. *Every day* was a late day for Stephanie.

"Whatever. I'm going in now. We have a ton of submissions to go over. One or two of them may even be bestsellers one day." I feigned hope, but I knew better. Everything I'd gotten lately was lame, romantic drab that would put the world's most boring bastard to sleep. Two people meet, fall in love, nause-ating cute scenes, inevitable break-up scene, proclamation of undying love, requisite happy ever after. *Blah, blah, fucking blah.*

Stephanie read most of the romance novels so that I didn't have to. But when the entire submission pool was littered with them, it became harder to pretend they didn't exist. I couldn't get through them, even if I forced as much of a smile as I was capable of and pretended the world was made of sunshine and unicorns.

But maybe I was being cynical. Maybe today would be a turning point for everything. Maybe tomorrow, I would wake up and crave a romance novel. Maybe I'd be happier...

Yeah, right.

"Don't be over an hour and bring coffee with you. Oh, and don't forget, I need you to work late tonight." I'd switched from friend to boss in under a second.

"Aye, aye, Captain." Stephanie rolled her eyes, lifting her hand to salute me, and left me alone to finish getting dressed. I breathed out relief, finally able do the one thing I'd wanted to do all morning: check my email. But as my eye caught sight of the time on the chrome clock on my chalkboard black wall, I realized I'd have to check it at work.

I grumbled, slipping my shoes on, and moved through my apartment. Grabbing an overcoat from the hook by the front door, I shouted my goodbyes to Stephanie before heading out the door and down to the building lobby. I ventured outside and pulled my coat on as I went, finding a much-needed pair of sunglasses in the pocket to guard my eyes from the after-effects of whiskey. It was warm, but the air threatened a bite that told me summer was over and fall was moving in. I rubbed the palms of my hands together and pushed my hands back into my pockets.

My office was a ten-minute walking distance from my apart-ment, but even that seemed too long. I moved fast, the desperation to check my email growing by the second. When I finally got to the thirty-seventh floor of the high-rise building, I made a direct beeline for my office—ignoring the repeated calls of my name—and locked the dark-wood double-doors behind me. The glare from the ceiling-to-floor windows was so bright, even past my glasses, and made me hiss. I lunged for the blinds, drawing them closed, and plunged my commodious office into darkness before landing with a thud onto my rolling chair.

Attacking the mouse button of my desktop computer like a madman, I waited for the screen to light up. It took too long, and my patience was running out. "Come the fuck on!" I whacked the side of the screen twice before it loaded up. My email was already logged-in, but nothing new waited in my personal inbox aside from a few messages from ex-hookups looking to rekindle. *No thanks. Into the trash they go.*

I checked my email again and again for over an hour but remained disappointed. It'd been a whole two days since I'd been desperate enough to email the *Love, Liana* website and still, I'd seen no response from the advice blog. I pursed my lips and frowned.

Clicking off my email, I made my way back to the site and reread the notice to make sure I read it right the first time. There it was in black and white: Guaranteed next-day reply. *Hmm.*

Gnawing on my cheek, I ground my back molars in frustration—almost to dust.

The site was brought to my attention by the after-sex ramblings of one of my one-night-stands, and I wondered if it would be able to help me understand my emotions. "...Apparently not."

The intercom buzzed me out of my thoughts as Stephanie's melodic voice came through loud and clear. "I'm here, your coffee is here... and there's a woman here to see you."

A woman? I wasn't expecting anyone. Opening my email

again, I clicked the refresh button and contemplated telling whoever she was to get lost, but as I clicked the button one more time and my inbox remained empty, annoyance tingled up my spine, and I relented.

"Send her in."

I unlocked the door and waited in my chair. Loosening my tie, my body flooded with white-hot electricity, surging to my manhood as a gorgeous brunette with hazel eyes entered my office. I recognized her as somebody I'd romanced—*fucked*—before but for the life of me, I couldn't remember her name. *Kaia? Kayla? Kylie?* It was something with a 'K.' We met at an industry party a couple of weeks ago, and I liked waking up to her smile—that was all I could recall.

Last I checked, I hadn't afforded her the golden ticket to my workplace, and a normal man would wonder how she found me. But sex was what I needed to blow off a little steam, and as she wordlessly crossed my office in her sultry stilettos and wrapped her arms around my neck, I asked *no* questions. Her lips crashed to mine with a soft moan as she guided my hand to the zipper of her skirt, above her ass. Smirking against her, I yanked it down and moved my attention to her jawline, nibbling my way down to her chest as the fabric covering her body dropped to the ground. I drunk her in, my eyes landing on lacy red panties that begged to be touched. Pressing my palm against her mound, my middle finger grazed her core through the thin lace, eliciting a delectable moan from her sweet mouth as she ground against my hand. Rousing my cock to half-mast, her right hand found the button of my jeans and wasted no time freeing me from the confines of denim before sliding beneath the elastic waistband of my boxer shorts. Her strawberry perfume filled my nose, too sweet for my liking, as I thrust my left hand into her hair and collided my mouth with hers. Deepening the kiss, I peeled her shirt from her body and caressed her nude back. I flicked my tongue against her lips one last time before moving my mouth down her body as we sunk to the ground.

When it was over, the woman—whose name I still didn't know—purred like a cat on my chest, tracing the shape of the geometric maze tattoo on my right pec.

"That was amazing," she moaned, lifting her head to nibble on my earlobe.

I forced a smile, moving away from her. As far as my track record with sex went, it was lackluster at best. It wasn't her fault though; it was mine. I'd grown distracted, unable to get *Love, Liana* out of my head. *Why hadn't they responded?*

I got to my feet and dragged my jeans over my legs, bouncing into them for the second time that day, before perching myself on the edge of my desk. Staring down at the beautiful woman, I wondered how much longer she intended to stay, and then my mind moved back to the blog. "Do you know anything about an advice blog called *Love, Liana... Katie*?" I took a shot.

"It's Amie. With an 'ie.'" Pushing herself up, she searched out her underwear. "Sure, I've heard of Liana."

I spotted them behind my desk and handed them over. "Who runs the blog?"

Her face contorted with confusion. "I don't understand what you mean?"

"Who runs it? How do I get in touch with one of their writers?"

"There are no writers, silly." Amie giggled, throwing her head back as though it was the funniest thing she'd ever heard. I didn't bother trying to hide the grimace that made its way onto my face. The piercing holler of her hyena calls made my brain tingle.

"Then who writes it?"

"*Liana* writes it."

My eyebrows lifted in surprise. "Liana is a real person?" I thought it was a brand.

"*Duh!*" Amie giggled again. I had a feeling she made the annoying sound often. Restraining myself from rolling my eyes, I hummed in consideration. "She's Eric Dawson's daughter. You know him, right?" She gave a dreamy sigh. "What am I saying? Of course, you know who he is. I bet he's, like, your idol."

Not fucking likely. I gritted my teeth. "No wonder she's having so much success so quickly."

Annoyance burned in my chest. I'd unwittingly sought advice from the daughter of my former mentor, and the man occupying the number two spot on my list of biggest pricks I'd ever met (the first going to myself, of course), *and* I'd been ignored by her. *I bet she and her jackass father were having a great day, laughing it up over how pathetic I was.*

"Oh, she doesn't speak to her father anymore. She wouldn't let him near the blog in a million," Amie said, moving to grab the rest of her clothes. "They fell out like five years back."

Huh. "Interesting. All of this is public knowledge?"

She shook her head. "I'm an assistant to her sister. I hear bits and pieces. Not enough to write a book, but enough to know Liana despises her father. Oh, and this has to stay between us, otherwise, I could lose my job."

With great difficulty, I bit back a snort as she held out her pinky toward me. Bile launched in my throat as her finger wrapped around mine for a juvenile pinky swear. I pursed my lips. *How absurd.* Two minutes ago, I wasn't sure of Amie's name and now we shared secrets. I nodded a promise to keep my mouth shut. But if someone asked me directly, I'd give her up without a second thought because I didn't care enough to lie for her.

Amie slid her skirt over her long legs, and I watched as she dressed. There was something sultry about a woman putting her clothes on after sex. It was the opposite of a striptease, but it had the same hardening effect on me. My arm almost reached out to stop her from leaving so we could go for a second round, but the intrigue of new information beckoned me.

Once Amie was clothed, I escorted her to the building's entrance and said goodbye at the door like a gentleman. She kissed my cheek, lingering for a moment by my ear, and whispered a promise of 'next time.'

I knew better. Seeing a woman a third time was dating—a mistake I didn't intend to make a second time. Never again would I experience the sting of the slap that came with a misunderstanding of casual sex. I shivered, remembering how much it hurt. Women had a special talent for finding the right angle to throw a slap to make sure the crack of skin hitting skin was earsplitting.

I sighed, looking into Amie's expectant gaze. "Amie, I'm not looking for anything serious. You said you weren't either. I'd appreciate it if we parted as acquaintances and remember this liaison for what it was—good sex." Deciding not to stick around to explain further, I turned my back and walked away, the muffled sound of her calling me a prick under her breath in my ear.

Can't say I disagreed.

Back in my office, I sent Stephanie for fresh coffee—earning an extra-dramatic eye-roll—and settled back in front of my computer. I pulled up a search engine and punched in Liana's name and waited a millennium for the results to load. We really needed better internet. A lot of links popped up to different articles, and I chose one at the very top, highlighting the points in her career. My eyes flicked through the results as I read everything I could until I came across a picture of her. I stopped scrolling.

My God, was she beautiful.

In my head, I'd painted an image of an older woman who

looked like her father in a wig. Someone well into their late-thirties or early-forties, seeing as how Eric was nearing seventy himself.

How wrong I'd been. I blinked, taken aback by her breath-taking eyes; lake green outlined with subtle hints of blue and silver. Her cute, button nose scrunched as she gave a million-dollar smile, standing outside a café in Italy with the sun beaming down on her subtly tanned skin. Her mass of unruly red hair hung loose around her dimpled cheeks, and her eyes shone with carefree happiness. I wondered what that felt like, to be so content and relaxed.

The photo cred said it was taken from her Instagram, linked underneath. I clicked on it and scrolled through her feed. There were only a few photos, with big chunks of time between them being posted. But one thing they had in common: They were all taken in different parts of Italy, which told me she visited annually. But not this year...

I sat back, staring at her, and scoffed. *This was the woman knowledgeable in all things romance?* How was that possible when she looked like she'd only left the Girl Scouts a few years back?

Pulling my eyes from her face—with great difficulty—I moved back to the article. Liana was twenty-three; barely more than a young adult. I scoffed, hunching forward, and winced; a nerve pinching in my nearing-thirty back. Disbelief rolled off my tongue in one word: "*Damn.*"

It seemed impossible a person so young could have so much insight. Scrolling up to read the headline of the article I'd clicked on, my amused smile turned into a full-blown grin.

'Love, Liana's' very own Liana Dawson to host a meet-and-greet with fans at a local bookstore.'

The event was scheduled for an hour later at Minnie's, a

bookstore a couple blocks over. I debated for half a second before grabbing my jacket and heading out.

"Hold my calls, Steph. I'll be back soon. Oh, and you can keep the coffee." I ran past the reception desk and out of the office like a man on a serious mission. I wished I could have cut my losses and let it go, but it was too important. I needed answers.

And if Liana wouldn't give me them in emails, then she would have to give me them in person.

~~~~~~~~~~

I stood amidst a rather impressive crowd; all bustled together, talking with the excitement of children on Christmas about how Liana changed their lives in the recent months.

"A total visionary. I divorced my possessive husband because of her." A blonde woman, middle-aged and dressed like a teenager in a cut-off t-shirt and a pleated skirt, beamed. "She gave me the strength to reclaim my youth. Now, I'm dating again for the first time in twenty years. This dating app business—it's a revelation."

"Really? Wow!" A younger woman with sleek black hair chimed in. "I had the opposite experience. My boyfriend asked to marry me, but I was freaking out about the commitment. Liana talked me through my panic attack and made me realize I didn't ever want to lose him." I watched as she thrust her hand out in front of her to show a sizable diamond on her perfectly manicured finger. "We're getting married in two months!"

Her eye caught mine and twinkled with attraction. Of course, she would be attracted. With a thick head of hair, a solid physique and cheekbones that could cut through steel, I was an attractive man. Some would say God-like, even.

I looked away. Her attraction didn't equate sexual desire but even if it did, I refused to go for women with rocks on their fingers. The last time I made that mistake, my nose had been knocked out of place so badly, the damage was permanent. Not that I minded. The crookedness and the scar from the ring the man wore gave me a bad boy look that women seemed to love.

I turned in time to see Liana be pushed in front of the podium. The pictures on the internet hadn't done her justice. She was far more beautiful in person, though a little paler, and a lot more jittery. Her smile was *too* wide, almost as if it were fake. It was a falsity I'd seen on many clients—the smile of a writer who'd never spoken in front of a crowd.

Liana shifted on the balls of her feet and practically shivered. There was something oddly endearing about her awkward disposition, and I couldn't help the tingles that shot through my body every time she bit her bottom lip.

I scolded myself. I wasn't there to ogle; I was there for answers. But as my eyes slid over to the woman behind Liana, my mouth zipped. She was holding up her phone, filming the whole event. I took a step back into the crowd and hid my face behind some guy's head. Her camera made me uncomfortable. The last thing I wanted was to go viral for being the freak who was alien to the concept of love.

"Hey, everyone," Liana finally spoke, and the room erupted into applause. "I'm so thankful to you for coming out to see me! I'm sorry I was late, traffic was—" The camera woman shook her head and Liana gave a cough. "Anyway, um, let's start with a Q and A! Does anybody have anything they need advice on? Or, um..."

Thirty or so hands flew into the air and her cheeks reddened. Her throat bobbed up and down as she swallowed her nerves. The sound echoed through the mic and her blush turned beet red. Wafting her hand at her face, she fanned herself until her cheeks cooled pink, and pointed to a random person in the crowd.

A short woman who looked to be in her thirties stepped forward. "Hi, my name is Julie. I've been following you since your career began at *Liberty*. I'm a big fan of you, and of your father, of course." Liana once again shifted on her feet and her lips pulled down into a frown. "What would you do if you were married and your husband wanted children, but you didn't?"

I flinched. It was a *very* personal question to ask in a crowd of people. The vibe in the room changed, thick with awkward pity. But Liana didn't seem affected. She smiled, her face taking on a professional look of understanding and compassion. Oh, she was *good* at what she did.

Liana nodded. "Well, Julie, I feel like this is an issue usually discussed before the long walk down the aisle."

"It was." Julie looked downcast. Her dark eyes landing on her feet, she heaved a sigh and whispered, "he's since changed his mind."

Liana's eyes softened. "I'm sorry. I can't imagine how heartbreaking it is to wake up and discover you and your partner want different things, especially when it comes to children. Neither of you should feel guilty or have to compromise the image of your life. My advice would be to discuss if those images include each other, and if they don't... maybe it's time you let each other go so you can both be happy."

Essentially, she'd advised a divorce. But the way she said it, with such emotion and care in her voice, made Julie feel heard and happy. I admired her ability to do that. I was way too forward to be able to give somebody advice in that way. If Julie asked me, I would've said the same, but in no-nonsense terms along the lines of, '*fucking leave him, Julie.*'

Next was a rotund man named Sully. He complained of his mother-in-law having too much impact in his and his wife's everyday life. Liana advised a sit-down over food, to discuss boundaries. "...In my experience, nobody can get angry with a really great lasagna and garlic bread in front of them."

A wave of laughter made its way through the room. Of all things intriguing about Liana, the most fascinating was her ability to compel a crowd. It was something I'd never been able to do. Charm a woman? Sure. Command the attention of every person in the room? Not a chance. Most of the time, I left the room feeling like a jackass, and everyone else left thinking I was one. If I wasn't so great at turning manuscripts into paper in more ways than one, I'd be a broke failure for my attitude alone.

A fundamental issue of my personality: I found it hard to give a fuck. Another reason I needed Liana's help.

"Any more questions?" Liana asked.

"What about sex?" Came a floating voice from the back of the crowd.

My interest is piqued. I watched Liana's cheeks flush and her fabricated confidence falter. She wasn't comfortable with the topic of sex. It was obvious, as her eyes darted in every direction; probably in search of the nearest exit.

"What *about* sex?" she choked out.

I sucked my bottom lip into my mouth and bit down, dropping my gaze to the floor. It was all I could do to stop from laughing at her.

The voice moved through the crowd. It belonged to a young-ish man, standing at over six feet tall with thick, circular glasses, dirty blonde hair to his shoulders, and a small recording device attached to his head. He pushed his way to the front, near the stage and looked up at Liana with a scowl. "Your fans have noticed you don't answer our questions when we ask about sex. Instead, you skirt over the sexual stuff and relate everything back to emotion..."

If Liana was flustered before, she was damn near hyperventilating now. "I—uh—To put it simply, I'm a love expert. I focus on keeping the emotions in your relationship alive. What you guys do in the bedroom is up to you." Whispers of discontent spread through the crowd. I blew out a low whistle. The fans weren't happy, and if I could see it, she could see it too.

"However," she cleared her throat and continued, her grip on the sides of the podium tightening so much, her knuckles turned white. "I'm aware sex and love go hand-in-hand, which is why I'm excited to announce a new section of my blog dedicated to answering all of your sex-based questions."

Cheers erupted around her, and the look on her face skipped past anxious and landed on panic-stricken—eyes wide, mouth open, chest heaving, and cheeks the color of sangria.

"When will this new section be available?" The man asked.

Liana went stiff and looked to her camerawoman who gave her a panicked shrug in return. "Two months," she said so fast; if one person coughed, the whole room would've missed it.

The crowd went wild as Liana stood, immobile. Not smiling, not frowning, she swallowed—her already pale skin turning translucent.

She'd been foolish enough to give a date... if it were me that the man approached with such vigor; I would have ignored him, or simply said, "Pipe down, John Lennon. It'll come when it comes." And left it at that. Now, Liana had given herself a deadline... and by the look of terror in her eyes, I guessed she wasn't the type to work well under pressure.

"Okay," the store owner said, ushering Liana swiftly offstage. "That'll be it for today. If you've paid for pictures and autographs, please make an orderly queue. And, *apparently*, to those of you who have yet to receive a response from Liana, as you can see, she's been busy. You'll get it by tonight. Thank you!"

Sated by this information, I resolved to spare myself the agony of standing in line with all the people waiting for autographs. Liana had enough on her plate with her newfound sex section without needing me in her face.

Consideration for others. I smiled. That was a definite check in the right column.

I left the store, deciding I would wait for my response from Liana like someone with patience. And when it came, she would teach me how love works, and then... maybe I could learn to fall in love. That might be nice.

Instead of going back to work, I took a left on Carnegie Hill and headed back to my apartment. The building Steph and I lived in was renowned for its lavish penthouses, owned by celebrities and millionaires alike, but I had never seen them— nor did I care to. We lived on the fourth floor, in an apartment that was spacious, modern, and closer to the high life than I thought we would ever get.

But every time I stepped off the elevator and twisted my keys in the lock, I sighed. The door swung open to show the clean gray and white décor of the open plan apartment. Something I used to dream of as a kid, before I realized dreaming hurt more than it helped. No matter how pretty my apartment was, contentment was out of reach. It was never home.

My laptop sat, open, on the glass table in the living room, waiting for me. Crossing the threshold, I tossed my keys on the side table, and wandered into the kitchen to make microwavable kettle corn. Dumping the toffee-flavored treats into a round, red bowl, I dove onto the leather couch where I spent the rest of the night watching the trash TV Stephanie loved so much, completing work... and refreshing my inbox.

Hours ticked by and I pushed through a lot of submissions but received nothing from Liana. I headed back to her blog— like I had countless times already—and checked her activity. My lips contorted into a tight, thin line, reading comments upon comments from new posters thanking Liana for getting back to them, and others writing how they understood about their late responses. It was clear she'd answered every email but mine.

I groaned. *What the hell did it take to get the guru to respond?* It was obvious that most of her fans were women, but if being a woman was the criteria for Liana, then I needed to accept I wasn't getting a response any time soon because—try as I might —I was fairly sure I couldn't sprout a vagina overnight.

I shrugged my shoulders and hunched back towards the laptop with my fingers laced together. Cracking them, and my neck, I again pulled up Liana's site... and clicked refresh.

Chapter 3

Liana

After the bookstore debacle, I stopped off at a dimly lit dive bar, or—as was more accurate—a Manhattan hipster bar that did its best to look like a dive bar, but with an upscale clientele and floors so polished, they shone like diamonds.

I sat at the bar, on a brand new stool purposely covered in duct tape to appear 'dinged up', drowning my stress in a vat of fruity drinks. I made a bet with myself that I could order every cocktail they had. My brain believed I could do it. My liver disagreed.

On my fourth drink, the bartender placed a blue concoction in front of me. Housed in a small fishbowl, it came with three straws to share, and one sip told me why. It was mostly tequila and packed enough of a punch that it wasn't long before a nice, fuzzy, warm feeling settled in my stomach, and the room started to swirl a little.

It was then my mind moved to Luka DiMaggio, as it so often did when I was drinking. *Oh, what might have been...*

I pushed the thought out of my head, and sucked down the remnants of the blue bowl, as it was so aptly named, enjoying the taste of raspberry and sugar. It went down so easily, I wanted another, but I was on a mission. I pushed on with the list and ordered a Skittles cocktail, hoping this would be the drink that made me forget my dumbass decision to lie to my readers.

Taste the rainbow, the tagline read, but all I could taste was grenadine with subtle hints of vodka.

God, I was stupid for making that damn proclamation. I didn't know the first thing about sex advice.

I moved on, tasting six out of fifteen before the bartender—who'd gotten marginally better looking while I was there—cut me off. Licking my lip, I smiled, thinking maybe he could teach me all the things I needed to know about sex. The tattoos on his arms, and the piercing through his nose, suggested he knew more about it than I did. But as a blonde woman came out from the back room and planted a slow one on his lips, my hopes dashed, and I decided it was time to go home and wallow in self-pity.

I stumbled from the stool and made my way outside to hail a cab. It was dark out, and it surprised me Kit wasn't blowing up my phone, wondering where I was. My hope was that she'd had a long day and gone straight to bed when she got home, but as a cab pulled up curbside and I clambered in the back of it, I got a sinking feeling in my stomach.

The cab rolled to a stop outside my apartment building, and I stepped out; the night air hitting me like a brick, I stumbled back before regaining my balance and headed for the door. The doorman opened it for me with a smile. I returned it as he clicked the elevator button for me.

The metal doors opened with a ding that reminded me of Minnie's store, and I stepped in, feeling queasy as the floor bobbed a little. *Would I have to pay a fine if I vomited in the elevator?*

Thankfully I didn't have to find out. I made it to my floor puke-free and stepped off, trundling down the hall like an inflatable tube man at a car lot, until I came to the end apartment.

I crashed through the door and made a beeline to the kitchen area to uncork a bottle of wine. Pouring two large glasses from the bottle, I smiled. "Portion control. *Good Liana...*"

Taking the glasses in hand, I emptied them down the drain and picked up the bottle before staggering my way to the living area. I took a swig and plopped down on the decadent, white plush sofa. Like everything else of expense in my apartment, Kit bought it when she moved in—and she would kill me if I spilled anything on it.

My brain told me to sit up and be careful, but I was riding the wave of all things good, and my ability to care was quickly becoming a thing of the past. I stretched out, running my fingers over the faux fur throw, and grinned as it brushed my skin, so soft and warm. I took another gulp as exhaustion set it and let my eyes flutter. They were halfway closed when I caught sight of something that made me jolt awake.

There were two suitcases in the corner.

Confused, I pushed myself to my feet and over to the foreign objects. Maybe they were Kit's... But none of Kit's suitcases were as big or as ostentatiously pink as the two in front of me. Lifting the tag, I read the initials. *ZPD.*

"ZPD?" I questioned. *I didn't know any*—I gasped, dropping the tag like it was on fire. I couldn't believe what I was seeing. A surprise solution to the rent issue, Kit said. But this wasn't a solution, it was my worst nightmare.

I sobered up fast, my fuzzy-drunk feelings replaced with white-hot rage, and I took a step back from the suitcases in case they were booby-trapped. It was a juvenile thought, I'll admit, but I wouldn't put anything past Zoe.

Moving through the apartment like a cheetah, I landed in

front of Kit's bedroom door and pounded with a closed fist. "Wake up, Katerina!"

I'd only hammered the door four times before Kit opened it, her expression that of a deer-in-headlights. "Don't freak out," she said, holding up both hands in surrender. "We had a third bedroom sitting empty, and I can't do the rent alone."

I understood her reasoning, and I hated that I put her in that position. *But of all roommates in the world...* "We could have put an ad out on Craigslist, in the paper, or even on goddamn social media."

Kit sighed. "Then we'd be living with a stranger who could be a psycho."

"That'd be better than—" I took a deep breath, trying to calm down. "I will find us a suitable roommate tomorrow, I promise. Get rid of her... *Please.*"

Kit winced, hearing the desperation in my voice, and scrunched her face. "I can't. She already paid half the rent for the next three months. She's got nowhere else to go. Besides... she's our sister."

Hearing Kit use *sister* in reference to my worst enemy was a punch to the gut. In an instant, I was hungover and ready to vomit.

"By blood, maybe," I spat. "But being dad's daughter doesn't make her our sister. It's not like being the offspring of Eric Dawson is an exclusive club. The man has more mistresses than I've had hot showers." I crossed my arms and squared my shoulders. I hadn't been this on edge around Kit since high school. "She can stay until she finds somewhere else, but then she's out... what is she even doing here? Doesn't she have a big house in Westchester somewhere?"

Kit shook her head, her grimace tightening. "Andy left her. He made her move out, they're getting a divorce." As she spoke, her hand instinctively moved to the vacant spot on her ring finger, and I knew why Kit had accepted Zoe's plea so easily.

"I guess Andy is smarter than I remember him being in high school. He should have dumped her then!" I winced, hearing my own voice laced with such venom. I wasn't that person, but the mention of Zoe brought out the worst possible side of me, surprisingly fast.

"Wow. Real nice, Liana," a voice like nails on a chalkboard said behind me. I turned to see Zoe—all four-foot-nine of the snarky blond—and growled. "You know, I could have stayed in a hotel or had daddy buy me a house, but I'm doing *you* a favor. After all, if you worked, I wouldn't be here."

I scoffed. "I work, Zoe. I may not have a steady income yet, but all of your money is Andy's. So unless..."

Zoe's eyes flicked to Kit, who was looking at the ground.

My mouth gaped. "Over my dead body is she staying here on Eric's dime! Kit, come on, it's so obvious she's here to spy on us like a good little Dawson lapdog." It was a reach, but not so out of the realm of possibility to rule it out. And I especially didn't like the way Zoe's thin mouth straightened into a pensive line as I said it.

Kit stuttered a laughed. "She is *not* a spy. Lee, you're drunk, and when you get drunk, you get paranoid. Dad doesn't care about what we're doing, remember? Odds are, he doesn't even know what he's paying for... Last time I bothered to count, there's twelve other kids to check up on. He's not giving a second thought to our living situation."

"Fourteen kids," Zoe corrected. "His newest mistress gave birth to twins."

I snorted, turning to Kit. "Are we counting them as siblings too?"

"No, but we never grew up with them," she said.

"We never grew up with *this* one!" I yelled. "She used to crash our summer vacations and went to our school long enough to torpedo my life. That's it."

"You quit a high-paying job to stay at home and send

messages to pitiful people online and you think *I* ruined your life?" Zoe scoffed, crossing her arms. Her eyes rolled and once again, she smirked. I wanted to rip it off her face. "Is this about Luka? Get over it, Liana. We were kids. Besides, it's not my fault I was hotter than you. Who could blame him for being tempted?"

Her smirk became an amused grin, and my veins lit up like they were turbo-charged, sending all the blood to my already pounding heart. I was so angry, I wanted to lunge out and wring her scrawny neck. Instead, I looked at Kit. Her eyes avoided mine again, and that was enough for me to know she felt guilty... *but not guilty enough to do anything about it.*

With a disappointed shake of my head, I nudged past Zoe, and made my way to my room, slamming the door behind me. I flung myself onto my bed like a teen in a snit and lifted a pillow to my face, screaming my frustrations out. Being around Zoe put me back in my feelings from high school, ripping open the wound on my heart that she and Luka left the night of my senior prom.

I sat up, reaching for my laptop, and Google searched the prison term of 'accidental' murder. It was all fantasy, of course, but it amused me to think how I'd explain my search history to the FBI.

"*Pfft.* If they ever met Zoe, they'd understand," I said out loud.

Closing the tab, and deciding I needed to do some real work, I opened my *Love, Liana* email account...

There it was, sitting in the same place I'd left it: the email from *sincerely, Kade*, mocking my ability to do my job. I sighed, double clicking on it, and my eyes skimmed its contents for the hundredth time.

I cracked my fingers, opened a blank page, and began outlining a response. But every few lines I got down, I deleted. With each word written and erased, I wanted nothing more than to punch a hole through the screen. I grumbled, slamming the lid, and threw myself back on my bed.

My head was spun by Zoe, and the migraine of a hangover was fast setting in. Kade was getting to me more than any other email I'd ever gotten in my career, and I'd gotten a *lot* of them. I'd dealt with commitment-phobes before. Why was this *one* so hard?

I melted back into my soft pillows and pulled the comforter over my body. All warm and toasty, I unclenched my shoulders and closed my eyes, the anger in my body being replaced by exhaustion.

Snuggling down, I declared I'd spend all day the next day in front of my laptop, writing, until something resembling advice appeared on the screen.

Kade had waited three days, and as I drifted into the sweet abyss of sleep... I swore I wouldn't make it four.

Chapter 4

Liana

My declaration proved worthless.

Three days passed, and Kade's email sat there like the ugly duckling in a pond of pretty, easy fixes. It was my fault. I'd spent more time plotting ways to get Zoe to move out than doing my job. The seventy-two hours she'd lived with us had been a hell of snarky looks and pointed comments about everything from her tryst with the ex-love-of-my-life, to jabs about my weight. Apparently, I was 'pudgier' than she remembered.

Bitch.

I wished she would disappear into an abyss of crocodiles and snakes. Instead, she sat in the armchair by the balcony, drinking her skinny latte and reading a crime novel in the light of the mid-morning sun—completely unaware that I was planning her own murder in my head.

I rolled my eyes at the back of her head, sipping my caramel latte with extra whipped cream—which Zoe informed me wouldn't make me happy... just fat.

I growled, taking a bigger swig, and swallowed with added rage.

Kit emerged from her bedroom where she'd been hiding for

three days, already dressed. I glared at her, expecting her to grab her bag and leave without coffee for the fourth morning in a row. So it shocked me when she stopped off in the kitchen to fill her to-go mug and turned to me with a small upturn at her lips. "I'm going to work... Maybe *you* should do the same?"

It was a critical comment that set my teeth on edge. I bit back the urge to tell her I'd have an easier time if she hadn't brought *Judas* into our home. Instead, I pursed my lips and nodded, keeping my feelings off my face the best I could.

As the door shut behind Kit, I took residence in front of my open laptop with my coffee in hand. Placing the mug on the desk with a purposeful clatter, I smirked when Zoe jumped at the sudden noise. Her eyes slithered over to me, glaring before moving back to her book.

Satisfied, I pulled my feet up on the chair and inched forward, covering my knees with my oversized, off-white hoodie. It was my favorite shirt to write in, but it wasn't the prettiest item of clothing... covered in unrelenting food and stains that wouldn't come out, no matter how hard I tried.

I took another sip of coffee, moaning as the caramel grazed my taste buds, and lifted the last bite of my toast to my mouth. I smiled.

Wouldn't make me happy, my 'pudgy' ass.

Scrolling over to Kade's email, I hit the button twice in fast succession and sighed. His words continued to stump me. Every night since his email came in, I read it like a bedtime story. It was so ingrained in me, I found myself reciting to the fill the silence. Yet as I sat staring at the screen, my fingers barely grazing the keyboard, inspiration was lost to me.

Half an hour passed by, and all I did was stare. I stared so much, I slipped into a trance-like state, twirling my pen and daydreaming, until an incoming message beeped me back to reality. It was Jana, getting on my back about making an Instagram account to connect with my fans.

I shook my head and deleted the email. Instagram wasn't my speed. As the owner of a personal account that saw no use beyond reminding me I wouldn't see Italy again anytime soon, I didn't need a professional one to go with it. Besides, pictures of me sipping caffeine in front of my laptop with tangled hair and syrup stains on my shirt seemed much more likely to lose me fans.

I snickered at the thought of the comments I'd get... The trolls would have a field day with my hair alone. Deciding Instagram wasn't for advice columnists with bad lighting who spent *way* too much time SVU live-tweeting, I set my phone down.

Then, my brain offered a debate on the matter: Maybe it wasn't such a bad idea. Maybe my fans would appreciate the candor of a daily bed selfie. (That is to say, a selfie in my PJ's, snuggled into my pillow and drooling, not a lingerie-clad photo of me in salacious positions.)

Convinced, I pulled my hair out of my bun, unlocked my phone, and snapped a quick selfie. I thought I looked great, but when I pulled up the photo, I realized the front-facing camera was a duplicitous bitch. It was as though it purposely highlighted the bags that told the world I was a coffee-addict who repelled sleep, and worse again... the stains.

Yeesh.

"No Instagram account for me." I voice-noted those exact words to Jana. "There aren't enough filters in the world..."

"Maybe you should try a skin-care regime," Zoe offered from the balcony. She shut her book and angled herself in my direction, upturning her lips into a small smile that on someone else may have looked sweet, but when paired with Zoe's snake eyes, was as bitter as an unripe lemon. "You're not going to stay twenty-three forever, you know?"

I gawped. "I was talking about the stains."

Zoe shrugged, standing from her chair. "Take the tip, trust

me." She moved inside, shutting the balcony door with a click, and huffed. "I'd appreciate it if you let up on the keyboard-tapping. You're ham-handed and it's distracting me from the words of a *real* writer. And since I'm paying rent and you're not..." She retreated to her bedroom, a sway in her hips, and shut the door.

I growled.

My fingers itched to Google more methods of forced eviction but if I didn't get to work on Kade's email soon, it would fester forever in my inbox. I opened up a blank document and typed with added ferocity, punching the keys like Muhammad Ali.

"Dear Kade," I spoke, loudly. "I understand your problem. My advice to you would be to..." I snapped my fingers and clicked my tongue, urging on the idea in the back of my mind. As quick as it landed, it disappeared. I groaned, fidgeting in my seat, and decided there was only one thing for it: *I needed more coffee*.

Standing from my laptop, I made my way to the kitchen, stomping my feet like cinderblocks past Zoe's closed door as I went.

"My advice to you would be to..." I replaced the coffee filter and filled the pot with water from the fridge door. Pouring the water into the machine, I put the pot back in its place and watched as it filled with heavenly nectar. I grabbed the pot and lifted it to my nose, inhaling deeply in hopes that the vapors would somehow bypass the drinking part of the deal and go straight from my nose to my brain.

No dice.

I refilled my mug, added creamer and two teaspoons of sugar, and trudged my way back to my desk to stare at a blank screen once again.

"Okay." I cracked my knuckles. "Kade, I understand your problem and my advice to you would be to..." I threw my head back and groaned so loud it echoed. "My advice to you would be to find an advice columnist who doesn't suck. Or how about get a new fucking therapist, hmm? They can't all be quacks! Why not try that instead of plaguing my every thought and moment? Well? What do you have to say for yourself? Huh? *Asshole!*"

"You do realize a laptop can't talk back?" I jumped at the male voice behind me, then growled when I realized who it belonged to. The jingling of keys in his hand enraged me as he moved. *Didn't need two guesses to know where he got those.* "I take it your little hobby isn't going well?"

"Get out," I demanded, my eyes trained on the screen.

"Is that any way to talk to your father?" He asked with an amused smirk on his self-satisfied face. Closing the door behind him, he dropped his six-foot frame down onto the couch and stretched out, swiping a hand through his graying hair. It hadn't occurred to me until now that he would know where I lived, and yet another reason to hate Zoe dropped in my lap: she'd given him my address.

Doing my best to act like he wasn't there, I kept my focus. But as the weight of his amused stare bore into me, I caved, narrowing my eyes in his direction. "What're you doing here?"

The grin that spread across his face unnerved me. Moving from the couch, he took a seat at the desk beside me. I scooted over, finding his cologne, *eau de self-centered*, repugnant.

"I heard about your bookstore appearance... I want to help." He clapped his hands together, as if his offer was the answer to my prayers and he, the angel who delivered it...

"Help how?" My eyes narrowing into dubious slits.

"I want to buy your blog."

Oh, this joke again... Ha-ha, your blog isn't worth anything so if you come back I'll buy it for you. At least that's one month's rent, right? My eyes blinked three times as I awaited the predictable punchline, but it didn't come. Eric leaned back and crossed his arms over his chest. When I realized he was dead serious, my shoulders shook in a silent laugh that became a howl. The more I replayed his words in my head, the funnier it became. I waited for him to join me, slap me on the back and say he was messing with me, but his face stayed expressionless. I laughed harder. "... You can't be serious?"

"Liana, I know what this venture of yours could be worth with the right person at the helm. Let me take the reins. I can get a fully qualified staff onboard and take your blog from thirty hits a day to millions. I'd even keep you on as a staff writer. You get the payout; I get the brand... it's a win-win."

My laughter, which bordered on aching, stopped dead. I stilled, curiosity clawing at me. "Why do you need *my* blog? You didn't believe in it when I pitched it to you five years ago."

Dad shifted uncomfortably, avoiding my glare. "... I'm retiring next month. Your brother is taking over. Since he is neither a writer nor an adept eye for talent, he needs a pet project to establish himself."

The sting of hearing him call my blog a 'pet project' punched a hole through my chest. I hated that I needed to remind myself his opinion meant nothing. Once again, I scoffed. "Except it wouldn't be *his*. It would be Dylan using *my* idea."

"Oh, don't be pedantic. It doesn't suit you..." He folded his arms. "We both know if my company doesn't captain this idea, it won't get the promotion or exposure it requires to succeed. You're an excellent writer, Liana, but you're no businesswoman. Without me, *Love, Liana* will stay an obscure blog in the far corners of the internet until you have no choice but to give up..." He stood, buttoning his suit jacket. It was a power-move he'd used to close meetings as far back as I remembered. And most of the time, it worked. This time...

I snorted. "You don't think *I* can do it, but you think *Dylan* can?"

"Frankly, no." He sat back down, this time on the edge of my desk, lording over me. "Your brother is an overgrown frat boy with no discernible skills, but with my resources and an admittedly *decent* idea, I have hope he'll become the leader I need him to be to run The Eric Dawson Talent Agency."

I stood from my desk, taller than he was sitting, and looked down on him. My lips pulled into a grin. "Get out," I repeated.

"Excuse me?"

My arms crossed over my chest. "You heard me. I refuse to put my blog in the hands of someone who would make *Dylan* their protégé."

His jaw slacked and his eyes widened, taken aback by my harsh tone. But in the five years I'd spent out of his shadow, I surpassed the need for an easy ride. His shoulders squared, then slumped. He sighed, dragging a hand through his hair, and his face turning pensive. For the first time since he walked into my apartment, I took in his appearance...

In his early-sixties, he did his best to stay youthful, but he was slipping. Thinner than I remembered, his once bright complexion appeared mottled and desiccated. Fine lines beneath his eyes and across his forehead added years to his face, and above all else, the old man looked tired. A small pang enveloped my chest, pulling for the father he was when I was a child. But he wasn't that man anymore. He'd been seduced by money and power and traded his soul to get it.

Turning my back, I stalked to the kitchen and put my coffee mug in the sink, hoping he would leave. Yet there he was, sat in the same spot.

"I'm sorry..." I said, my voice soft, and then flinched hearing my own vulnerability. I cleared my throat and put some power behind it. "Why should I risk my career to help you? You never gave a second thought to me or Kit before handing Dylan the agency on a platter."

His eyes sullen, he hung his head. "Liana, women... they're not as business savvy as men. Nobody takes them seriously."

The small amount of sympathy I had dried up at his words.

"Get out!" I barked, wishing I held something big and weighty in my hand to throw at him. "Kit studied marketing at your request, I spent my teen years pouring over manuscripts you couldn't be bothered to read and killing myself to get good grades. For what?"

"So you could both be self-sufficient." He shook his head. "Though since I'm paying half of your rent, I suppose only one of you managed that feat."

A knife twisted in my gut; the word *failure* imprinted on the steel of the blade, burning my insides.

He sighed. "See reason. If we took control, we would be setting up a social media presence, doing radio shows, podcasts, webisodes... Ads all over this goddamn city. We have money to throw at this thing and turn it into the next big phenomenon. We can do what you can't. We can turn the blog into a brand."

I stumbled back, feeling the brunt of his words.

"What do you even know about love?" He continued. "Everything you know comes from cookie-cutter examples people want to believe in, and you basing your advice on them is fraudulent. Once your readers figure that out, your career is over. I can utilize writers with more tenure, resources, and web designers far better than your little subpar wannabe-influencer friend, Jenny... Your brother needs this to step up."

My face took on an amused smile, but inside, I was bubbling. "Maybe you wouldn't be in this mess if you dropped the misogynistic values and entered the twenty-first century. But since you won't..." I stormed for the door and ripped it open for him to leave.

He crossed the threshold with an arrogant smile. Turning his back, he strode toward the elevator and clicked the down button. His grin widening, he looked at me. "You should know, if Dylan fails and a daughter takes charge, it won't be by seniority... You just don't have the skill, kid."

Tears pricked in my eyes and my blood boiled. As much as I didn't want to give him the satisfaction of showing I cared, I couldn't help myself in asking, "Who is next in line?"

Eric's smirk became a grin. "You know, this is better actually... because when you crash and burn, you'll be begging me to make an offer and I can get your blog for a discounted price. But don't worry, you'll always have a job with me. Maybe my assistant could use an assistant."

He wasn't going to tell me, which spoke louder than words. He wanted Kit back. My jaw set. "Speaking of your assistant, maybe you should spend less time bedding her and more time with your wife," I spat. "And don't worry about me, *Dad*. I'll figure it out, like I always do."

He laughed, stepping onto the elevator. "What're you going to do, Liana? Hire a consultant? You can barely afford to eat."

I slammed the door as a response and stomped past my laptop, showing Kade's email, and headed for my room so I had another door to slam.

Chapter 5

Liana

It took a while, an Irish coffee, and a relaxing bath in Kit's tub before I cooled down enough to sit back at my laptop. My damp hair smelling like lemons, and in a fresh lounge set I'd bought cheap online, I felt better. For the price, the blue sweatpants were stylish and comfortable, and the cotton, long-sleeved T-shirt fit my figure so perfectly, it moved like a second-skin. My feet, covered in soft bouncy slippers shaped like rabbits, felt like walking on clouds.

Letting out a shaky breath, I did my best to forget my father and get to work. I closed the draft-email to Kade and pulled up my website. My chest burst with a sense of pride as it loaded on my screen and reminded me how far I'd come without his help. He was wrong about Jana being subpar. The website: light and fun with a palette of pastel pinks and white, was cute and inviting. It was perfect for my brand.

The two hours I spent in the tub, in deep reflection, hit me with a realization: I was pining for a father who never existed. Manipulation was always his most fluent language in everything he did, and the image of the dad I wanted clouded the one I had.

I came to a startling conclusion as the water turned cold—I hated my father. For the way he raised us, and for what he did to my mother.

I shook my head, refusing to go there, and pushed the bitter memories aside. Choosing to focus on Kade, I closed my site and reopened my inbox where I found Kade's email, mocking me.

Panic attacked my chest, making it heave up-and-down. *Fraudulent. No skill.*

Eric was right. I was giving advice in areas I had no experience. No idea what I was doing...

With the blog, not the sex.

I'd had sex before, of course, and I knew how it worked in a technical where-everything-goes way, but I wasn't on the short-list to star as Gloria Leonard in a biopic anytime soon. Sex for me was bland. No passion, angels never sang, and the earth never quaked.

My only hope was to do some research. I started by looking up the most common bedroom questions asked on Google, but by the end of that search I was more confused than ever. God help me, I gave credence to my father's idea of hiring a consultant.

I was ready to scream when my laptop gave another ding, reminding me of my other readers. I scrolled through the unanswered emails and cursed. A lot piled up.

Picking one from the bunch, I got to work.

The first, a guy in love with his best friend's girlfriend. Or at least, *he* thought he was. I wasn't too sure. To me, it seemed he wanted what he couldn't have. I advised making sure his feelings weren't part of a fantasy, and to talk to his friend before he did anything about them.

Happy with the advice, I clicked send and moved on. Two hours later, I was nearing an empty inbox, with only one email left to answer. I brewed myself one last cup of coffee and double-clicked.

As always, I started with the subject line and shifted in my seat, sitting up straight as a familiar name caught my eye. Pressure mounted in my head and my heart raced as I forgot to breathe. I moved my eyes down and read.

'Dear Liana,

Hi. It's me... Kade.

I'm writing this follow-up email for fear you never received my first. If not, I'm afraid writing 'It's me' as though you know me might come across as a little weird, bordering on narcissistic.

I've attached the contents of my original email above, just in case. I don't know how your system works, but I'm sure one or two slip through the cracks from time to time. Don't worry about it.'

My face scrunched. He was wrong. Not once had I let an email go unanswered. His was the first.

But maybe people would have been better off if I had.

Eric's voice echoed in my ear calling me a fraud again. Raking a hand through my hair, I was too hot. I bolted from my chair to the other side of the living area and cracked the window; not able to breathe until I inhaled the crisp fall air. I savored the aroma of oncoming rain and let out a slow breath.

Leaving the window open, I moved back to my laptop and continued to read.

'In the past two days, fears of something being wrong with me have increased. In fact, I think I might be a mild sociopath. I've done extensive research on the condition and ooh boy! I check a lot off the symptom list...'

I shook my head. Kade was not a sociopath. I wasn't an

expert, but I had an inkling that if he was, he probably wouldn't care.

'Since my self-diagnosis, I've been forcing myself to interact with people other than my best friend, Stephanie. Turns out, I don't like people.

Stephanie says not to give up until I make a connection, so I tried a different bar. There were many amazing women there, but they were all like me—career focused and looking for a one-night deal. Which is fine. I didn't want more. But isn't that the problem? Aren't I meant to want to meet someone I would want to stick around?

I want to want that.

In another attempt to meet people, I allowed Stephanie to drag me to the Walmart in the Green Acres Mall where I stocked up on my monthly supply of protection and post-coital snacks. I'm sure the manager, Frederick, thinks I'm hosting sex parties. I've been back twice since, and now he's angling for an invitation. Let me tell you, if I ever were to throw an X-rated gathering, he would not get within fifty yards of it. He has a handlebar mustache and looks like he idolizes Norman Bates.

I may have issues, Liana, but at least when my mother died, I didn't stuff and keep her.

Anyway, I look forward to hearing from you. Until then, I will sleep secure knowing life could always be worse. After all, I may be fucked in the head... but at least I'm not Frederick from Walmart.

Sincerely, Kade.'

Oh my god. I snorted. How did I respond to a guy like Kade?

Scrolling back, I reread his first email, and then his latest. Essentially, he wanted to know about the fundamentals of love, just as I needed to know about sex. Ironic that we each hoarded information the other needed. If only we could've switched minds for the day. Or maybe—

Eric's mocking words about hiring a consultant unexpectedly seemed like a stroke of genius. But I wouldn't pay someone to teach me about sex... I didn't have to. I had a bargaining chip to trade.

With a grin, I outstretched my fingers and started typing...

CHAPTER 6

KADE

She wanted to meet in person. That's all that Liana's email said. No fix-it for being emotionless... Nothing useful whatsoever. I'd sent two meaningful emails and got zilch in return.

I glared at the screen of my office computer and read its contents over and over, as though more would appear if I looked hard enough. I scrolled up and down, searching for hidden messages, and blinked to make sure I was reading it right.

A date, a time, an address, and the vague mention of a 'chat' about a business proposal. That was all I got after days of waiting? *A fucking joke.* My mouth pulled into a tight line as I waited for her words to make sense, but no matter which way I read them, they didn't add up to advice.

I Googled the address to discover a quaint café a block away from my office, and sat back, indignant at the whole process. Why hadn't I been one of the many who got their advice to go? I'd never intended on meeting Liana in person—*unless, of course, I was crashing her meet-and-greet to confront her.* But that was the act of a desperate man in search of answers. Liana proposing the meet-up was... weird.

Why would *she* need to meet *me*? She was the adviser; I was the one in need of advice. I shook my head, dejected. "I swear her website didn't say this would be so damn complicated."

"Talking to yourself again, Kade?" An amused voice appeared at my office door. "You should really see somebody about that."

My mouth twitched up at the corners, the pissed off feeling in my stomach dispersing. "Steph, how many times have I told you it's Mr. Jennings when we're at work?" I forced self-importance behind my tone, but the smirk gave me away.

Stephanie rolled her eyes and entered my office, shutting the door behind her. Her braided, magenta hair was pulled into an unmoving bun that sat atop of her head. Once again, I wondered if it hurt to pull her hair that tight, and then I noticed the delicate features on her heart-shaped face.

Her eyes were deep-set and oval, her cheekbones high, and sharp enough to be visible under her dimpled, round cheeks; and her lips were plump and looked soft to the touch. But really, what made Stephanie so beautiful was her smile. When she smiled, she could light up a room and most days, that smile was the only thing that made me feel a little less like an alien.

"You've been acting weird for days." She dropped her purse to the ground and unlocked the cabinet in the corner—the one that housed the bottle of single malt I kept for special occasions. Whiskey in hand, she placed two small glasses on my desk and filled them up until they overflowed. Sliding one glass in my direction, she took a seat and brought the other to her lips, her dark eyes bright with curiosity. "I noticed you seemed pretty enthralled by your computer screen, *again*... Are you addicted to porn, or searching for a soulmate?"

A small laugh escaped my lips. "Steph, don't tell me you believe in all that love and destiny, *Hallmark*, *Lifetime* movie bullshit? Trust that I'm not searching for a soulmate, only answers."

"To what question?" Again, her eyebrow quirked. I rolled my eyes and considered telling her to fuck off, but by now that brash suggestion was like water rolling off a duck's back to Stephanie and it didn't do shit to make her leave. I took another sip and kept my lips tight.

"Come on, Kade, don't make me beg for it..."

Letting out a low laugh, I downed the rest of the glass and reached for the bottle. "Ever heard of Liana Dawson?"

I echoed the story so far to Steph as she got herself comfortable, slipping her panty-hose covered feet from her stilettos and placing them on my desk. She sat back and pondered the tale, her eyebrows hunched, her tongue in her cheek and her mouth drawn into a pout. "And you have no idea *why* she wants to meet you?"

"Not a clue." I sucked down on the remnants of my second glass and shrugged, sitting back in my chair. It was good whiskey—tangy and old, leaving an oaky taste in my mouth with hints of vanilla and caramel. In fact, it was sacrilege that it was being drunk on a random Tuesday, and not in celebration of closing a lucrative deal. "Maybe she figured out who I am and wants an agent. I Googled. She doesn't have one yet."

Steph stuck her tongue between her teeth. "Or maybe you're so fucked up, she needs to evaluate you in person," she said, a laugh at her lips. I didn't find it funny. Rolling her eyes, she dropped her feet to the ground and sat forward. "Representing her might not be a terrible idea. If she plays her cards right, she could be on the come up. You could do worse for a client."

I shrugged. Her point was noted, but I wasn't sold on Liana's skill—or my desire to get into the business of romance. "It took a long time for her to respond, and when she did, she didn't help me. I don't think she's anything special."

Stephanie finished her drink and set her glass down, getting to her feet. "I think you're underestimating her. Go for a cup of coffee and find out what she wants. What's the worst that can happen?"

"She can't help me, and I've wasted an afternoon," I said.

"An afternoon you'd waste obsessing over it anyway."

I grunted. She was right, I would only spend the time staring out of the window wondering what words Liana had for me a block away, and though I'd never admit it out loud, I was intrigued. The tingle in my spine told me so.

"Okay, fine." I caved.

Stephanie clapped her hands like one of those robotic animal toys banging cymbals. Annoying and repetitive. I scrunched my nose. "Don't you have work to do?"

She nodded, pushing her glass toward me. "Yes. But the whiskey has gone to my head, so I apologize if your calendar has typos." Digging in the purse, she emerged with breath spray and shot two pumps into her mouth to cover the smell of alcohol. The air filled with cool mint and blueberry. "Oh, and Liana's email said *business* arrangement... Don't hit on her."

I narrowed my eyes, confused, as she departed my office and left me to mull over her words in my already too loud head. I wasn't intending to hit on Liana. Then again, I never intended to hit on anyone, it just happened. Most of the time, it resulted in the exact same outcome: sweaty and naked on the flattest surface nearby, hearing my named screamed without ever learning theirs.

But it wouldn't be that way with Liana. It *couldn't* be... I already knew her name.

I was yet to reply to her email with a confirmation because that would set my decision in stone. I pondered if I would show up. In my mind, it was final. I would meet Liana at the coffee shop in less than twenty-four-hours and we would—to use her word— 'chat.' But who knows what the me of my future would decide. As long as it was up-in-the-air from Liana's perspective, I could back out.

I contemplated the art of chatting with a scowl on my face. "What constitutes the difference between a conversation and a chat?" I mused aloud and decided to look it up. That way, I could practice.

According to Google, a chat was less time consuming, involved casual topics, and incorporated jokes of some kind. Huh, I was more adept in chatting than I thought. *Practice done.* I closed the browser and opened a manuscript that had been on my desk for over a fortnight to read the first sentence.

Is obsession with researching things a sign of being a sociopath? I stopped. Closing the manuscript, I dropped it back onto my desk with a slap. "I should look that up."

One search led to another, and three hours later I was down a Google rabbit hole with so much new knowledge, I became a self-taught psychologist, better than any quack I'd ever paid. If I owned an official leather-bound notebook and fountain pen, I would have lain on my own couch and talked to myself for free. Then, I would write myself a big ol' prescription for something fun.

I stretched out in my desk chair, my eye catching a glimpse of the moonlight through my closed shades. Outside of my window, the skies were dark. Usually, that meant quitting time, but as a small pile of unread manuscripts stared up at me, I sighed and grasped the thickly-bound, three-hundred pages of something fantasy-based in my hands. It would be a late night. Licking my thumb, I turned the first page and dove into the story.

By the third chapter, a knock at the door was a welcome distraction. "Come in," I yelled, dropping the manuscript into the red box under my desk. I made a note to have Stephanie email the author the bad news as her head popped around the door.

"I'm heading out. See you at home?"

"Not for a while." I sighed. "Goodnight. Oh, and thanks for the *chat*..."

Steph's eyebrows wrinkled, she giggled. The sides of my mouth pushed up into a half-smile. She retreated, almost out of my eyeline when I called her back.

Thinking of her earlier mention of soulmates, I let myself linger on the thought. While I didn't subscribe to the notion myself, I wished it true for Stephanie. She deserved that fairy-tale ending more than anyone I knew. "Whoever your hypo-thetical soulmate is, I look forward to meeting them someday. He, or she, is one lucky bastard."

I expected her to laugh or smile, or even roll her eyes and call me sappy. Instead, her eyes narrowed into slits, and her arms folded across her chest as she stepped fully into my office.

"You don't think Cleo and I are meant to be together?"

Shit. My mouth clamped shut and my eyes landed on the title page of the next manuscript on the pile. "Shut the door when you leave, please." I refused to engage in the same argu-ment one more time.

Steph stayed put and scoffed. "Look, I know she and I haven't had the easiest go of it, and you think she's—"

"A manipulative, abusive bitch," I offered, my back molars grinding together as my jaw clamped.

"Cleo's never hit me, Kade."

I didn't believe that, and even so, I held an unwavering belief that Stephanie deserved better. Keeping my focus on my computer and my mouth shut, I suffered the weight of her stare.

Stephanie dropped her arms, balling her hands into tight ball, and gritted her teeth. "If you gave her a chance, you'd see she's the most amazing person. Nobody will ever love me like she does."

"It's sad that you believe that." I repositioned my keyboard and typed a response to a submission that had sat in my inbox for months, willing her to go away before one, or both, of us crossed a line.

"No, Kade. What's sad is you pushing your childhood trauma onto my relationship. Cleo isn't Garret, and I'm not your mom," she spat, taking a running start and goddamn long-jumping over the line.

I stopped typing, my eyes flitting to her. The silence around us settled so thick, it was choking. Steph's mouth hung open, her eyes wide as though she couldn't believe what she said. I couldn't believe it either.

"Oh, God. I didn't—"

"Miss Taylor, you have some vacation days left over. I suggest you take them. Now, get the fuck out of my office."

Steph didn't argue. Her bottom lip wobbled as she rushed out, closing the door behind her without another word. My anger, palpable, stuck in my throat. I stood from my desk, pacing back and forward in a lame attempt to fight off the attack of my own mind, forcing flashbacks in front of my eyes.

My chest constricted. *Where was the air? Why were the goddamn windows sealed shut?* I wasn't suicidal, I was fucking suffocating.

I stumbled toward my desk in search of more whiskey, anything to numb my mind. The bottle sat on the other side of the mahogany, where Steph had been. Grabbing for it, I lurched too fast and struck the corner of my computer screen with my shoulder, sending it hurtling to the floor.

Oh, shit! I tried to catch it, but I was too late. It crashed to the ground on an angle and bounced before landing on its back. Cracked plastic casing captivated my thoughts; the sweet pop of the computer screen bleeding blue as a sharp edge pierced it. The images in my head stopped, too focused on how fucked I was. I was able to breathe again.

"Fuck," I huffed, scratching at the nape of my neck. Without a computer, working became impossible, and I had no other reason to stay at the office. But the prospect of going home was so uninviting, it threatened to rise in my throat.

I grabbed my jacket from the back of my chair and headed out of the building, finding myself at a crossroads; each of my feet pointing in a different direction. If I turned right, I'd spend the night at a bar, hammering shots of Jameson until I found someone to take me home. If I turned left, I'd go back to the apartment where Stephanie would likely be swallowing down a pint of cookie dough and crying. My stomach revolting at the thought of her being sad and alone, my right foot twisted an inch to the left.

A gust of cold air whipped around me, reminding me summer was over. Pretty soon, the bitter sting of Christmas would follow—*another I would celebrate alone; drinking and watching the snowfall as Stephanie abandoned me for Cleo.*

I turned right.

M y eyes ripped open—the images forcing me, in a fit of sweat and groaning, to jolt awake before my body was ready. Blinking, I took a deep breath and focused my eyes to find the unfamiliar setting of a small loft in Queens. I knew I was in Queens because the cab fare from the bar had been so high, I remembered wondering if getting laid was worth it.

Christ, my head hurt, like a nest of birds were pecking at my brain with a mouthful of rocks. The time flashed on M-something's alarm clock, staring at me from an interwoven wicker stand. Already eight a.m. I was going to be late to the office. Not that it mattered much without a computer.

Turning over, I expected to find the gorgeous brunette I'd left the bar with beside me. To my pleasure, I found the sheets empty, and spread out like a starfish, melting into the cotton heaven. I closed my eyes and hummed. M-something's bed was *insanely* comfortable, with a mattress made of foam and pillows so soft, they were like sleeping on clouds.

"I need this bed," I murmured intoxicated by the smell of peach softener.

A giggle came from across the room. I flinched, my eyes springing open again to find last night's bed-buddy, half-dressed. I hardened below the waist watching her zip her skirt and button her top.

Slipping on her heels, she brushed her full lips with the color of cherries and snapped a photo of herself with the Polaroid camera that sat atop of her chest drawers. Seeing me staring, she smiled. "Look, I gotta go, so..." She turned, pointing the camera in my direction, and snapped a photo. "If I come back to my place ransacked and my cash gone, this photo goes straight to the cops along with your name. Which I know begins with a C? Caleb? Calen?"

My eyebrows lifted. I couldn't remember the last time a woman hadn't remembered my name. "Kade."

"Oof, I was way off. I'm Nikki." She smiled, and then gave a small laugh. "That'll be a nice little tidbit to tell our children one day."

I blinked. "*Excuse me*?"

"What?"

I cleared my throat of the panic that launched itself into my esophagus. "You said *our* children?"

Her eyebrows pulled forward. "You are planning on marrying me, right? Because I already told my mom we were engaged. I sent her a photo of you sleeping and she's so excited. She can't wait to meet you and she's already bought outfits for our baby." Her lip began to quiver, and tears pricked in her dark eyes. "What kind of man sleeps with a woman they don't plan to marry?"

What the fuck?

Her quivering lip inched up into an amused smirk. "Relax, I'm messing with you."

I breathed an audible sigh of relief.

She giggled. "I better be going. Lock up when you leave. Keys are on the side table by the door. Put them in the fake plant pot outside. Thanks for last night. Enjoy my bed... and, uh, don't be here when I get back, kay?"

Nikki left me confused with a headache and a serious case of cotton mouth. The rational part of my brain told me to collect my stuff and leave, but as my body ached, the opportunity to revel in her divine bed became too appealing to pass up.

I set Nikki's alarm with enough time for me to get up, go home, shower and change before my big coffee date with Liana Dawson. But as I snuggled back down into her sheets and the sweet stretching of my muscles gave way to pleasure, I knew it was a dangerous game to play...

And it was a game I lost.

Chapter 7

Liana

I sat at the back of a coffee house, admiring the black and white modern décor. The diamond speckled counters shone, wiped down after every order, and the walls were a white brick adorned by a giant iron clock letting me know how late Kade was. The jukebox played an early nineties punk rock song about someone with a fat lip, picked out by the tattooed Gen-Z's with skateboards in the far booth. Aside from me, the custom held an almost exclusive teen vibe—not enough to make me feel old, but one too many beanies for me to be all the way comfortable.

I'd been there for over an hour and my nail beds were fast becoming stumps with how far down I chewed them. It was a comfort, and I needed all the comfort I could get. My stomach wound in knots at the thought of meeting a reader outside of a professional setting for the first time. Especially one I had every intention of pumping for information...

The music changed to Ed Sheeran and my shoulders relaxed, but I knew it wouldn't be long before another rock anthem belted through the speakers. As my Spotify could attest, I liked an array of musical genres from The Beach Boys to Ariana Grande with regular pitstops in AC/DC and Fleetwood Mac. But the erratic tempo changes were spiking my already climbing anxiety, propelling my nail biting to a level near cannibalistic.

I took a sip from my second frappé and looked at the clock again. I didn't know if Kade was coming or not. He hadn't emailed to say he was.

I wouldn't have if the tables were turned.

I glanced around for any sign of him, then remembered... I had no idea what he looked like. As far as I knew, he could've been one of the many men in the café. Though, a gut feeling told me he wasn't hiding under a beanie, which eliminated seventy percent of suspects. And the presence of partners, plus the age bracket, shot down the last thirty. Most were barely twenty, if I had to guess, and none radiated the sex appeal I imagined Kade would have.

If I were to believe his vision of himself, I was seeking out a mix of Khal Drogo and Thor.

There was one man in the corner who looked to be the right age, and he wasn't bad looking with thick brown hair and a sharp jaw line. His eyes met mine, a deep green, and he gave me a crooked smile. I gave a warm smile back and dropped my head. Though not to my taste, I could see many women falling for his charm. He emitted a sort of *je ne sais quoi*. Enough to have an ego, at least.

I sucked in a breath and debated how best to approach the situation. Shouting his name was out of the question, and I couldn't walk up to him and ask if he knew who I was without looking like a crazy person. I stayed put, remembering a picture of me was on the 'about me' section of my blog. Kade would know what I looked like if he was smart.

Another hour moved by with two sugar-filled frappés with extra whipped cream. I licked my lip, sucking the remnants through the straw, and tapping my fingers on the pinewood table.

Maybe he's not smart, I thought, *or maybe he forgot...*

Then there was the third option—the one where he was standing me up as a punishment for not getting back to him in time. *Honestly, I couldn't blame him.*

"I'll be okay," I murmured in an attempt to convince myself I didn't need his help. "I'll write it myself and it'll suck, and all of my readers will leave me for a sex-worker-turned-advice-columnist named *Lust, Lizzy*. Oh god!" Panic attacked my chest.

No. Being stood up was not an option.

I pulled out my phone, my fingers battering the screen until an impromptu, admittedly manipulative, email appeared. I proofread once and clicked Send.

'Kade,

I'm sitting at the back of the café I told you about... alone. I hope you're nearby, or at least on your way.

If you're thinking about standing me up, I believe it's in your best interest to reconsider.

I hope to see you soon.

Love, Liana.'

"There, that oughta do it."

<hr>

I t did not, in fact, do it. I checked the clock on the wall for the hundredth time. Another sixteen minutes, and four genre-jumping songs, passed since my last check and Kade was nowhere to be seen—in real-life or in my emails.

"Another?" The barista approached with a smile; her green hair tucked behind her thrice pierced ears.

"I better not." I sucked down the caramel at the bottom of my third frappé and packed my stuff into my bag, ready to leave. I sighed.

Kade's absence burned my brilliant idea to dust. I stood from the table, pulling my denim jacket over my arms, and dug my hair out of the back. Hanging around the café while crowds of people moved in and out was getting steadily more pathetic. I pulled my bag onto my shoulder and turned to leave. With an oomph, I collided with something hard, sending me stumbling back. A hand reached out to steady me, and when I looked up, my eyes widened beyond what I thought was possible; landing on a stranger with eyes so beautiful, they reminded me of the sky in December—an array of grays, teals, and blues, with flecks of black like skyscrapers.

"Are you okay?" He asked, his voice deep. A man, standing at least at six-foot-two with a mass of dark hair. His face was lined in thin stubble that ranged from his jawline to below his somewhat crooked nose; framing a pair of thick lips that could only be described in three words:

Pretty. Damn. Kissable.

I looked him up-and-down twice before I was able to compose myself. "Hi," I said, in an octave above audible.

"Hi," he replied with a grin. "Sorry about that. Can I get you a coffee to apologize?"

I nodded without a word and reclaimed my seat. He asked the barista what I liked and ordered himself a black coffee with a double shot of espresso. *Manly*, I thought, until he added the request for extra whipped cream and multi-colored sprinkles on top. My mouth pushed up into what I hoped was a cute smile as he took the seat across from me.

"Adorable."

He smirked. "I'm a man who likes the finer things. Sprinkles on a coffee may be the difference between a good afternoon and a bad one."

"Agreed." I tucked my hair behind my ear then extended my hand. "I'm Liana."

His face lit up in an amused smile as his warm palm slid into mine, pulsing against my skin. "Casper."

Oh, not Kade... "As in the ghost?"

"As in my uncle." He laughed, dropping his hand, which I hadn't realized I'd kept a firm grasp of until my skin felt naked without it. "It's nice to meet you, Leela."

"Liana," I corrected.

Casper nodded, sipping his coffee. He placed his mug onto the saucer, a little spilling over, and sat back in his chair. "So, are you on a blind date? You looked like you were waiting for someone."

"No. No blind date, really. More like, research, I guess."

"Well," he sat back with a twinkle in his eye, "that doesn't sound at all kinky."

My airway constricted as I rushed to deny it, only to realize I couldn't. Technically, I was in a coffee house to meet a strange man about sex. "It's..." I racked my brain and came up blank. Finally, I spat out the only word in my head. "Complicated."

"Anything I can help with?"

Oh, that was a loaded question. Heat crept up my spine and my body convulsed with desire as a list of ways he could help me ran through my mind—images included. I pushed my urges away and shook my head. I'd never met Casper the Smoldering Ghost, but the thought of jumping his bones in a café full of people was as strange and appealing to me as he was.

I shook my head because I didn't trust my voice not to yell out *take me now!*

Swallowing down the lump in my throat, I stood up. "I better get going. My, uh, coffee is cold."

"... It's a frappé."

"Right." I bit my lip, blushing, and pulled my bag onto my shoulder. "But I think if I stay here any longer, they're gonna start charging me rent." *And since I couldn't afford my own...*

"Okay," he said with an amused smile. "How about I take

you out sometime? Purely business, of course. I want to help you with your problems. Maybe we could think of a way that could be possible?"

Every word he spoke dripped with sexual innuendo. I could see sex in his eyes, the way he licked his lips, the twitch of his jaw as he smirked, and the tightening of his arm muscles under his gray shirt. I found it hard to breathe, never mind give an answer. The door dinged open with new customers, giving me an escape hatch. But as I turned on my heel, a shivering radiated from my tiny, blue lady-balls that stopped me in my tracks.

Okay, time to act sexy. I flicked my hair over my shoulder and brushed my hands down to my waist, letting them linger there. In my head, I built a list of sweet, flirtatious ways of asking for his number. My options ranged from the simple and straight-forward, 'can I have your phone number?' to handing him my phone and asking for his 'digits' with a wink.

With the way he was staring, I couldn't go wrong. But, as I opened my mouth, my brain froze and what came out was a jumble of words. "Num-gits. Phone." I threw my phone at him, my cheeks stinging with a blush as he scrambled to catch it.

"You've never done this before, have you?" He laughed, his shoulders shaking, a bemused smile on his glorious face. I shook my head and bit my lip. "There's a lock on your phone, gorgeous."

Casper passed it back, and I typed my code in with shaky hands; wrong three times, and right the fourth. I handed it back to him, calmly this time, and watched as he clicked save on his contact information and drop-called his cell.

"There, now I have yours..." He slipped my phone into my hand, grazing my palm and sending shock waves through me, my legs and arms turning to jelly. "I assume we'll fuck at some point?"

My lungs took in so much air, I almost asphyxiated. I sputtered, heat rising from my toes to my head—a mix of shock, embarrassment and... horniness. Everything below my waist clenched.

"I'm sorry, was that too forward?" He smirked. "I've been told I have issues with what is, and isn't, socially acceptable decorum."

I nodded because it *was* forward, but it was also all I could think of since I first saw him. He wasn't marriage material as far as I could see, but standing there, staring with lust in his eyes, he screamed the potential for a new experience: casual sex.

With my lip between my teeth, I nodded again with a small smile. Casper's eyebrows lifted, surprised, and my smile widened as I turned to leave. I was almost out of the door when I heard him say a goodbye, and my stomach flipped as he added a suggestive *for now*...

I didn't turn back, instead I hurried over the threshold like a bat out of hell and only when I got halfway down the block, did I feel like I could think straight again. My head was so light, it floated, and I walked with my knees so far apart I risked bowleggedness rather than walk with them together, for fear they'd stick for another three years.

My dizziness was unexpected. I'd never been shy around guys, even the ones I crushed out on. My ex-best friend, and most devastating love story, was Luka DiMaggio.

But when sex entered the equation, I was perplexed by my inability to follow through. And when I saw Casper, sex wasn't only in my mind, it was in my entire body. My hands ached to touch him, my lips tingled to kiss him, my legs wanted to wrap around him, and my core trembled for him.

I forced my mind onto another subject and wished I hadn't when it landed on my blog. I groaned realizing how monumentally screwed I was. I couldn't write about sex. I could barely get a sentence out to a guy I wanted to *have* sex with.

Kade being a no-show threw a major wrench in my plans, but perhaps it was unfair of me to put him in that position in the first place. He was a reader who asked for my advice. And what did I do? I gave him nothing and asked him for a favor...

I sucked.

Resolving to go home and make things right, I picked up my pace. Avoiding knocking into people the best I could on the crowded sidewalk, I power walked with purpose all the way back home.

As the doors of the elevator dinged on my floor, I dreaded the company waiting inside. I sighed, taking a long walk down the corridor, and louder again as I inserted the key into my apartment door. But to my surprise, I pushed the door open and found the apartment empty. Relief flooded me.

Thank God, I wouldn't have to deal with Zoe.

I dropped my bag by the door and reclaimed residence in my desk chair; clicking at my computer mouse until the screen loaded onto my email. Sitting forward, I opened a new email to Kade and bit my lip as my fingers punched the words of a fairly desperate message.

If I saw any other option, I would've sent Kade whatever lackluster advice I could come up with and let him go on his way. Now, he was my only hope of pulling off a sex-section without making an ass out of myself and losing my readership. I couldn't let that happen. The thought of admitting failure to my father was incapacitating.

My only back-up plan was for Casper to teach me all the knowledge I needed firsthand, but that came with pressure. Kade was a talking deal, and while my motives were somewhat selfish, I really did want to help him.

He seemed... *lonely.*

I imagined him in the bed of his latest concubine, his chest aching, and pity wormed its way into my heart. Love wasn't something I was in an abundance of, personally, but I saw it everywhere I went in New York. In the couples who walked hand in hand through Central Park, the families ice skating together at Rockefeller Center every Christmas, first dates in coffee houses, second dates in restaurants, even in the wide eyes of tourists taking pictures of the Empire State Building and experiencing the city for the first time... Love was a staple in my everyday life.

And knowing Kade was moving through the monotonous gray of the concrete buildings without the ability to experience the vivid expressions of life around him—I couldn't imagine how desolate he felt and trying to... Broke my heart.

CHAPTER 8

KADE

O f all names in the history of the world, I seriously questioned my decision of going with Casper. Since my meeting with Liana, I hadn't stopped muttering about my own stupidity.

"What kind of psycho creates a whole new persona?" I scolded myself. Why couldn't I have sat down, introduced myself and found out what she wanted like a normal person? *Idiot!*

I slipped my key into the lock of my apartment door and pushed it open. In all the excitement of creating a catfish, I'd forgotten about my fight with Stephanie. There she was on the other side of the door with puffy red eyes and messy hair, crying on the couch in her pink, bunny rabbit pajamas.

Spotting me, she jumped to her feet, ready to apologize. "I'm so sorry, Kade. I—"

I waved my hand and headed straight for the bar. "Yesterday's news, Steph. I'm in crisis. Pull up a chair and revel in my goddamn stupidity!"

Her mouth dropped open. "But, we had a fight. I need you to let me apologize."

I waved another hand, twisting the cap off a bottle of

Jameson whiskey. "Over it. Apology accepted. Need advice." I poured the whiskey over ice and took a sip. "Drink?"

Nodding, she sat down with her eyebrows knitted together. "So, we're cool?"

"What? *Oh!* Yeah, sure." I handed her a glass. "So, about my being a moron..."

I recounted the tale of my morning and watched Stephanie's eyes widen more with every word. Finally, when I got to the part about Casper, they were near ready to pop out of her head.

"*Casper*?" She burst into maniacal laughter.

I growled, swirling the ice around in my glass. "Named after my uncle, apparently... I don't have a fucking uncle."

Stephanie hid her snort behind her hand.

"I'm done with advice columnists," I bit. "This whole experience has been a shit-show pain in my ass from the beginning." I dropped down on my leather sofa, stretching my legs out, and grumbled. "Getting involved with Liana was a mistake. She hasn't helped me at all with my problems."

Sensing an opening, Stephanie took a shot. "What are these deep-seated issues?"

"They're none of your damn business, for a start." I shut her down and continued my rant. "Liana's guaranteed insightful advice was a load of bullshit. Whatever, it's over, anyway. She won't contact me, I'm not going to contact her, and Casper-the-friendly-psycho is *definitely*—" I was interrupted by my laptop giving an almighty ding from where it sat on my desk in the corner of the room. I groaned, my eyes rolling to the back of my head. "Whoever that is, send them an automated message. I'm in no mood to work tonight."

Stephanie made her way over to my desk. "What do you want it to say?"

"Fuck off should do the trick." I shrugged, lifting the glass to my lips. I inhaled the scents of malted barley, butter, and oak and gave a content sigh. "As I was saying, neither of my personas are going to contact Liana, so I see no reason that the café run-in shouldn't be the end of this whole situation."

Stephanie grimaced. "Well, there's the fact she emailed you..."

I stopped mid-drink, slammed the glass down on the table, and joined Stephanie's side to read the email.

'Dear Kade,

I realize asking you to meet-up might have come across as... strange, and totally not what you emailed me for.

I don't blame you for not coming.

I should have elaborated on what I meant when I said business arrangement. Long story short, my fans have demanded advice from me... about sex.

I bet that got your attention, right?

Anyway, I had this crazy idea that talking with you might be insightful and help me learn how to give the fans what they want. I don't have a specific plan mapped out yet. I hoped we could figure it out together.

But you should know, your decision won't affect my helping you. If you want to learn about all things love, Kade, I'll teach you... Hell, I'll even dress up in a cupid's outfit if you need me to!

I hope you don't ignore this email... but if you do, I'll respect your choice.

Love, Liana.'

"What are you going to say to her?" Stephanie stared expectantly.

I scoffed. "You don't honestly think I should reply?"

She folded her arms across her chest. "You left her sitting in a café for over an hour. If you don't email her back, I will."

"*Technically*, I was there." I could tell by her scowl she wasn't swayed by semantics. I growled. "Fine, I'll email her back in the morning on the condition you leave me alone to drink in peace... Buh-bye."

Stephanie threw her middle finger up and headed for her bedroom. She got halfway before she stopped and turned back, dubiously. She danced by the door of her bedroom, shifting from one foot to the other. "You want to learn about love?"

I winced, wishing she hadn't read that bit. "Why do you care?"

Steph shrugged with a small smile and left the room. I poured another glass, and then another. With each glass down, another was poured, and before I knew what was happening, I was drunk off my ass, again. I sat at my desk, waiting for the numbness to plunge me into a deep, dreamless sleep. As my head hit my desk, my eyes near-closed, I edged into the sweet abyss; cursing when my phone blared out an annoying sound.

I lifted my head from the cool glass and dug in my jean pocket until my hand grasped my phone. Blinking away the blurriness in my eyes until the screen came into focus, I read the words three times before they registered. "Oh, sweet baby Jesus on a holy tricycle."

'Hey, Casper. I was wondering if you'd like to grab dinner sometime this week? Let me know!'

Dinner with Liana? It was stupid to even consider it. As Kade, it'd be a risk, but as Casper? It was begging for trouble. One wrong slip and the whole charade would be blown to bits.

No! It wasn't happening. That was final.

'Hi, Liana.
Dinner sounds amazing. Seven-pm on Thursday good for you?
Looking forward to it!'

"Shit."

Chapter 9

Liana

A date with *Casper* and an email back from Kade. My night was going great...

Except for the demon that crawled its way out of hell and into a four-foot-nine blonde who lived in my home. I checked the clock on my desk, wondering how long it would take Beelzebub to send a search party for her.

Being around her was like being hit with snowballs—icy, hard, and left a stinging red rash on my skin. Everything she did seemed purposeful to get on my nerves, whether it was popping her gum non-stop while I was trying to work, painting her nails with what smelled like acetone and propane in the living room when I had a migraine, or disrupting my writing hot-streak by making an abundance of green juices every day. Most of which ended up down the drain after a sip.

Today, she was on a roll with a trifecta of noise. In the midst of drying her hair in the living room, she decided to blend herself a smoothie for dinner because the pizza I ordered was '*a grievous desecration of the human temple.*' And, to top it off, the vacuum was on full power because Zoe had 'accidentally' dropped a full bag of granola on the carpet and placed the vacuum over the patch to do all the work without her lifting a finger.

I switched my headphones to the highest volume setting and put my focus on Kade's newest email, but even blasting eighties rock ballads couldn't drown out the noise. It was like waterboarding for the ears, perforating my brain. I gritted my teeth, telling myself it couldn't be much longer, but as the time ticked on and Zoe's hair got dryer than the Sahara, I realized she was doing it to get a rise out of me.

With a huff, I stood from my chair, and stormed to the kitchen. I pulled the blender plug from the wall with such force, I half-expected the socket to come with it.

"Hey!" Zoe scolded, shutting off the hairdryer at last. "It's not done. I like my smoothies *extra* smooth!"

"And I like being able to focus," I bit, emptying the mixture of green into a glass, and placing the blender in the sink.

Zoe scrunched her face into a punch-able sneer. "Hmm, maybe you should've thought about that before you became a freeloader. Don't forget, I pay the rent!" My hands balled into fists at my side.

"*Eric* pays the rent... Grow up, Zoe."

Zoe turned so red, I thought steam was going to burst out of her ears like a British teapot. She scoffed and nudged past me, stronger than I thought she was. I held my groan in, not giving her the satisfaction. Fishing the blender out of the sink, Zoe emptied the smoothie back into it and plugged the blender into the socket. Smirking, she hovered her finger over the switch.

Annoyance tingled its way up my spine. "I swear to *Lucifer*, if you press that button, I'm going to blend *you* up into tiny pieces."

"Oh my God." Zoe backed away from the blender. "You're a psycho."

"*Ha*! You wanna see psycho? I'll show you psycho!"

The front door opened, and Kit sighed as she took in the scene. "How is it possible I'm the youngest one here?"

Her light toned remark was meant to ease the situation, but all it did was add an extra layer of tension, reminding me that Zoe was born before Kit as a result of Eric's betrayal to our mother.

Zoe poured her smoothie down the drain and pushed past me with a smirk on her way to her room, leaving me to turn on Kit.

"Why?" I asked as Zoe's door slammed shut. "Charles Manson would be a better roommate than Zoe! Hell, if you wanted to move a sister in, why not Rhian? She's a freshman at F.I.T. She would've jumped at the chance to split the rent, she hates Eric as much as we do, and—"

"She was born after mom left?"

I scoffed but couldn't deny it. Zoe's birth was the straw that broke my mother. After that, she was never the same happy-go-lucky woman I knew. "How about the fact Rhian never—" I stopped myself reopening old wounds.

Kit's eyes softened. "Lee, that was *so* long ago. We were teenagers. You need to let it go and maybe give Zo a second chance?"

Zo.

I almost gagged, my skin crawling so fervently, I wanted to peel it off with a potato knife. Along with my ears so I wouldn't have to hear the justifications of how *Zo* wasn't the same back-stabbing, vindictive bitch she was in high school.

Kit opened her mouth again, ready to be the great Zoe-defender she'd always been, but I was tired of hearing it. I held up my hand and shook my head. "I can't convince you she's evil, and you can't convince me she's not, so let's... not." I gathered my laptop from my desk and decided to work in bed.

I shut my bedroom door, furious at myself for letting Zoe gain the upper hand. I'd made it too easy for me to look like the irrational troublemaker to Kit. Zoe strung me up and played me like a fiddle, and worse—*I'd let her.*

I hunkered down under my duvet, perching my laptop on my knees, and opened up Kade's newest email, only to close it again without reading a word. My mind was too unfocused. Even the brief alluding to Zoe and Luka ripped open the past, rubbing salt in the wounds I thought were healed.

"I should be over this by now!" I scolded myself for feeling the hurt over again.

I raked a hand through my hair and sighed. Hiding away in my bedroom was no way to handle my problems but being around Zoe was driving me insane, like being back in high school where she was the prom queen, and I had no one except Luka. And pretty soon, I didn't have him either. *She did.*

I grumbled. Deciding to take a walk, I slipped on the first pair of sneakers I could find in my mountain of shoes, plain white converse, and left the apartment—sure to slam the front door on my way out.

I was already outside by the time I realized I had forgotten a jacket. The air was damp, drizzling, and crisp, blowing my hair in every direction. I spat a lock out of my mouth, shivering as the skin of my arms prickled. I wrapped them around myself and battled the urge to go back home.

I'd rather freeze.

I took a long stroll around the block, inattentive of destination. I stared down at my feet as my mind swirled through an array of topics. Luka, Zoe, my father, my mother, a pitstop in my blog, and ultimately, Kade.

Maybe he was better off without love.

I winced, abandoning my belief system, and plopped down on a wooden bench. It was then I looked up to find I was in the park. The trees already began to wilt, dropping the first of their auburn leaves on the shoulder of an old man. He glanced up, smiling, and brushed it off before rejoining the side of his wife. He slid his hand into hers, and I couldn't look away.

Laying a sweet kiss on her cheek, he whispered sweet-nothings into her hearing aid, and then... The old dog pinched his wife's ass. I mean, his fingers were arthritic so they couldn't really *pinch*, and he got mostly bone because she was kinda frail... but the pink blush that spread across her face filled her with a youthful exuberance as her eyes became alight with new confidence. They turned playful as she leaned in and kissed his lips.

The sweetest thing I'd ever seen.

That is why I believed in love. For couples in their eighties still playing grab-ass and making out in the park. Suddenly, I became very aware it was Wednesday, and my date with Casper was only a night away. I held no illusions I'd be ninety, grabbing his ass in the park, but the prospect made me giggle.

My smile stayed on my face as I sat people watching for over an hour, hoping to catch more glimpses of love. It stayed as I walked from the park, all the way back home; it stayed as the doorman opened the glass doors for me, and it stayed as I rode the elevator to my floor and unlocked the door to my apartment.

Then it dropped, replaced by a sneer.

I found Kit and Zoe, having a sister night I wasn't invited to. They were giving each other pedicures on the sofa as a playlist of modern pop hits played on the speaker. In the air, a smell so violently strawberry, assaulted my gag reflex and made me choke, and if that wasn't enough for vomit to rise in my throat, Eric's face lighting up Kit's screen was. Covering my mouth, I bypassed them in silence and moved to my room where I threw myself onto my bed.

A sharp pain jabbed my stomach, but I refused to let them get me down. Casper willing, I'd get laid in less than twenty-four hours... and that was something worth smiling about.

I kicked off my jeans as I slipped between my sheets. The coolness of the linen against my warm skin offered me comfort, and I sighed happily; the images of the old couple in love lulling me into a nice, deep sleep where all I dreamt of was glorious black hair, magnificent height, and eyes an unnamable color...

Chapter 10

Liana

I'd almost forgotten what it was like to be in the zone. At last, I could work. The only thing I was short on was time. It was already three p.m., giving me only four hours to reply to forty-two emails before I had to get dressed for my date.

I started with the most obvious, and the one I considered most vital: Kade's.

Double clicking on the email, I held my coffee to my lips, inhaled deeply, and read.

'Dear Liana,

First, allow me to apologize for not showing up. I'm a dick.

That being said, we can't meet. Ever! I would appreciate it if you would accept that at face value and not probe.

As for your proposal of a mutual teaching scenario, I am intrigued. As for your offer to wear a cupid's outfit, I am aroused. If this was your attempt at comedy, I may die of despair. If it was not, then please, I encourage you to attach all photographic evidence in your next email—purely for business, of course; to keep me motivated in finding love.

See? There I go again, flirting with another beautiful woman. I *believe you have your work cut out for you. I hope you're up to the task.*

How do you propose this arrangement is going to work? I await your instruction.

Sincerely, Kade.'

"Who knew being so desperate got results?" I said aloud, with a grin stretching across my face. It dropped hearing Zoe snicker across the room.

"No, it doesn't. If it did, you would have been prom queen, not me..."

I glared.

With Kit at work, Zoe had nothing better to do than sit in expensive negligée and read bridal magazines with a glass of rosé and offer the occasional insult when the mood struck her.

"Don't most people have a ring on their finger when they scroll through those things?" I regretted asking as Zoe's death stare burned a hole in my face.

"If that's true then you'll never read one," she snarled.

Ouch. My eyes narrowed into slits as venom burned in my throat demanding I took the cheap shot. "Speaking of marriage, when is your divorce hearing?"

She stilled, slapping the pages together. Her face was thunderous, but there was a hint of pain in her eyes. I hated the satisfaction it gave. "Seems to me like Andy got a lucky escape. Did he ever find out about you and Luka on prom night?" Zoe's lips pursed and her cheeks reddened. "Oh my God, he did. Is that what put the final nail in the coffin?"

"Shut up!" Tears pricked in Zoe's eyes. It was the first time I'd ever seen her show any emotion.

I tried to, but all the anger I'd built up over the years continued to spew out like an erupting volcano. "Cry all you want, Zoe. But I will *never* feel sorry for you because everything wrong in your life, you did to yourself."

Zoe wet eyes met mine, she pursed her quivering lips. "Are you done?"

Finally, I was.

My chest heaved. I focused my eyes back on the screen as Zoe got to her feet and left the room in a hurry, but not fast enough for me not to hear her sniffling. I knew I'd gone too far, and yet I was lighter, somehow—like hurting Zoe acted as a therapy session.

It made my skin itch.

Shifting in my seat, I clicked on the first email under Kade's and welcomed the onslaught of someone else's problems with the hope that offering advice would lessen my conscience plunging daggers into my stomach.

I managed to respond to twenty-six emails, and was halfway through answering the next, when my phone lit up with an incoming call from an unknown number. I narrowed my eyes, the curiosity niggling.

"Hello," I answered with hesitation.

"Liana!" Came a cheery voice that made me flinch. At once, I understood how curiosity killed the cat: *The cat killed itself.* "Have you given any more thought to my offer?"

I groaned. "I already gave you my answer, *Eric.* Don't call me unless you're dying and I'm the first name on your contact list. Even then, you might want to pray I'm in a good mood. Goodbye."

He gave a cold chortle that sounded like bribery. "Don't be so stupid to delude yourself into thinking you're independent. Think of all those unpaid bills. You *need* me."

"Like a goddamn crater in my cranium," I spat and hung up, not giving him a chance to respond. Sighing, I massaged my temples in an attempt to fend off the sudden migraine. It didn't help, so I brewed a cup of coffee, took two aspirin, cracked my fingers, and got back to work.

An hour later, I was thirty-four emails deep and opening

another when I glimpsed my reflection in the mirror—hair unbrushed, glasses askew, and in a set of pajamas I'd worn for two days—and realized it was time to log-off and get dressed for my date.

Standing from my seat, I headed for Kit's bathroom again, stalling at Zoe's door. Soft whimpers and sniffling rubbed the gaping guilt wounds in my stomach with a layer of salt. I reached out to knock when my mind offered a debate. *Zoe was worse. She liked to see people upset. She cheated. She hurt people and she didn't care...*

But I wasn't like Zoe—and that was the thought that solidified my next move.

Lifting my knuckles, I knocked twice and opened the door. My mouth gawped seeing Zoe's room for the first time since she moved in. It was far from what it was before. The once white walls were an obnoxious hue of flamingo-pink, and my bouncy, black carpet was now an oakwood floor, decorated with three fluffy white rugs.

The window, which once wore metal shades, now donned extravagant white curtains that could have been plucked from *Miss Havisham's* mansion—though immaculately clean—and gone was the old run-of-the-mill bed. In its place stood a queen-size, four-poster bed that cost more than all my possessions combined. Every inch of her room screamed expense. Even the air reeked of aldehydes and florals distinct to Chanel No. 5.

My eyebrows drew together. I'd been home every day, so when did she have the time to get workers in?

When Kit's bathroom was renovated. My teeth ground. The workers were in-and-out of this room, but Kit told me it was where they kept their tools. She knew, all those months ago, when she would tell me traffic would pick up and I'd be making enough to cover the rent in no time, that Zoe was moving in.

Unbelievable.

"What do *you* want?" Zoe sneered, curled into a thousand-dollar pillow with a strawberry face and eyeliner running down her cheeks.

I cleared my throat, the words like acid on my tongue. "To apologize..."

"Why?" Zoe scoffed, wiping her eyes. "So you can pretend you're better than me because I didn't apologize? I'm *not* sorry. I slept with Luka because I knew it hurt you, and nothing gave me greater pleasure than taking you down."

My heart panged in my chest. The venom and the anger on her face surprised me. I knew she was malevolent, but I never thought her sole purpose of sleeping with Luka was to hurt me. "... I feel sorry for you, Zoe. I can't imagine being so sad that I have to one-up every person in my life to feel worth something."

"Oh, save your worthless advice for someone who needs it, you hack!"

Anger attacked my chest, burning like she'd stabbed me with a hot poker. I scoffed, unable to believe I'd ever felt bad for her. Turning on my heel, I left Zoe's room in time to see Kit coming in the door. Her eyes squinted, quizzical as to why I was in there, and then widened as she realized I'd pieced the puzzle together.

Crossing my arms, I headed for my own room and slammed the door before Kit had the chance to open her mouth. I didn't want to hear it.

Heading for my shower, I stepped under the downpour of sweltering lava and let out a sob built of frustration and residual heartache. As much as I wished I could blame it all on Zoe, I couldn't saddle her with all the culpability and let her co-conspirator off scot-free. Luka was a fool used as a pawn in the game she played against me, but it didn't make him any less to blame.

I couldn't dwell on it for too long. I had a date. One I hoped would end in sex—anything to jolt me forward to the point I wouldn't care anymore...

I stepped out of the shower and dried myself off, wiping the rest of my tears away before blow-drying my hair. I styled the top into a French braid, stopping at the crown of my head and left the rest down in flowing waves. Next, I moved onto makeup. I applied foundation, a light smoky-eyed look, and a red lipstick.

My outfit was prepicked to save time. A black romper dress hybrid, low cut enough to make me feel sexy but not enough to make me panic every time I reached for the breadbasket. It hemmed mid-thigh, could pass as both classy and racy; and would work for any date situation that could arise—except maybe rock climbing, but the only thing I planned on climbing was Casper... and I wouldn't need my dress for that.

Picking out a pair of flat ankle boots, I zipped them up and checked the time on my phone. Casper would be here any minute, and the thought of him walking into the madhouse, or Zoe setting her sights on him, made me squirm. I decided not to risk it.

I grabbed my jacket, slipped it over my shoulders, and headed out of the building to wait for Casper curbside instead. Kit yelled my name as I left the apartment, but I didn't turn back. If anything, I sped up into a run and didn't stop until I got outside.

Leaning my back against the cold walls of my building, I grit my teeth to bare the cold, and waited... Sure he would arrive any minute.

CHAPTER 11

KADE

I wasn't going.

I made the decision in the shower, and now, as I sat on my sofa with a stiff drink in my hand, looking over a pros and cons PowerPoint I'd made, I knew more than ever that standing Liana up, *again*, was the right thing to do. After all, I wasn't romantic, and she was all about romance. I sat back, finished my drink, and wished I could turn back time.

Seeking advice from Liana? *Mistake.* Agreeing to date Liana? *Big fucking mistake.* Dating Liana as a second persona? *There weren't enough pills in the world to make even me think that was a good idea.*

Besides, standing her up cold—or 'ghosting' her, as the kids say—eliminated her wanting to reschedule. Though I was sure Casper could expect a strongly worded text sometime soon.

"What a great time not to exist, ay, Casper?" I chuckled to myself.

The door to Stephanie's bedroom opened and the sound of heels click-clacked across my tiled floors. "Don't you have a hot date tonight?" she asked, checking her hair in the mirror.

"Fuck off, Stephanie."

She rolled her eyes. "I guess in Kade-language, that could translate as: 'Gee, Steph, you look beautiful. Enjoy your night.' So, if it's all the same to you, I'm going to take it that way."

"Take it as you please." I lifted my eyes to look at her, and smirked. She was wearing a gorgeous, skin-tight beige dress and her grandmother's small diamond earrings she only wore on dates. "You look great."

Steph smiled, applying an extra coat of lipstick. "Look, I know this is none of my business, but tell me you're not standing the poor girl up for a second time."

"No, this time *Casper* is standing her up. He and I have discussed it at length. We agree it's for the best."

"Well, I think you're both abhorrent."

I shrugged, reaching for the TV remote. "We don't care."

Steph finished fixing her makeup and turned to me, her left hand on her hip. "Kade, so we're clear... Casper isn't real. *Right*?"

"Seriously?" I sat forward in my seat and shook my head. "I can assure you, at the present moment, there is no Casper in my brain, pulling the strings like some sadistic, S and M version of Geppetto on crack cocaine..."

"I'm just making sure." She held her hands up in defense. "After all, you're the one with a checklist to test if you're a sociopath, *Pinocchio*."

"Yes. True. But I'm the type of nutcase who is incapable of love and dies alone; old and decrepit on my deathbed with nothing but money to hug. Not the type to have a serial-killing alter ego who takes over when he feels like being a real live boy for the night."

"Thin line, Kade." Stephanie teased. "*Thin. Line.*"

"Aren't you leaving?" I spat.

Steph rolled her eyes again and picked her purse up from the ground. "At least have the decency to call her this time." She opened the apartment door. "And if you do decide to go, be careful. What if she likes you?"

"A lot of women like me."

"But it won't be *you* she likes. This could get ugly, fast."

"It couldn't possibly get uglier." As if on cue, my laptop dinged with an incoming email.

"We'll agree to disagree on that one." Steph walked backwards out the door. "You should take her to *Rosario's*; it's not at all romantic. Don't wait up for me. I'm staying at Cleo's tonight."

"And we'll continue to disagree on that one, too. Be careful!" I yelled as the door swung closed. I dragged my laptop onto my knee and double-clicked the new email from Liana.

'Now, Now, Kade... Photographs like the ones you're talking about are only sent to trustworthy people; and so far, the only thing I trust about you is your ability to talk a woman's panties off.

Besides, if I dress up, you have to, too! Hmm. What is the sexual equivalent of cupid?

Your move, Kade.

As far as the arrangement goes, I was hoping you'd have some ideas. Perhaps question for question? Although, I may not need your help at all. I happen to be on a date tonight with a ridiculously hot guy! If things go well, I could be a porn star by morning.

If he ever shows up, that is. He's already fifteen minutes late. I'm standing outside of my apartment building. Hence the 'sent from iPhone' at the bottom of this email.

Wish me luck.

Love, Liana.'

My body twitched from head to well... *head.* If I played my cards right, I could have a gorgeous woman in my bed by nightfall. All I had to do was: a.) show up; and b.) make sure she had a good time in my—*or rather, Casper's*—presence.

Rushing from my living room, I moved to get dressed; my decision not to go overturned by the court in my head. Strategies and tactics were already falling into place based on what I knew of her.

I stopped. *Was strategizing dates normal?* "I should ask."

Stepping into my bathroom, I wrote half of the email before I smothered my face in tea tree and mint shaving cream, and got to work making my stubble look presentable, careful not to shave it off altogether.

When I was done, I slapped my face with peppermint-infused aftershave, and finished typing the email. Reading it over once, I clicked send.

'... *I go over my plans for the night like a seasoned psycho. What I'll say, how she'll react—the endless possible scenarios each word could result in. Not to brag, but I've never met a single woman who this hasn't worked on. The problem is, I'm starting to think, like everything else in my life, this isn't a normal thing to do.*

I equate the amount of preparation I put into ensuring a date is successful to the effort serial killers put into securing their victims. Of course, I'm not a serial killer. Let's get that clear. I'm just saying... if I did decide to become one, I don't think I'd have a problem.

I am very charming.

As was Ted Bundy, Dahmer... Christ, Manson was so charming; he created a whole family.

I'm getting off-topic.

Is it weird?

Sincerely, Kade.'

Ripping through my ash wood wardrobe like a tornado, I discarded five shirts and four pairs of pants before deciding on a dark blue suit. I slipped my feet into leather loafers, dropped my phone into my breast pocket, and grabbed my keys from the table.

Heading out, I caught the time on the clock in the lobby and swore under my breath. I was so late. The proper date etiquette demanded I offer some sort of lie as an explanation. I waited until I hit the lobby and the signal picked up before hitting call.

"Hey, sorry, I was caught up at the office," I said as the call connected.

"Oh. You work in an office? What do you do?"

I blinked. *Fuck*, I wasn't prepared for follow-up questions. I panicked and hung up, scratching the back of my head. My lack of backstory for the character I created would be a sure giveaway.

Hailing a cab, I sat in the back and got to work creating a whole new life. Casper needed a job, and a happy childhood. *A house. A white picket fence. A dog. Two loving parents. Spoiled as a kid.* That was Casper's life—and it was a far cry from my own.

"Now for a job..." I clicked my tongue, going over Google's list of office jobs. "Lawyer. *Hm.*"

It wasn't totally ridiculous. I already mastered the pompous ass vibe down to a science, the night terrors gave me eyebags dark enough to look as though I spent my nights prepping for cases and, of course, my impressive looks and charm would make me likable to a jury.

I could be a lawyer, I smirked. And then stopped smirking. What if she knew about law? "Oh, fuck me."

I went back to the list, but none of them seemed to fit. And they all seemed to have a 'one wrong answer' downfall. Assistant? *Yeah, right.* As if I could assist anyone. I'd been a PA before and lasted a day before my rightful firing. Receptionist? Nobody would believe I'd have the patience or manners. Tech guy? I was tech-challenged.

I groaned.

"Hey." I caught the attention of the driver as we rolled to a stop at a traffic light. "When you look at me, what job do you see me doing?"

His eyes flicked to see me in his rearview mirror. "Accountant."

Accountant? Stiff upper lip, boring bastard, good at algebra —all things I was not.

I scowled. "What kind of fucking useless answer is that?"

The driver scoffed and called me a prick under his breath. I didn't mind. I deserved it.

Twenty minutes later, the car rolled to a stop outside of Liana's building and sure enough, there she was, curbside— breathtakingly beautiful.

Lawyer it is.

⁓⁓⁓

"S o, where're we going?" Liana asked, and that was when I realized I didn't have a place in mind.

"How about Italian?" I offered. "Ever been to *Rosario's*? It's a back alley secret."

"Perfect." She smiled, walking ahead.

I huffed out a low sigh, realizing I was, in essence, luring her into a dark alley. "Great job, Kade," I whispered to myself and blew out a breath. "That's not serial killer-y at all."

"Sorry, what?" Liana asked, turning back.

"I... didn't realize you were so tall."

Liana's lips pulled into a lopsided smile and her eyebrows pulled forward. My heart dropped, convinced the jig was up, but when she laughed like honey and kept walking, I let out a relieved breath; unable to believe she bought it. We arrived at the restaurant and were seated at a table in the far back, pressed against a rockery wall, next to a lightly burning fireplace. I looked around, taking in the atmosphere of the restaurant, and cursed Stephanie Taylor's existence.

Not at all romantic, my goddamn ass. The only light came from the flickering of the fire and the candles on each table, and there were only eight tables in the entire restaurant—all with two chairs, and all with couples sitting in them. Not first date couples like Liana and I, but couples in sickening love. One couple whispered sweet nothings back and forth, their hands clasped together, while others stared intensely at each other, without blinking, and didn't say a word. *What?* And the rest, well... the food would go cold before their mouths were free to eat it.

The air was filled with the aroma of roses and freshly baked bread. Even the table dressings were a romantic red, decorated in small white polka dots that, up close, were revealed to be tiny hearts. I grimaced at the image of Stephanie laughing her ass off somewhere, and near ground my back molars down to stubs.

A waiter dressed in a black and white suit arrived with complimentary water and the wine list. He stood, his ballpoint pen pressed to his notepad, ready to write our order.

"I'll take a vodka soda. Thank you." Liana smiled.

"Whiskey. Top shelf Jameson. Bring the bottle. Charge everything to this, thanks." I handed over my credit card as the waiter offered us each a food menu and left to collect our drinks.

"What's good to eat here?" she asked.

"Don't know. I've never been here before," I said, my throat dry. I took down a gulp of water.

Liana's eyebrows pulled forward. "Then why did you suggest it?"

Panic constricted my throat, the water lodging in my esophagus. I coughed, sputtering like a broken sprinkler, and fought for air.

"Oh my god. Are you okay?" she asked, throwing napkins with wide eyes. What were napkins meant to do? *Unchoke me*? I waved a reassuring hand, hacking until the last of the water in my throat landed in my mouth. Finally, I was able to breathe.

"Sorry about that," I said, my voice hoarse. "To answer your question, *I* haven't been here before, but I've heard great things. My best friend brought her girlfriend a while ago and she said it was delicious."

The table descended into silence, broken only by the waiter coming to take our orders, and the occasional slurping of Liana drinking through a straw. I cleared my throat as she moved forward and placed her elbows on the table.

"So, Casper, what do you do? Where did you grow up?" Her eyes flickered with the reflection of the candlelight. My breath hitched. "I want to hear the whole origin story."

I took a deep breath and recanted the tale I'd made up in the car. "Casper Daniels. I'm a lawyer. I grew up in a nice house in the suburbs with two adoring parents, God rest, and a dog. I was an only child. So, obviously I was spoiled. All in all, I've lived a pretty picturesque life. Not much more to tell." I finished the whole story in one breath. "Your turn."

Liana narrowed her eyes, a knowing smirk twitching at her lips unnerved me. I shifted in my seat.

"Liana Dawson," she said, finally. I relaxed. "I'm an advice blogger. I had a similar set up. Only, I grew up in Manhattan, in a lavish apartment with a brother, a sister, and parents who hated each other… so, not similar at all." She laughed and I nodded, my lips in a tight line.

I didn't know what to say next. Liana stared at me as though expecting a response, but whatever words were in my head refused to leave my mouth. A well-timed chime emitted from her jacket pocket, giving me a much needed moment to organize my thoughts; too loud and vast for me to pick a coherent one from the din.

Digging in her pocket, Liana emerged with her phone. "Oh. It's my work email. It sets up a reminder when I've been inactive for a while. Give me a sec while I put it on vibrate."

"My personal favorite mode." I smirked, finding my footing along with a suitable topic. "Speaking of your work, did the research guy ever give you an explanation for standing you up?"

"He did." Liana grinned, and then she rolled her eyes. "It was *lame*. Some cryptic email about how we can't ever meet in person. I don't know, maybe he's self-conscious about his looks."

I almost snorted, covering it with a low chuckle. "I don't think it's that..."

"And why do you say that?"

I sat back in my chair and shrugged. "I may have Googled you after we met and read that you're opening a sex section of your blog. I assume this is the research you were referring to?"

She nodded.

"Seems to me, a guy so self-conscious he won't meet you for coffee couldn't have racked up the amount of experience he'd need to help you out."

"Or the amount he *claims* to have." She laughed.

My shoulders squared. I pressed my elbows to the table, sitting up straight. "You think he's lying?"

"Of course he is. I read a study that the number of women guys claim to have slept with is double the number of women they've actually slept with." Liana sipped her drink. "He's a sad male statistic."

I scoffed. "Not all men lie, Liana. I, myself, am quite experienced."

"Yeah, but look at you... You're a good-looking guy who oozes charisma. Kade is probably some sad sack shut in, emailing me from his parent's bathroom with his hand firmly wrapped around his shaft." She laughed, and fury scorched a hole in my stomach.

A heavy weight bore down on my chest and my neck burned. Beneath the anger something else niggled. A new feeling I couldn't decipher. It wasn't embarrassment or annoyance, it was... offense. She was offending me—*to my face.*

"I don't understand why you think he's lying," I bit. "What kind of self-respecting man would subject himself to emailing a fucking chick site for help if he wasn't desperate?"

"*Excuse me*?" Liana's mouth gaped. "Did you call my blog a chick site?"

"Well that's what it is, isn't it?"

She harrumphed, a cute wrinkle appearing between her eyebrows. It was delightful. "I'll have you know men are at least a third of my readership." She sat tall with her chin raised. "I think you underestimate how much men need advice on love."

I rolled my eyes, a question popping into my head. "Why do you even need my help? You're a beautiful woman. Your sex life should be thriving."

"Not that it's any of your business, but I've been busy trying to make a career for myself, and after my first boyfriend and I broke up, my personal love life took a backseat. So, no, my sex life is not thriving."

One guy? I blew out a low whistle.

Liana scoffed. "What? Does the fact I've only been with one guy impress you?"

Why would it? I thought, a sneer at my lips. If anything, I pitied her. No wonder she was wound so tight. I snorted, shaking my head. "Sex isn't about numbers, it's about fun, spontaneity and, of course, safety. For me, sex got better with experienced partners. The more adept, the better. The kinkier, the better. The *dirtier*, the better..."

Liana chewed on the inside of her cheek, her skin flushed red.

"A woman's past has no place in my head in the bedroom, or anywhere else for that matter," I continued. "But you're right, I am impressed. Your drive and ability are remarkable, and your blog is an accomplishment... But as far as sex goes, I think you're depriving yourself. You want to learn about sex? Lesson number one: Get out of your own head and enjoy yourself."

She squinted her eyes and crossed her arms on her chest. "That is such an easy thing for a man to say. Guys don't have to deal with the judgement us women do. You walk through life windmilling your average-sized penises like they're anvils, without a care in the world."

Average? Pfft. "Sweetheart, average isn't a word than can be used to describe me, or my cock."

Liana's face scrunched. "*Ugh.* You know something? Men like you go around sleeping with anything that walks, talks, and breathes, don't you? I bet you and Kade are like the same person..."

Well, I couldn't deny she had a point.

"What's wrong with that? You're being very harsh on Kade. I happen to think he sounds like a stand-up fellow... I think I'd like him a lot."

"Funny, I think he sounds like a petulant child who does stupid things and boasts about his conquests like he's some kind of mysterious Hugh Hefner when the truth is he's a transparent asshole, and probably a thirty-year-old virgin."

I finally snapped, unable to take anymore slander. My teeth clamped together as I spat my words through them. "Like fuck I am! Jeez, what kind of advice blogger are you? You shouldn't be discussing my personal and private business with anybody. Isn't there some kind of confidentiality agreement on your goddamn site? I could sue you."

"There is a confidentiality agreement, *Kade*. But since I'm talking about you to you, I figured it didn't apply," she whispered-yelled, a pink blush creeping up her cheeks as murmurs spread around us.

My mouth gawped, and my mind went blank—jumbling my entire grasp on the English vocabulary into one long, mixed-up word. Liana quirked an eyebrow, waiting for me to offer some kind of excuse, but as I tried my best to string a sentence together, only one word rolled off my tongue:

"Fuck."

Chapter 12

Liana

I arched my eyebrow at him and sat back, taking a sip of my drink as I bathed in the smugness of catching him in a lie. "Why pretend to be someone else?"

He stammered, sputtered, and coughed. But nothing resembling words trundled out of his glorious mouth. *God, those lips...* Suddenly everything in his email made sense. It was no wonder Kade left the bar with a new woman almost every night. He exuded charm and looked like... *not a model*—he wasn't picture perfect enough. He was raw, had a scar spreading from his lip to the side of his nose that I hadn't noticed at first glance, and he was breathtakingly sharp. Every feature on his face had a razor edge, from the underside of his jaw to his cheekbones, and even the bridge of his crooked nose that gave the impression of a badly-set break. Somehow, they all added to the package of Kade. My throat dried as my core tightened, and for a split second, I forgot why I was pissed.

Oh, he'd created a persona out of thin air and used it to catfish me. Now I remembered.

"What? You think I didn't hear you muttering to yourself." I snorted and put on a deep voice. "'*Great Job, Kade... That's not serial killer-y at all.*' You suck at whispering. And next time you want to personality-catfish someone, hide your name on your credit card when you give it to the waiter." I rolled my eyes, calling him an amateur under my breath.

With one last clearing of his throat, Kade finally found his words. "You've known this *whole* time?"

I nodded my head. "By the way, your *smooth* cover jab at my height?" I snorted. "Not so smooth. I thought you said you had game?"

Kade sat forward in his chair, squinting his eyes, his lips tightening. "Oh, I have game. Believe me."

A tiny laugh escaped my throat, thrilled by the idea of riling him up. I sat forward, matching his stance and crossed my arms, my elbows atop the table. Smirking, I said, "Well, you must have misplaced it because right now, you're like a round of *Operation* without the tweezers."

Kade bellowed a disbelieving *ha*. "Sweetheart, you have no business playing Operation. You can't even find the bone."

Fire burned in the pit of my stomach, and my palm itched to toss my drink in his face; my blood coursing with the furious adrenaline of our hurtful tennis match. "Oh, I can find the bone. I choose not to."

"Why? Because you're an uptight sexless bore?"

I arched an eyebrow. "Opposed to a guy who's apparently sleeping his way through New York. Hey, how many kids have you spawned, Hefner?"

"None. Safety is key." He said, but by the bopping of the apple in his throat, I could see his momentary panic—going over the list of one-night stands in his head and wondering if any of the condoms broke.

Seizing my opportunity to get to him, I inched forward again. "I bet you've got at least five lovechildren out there."

He'd recovered from his panic. Back on form with that dangerous smirk, he winked. "Maybe, but none of them will ever call you mommy."

My eyes widened. "Ha. As if I'd ever want to bear children that were half spawn-of-Satan."

"*Right...*" Kade laughed. "As if you weren't hellbent on me bending you over the second you agreed to this date?"

Embarrassment tingled up my spine, and my mouth made a perfect 'O' of its own accord. He was right. Even as he sat glaring, I wanted him to take me in the bathroom and push me up against the cold tile. But I'd be damned if I'd give him the satisfaction of knowing that. I swiped a finger through my loose waves and played it cool. "Umm, says who?"

Kade's mouth inched up into a half-smirk, calm, collected, and... hot as hell. "Oh, selective memory loss? Well, allow me to give you a quick recap. I believe the words were, 'If things go well, I could be a porn star by morning.' Not sure I could get you to that level in one night, but hey, I'm willing to try."

My core burned of pent-up frustration, "In your dreams!" I seethed. *Or in mine...*

The waiter arrived with our food, a spaghetti carbonara for me, and a lasagna for Kade. My chest heaved as I sat back, enraged... and turned on. We zipped our lips until the waiter did a whole song and dance of '*Parmesan? Pepper? Salt? Refills? Enjoy your meal.*'

Kade bit his lip like he attempted to hold back a laugh until the waiter left us alone.

"What's so funny?" I asked.

Sitting forward, he smirked. "Believe it or not, I didn't go to the café with the intention of creating a persona. It happened in the moment. I realize it's not a normal thing to do, but in case it escaped your keen notice, I'm not fucking normal."

A small strike of amusement forced an upturn of my lips. "Oh, I got that. Trust me."

"Hence, why I emailed your chick site."

"It. Is. Not. A. Chick. Site!" My teeth clenched.

He gave a small snort, and I knew he'd said it to get to me.

"... The point is, whether we like it or not, we need each other. I would like to be a human someday, and you would like... to be a porn star, apparently."

I couldn't help the half-smile that cracked its way onto my face. Sensing an opening, Kade moved forward in his seat, amused. "Out of curiosity, sweetheart, how dirty were those dreams?"

I snickered, rolling my eyes. "Relax, *Fifty Shades*. They were vanilla at best."

"You severely underestimate me."

⌢⌣⌢⌣⌢

His lips crashed against the underside of my jaw, leaving a trail of hot kisses on my neck. I moaned as his hands trailed down to my hips, pushing me against the wall on the inside of my apartment door. I'd never been more thankful to find my apartment empty with a note on the table to tell me Kit and Zoe had gone clubbing. I didn't even care Kit hadn't invited me.

After Kade and I finished eating, we'd ordered two pitchers of margaritas, and as the last glass emptied, Kade and I started a game of footsie under the table, and we wasted no time in talking filth like seasoned professionals—or rather, he talked while I listened, feeling every word brush over my already too hot skin and between my legs.

Now, his hands moved down to my thighs and covered parts of me even I hadn't palmed in a long while. His kisses traveled to my bare chest and up again to the other side of my neck, nibbling my left earlobe. *Heaven.* My knees buckled under me as a moan ripped from my throat, Kade's strong hands kept me in place, his teeth nibbling on my skin through an amused smile.

I couldn't take it anymore, my hands wound up into his hair

and pushed him back with every intention of pulling him forward again and colliding our mouths in a hot, passionate kiss that led to the bedroom. But as my eyes met his, the profound sadness concealed behind fiery lust stopped me dead. I felt wretched. *What was I doing?*

Kade emailed my site for help, and here I stood, breasts heaving, becoming part of his problem. Another notch on his bedpost he would move on from in the morning and be alone forever—lost in the abyss of one-night stands, never getting close to another person.

And I'd be down a sex expert, forced to tackle the blog alone.

My hands dropped to his chest, flat and outstretched. I pushed him away with the edges of my fingertips.

Kade stepped back, leaving my body cold. "Everything okay?"

I fanned myself in an attempt to cool down. "Maybe this isn't such a good idea. We need each other, and sex... complicates things."

Kade's lips pursed as he pondered my statement for a long minute before he nodded. "You're right. So, I say we get on with it then. The sooner we help each other out, the sooner we can fuck our brains out. I'm thinking we do it right on your dining table..."

He turned his back, walking further into my apartment and took a seat on the floor as I worked hard not to swallow my tongue in shock. *Oh boy.* Working with someone as brash and forward as Kade would be hard but keeping my hands off him in the process—absolutely torturous.

My limbs on fire, I grabbed a bottle of whiskey and two glasses from the kitchen cupboard and joined Kade on the floor of the living room. His back pressed against the softness of Kit's sofa, but his head turned in my direction, watching my legs with hunger as I walked. The way I tingled *every-*

where seemed an impossible reaction to a simple look. I pushed my urges away and plopped down beside him, a little too close for my lack of willpower, leaving only a modicum of space between our hot bodies. I gulped and clicked play on an upbeat pop playlist, sure to exclude anything slow or sensual.

Kade smirked, reaching for the bottle. He uncapped it, licking at his bottom lip as his eyes bore into mine. "Shall I start?"

I bit my lip and raised my glass. "Hit me."

He poured me a double, and one for himself. "Do you think I'm a sociopath?"

"*Hmm.* I didn't until you faked a whole new life," I teased. He nudged me and raised an eyebrow as if to tell me to be serious. My smirk dropped. "No, I don't think you're a sociopath." He seemed relieved by my answer and his shoulders relaxed. "My turn. Do you really think I'm a sexless bore?"

"Definitely," he said without pause. Well, I couldn't fault him for being truthful.

I groaned. "Why do you think you're incapable of love?"

Kade shrugged. "I've never loved anyone. Not really. I care for Stephanie, so much so, I think I'd lose my mind without her. But I'm not sure I *love* her. Rather, I've grown used to her."

I stretched out, propping my head up on my hand as I leaned my elbow on the couch. I angled my body toward him and tried to figure him out. "What would it take for you to be sure?"

"I wish I knew." His eyes dropped to his feet.

Worried I overstepped too soon, I pulled it back to a more general question. "You've never had a girlfriend?"

He shook his head.

"Do you want one?"

"Someday." He smirked, eyeing me with mischief. I narrowed my eyes, waiting for the punch line, but it never came. Lifting my drink to my lips, I took down a quart of the glass, and that's when he struck. "I did have a wife once."

The burning liquid launched into my esophagus and shot out of my nose. I sputtered whiskey and coughed, clamoring for breath with wide eyes. When I could breathe, I inhaled three fast breaths, my chest burning, and shook my head. "You're messing with me, aren't you?"

Kade laughed, holding up a hand. "Honest to god. I was twenty-four. Her name was Melissa, I think... or maybe Cassidy. Could've been Sarah... or was it Aubrey?"

I snorted, my eyebrows crinkling. "Such similar names, how could anyone decipher between them?"

"Give me a break, we were married for seventeen hours..." His smirk turned to a grin. "What happens in Vegas..."

I marveled. Kade was fast becoming the most interesting specimen I'd ever met. I wanted the full story on how a person gets so drunk they get married to a stranger, but more pressing matters called me. With difficulty, I moved on. "Are you on any dating apps?"

Kade scoffed. "They're more like booty call apps. You really get paid for this?"

"*Shut up*," I laughed. "Some married couples met on dating apps."

He rolled his eyes.

"You're really pessimistic, has anyone ever told you that?" I teased, narrowing my eyes, my tongue between my teeth.

"They have. But they used it in a way it was somehow synonymous with asshole."

My shoulders shook in a small laugh. "You need to establish an intellectual and emotional connection... learn to talk to a woman without the possibility of touching her."

"But touching her is the fun part." He whined.

I nudged him. "You need to learn how to date. Long-term, not for a night."

He winked. "And you need to do the opposite. A couple of one-night stands should do it. I offer myself as tribute to the cause."

I scowled. "I was thinking I could open my blog up to beta questions from a select few readers and have you answer them. That way, I can observe and learn."

Kade shook his head, finishing his glass. "Sorry, but if you're going to teach me to fall in love, I'm going to loosen you up a little. Was this one guy even good?"

My face, burning hot with embarrassment, said it all.

"Did he at least make you orgasm?" He asked, and I bit my lip as a response. Kade scowled. "*Rough.*"

I agreed, but we weren't there to talk over my lack of orgasms or Ronnie's seeming want to be a racer boy, completing the course faster each time. "We're not talking about him, Kade. This is about you. What was your childhood really like?"

He clammed up.

"Kade?"

"We're not talking about that, either." His eyes, and the way his mouth settled into a line, told me not to push. I let it go and checked my phone, waiting for the tension to ease. I realized I had an email from him and snorted.

"*Manson created a whole family?* You have... a way with words."

"Hence my ability to be a damn good literary agent in spite of my personality."

A lit agent? My eyes narrowed as I went over the list of agents in New York in my head. "Kade... *Jennings*?"

He nodded. I put my glass down, hit with a wave of doubt and suspicion as my spine tingled. "... You interned for my father back when The Dawson Talent Agency was purely lit based."

"I did."

"Did he tell you to email me?" I bristled, the urge to throw him out overwhelming me. I wouldn't put it past the old man to send Kade in as a plant and destroy my chance to expand the blog so he could sweep in and 'save' me as I went under. My jaw set, expletives on the edge of my tongue. I looked to Kade with a face made of stone, only to find him smirking.

"Liana, I wouldn't piss on Eric Dawson if he were on fire, much less do a thing he said. He's a pretentious prick with an arrogant attitude, and coming from me?"

That was bad. My nerves relaxed as a whole new surge of intrigue hit me. "You were what? Nineteen?"

"Fresh out of high school, a few months into my first year of college. Imagine my luck at scoring an internship with *the* Eric Dawson." He grinned. "What a dick."

"*That's Daddy,*" I sang, knowing how right he was. "How long were you there?"

"Four *long* years." He licked his bottom lip and drew in a breath. "I quit the day Steph and I decided to go out on our own."

"How'd you and Stephanie meet?"

Kade bit his bottom lip and laughed. "My last therapist asked me that same fucking question."

"Your answer?"

"He's still waiting on it."

I sighed, refilling our glasses. I lifted mine to my lips and took it down like a shot before refilling the glass. "You gotta give me something here, Kade. I can't help you if I don't know how you ended up like this."

Kade followed my lead, downing his drink. "Fine. Steph and I met when I was eleven, at a time when I had nobody else." He blew out his cheeks as though the next part was hard to admit. "When I lived on the streets."

I stopped my drink, mid-sip. My heart panged as I imagined Kade as a young boy, alone on the streets.

LOVE, LIANA... SINCERELY, KADE

"Where was your mom?" I asked and flinched, wishing instantly that I hadn't.

It seemed those were the magic words. His mouth clamped shut, his demeanor changed, and he decided it was time to go. He got up and left without a single syllable passing his lips.

He didn't even say goodbye.

CHAPTER 13

KADE

When I got home, I drank so much that 'passed out' wasn't dramatic enough to describe what I'd done. Liana bringing up my mom had slammed everything back into the forefront of my mind and drinking to excess seemed the only thing that made it go away. Though my liver, a hostage in my plight, had become an unwitting victim —*collateral damage.*

Peeling my head off my desk, I wiped the slobbering drool from my mouth and covered my eyes with my hands, the moonlight shining through the ceiling-to-floor window of my apartment burned my corneas. When I first moved in, I thought they were a great feature. Now, I wanted to spray them black and exist in darkness.

My head was already heavy, but the weight intensified when the overhead lights flicked on, bathing the room in a white beam so bright, I wondered if I died in my sleep and approached the pearly gates. *Fat chance.*

"Rough night, *Casper*?" Steph appeared, placing a bottle of water and two aspirin in front of me. "You came home, so it couldn't have gone well."

I tried to shrug, but my motor skills were short-circuiting.

"You're home. How'd your night go?" I lifted my head high enough to look at her and flinched at the sight. My answer, written on her swollen face in bruising, made me gasp. My jaw locked as rage spread through my veins like molten rock.

Tear lines stained with the remnants of her mascara decorated her face, covering a fast-emerging blue and purple bruise on her right cheekbone. Her eye swelled—so rapidly, it was near closed—and her bottom lip trailed only a moment behind. Thick, dark blood trickled from her nose and dripped down to the scratch on her chin.

"What the fuck?"

"It wasn't her fault," she was quick to say. "It was an accident. We were at a bar, and we shouldn't have been. She's sober. It was selfish of me to take her there. There was this guy, and I shouldn't have been talking to him. I had no reason to be, I know how jealous Cleo gets. I riled her up."

The nausea that crept up my throat tasted of vitriol and disgust. "How many fucking times are you going to make excuses for her?"

"She didn't hit me, I swear," Stephanie cried. "We started to argue, and she stormed out. I went after her, and tripped, hitting my face on the concrete outside." Her words were delivered like a performance, and I wasn't sure which of us she was trying to convince.

"Steph..." I shook my head, pulling her into my arms. Her shoulders shook with sobs, and when she pulled away, blood stained my shirt as her nose gushed like Niagara Falls. I studied her face to see if she needed a doctor or not. Faintly, under the mess of make-up and bruising; the unmistakable mark of knuckle-to-skin impact.

"She didn't mean to. I got her mad." Her words contradicted her story. I pulled my bottom lip into my mouth and bit down, saying nothing. She didn't need a lecture, not now.

I took her hand and guided her to my bathroom. On the

way, I grabbed a pair of my boxers and an old, ratty T-shirt. Handing them to her, I turned my back and drew a bath while she got changed. When she was decent, I craned my neck to look at her and my eyes focused in on her legs. Blood, cuts and bruises on her shins and thighs told me all I needed to know about how her mid-section would look. She hadn't been lying about hitting the concrete—the layer of dirt on her knees proved it—but I doubted she'd tripped like she said. It looked more like she was knocked to the ground and stomped on.

Shutting the faucet off, I checked the temperature was luke-warm before I helped her into the tub. She hissed as she sank down, the water sloshing against her cuts, and pulled her knees to her chin—burying her head between her thighs.

I didn't know what to do next. Every instinct urged me away, to leave her to her thoughts. But as more water grazed her cuts and she let out another low hiss, I closed the door and rolled my sleeves to my elbows.

Seeking out a white cloth in the cabinet below my basin, I dipped it in the water and wrung it out. I approached her face first, dabbing it with care until all of the mascara and blood washed away. Stephanie's eye was completely shut by the time her face was cleaned. I wrung out the cloth and brushed under her eye. She winced, shrinking back.

"I gotta get the dirt, Steph. You don't want an infection. Your eyes are too pretty for you to lose one," I whispered. My chest ached seeing her in pain. Not for the first time, I wished Cleo would stumble into traffic.

Gritting my teeth, I added antiseptic to the edge of the fabric and approached gently. She recoiled again, and my sorrow turned to anger. I wanted to scream, shout, break things and threaten to kill Cleo for what she'd done. But none of that would help Stephanie.

For her, I kept my temper in check.

I rinsed the cloth—the blood and muck running russet in the clear water—and rang it out again.

Placing my hands under her chin, I tipped her head back. Her nose, crooked and swollen, pissed blood like a busted pipe. It would need medical attention, but I didn't want to worry her with it yet. Instead, I handed her the cloth and told her to apply pressure to stop the bleeding as I moved onto the open wounds. Starting with her lip, I used a fresh cloth doused in disinfectant.

"This might sting," I warned.

"More than it already does?" She tried to laugh, but it came out strangled.

I grimaced and pressed gently to her lip. She bucked, hissing and groaning, until the sting wore off. "I'm sorry."

With a small smile, she lay the side of her face that didn't look like a golf-ball on the edge of the bath and uncovered her legs for me. The thick layer of dirt demanded I be less gentle on her knees. I scrubbed, hard, until the debris of the street washed away. Under it, lacerations where her skin met the pavement were deeper than I thought.

She stayed still the entire time I cleansed them, and when I looked at her, her lip quaked, and tears pooled in her eyes.

"She loves me," she whispered, more to herself than me. "I know she does."

I pretended not to hear. "Dry off. I'll go get you some clothes."

I turned my back, my stomach panging as I heard the crack of her sobs straining free from her body. I headed to her room in search of some comfortable clothes; chewing the inside of my cheeks like chunks of overdone steak until they were sore.

Emerging with her favorite onesie, I stopped off in the laundry room and heated it up in the dryer so it would be warm when she put it on. Next, I collected her favorite pair of slippers—more like gray cotton boots—and put them on the radiator so her feet would be toasty too.

I knocked twice on the bathroom door before entering. That was always our signal. If she was indecent, she would yell out before I pressed down the handle. She didn't. Opening the door, I found her in a towel, the t-shirt and boxers discarded to the floor. Perched on the edge of the bath, she held her left side, above her ribs, and shuddered.

"Can I see?" I asked and she nodded. Standing up, she parted the towel ever-so-slightly to reveal her side without compromising her modesty. It was worse than I thought. Black, blue, purple, and red bruising covered her ribcage on one side, and again, the unmistakable markings of fists on flesh.

Every movement she made was accompanied by a flinch and a small cry. I raised my fingers to feel for cracks in her bones, but I barely brushed her before she let out an ear-splitting squeal.

I jumped back, my jaw hardening. "I'm taking you to the hospital. You might have a broken rib."

"Oh, more than one," she wheezed. "I remember how it felt last time. This is worse." I moved for my phone to call an ambulance. "No." She grasped my arm. "I'll go tomorrow, I promise. Tonight, I need sleep."

I didn't like it but arguing with Stephanie when her mind was made up was akin to barking at dogs and expecting them to talk back. My nostrils flared as I handed over the onesie and left her to get dressed. While she was doing that, I made up the sofa for her with a sheet, a pillow, and her comforter. And then, I did the same with the smaller sofa so I could keep an eye on her.

She emerged a few minutes later, the swelling on her face somehow worse than it was a minute ago. Pursing my lips, I fished the ice pack out of the freezer and handed it to her along with some heavy-duty pain meds.

"Can we watch trash shows?" Her lips turned up into a soft smile as her eyes shone with tears.

Taking my space on the sofa across from her, I nodded, and reached for the remote. Pressing play on some reality show, I didn't watch a single second of it—my eyes never left Stephanie, even after she'd fallen asleep.

I stayed awake most of the night watching her, terrified she was bleeding internally. The voice in my head urged me to wake her up, drag her into a cab, or call an ambulance. But the other side of my brain told me to keep her out of the conscious world for as long as possible. When she woke up, she'd have to address a lot more than her injuries, and so I left her sleeping, hoping the meds would keep her sedated through the worst of it.

But they didn't. It got to four a.m. before the guilt of not dragging her to the hospital began to suffocate me. Every time she groaned with pain, I flinched. She turned on her injured side and whimpered like a wounded animal. I swore under my breath.

I wanted to rip Cleo open and sell her for parts on the dark web. But that wasn't the healthy response to have. In fact, it added six or seven marks to my now called *potential serial killer* column. Shaking my head, I realized killing Cleo wasn't a viable option. For one thing, Steph would never forgive me. For another, I wasn't sure how I'd fair with a face like mine in the pen.

But no matter how I did it, I swore I would make Cleo hurt.

Stephanie groaned again as I woke her and administered the final round of painkillers for the night. When she was out, I reached for my phone and took detailed close-ups of the marks on her face and neck, saving the pictures to a secure file on my phone.

I sat at my desk, accepting *most* of the night was becoming *all* night, and watched the sky lighten outside of my window. The sun rising over the Manhattan skyline was a breathtaking sight the likes of which I'd never seen growing up in Chicago. It served as a reminder of how far I'd come—and how far Stephanie should have.

Gnawing what was left of the inside of my cheek, I repressed the urge to scream. With no other option, I decided to be semi-healthy about my thoughts and vent them to the one person who I knew would care.

'Dear Liana,

My best friend came home beat up and bruised at the hands of her abusive girlfriend.

When we were kids, Steph and I lived in a halfway home for homeless teenagers ran by Cleo, a narcissistic bitch who called herself a beacon for the lost, but all she really wanted was vulnerable kids to sell drugs for her.

After a while, I couldn't stay there anymore. My dreams were bigger than slinging coke on the corner, and as Cleo became an addict—pushing drugs on everyone—she got dangerous. The day she handed Steph a needle was the day we left. We got our first shitty apartment in Weehawken where, a few years later, The Jennings & Taylor Literary Agency was born. It could've been great, but only a month in business, Cleo showed up broke and addicted, and wormed her way back in.

Like that, Steph disregarded all of her hard work and assigned herself to desk duty and coffee fetching so Cleo wouldn't think she was out of her league.

I should have thrown Cleo out when I had the chance.

Stephanie would have stayed with me, then. If I gave her the same ultimatum now, I'm not sure she would make the same call. I couldn't survive knowing she was out there, in the grasps of someone like Cleo, without me to come home to. I fear she'd end up dead.

And as selfish as it sounds, I need her. She's all I have in this world—my only humanizing influence.

You asked me what it would take for me to be sure if I loved

Stephanie. This is what it took. I know now what she means to me. Stephanie Taylor is the only real family I've ever had—the closest thing I'll ever have to a sister.

And I think I love her.

Sincerely, Kade.'

CHAPTER 14

KADE

The beeps of the hospital machines were driving me insane.

Stephanie had been lying on her assigned bed in a fluorescent-lit, battleship gray room that stank of ethanol for over an hour waiting for a doctor. One had already been by to assess her injuries. He, of course, ordered a scan to see if anything internal was broken. But since she'd gone in for it, we'd heard nothing.

"What the fuck is taking so long?" I paced back and forth.

Stephanie stayed silent, as she had the nine other times I'd asked the same question. I didn't like her so quiet, without her usual level of snark. It seemed unnatural. I wished she would talk, laugh... *look alive.*

Pulling up a chair by her bed, I enticed her. "Did I tell you about my date with Liana?"

Her attention peaked. "How did you mess it up?"

"Oh, let me count the ways." I snorted. "For starters, she's as smart as she is insightful and beautiful. She made me within the first five minutes. Casper is dead and buried."

"Of course, she did. You're not slick." Steph tried to smile, wincing as the muscles pulled in her cheeks. "What tipped her off?"

"Me muttering to myself in third person, and then to add idiocy to stupidity, I decided to hand over my credit card with my name looking all pretty there on the front."

Steph shook her head and winced again. "I think my nose is broken."

"It is. I saw the doctor write it on his pad. They're going to set it soon..." I sighed. "Of course, to them, soon seems to be in *ten-fucking-years!*" I raised my voice so the workers outside could hear me, and then I felt like a jackass.

Doctors were overworked, nurses were underpaid, a hospital had many pressing emergencies—all of this, I knew. But every time Stephanie whimpered, my ability to give a shit flew out of the window, replaced by the urge to yell until someone came and took her pain away.

As if on cue, the doctor finally returned... and he wasn't alone. Behind him stood two unremarkable uniformed police officers, and a brunette woman in an ashen suit. The eyes of all three people surveyed me in a way that unnerved me.

"Hi, Stephanie. I'm Detective Hart." The woman introduced herself, and then her dark eyes landed on me again. Her steel jaw pushed forward as she scowled. "Would you wait outside please, *sir*?"

I scoffed, folding my arms over my chest. "I'm not leaving her alone."

They all exchanged glances and moved to Stephanie, creating a barricade around her as Detective Hart leaned forward and whispered in her ear.

"Please, sir," Detective Hart spoke to me again. "Your girl-friend needs to speak with us. *Privately.*"

"Girlfriend?" I blinked, suddenly aware of what was happening. "You've got it wrong. I didn't do this to her. I'm not her boyfriend, I'm her… brother." Stephanie did a double take hearing the word come out of my mouth. Her lips twitched up at the corners, and her eyes filled with tears.

Stephanie reached out past one of the uniformed officers and grabbed my hand. "Please, I don't want him to leave."

"Okay." Detective Hart nodded. "Stephanie, what we do in situations where abuse is evident is—"

"I fell," Steph rushed out. "I wasn't abused."

"Steph, come on," I scorned, dropping her hand.

"Shut up," she glared through narrow eyes, then turned her scowl on Detective Hart. "There's nothing you can do for me. I'm fine. I need to be more careful when I walk, is all."

The police officers shared a knowing look, their mouths turning down into tired frowns, but no surprise flashed in their eyes. In fact, one of them gave a sigh as though he expected Stephanie's response.

"Stephanie… we can help you."

"I don't need any help," Steph spat, forcing a wry smile. "Thank you, Detective."

Detective Hart nodded, somber in her failed attempt to help. She left her card on the side table in the corner of the room and escorted the officers out as the doctor moved to Steph's side and talked treatment plans.

Sensing an opportunity while Stephanie was preoccupied, I ran after Detective Hart, catching up with her in the hallway.

"Her name is Cleo Kilmer," I yelled.

The Detective turned to face me. "Excuse me?"

"She's a recovering drug addict and 'former' dealer from Chicago. She moved to New York almost eight years ago to be with Stephanie. She doesn't work, but always has hard cash," I quirked an eyebrow, highlighting the implication. "And this isn't the first time Steph has come home with injuries this severe. But Cleo has a hold over her that I can't break. *Please…* Is there anything you can do?"

Detective Hart's face contorted with sympathy. "Sir, without your sister's statement, I'm afraid we can't lay charges of assault against Cleo Kilmer... But we *can* investigate her income." She reached into her pocket and emerged with a card. "Take my number. If you can think of anything else that would be of help to us, give me a call. If we find something illicit, would you be willing to testify?"

"Anything you need," I vowed, taking the card. "I want to see the bitch in prison."

T he cab rolled to a stop in the middle of a pretty bad traffic jam at the corner of Columbus Avenue and West 81st Street. Raindrops pelted the cab windows like small rocks as I checked my email, hoping to find something from Liana. I sighed seeing it empty.

Leaving the hospital without Stephanie was weird. The doctors recommended she stay overnight for observation, and I agreed, but the thought of going home alone, to sit in the silence with my tsunami of inner conflict... *scared me.*

I hunkered down in the leather seat, raking a hand through my sopping wet hair. My head hurt from all the thoughts tumbling around in there, the throbbing added to by the incessant EDM playlist the driver insisted on deafening me with.

Unable to take anymore bass, I decided it would be faster—and less painful—to get out and walk home. I tossed the guy twenty bucks and bailed, pulling my jacket closed as the harsh weather beat around me. It took only a moment before my attire was drenched through to the bone.

I hunkered down, heading for the park, when I realized Liana's apartment was only three blocks away.

Would it be too much to stop by? I pondered. I'd only met the woman twice. Showing up at her doorstep the day after storming out of her apartment was most likely unacceptable social etiquette. Not to mention, weird.

But you're kind of weird. My inner monologue spoke logic.

The rain hammered down harder, pelting my skin with the force of paint gun pellets. I shivered, my arms wrapped around myself, and ran in the direction of Liana's building before I could talk myself out of it. Giving it my all, I bounced on the pads of my feet and took off in a vigorous sprint.

By the time I got to her door, I was breathless, and my suit clung to my body as though stuck by a layer of invisible adhesive. Knocking on her door, I pushed a hand through my sopping wet hair, slicking it back like I was auditioning for a role in a low-budget stage production of *Grease*.

Liana answered on the third knock and her mouth dropped open at the sight of a drowned rat with an impeccable face on her doorstep. Her eyes moved down, landing on my body, and spent a little extra time on my abs—visible through my transparent white shirt. Then, as they moved down again, I realized my pants were no longer on securely. The waistband of my boxer shorts, and a glimpse of the hammock hole, were on show. My manhood quivered, hardening under her gaze.

Oh, God. Not the time.... "Dead cats. Dead cats. Dead cats," I repeated until I deflated. Liana raised an eyebrow. "A little trick for the—uh—mind."

She smirked, opening the door wide and turning back into the apartment. "I got your email. I was in the middle of replying to it."

"What do you have so far?" I followed her in, taking my jacket off, and hung it on the coat stand by her door.

"The gist of it was me apologizing for bringing up a sore spot for you last night, and then I asked about Stephanie. Are the cops involved?"

"They were at the hospital, but—hey, do you mind if I take

these off?" I stripped off my shirt and trousers and balled them up in my arms. "You got a dryer around here?"

Liana's eyes bugged out of her skull as her mouth dropped open. She pointed in a direction to my right. I followed her hand and found the laundry room at the end of the hall. It was a simple room. White walls with black shelves housing the detergents, and two machines—one for washing, the other for drying—and an empty hamper in the corner. My nose tipped up, inhaling the sweet scent of lavender and lemon. I piled my clothes into the machine and hit the start button, leaving my clothes to dry.

Back in her living room, I found Liana on the sofa and stretched out on the seat beside her. I was thankful her apartment was warm and comfortable, though the texture of her faux fur sofa tickled my back relentlessly. There was a faint smell of cinnamon toast in the air and residue of syrup on Liana's bottom lip.

Suddenly, I had a craving. Forcing my eyes from her lips, I blinked at her. "What was I saying?"

"Stephanie..."

"Oh, right. She refused to give Cleo up to the cops. I gave them the info I had. It might lead to an arrest, but it's a long shot."

Liana's mouth moved into a straight line, but her eyes were roaming all over my bare chest, examining every detail. I let her stare as long as I could without getting aroused, clearing my throat when it got too much to handle. "*Liana*?"

"Sorry," she said, eyes wide. Her face developed a sudden sunburn. "I was..."

"Ogling me?" I offered. "Don't worry; I don't mind."

Ripping her sights away, Liana composed herself, the red in her cheeks now a light blush. "I think some people become so used to abuse, they mistake it for love. My mom did." Her green eyes darkened, turning sad. "It wasn't physical, but the torment she went through every time my father stayed out all night was debilitating. Eventually, it became something she got used to. And every time he would come back home and treat her nice, it was like she would forget all of the bad stuff and be grateful for the attention."

"That's awful," I said, my voice soft. I slid my hand into hers and gave it a light squeeze.

"You know the worst thing? I kind of hated her for not leaving. I wanted to scream in her face every single day until she realized she deserved more... So, I guess what I'm saying is, it's okay for you to resent Stephanie's decision."

I breathed out, hard, and hung my head. "I think I do a little... I hate that she goes back every time, I hate that the next time she could end up dead, I hate that she doesn't seem to care. And I hate that she doesn't think about how alone I'd be without her. She only cares about protecting Cleo, that goddamn bitch. I hate her so much."

Liana inched closer, making me rapidly regret my decision to strip. As her hand brushed the naked skin of my bicep, dead cats weren't enough to stop my biological responses.

Her eyes moving down to my engorged penis, she bit her lip. "You really are ready to go at all times, aren't you?" Her voice, breathy and soft, sent a surge through my body.

"It's a gift and a curse," I said.

The air, electrified around us, didn't help my situation. Neither did the way her eyes locked on mine and seemed to light up with the images of everything I wanted to do to her. My breath labored as I drank her in—so beautiful, it seemed impossible she'd never been satisfied. God, how I wanted to be the man to give her a toe-curling, earth-shattering experience...

We moved in, millimeters off each other's lips, and froze. The smell of her perfume, a warm vanilla with hints of amber and cedar wood, mixed with her fabric softener to become the most intoxicating aroma I'd ever smelled.

I ached against the waistband of my boxers, begging to be set free. A red-hot pocket rocket, ready for lift-off as Liana's timid hands reached out, grazing the hair on my chest before moving down between my pecs. I groaned, every inch of each delicate finger sending shockwaves through my nervous system. Her touch felt so good, it stung. And suddenly, I was a sadomasochist addicted to the pain. I shivered, wishing she would dig her nails in so hard the skin would break.

She licked her lips, giving them a shine that beckoned me. My hand wound up her neck, brushing the mane of hair away from her glorious face. Only then did I notice she was wearing her glasses. It was the first time I'd seen her in them, and holy hell, were they sexy.

Her lips parted, a shiver of a breath escaping as her hand moved to my back, tracing the edge of my shoulder blade as though searching for the remnants of a broken wing.

"I'm no fallen angel, Liana," I whispered.

"I was searching for the markings of a devil in disguise."

I grinned, taking her hand in mine, and placed it at the base of my abdomen, pushing down. "Search lower."

She swallowed the lump in her throat, inching her hands down at a painfully slow pace. I bit back a groan. Untrained or not, she was a pro at the slow burn tease, lingering by the waistband of my boxers in an effort to torture me. I closed my eyes and waited for the impact of her hand on my most intimate part. Instead, she let out a soft giggle like a whisper from the divine, and her lips landed on my neck.

Her moan in my ear broke the last straw of my self-control. I wrapped my arms around Liana's body and pulled her to me. Her legs parted, landing at either side of my lap. My mouth arriving on her neck, I nibbled the sweet spot above her collarbone. Shuddering a moan, she threw her head back, allowing me more access. I kissed down her chest, my hands kneading her breasts.

"Holy fuck," I whispered against her skin. "No bra? I'm appalled."

Her scoff turned to a giggle. "I wasn't expecting company."

"I wasn't expecting this."

She smirked. "Me neither. Maybe you should hurry up and kiss me before we realize how much of a bad idea this is."

"It is a bad idea, isn't it?" I grinned.

"*Disastrous.*"

Our noses bumped together, every breath she took fanning my face. Her lids fluttered closed as she licked at her bottom lip and trembled in desperation for my kiss.

But she'd slow-burned me... and now it was my turn.

Starting at the edge of her jaw, I moved meticulously slow, sure to hit every mark on the treasure trail of her face before I reached the chest of gold in the middle. Placing one last kiss at the corner of her mouth, I licked my lips and moved in, ready to—

"I'm home!" A woman's high-pitched squeal shot through my ear. Liana jumped back, her body leaving me cold as she landed on the other side of the sofa. Sitting up straight, she adjusted her t-shirt and flattened her hair in an attempt to look nonchalant.

"Hey, Kit." Liana breathed out as a small brunette rounded the corner. "How was work?"

The woman, *Kit*, moved her suspecting eyes from Liana to me. She arched her left eyebrow, and asked, "Who are you?"

To be polite, I stood up to introduce myself. Bad idea, I realized, when her gaze landed on the tent in my shorts. Kit's mouth crept into an amused smile. Her eyes moved from my crotch over to her sister.

"On my faux fur, Lee? *Really*?"

Liana turned beet red and shook her head, tripping over

her own tongue trying to deny it. Her mouth opened and closed, the words on her tongue getting stuck in her throat. She squeaked, taking another calming breath, and her mouth opened again.

When it did, I could hardly believe the words that tumbled out...

Chapter 15

Liana

"I was wet."

If my cheeks were red before, they'd since become an undiscovered shade of vermillion. I closed my eyes and let the embarrassment wash over me for a moment before trying again. "I mean *he* was wet."

Kit snorted, turning to Kade. "Ah, don't worry, you're not the first pre-ejaculator to roll through this place. Though the first to be in Liana's bed." She winked, and I could have died on the spot.

"Excuse me?" Kade scoffed. "I'll have you know —"

I held up a hand and his lips zipped. "Knock it off, Kit. *Kade* here got caught in the rain on his way over. Drenched to the bone, he stripped off, and—"

"Got hard?" Kit chewed her lip and stared me down like she didn't believe a word I was saying, then something dawned on her, and her mouth made an 'O.' "Wait. Kade as in *the* Kade?"

"What the fuck does that mean?" he demanded.

The burning in my chest lurched into my throat and asphyxiated me. "Nothing," I swore, "I told her you catfished me is all, nothing else."

Kit's eyebrow twitched. "What else is there?"

"None of your business," Kade bit.

She laughed. "Oh, you're sensitive... no wonder you pre—"

I gave Kit a look that told her to shut her mouth. The last thing I wanted was for Kade to get worked up and storm out again, especially after the night he'd had. He was already a flight risk, and while I knew Kit was kidding, her tone of voice stayed even in fluent sarcasm that came off cold and bitchy to a stranger. Almost Zoe-like.

"Relax, Kade. Kit's just playful." My face hit burned so hot it stung. I fanned myself and tried to return to my normal color. "Go get your clothes. They'll be dry by now."

He nodded and made his way to the laundry room.

"With a face like that, I don't even mind his off-putting attitude." Kit wasted no time in lusting. "Are you fucking him?"

"No!" I protested. "Of course not, he's a client. It's all business..."

"You know that doesn't sound any less sexual, right?" she said, and my lips pursed, unamused. "Okay. I believe you." Kit held up her hands, her shoulders shaking with laughter through her salmon-pink club dress.

My eyes narrowed. It was my turn to interrogate. "Did you not come home last night?"

Kit's mouth opened and closed as Kade rounded the corner, fully dressed.

I let out a breath, a mix of relief and disappointment. It was for the best Kit interrupted us. Technically, his side of the bargain was to loosen me up, and I bet sex with him would have done that and more, but it was up to me to get his mind off sex and onto emotional bonding. Meaning, no matter how attractive he was, I had to stay chaste and concentrated when it came to Kade. God knows I couldn't trust him to keep me eligible for the convent. He'd condemn us both if given the chance.

But Kade was in a vulnerable place—worried about his best

friend—and it wasn't right of me to take advantage, especially since where most people had fight or flight in response to stress, Kade had fuck.

Honestly, I couldn't believe how brazen and ready I'd been to sleep with him in the first place. We were strangers, and I'd almost messed up a career-altering deal with my sudden burst of insatiable… *horniness.*

"Should I head out?" Kade straightened his tie by the door.

"No," I decided. "We have work to do. But maybe we should talk in my bedroom for privacy."

Kit's eyebrow shot up, again, her eyes landing on me, she tsked. It sounded like an accusation.

"On second thought, maybe *we* should head out." I grabbed my denim jacket from the hook by the door. "Feel like a long walk in the park?"

With a half-grin, Kade nodded.

⌇⌇⌇

Walking through Central Park after a rainfall was always so beautiful and my favorite thing about living in New York. The overhead clouds painted the scene varying hues of gray, and the smell of the wet leaves in the air filled me with a wistful desire to run and kick them as they fell. Despite the cold, the park was bustling with people— tourists, mostly—taking photos by Bethesda fountain, jogging; and some, like Kade and I, were taking a slow walk with cups of searing hot coffee to keep warm in the cold.

"You really meant a walk in the park, huh?" Kade sounded disappointed. "I thought that was code for going back to my apartment and—"

"About that…" I cut him off with a shake of my head. My core had cooled down and I didn't need him talking about sex to burn me up again. "It's a bad idea."

He smirked. "We established that."

"I mean, it can't happen. *Ever.*"

He sighed, taking a moment to ponder my words. He nodded. "So, what do you want to do if you don't want to *do me*?"

I shrugged, sipping my coffee. It burned my tongue and I flinched, swallowing it down. I stuck my tongue out and made a 'bleh' sound. Kade laughed as I moved my tongue from side to side in the cold wind.

"Maybe we thould do an exerthise," I said, my burnt tongue muffling my words.

"You want me to start a round of pull-ups in Central Park?" He shook his head. "Sweetheart, I'm all for staying in shape, but if I pop my shirt off like some of these dickbags—" He pointed to the runners glistening in sweat despite their eight-packs being tinged with frostbite. "—I'll start a fucking frenzy. Women crying, screaming, clawing their way through the crowds to get to me... I don't want to risk your safety."

I snorted and nudged his shoulder. "No, dummy. I mean, we should each pick a person for the other to talk to and give each other a task to accomplish."

"Example?"

"Well..." I blew on my coffee through the mouthpiece in the lid. "I could give you the task of talking to a woman, getting her number, and setting up a date without being at all sexual. But we may need to find a way to ugly you up a little. You're too hot..."

"I know." He deadpanned. "But alas, making me ugly is impossible, so let's not."

I rolled my eyes. "At least ruffle your hair and loosen the tie. Give the appearance you're anything other than sculpted by gods."

He did, and *holy moly*, it had the opposite effect. I silently groaned, squeezing my thighs together, and did my best to ignore the fluttering south of the equator as we walked on. I took my focus off him and surveyed the prospects.

"So, I could give you the same task in reverse?" He asked. "Talk to a guy in nothing but innuendos? Get his number, set up a sex-date? That kind of thing?"

I grimaced. "Sex-dates aren't my thing."

"You should try it, Liana. I think you'll find you've been depriving yourself of the good things for a long time." It was the second time he'd said I was depriving myself and it bothered me enough to prove him wrong.

"Okay, you're on! Find me a guy."

Kade smirked. "Do you have a preference?"

"If we're talking purely sexual attraction, I like the cliché tall, dark, and handsome." My tongue tingled as I took a small sip of coffee. Still too hot.

He nudged my arm and winked. "I already offered you that."

"What about you?" I moved on. "Go past the sexual stuff and think long-term. Describe your perfect woman."

"*Woman.*" He smiled. "I don't have a type. Every woman has something uniquely intriguing about her. I'm drawn to a different thing each time."

"That's... sweet. But I'm talking about the ultimate, *Weird Science*, make her in a computer, everything you want a woman to be... *The* perfect girl for you. What's she like?"

Kade shrugged, pulling his lips into a thoughtful line. "Well, I guess she would have a nice, curvy figure, particularly around the thigh area... you've got nice thighs," he said, so casual—as though his words didn't affect every inch of my body. "Aside from that, I like long hair and gorgeous eyes. Preferably dark or green. Oh, and a cute button nose... Kind of like yours."

"Okay." I nodded, surveying the area. I angled my face away

from him so he couldn't see the red hue coloring my neck. "What about personality, clothes and attitude?"

"I have no idea. Personality isn't the first thing I notice. As for clothes, I like women who wear clothes by the brands, '*are you fucking serious?*' and '*what makes you think I know anything about women's clothing?*'"

I scoffed and flipped him the bird. "What about attitude?"

"Feisty with a sweet side. I need someone who will make allowances for my..." he cleared his throat, "eccentricities, but will call me out if I'm being a dick."

"Which is ninety-percent of the time, as far as I can see," I said, my tongue between my teeth.

Kade rolled his eyes, sardonically. "...*Ooh, burn.*"

I grinned. "While we look. why don't you tell me a little bit more about the mystery that is Kade Jennings?"

He shrugged. "What do you want to know?"

It was my first opportunity to ask the list of questions in my head, but he'd already proven himself skittish. One wrong word, he could take off in the opposite direction like a greyhound on meth, so I started out easy. "Did you always want to be an agent?"

"No. I was... a slow learner." Kade cleared his throat again, something I'd observed as a vulnerability response. "The first thing I got a handle on was words. Writing was the only time I didn't feel stupid. So, I guess the first thing I wanted to be was an author."

"So why didn't you pursue that?"

He shrugged, sliding his hands into his pants pockets, creating a tent around his crotch. *Don't look, don't look, don't look.* "Most books need an element of romance to carry the plot. It's a big appeal to readers and gives them something to root for. But I could never pull it off. All of my romantic scenes frustrated the hell out of me, so fucking pathetic that I gave up. I couldn't do it. It was then that I realized, just because I can write, doesn't make me a writer."

I nudged his arm. "Not all books need romance," I reasoned, pushing as much belief as I could into my words, but even I could tell they didn't sound sincere. Every book I'd ever loved encompassed an earth-moving romance that left me warm and toasty, reeling from a heartbreak or bursting with a happily-ever-after. I couldn't get through a three-hundred-pager without it.

"But the best ones do," he said, and I couldn't pretend to disagree, and so I stayed silent.

We walked in silence for a while until our hands brushed on accident. My palm burning, I jumped further to the side, putting an appropriate amount of space between us, and tried to act like I wasn't on fire inside. I cleared my throat and picked up the conversation again. "So that's when you decided to take on the other side of books instead?"

Kade's eyes moved to the ground, and I swore I could see the faintest blush creeping up his neck. "After my failed run at writing, and before the agent dream took hold, I... wanted to be a news anchor."

I bit my lip to stop the laughter in my throat and stepped back to observe Kade—with his head full of near-black hair and piercing eyes, he'd make a fine news anchor.

Hell, half the city would tune in just to stare at him.

"Okay, give me a show..." I demanded, snickering as confusion crossed his handsome face. "Narrate the scene..."

Kade shook his head with a chuckle. He cleared his throat twice, a smirk crossing his lips, and stopped dead in his tracks. With an even voice deeper than his usual tone, he announced, "Today's celebrity report: Up-and-coming advice blogger, Liana Dawson missed out on incredibly steamy sex with red-hot Adonis, Kade Jennings. It is a decision he, and the masses, think Liana will regret one day. More on this story as it develops…"

A laugh like starting a vintage car erupted from my open mouth. I pushed him. "Jerk."

"This just in, Liana states the obvious." He smiled and for the first time since we met, it reached his eyes. It dazzled me how young he looked with that smile. I couldn't believe he'd never experienced being loved.

Again, my mind went back to his mom—as it had a million times since he stormed out of my apartment. I knew his mother was dead, but his reaction said there was more to the story. No kid ended up on the streets without someone knowing he was missing unless he'd gone out on his own before his mom died, for a bad reason.

And that was too sad to think about…

I forced my attention on the task at hand. There were so many gorgeous women in Central Park, I had to narrow it down.

I decided against the joggers, not wanting to chase a woman down for him to talk to. My best bet were the women taking slow strolls alone with their heads in the clouds, or the few on benches reading. They screamed rom-com leading ladies.

My eyes settled on a brunette woman sitting by the fountain. Long hair? *Check.* A curvaceous figure? *Check.* Cute button nose? *Check.* The only thing she seemed to lack was the feisty component. From afar, she looked timid.

I opened my mouth to inform Kade of my choice, but then a glimmering caught my eye. I stalled and groaned as the woman raised her hand to brush a strand of her hair behind her ear, and there it was: The rock, and the band. Married. "Dammit."

"Not for me, anyways." Kade shrugged. "Beautiful, but… she's reading *Twilight*."

I looked again, and sure enough, the third installment of the franchise was glued to her hand and tears glazed her eyes. I couldn't help but snort at the thought of what Kade would say if he knew I'd been a *Team Edward* girl in my youth.

"I'm open to role play... But I point blank refuse to cover myself in glue and roll around in glitter," Kade said.

Oh... The mental image of him shimmering with a hard-on and vampire teeth blessed my mind, sending shivers down my spine. I was so glad I wasn't packing a penis in my tight jeans because there'd be no hiding my erection. I imagined it would be big, standing at least to my belly button, and screaming *Sex! Sex! Sex!* Like a horny fire alarm.

"Moving on. Oh, what about her?" I pointed to a beautiful woman in a biker jacket and jeans. Her hair was long, she had good hips, a nice butt, and a gorgeous smile. No button-nose, though. Her nose was elongated and turned up at the end like a supermodel from *Whoville...*

She was also arguing with a hot-dog vendor, trying to negotiate some kind of discount for being a 'long-time customer.'

Feisty? Check.

"I choose her." I pointed.

Kade's eyes followed my finger and landed on the woman. His mouth made an 'O' shape. He half-smiled. "That's Nikki."

"*Nikki*?"

Kade nodded. "We met the night before Caspergate. She's why I was late to the café. Her mattress is amazing. I couldn't leave. And she pulled this prank..." I flicked an eyebrow, waiting to hear the prank as Kade's mouth pulled into a small smirk. "Let's just say she made an impression."

Ahh! My movie-obsessed mind screamed *this could be it*! The girl meets guy, guy runs into girl at the park scenario was a staple in some of the best romantic comedies ever made. And when *Nade* got married, I'd be the one they'd thank in their toasts.

"Relax," Kade said. "I can see the cogs turning in that

gorgeous head of yours. I said she made an impression, not that I was ready to buy a house in the suburbs."

I rolled my eyes. "Go ask her on a date... but first, I would like to make an amendment to my task." I bit my lip and brought her clasped hands to my mouth, not knowing how he was going to react. My mouth upturned in a nervous smirk. "No sex until you reach the third date."

Kade's shoulders stiffened.

He blinked twice before he registered what I'd said. His eyebrows hunched, dumbfounded, and his jaw slacked. "Are you kidding?" He asked, with a look like I'd offered him a golden baseball bat decorated in diamonds under the condition that he could only ever use it to bash his own brains in. "But Nikki doesn't count, right? I've already slept with her."

I shook my head. "Celibate, Kade. Own hand only. The next time you see her naked will be on your third date."

He threw his head back and groaned, so loud a flock of pigeons nearby took to the skies in fright. "I've never been on more than a first date. I'll be ninety before I ever see a pair of breasts again."

I rolled my eyes at his dramatics. He was *Liz Taylor* with a penis. "Who knows? Milly might be the one you want to see again."

"Nikki," he corrected. "And maybe it's Nikki who won't want see me again. In case it's escaped your keen notice, Liana, I'm not the easiest person to be around."

I chortled. "Trust me, I've noticed." *In more ways than one.* "Just go over there..."

With a groan, off he went in the direction of Nikki. I watched him, his slumped shoulders becoming taut and strong as he pushed them back, standing tall. His ruffled hair pushed back into a suave side-part as he slipped his suit jacket from his torso like he'd rehearsed it, slinging it carelessly over his shoulder. Even his stride changed as he got closer to Nikki. His dragging steps became fast and confident, and his nose which had been pointed toward the ground, was so high in the air he could snort a cloud. The Kade I'd joked with became a cocky son of a bitch before my eyes, and I couldn't help but wish I could be on the other side of his charm—for observation purposes, of course. I'd never truly seen him in his prime. Not as Casper, not as Kade, not even as our bodies tangled on the couch...

Was it so preposterous that not an hour before, it had been *my* inner thigh his manhood pressed against and now I was sending him off in the direction of a beautiful woman he'd already slept with?

The answer was yes.

Which is why, as Kade flexed his muscles beneath his shirt and batted his dazzling eyes at Nikki, I turned away.

CHAPTER 16

KADE

"Come on, Simon. I've been eating at this cart since I got to this city," Nikki waved her arms at the hot dog on wheels guy as I approached. She scoffed, flicking her black hair over her shoulder, the scent of strawberry wafting up my nose. It paled in comparison to lavender and lemon, but it wasn't an awful smell.

Simon sighed. "Can't do it. You owe me at least a thousand dollars in dog debt."

I coughed in an effort to gain her attention.

"Oh, that is such bullshit!" Nikki argued, ignoring me. Her brown eyes sparkled mischievously. "I paid you last time."

"One hot dog out of hundreds. I wouldn't brag too hard, Nik."

"Yeah?" she sneered, her thick pout pushing into a scowl. "Well I wouldn't brag about your face, Simon."

Simon frowned, his hand tracing the contours of his face. "What's wrong with my face?" He asked, as though genuinely curious. He touched his chin and nose before landing by his forehead. "Is it the eyebrows?"

Nikki smirked. "You look like Jim Levenstein's dad, you creeper."

I watched their exchange like a tennis tournament, my mouth hanging open with each insult.

"No, I don't," he insisted, before conceding her point. "Well, maybe a little. But you look like the result of a botched cloning experiment splicing Lucy Hale and Cara Delevingne."

She snorted. "Whatever. Give me the dog, you sewer-dwelling perv."

"Give me the money," Simon leaned on the cart and sneered. "You basement rat."

I groaned, reaching for my wallet. "Here, allow me," I interjected, refusing to lose the last of my sanity over a hot dog.

Finally, Nikki looked at me. "Oh, hey, Kade." She smiled as the vendor finished putting the dog in the bun and gave it to Nikki. She took it and applied an obscene amount of ketchup.

"Oh, come on. That shit's expensive to refill," Simon whined.

Nikki sniggered. "Kade paid for the dog, tiny-head-big-eyebrows. The condiment comes free. *Yum.*" She flicked her eyebrows and smirked before taking a big bite. Then, she dug her hand into her pocket and emerged with a rolled-up five-dollar bill. "Hey, Simon. You got change?"

Simon gawped, and Nikki giggled. "No? Okay then, I'll take a soda and a dog for my friend here."

My brow crinkled. The whole ordeal seemed strange, even for me.

His jaw hard, Simon all but threw the hot dog at me along with a can of soda as Nikki handed over the bill.

"Why do you mess with me?" he asked.

"Because it's fun to hear you say mean things." Nikki grinned, biting down on her food.

Her arm nudged mine, signaling it was time for us to walk away. But we only got a few steps from the cart when she spun back around to deliver a final blow to Simon's existence. "Your father should've held you in."

"Your mother should've—" Simon stopped himself. "I'm not stooping to your childish remarks."

Nikki smirked, self-satisfied at having broken the man down so much he refused to communicate with her anymore, she turned her attention on me. "So, what brings you to my neck of the park?"

My mind flooded with a load of contrived bullshit I could say to convince her to go on the date, but craning my neck to look back at Liana, I found her staring up at a warbler in a nearby tree, and for the first time in my life, I told a woman the truth. From start to finish, I recanted the tale of mine and Liana's questionable partnership; the parts of our bodies pressing together on her couch conveniently left out.

"Let me see if I'm following this," Nikki said as I finished talking. "Your friend, Liana, gave you a task to ask me out? But if I say yes, I don't get sex for three dates?"

"More of an associate than a friend, but in a nutshell."

Nikki nodded. "Because she's trying to teach you to fall in love... *with me*?"

Air caught in my throat, choking me. "Not you specifically," I said, fast. Too fast. Offensively fast. I sighed.

"Relax." Nikki smiled. "It's a noble cause, albeit a boring one. But sure, I'm willing to be in this experiment with you. Question, though: if the first two dates are terrible, can we go on the third and have sex again?"

I laughed, pretending to mull it over. "That sounds like acceptable terms."

"Then you've got yourself a deal."

I sauntered over to Liana, triumphant in my mission. "I have a date. Now, time to get you laid." Surveying the area, I searched out a suitable guy to make Liana orgasm, but no tall, dark and sex appeal jumped out of the crowds.

More pressure was on me than Liana. All she had to do was make sure I didn't wimp out on my date... Meanwhile, I needed to find a man who looked like he was good in bed, and that's not something that could always be deduced based on looks alone. Most men would give their left nut to sleep with a woman like Liana, but not all of them could, or cared enough, to make her come.

If I had my way, I would have already completed the mission on her couch. At least that way, I could've been sure she was getting top-notch sex. I sighed, wishing I had a time machine. I would have moved us to her bedroom and spent hours getting to know her body before her munchkin sister interrupted us.

"I should go home and get some work done. Besides, maybe the park isn't the place to prowl for guys," she said, and my stomach panged. Going back to an empty apartment for the night when my mind was so vulnerable felt eerily akin to climbing into a coffin. Liana caught my eye, a fleeting look of pity crossing her face. "If you don't feel like staying in, we could go out tonight? I have a friend who is like an all-access pass to clubs."

"Okay," I agreed, a little too hastily, relief expanding in my chest. That took care of the night, but there were hours left between now and then. I wasn't ready to go home yet. "Allow me to walk you back?" I offered. "You can tell me more about yourself on the way."

Her lips curving into a smile, Liana nodded.

As we walked our hands brushed together. My palm itched,

begging me to slide it against hers and entwine our fingers. Refraining, I shoved my hands into my jacket pockets and made copious amounts of small talk. The rest of our journey flittered by to the soundtrack of beeping cars, and two-second insights into the lives of strangers yelling on their phones.

By the time we got to her building, I'd learned some new Liana facts. She liked an Irish band called *The Script*, her hair was so long because she cut it all off on a whim when she was fourteen and cried for three days straight, and her middle name was Jude, after *The Beatles* song 'Hey, Jude.' And we shared a mutual love of *Great Expectations* by Charles Dickens.

They weren't personal facts, but I was honored to know them all the same.

"I know it's not the best book in the world," I said as we reached the door to her lobby. "But it was one of the first I ever read, and for that reason I think I'll always have a soft spot for it."

Liana agreed. "Though I will admit I would have preferred an ending where Pip and Estella ended up together."

"Of course, you would," I said, amused. Standing outside her apartment building, laughing together, felt a lot like the ending of a really great date. It wasn't, of course, because I had a date lined up with Nikki and a mission to get Liana a man for the night.

But as Liana reached up, placing a small kiss on my cheek, and whispered, "Be at my place for eight? I may need a little training before we go."

I couldn't help wishing I could be the man who would wake up in Liana's bed in the morning. I watched as she made her way inside before starting the slow stroll back home with a smile on my face. It had been a relatively good day, all in all, and I was flying high. Nothing could bring me down from the cloud I floated on, I thought.

My phone vibrated in my breast pocket. I fished it out to find a frantic text from Stephanie, and my slow stroll turned to a brisk jog.

Well, almost nothing.

Chapter 17

Liana

My hair, beautiful, hung in loose curls trailing down my back. My makeup, flawless, consisted of a bronze smoky eye, dark lips, and, for the first time, I'd pulled off the perfect eyeliner flick all the women on Instagram wore. I grinned in the mirror as I sprayed myself with the scent of cherry vanilla from a bottle I'd bought for six bucks at a half-off sale. The only thing left to do: get dressed.

"You look nice," A voice chimed in behind me.

"Thanks, Kit." I turned. "*Oh...*"

Zoe stood at my bedroom door, observing the fire engine red blouse and matching skirt laid out on my bed. "You should go with a black skirt instead, or maybe an LBD. I have one that'll accentuate your figure and match the shoes."

I blinked in shock. Was this *The Twilight Zone*? Had Zoe been taken over by an alien life-form nicer than her? With a scary nice smile, she slinked away and came back a few seconds later with a gorgeous little black dress. It was plain, but sexy. A tight A-line, spaghetti-strapped bodycon dress with a small slit up the side of the left leg and a low-cut cleavage line.

And it looked like it cost more than I earned all year. I eyed Zoe, smiling creepily at my door, and my hackles rose trying to work out her angle. It was of course possible the dress was an olive branch, but it was more likely—*much more likely*—Zoe was fucking with me, offering me an expensive dress I'd look amazing in and then ripping it out of my hands with a smirk.

I clutched it tight, envisioning myself in it—*and I looked good*—but gazing at it, I could tell it was at least two sizes too big for Zoe, which raised the question. "Why did you buy it so big?"

"It was a gift."

A snort ripped from my nose. "Someone looked at you and saw a size other than zero or, at a push, two?"

"Oh, please," Zoe waved her hand, entering my room and perching herself, much too comfortable for my liking, on the edge of my bed. "I *wish* I was a two. I'm cursed with perpetual thinness."

I shrugged. "Worse things to be cursed with, right?"

"I guess you'd assume that. The truth is, I would kill for your figure, Liana."

My eyes narrowed, remembering her fat comment, but I couldn't help the small smile stretching onto my face. "Still, I can't believe someone could be so wrong in measurements," I said, moving the conversation along, "It *had* to be a guy, right?"

Zoe shook her head. "It's not mine. It was a gift *from* me. I, uh, thought it'd be a peace offering when I moved in."

"You mean it's *mine*?" My body froze in shock

She nodded. "Try it on. I think it'll look good."

Catching up with my brain, my feet turned in the direction of my en-suite where I slipped on the dress. It fit like a second skin and looked incredible. Zoe had good taste in clothing—if nothing else.

Unable to say it out loud, I stayed silent, letting my grin do the talking instead as I emerged to Zoe's mouth agape, telling me how great I looked. But I couldn't get past the niggling cynicism in the back of my mind, screaming she was not to be trusted.

I pursed my lips. "Not to start an argument, Zoe, but... why're you helping me?"

She shrugged, grinning. "What're sisters for, right?"

"We're not sisters." The words were out before I could stop them. Zoe's grin dropped as her eyes flicked to the floor. I bit down on my lip and sighed. "I mean we don't *act* like sisters. Why now?"

Zoe sighed, her eyes finding mine and then flitting away again. "Kit isn't here. She was supposed to be home from work an hour ago, but every night it gets later." She looked downcast, her eyes glazing in tears. "I guess I'm lonely."

My stomach panged in annoyance tinged with a little bit of sympathy. "You can't use me because you're not happy being on your own. Not with our history."

Zoe nodded. "About that... You were right. I don't have the right to bitch about being single when I did what I did to Andy. Hurting him made me realize how bad I hurt you. I know now how wrong I was for sleeping with Luka... so I'm sorry."

Dumbfounded, I blinked. Most shocking to me was how little I cared about Zoe's apology. It was all I'd wanted for so many years, but it no longer mattered. It didn't rewrite history or change how it hurt, it didn't magically glue Zoe and I back together or fix me and Luka. It changed nothing.

"What brought this on?" I asked, my voice laced with doubt.

Zoe's eyes coated in tears. "I know you have no reason to believe me, but I realized today how much I could lose when I saw Andy at the lawyer's office. I expected to go in there and have him treat me like a stranger, but he didn't. He was kind and gracious, and he wavered when his lawyer talked about divorce papers... I think there's hope to get my family back, and that includes you whether you like it or not."

I brushed a hand through my curls and added hairspray to keep them in place. Zoe looked so pitiful. I grimaced, the overwhelming urge to be a nice person like a knife in my gut. "What're your plans tonight?"

"Wine and TV." She shrugged. "Glamorous, I know..."

"Get ready." I forced the words before I had a chance to change my mind. "You're coming out."

"Really?" She looked surprised and sat up straight, smiling.

I dug through my pile of shoes, finding a pair of knee-length block heels. Resting on the edge of my bed, I pulled them over my legs.

"Why not?" I tried to quiet my mind screaming it was a bad idea as Zoe bounced to her feet and left to get dressed.

My tongue caressed the inside of my cheek as my mind wandered to Kit. Zoe made a good point; Kit was coming home later every night. It wasn't like I hadn't noticed, but my mind was on Kade and I, and Kit slipped into the background. Now that Zoe said it outright, I wanted to know why.

Maybe it was because Kit didn't want to have to deal with the hostility of Zoe and I's never-ending turf war, or maybe she was gunning for yet another promotion. But if I knew my sister —and I did—I wagered Kit wasn't coming and going at all hours of the day and night because she loved her job...

Making sure Zoe's door was shut, I tip-toed past—careful not to hit the creaky spots on the hardwood floors—and into Kit's room. "If I was a laptop that I didn't want my sister to see, where would I be?" I pondered, observing the room through narrowed eyes.

Sure, it was snooping, and sure again, it was reprehensible —ethically, it was as bad as reading Kit's diary—but only a day ago, Kit walked in on me straddling a half-naked Kade. So, in my opinion, it was justified. (*Or rather, pretending it was made it easier to do.*)

My first stop was the chest of drawers at the end of the room. Then, I tried the laundry basket in the en-suite. And, finally, the closet. Coming up empty, I became aware of two things: Kit was good at hiding things, and her laptop was purposely hidden.

With a groan, I walked back toward the door, ready to give up, but then something strange caught my eye... Kit's bed was made up. No comforter heap in the middle, no sheets hanging off, and not a pillow out of place.

"Dead giveaway."

Ripping the pillows off like the hulk, I surmised Kit hid the laptop under her mattress. But as I got down to the final pillow, I noticed it was less soft than the others. I popped the buttons on the case, turned it upside down and shook. The pillow got half-way out before the laptop dropped and bounced onto the bed. My skin slithered at the thought of breaking Kit's trust, but something in my stomach said she was in trouble, and I couldn't shake it.

Opening it, I typed in the obvious password: *KDawson229*.

Every year Kit changed her password, but it was always the *same* password. Last year, it'd been 219, and the year before, 209. Her age, and the month she was born.

"Get a better password, Kit," I muttered.

The screen opened onto her email. And *boy*, were they steamy. I blushed and stopped reading, feeling relieved. A secret boyfriend was nothing to stress over. I blew out a breath and moved to close the laptop... but then I saw who the emails were from.

Every email was signed with a sweet *'Yours, J.'* at the bottom. The *J* could've been a million people in New York, but the email itself was sent from MrJReece@gmail.com. And right at the bottom of the electronic love letter was an automated signature.

Mr. Jacob Reece. CMO of J.R. Marketing firm.

Oh no... I covered my mouth with my hand as under-standing settled in my mind. I knew exactly why Kit kept me in the dark—she was sleeping with her boss. And, unless you're a quirky brunette in a Netflix original movie, that rarely ended well.

I sighed and put her laptop back in her pillow, making sure everything was left as I found it before I moved to the living room where I stewed on new information and waited for Zoe to get dressed and Jana to arrive.

It was nine forty-five p.m. when Zoe emerged in an off-the-shoulder, teal Gucci dress that would be more fitted to brunch than a club. Moments later, the door knocked, and Jana entered. Her sleek, straight pink hair looked amazing with her outfit of blue denim shorts, a white crop-top, and a black leather jacket.

Both Zoe and Jana leaned on the wall near the apartment door looking bored as we waited for Kade. I sat at my desk, checking the time again.

I'd emailed, called, texted, and left six voice messages. He hadn't responded.

"Should we go?" Zoe asked. "Doesn't look like he's coming."

"Or maybe cancel?" I suggested, my mood dampened by his no-show behavior. The night was his idea, and I wasn't sure I had the gumption to go at it without him. Sure, Jana would back my play, but I was hesitant when it came to Zoe. And now, I couldn't stop thinking about Kit.

"Not happening!" Jana declared. "I left a hot guy offering me pizza in bed and got dressed up to get you laid. We're going."

I relented. "Fine. Let me shoot off a text to my sister before we go."

"Speaking of, when do I get to meet the whore-sister who screwed your man in high school?" Jana asked.

Zoe's eyes landed on me and scowled. "That would be me. We're... *working on things*."

"...Oh." Jana's cheeks turned scarlet, and her mouth contorted into a perfect 'O.'

Great start to the night. Zoe was pissed, Jana was embarrassed, and all I wanted was to curl up in my PJ's and watch Olivia Benson kick butt on *Law & Order: Special Victims Unit*.

"Shall we go?" Zoe made her way past Jana and out of the apartment.

It hadn't occurred to me that Zoe thought a night out on the town was us 'working on things.' The only reason I'd invited her was because, try as I might, I couldn't be the girl who left someone on their own when they looked on the verge of bursting into tears. Especially after Zoe gave me the dress.

"Damn morality," I whispered.

~~~

Remixes of old rock songs pumped through speakers so loud, the stone floor of club Eden quaked. The place was packed wall-to-wall with people, dancing and making out. A suffocating odor of sex, sweat, and liquor hung in the air as the seizure-inducing lights blinded me, and the sweet taste of a grenadine and pineapple-vodka cocktail cooled my throat as I drank it through a straw, straight from a sharing pitcher.

I was drunk. No denying it. I could barely speak a word that wasn't slurred, and if that wasn't enough proof, the fact Zoe and I smiled and laughed like best friends was...

Jana, by far the least drunk of the group, was the only one focused on the mission of finding me a man for the night. I'd long given up after the first dozen duds tried to get me to go home with them.

"Liana!" she shouted from across the club. "What about him?" My head turn to find Jana pointing to a tall guy with big shoulders and bigger... *hands*. He turned and smiled, flashing me a wink. "His name is Derek. He thinks you're hot. He wants to see your—"

The DJ picked the perfect time to yell out to the crowd. I cracked up. Derek was big, beautiful, blue-eyed, and blond, but he wasn't my type. I shook my head. Turns out, I could no longer judge guys without prejudice. Every man who approached me was subjected to a new, one-item checklist I wasn't aware I had...

If I closed my eyes, could they replace the image of Kade in my head? So far, the collective answer was no. Every time I pictured rolling around with a man, I'd go straight back to the memory of Kade touching me.

Derek took it in stride and moved on with his friends. I appreciated that. It hadn't been that way when I'd turned down a guy named Mike early in the night. Before I brushed him off, I was a 'goddess, the likes of which had never been seen'. After, I was a 'ginger, fat whore with a big nose' and he could 'do better.'

Good luck, Mike.

Zoe, Jana, and I huddled together and danced in the middle of the dance floor, surrounded by an inhumane amount of Axe body spray that smelled like coconut, pinewood, and desperation. I almost gagged as Jana pulled me in and whispered a reminder of why we were out in the first place. I tried to find a tenacity in myself to get to it, but the thought of that stench in my nose as some guy slid between my legs was enough reason to go home alone. Worse again, the risk the pungent stink would be absorbed by my satin sheets and survive a myriad of washes... My nose wrinkled.

"Let yourself go. Take a chance, Liana." Jana gave an encouraging smile, and I dropped my attitude and decided to try. There were many men who could grace the cover of *GQ* or *Esquire*, but they weren't doing it for me.

My nerves weren't helping, either. They were prickling like poison ivy. I'd never in my life picked up a guy at the club. I wished Kade could give me pep talk. His brash 'no fucks given' attitude gave me more encouragement than Jana pointing to guys and gyrating her hips or doing obscene gestures with her hands. As strange as it was, I'd become comfortable with him in such a short amount of time. He'd never poke fun if I freaked out, whereas I knew Jana would roll her eyes and tell me I'm being silly if she could hear my thoughts, and Zoe was a no-go.

"Should we try somewhere else?" Zoe offered. "I saw a couple hot guys go into Jubilee down the street. Want to go there, sis?"

Sis. I bristled. It sounded plain weird coming from Zoe. I forced a smile and nodded to hide my teeth, set firmly on edge. "Sure, let's go..."

She linked my arm as we made our way through a narrow hallway and out into the cold. Stumbling a little on the cobblestone, we pushed through the crowds, taking in the crisp air of the night, and started toward Jubilee. I was high on life and alcohol, amused by every little thing... But I couldn't stop wondering where Kade was, and why he hadn't turned up.

Then, out of the corner of her eye, I found out.

Walking down a back alley was the unmistakable shape of Kade, his strong arms wrapped around a woman, and his luscious lips planted atop of her head.

Even after his vow of celibacy, he'd blown me off to have sex.

"Asshole!" The word burst out of my mouth in a shout, but he was too far away to hear it. I almost chased him down and would have if not for my heels.

Dejected, I was ready to pack it up and go home, but Zoe and Jana were having a blast. For them, I persevered, deciding that even if he didn't hold up his end, I would hold up mine.

The line to Jubilee wound down the block, but it seemed Jana was an all-access fast pass because of her connections and following on some clock-related app I didn't know.

She took my hand and guided me through the windowless double doors, down a long twisting hallway that led to another set of doors. Pulling them open, she grinned as though she'd found the promised land, but I wasn't so sure. Jubilee held a vastly different vibe than the club we had been in. Compared to Eden, Jubilee was louder, but not necessarily better. Rather than nostalgic crowd pleasers, the speakers pumped out chaotic mixtures of bass and electronic synthpop interjected with lyrics ripped from the latest chart toppers. My brain tingled, short-circuiting with all of the new sounds and laser lights.

The only thing Jubilee had over Eden was space. With three floors, all with their own bar and theme, it was easier to find my footing without knocking into the crowds. We were on the second floor where the VIP section was. Jana blushed as the manager offered her a booth but took it with thanks. I furrowed my eyebrows, reaching for her arm. It seemed strange to me that she was so well-known on this *Tick-Tock* app that she was being comped bottles of champagne and free booths in exclusive sections, but she worked for me for dimes.

"Do I pay you enough?" I asked, despite having no additional funds to pay her more.

Her mouth inched up, amused. "Definitely not. But when you're rolling in cash and fame, I'm planning on reaping the rewards and name-dropping you whenever I can. So, for now, we're good."

She took my hand and gave it a squeeze, leading me to the bar where she shouted over the music six times before the bartender supplied her with three of something fruity she hadn't ordered. It tasted of kiwi and strawberry with undertones of vodka, and went down as easy as soda. I ordered another.

Moving past drunk, I paid rent at hammered, and landed on shitfaced where I set up four houses and a hotel. I did not pass *Go*; I did not collect two hundred dollars.

I stayed at the bar, losing the girls in the crowds, and sat alone for a while—my already waning mood dashed by seeing Kade with the girl. But as crystal blue eyes met mine across the bar, and the tall guy they came with smiled in my direction, I got the feeling my night was about to get a whole lot better.

T he room started to spin, but in a good way. Like being on a merry-go-round at the playground, or an exhilarating roller coaster I never wanted to get off. The music was so loud I couldn't hear myself think and while not a fan, I let go enough to enjoy it.

And then there was Gregg.

Six-foot-three, wide-shouldered, well-muscled, and perfect hair-having, fireman Gregg. He was handsome, and smoother than a greased-up slide—the kind of charm that couldn't be trusted to stick around the day after the night before, but that was good with me. I wasn't in the market for a breakfast buddy. I wanted one night only, and the look in Gregg's eyes, coupled with the fact his hands were south of my waist, told me everything I needed to know about his intentions.

The way his body held me close screamed the potential for *dirty sex.*

'*The dirtier the better.*' Kade's words echoed in my ear. I flinched, my jaw set, and stepped back from Gregg, feeling like someone punched me in the gut. Gregg eyed me curiously, wondering what went wrong.

"I need another drink," I told him through a fake smile.

I left him on the dance floor with Zoe, Jana, and his friend —who was not called Sam, but had a name with a similar sound that, for the life of me, I couldn't remember—and pushed through the crowds like I didn't care if I got beat up.

Taking a seat back at the bar, I put my spinning head in my

hands. "What am I doing?" I scolded myself. "I should be all over that dude!"

It was the thought of Kade stopping me. I couldn't get over how quick he'd ditched our plans to hook up when I was committed to having a bunch of nookie with a random guy.

I bet he's having sex right now. I seethed. *They're probably doing things even the Kama-fucking-Sutra hasn't discovered yet.*

I downed a shot as it was put in front of me, thinking of Kade merrily fucking his way through life without a care in the world. Meanwhile, I had to get drunk to find the courage to ask Gregg back. I sighed, ordering one more drink—a Grey Goose vodka with cola—and thought about my next move.

To sex, or not to sex?

As my glass neared empty, I made my decision. But first, I needed to make a phone call.

I wasn't expecting him to pick up—my plan was to leave a passive-aggressive voice message on his cell—so when I heard his voice telling me it wasn't a good time, I was hit with a spike of anger, and passive became aggravated.

"Yeah, I bet it's not a good time, you smug, back alley urchin." The music in the club was so loud, I screamed down the phone.

"What? Miss Dawson, are you drunk?"

"Well fucking clearly!" I scoffed. "I hope you're having a fantastic time breaking our rules, Kade, or Casper, or whoever the hell you are tonight. But I want you to know that unlike you, I keep my word! I'm at Jubilee, very drunk, and dancing with a guy! Not just any guy—*a red-hot fireman!* And guess what, Mr. 'I think you're depriving yourself'? I'm going home with him!"

With a satisfied humph, I disconnected the call and made my way back through the crowds with fire tingling in my core, ready to climb Gregg like he was a tree, and I, a horny orangutan.

Fluffing my hair, I pulled my dress down a little and smacked my glossed lips together. Suitably spruced up, I headed back out on the dance floor. Only when I got there, the girls, not-Sam, and Gregg were nowhere to be seen.

Intuition told me to check the VIP booths at the back of the club, and lo and behold, there they were huddled together in the velvet red seats. I stopped in my tracks, my smile dropping, and took in the scene.

Jana draped all over not-Sam; her lips planted so firmly on his, I couldn't tell where she ended, and he began. And Zoe with her tongue so far down Gregg's throat, she could play his ribcage like a xylophone and his pancreas as a drum. In fact, she was using her tongue with such vigor, I reckoned she could slurp whatever alcohol Gregg consumed directly from his liver.

I let out a cold laugh. It shouldn't have surprised me, but it did. I was an idiot for allowing myself to be manipulated by the doe eyes and lonely façade. Zoe took her first chance to jump on a guy I wanted. *Again.* It was what she did; she was a viper, and I'd made the mistake of letting my guard down. Her venom wormed its way into me like it did into everyone in her life. But just because I'd been fooled twice by her, didn't mean I couldn't save somebody else from my fate.

I shook my head and took a video snap of the scene and saved it to my phone.

The night was a bust. Kade was getting some, I was getting none, and Zoe… was getting a divorce—I'd make sure of it. Not for revenge or out of spite, but because Andy deserved better.

I sat back at the bar and ordered a water, hoping to stave off the hangover in the morning.

"This night couldn't possibly get any worse!" I winced, wishing I hadn't spoken those words aloud. The universe proved itself a finicky bastard who loved to screw with me.

And as fate would have it…

"Say, don't I know you from somewhere?" A dreadfully

familiar, silky-smooth voice asked, and my body turned rigid. *Holy shit*. Even after all this time, the sound was like music to my ears. I gripped the bar with my hands, desperate not to fall out of my chair as I twisted my neck to see his face for the first time in five years.

"Luka..."

CHAPTER 18

KADE

Stephanie's text said nothing that made sense. *Help. I need you.* And *Hurry.* written just like that. Five words that insighted a vast amount of crushing panic in my chest, but no details on where she was or how I was supposed to help.

I tried the hospital first, only to be informed she discharged herself against doctor's recommendation as soon as I left. *Unbelievable.*

Next, I checked our apartment in case she went home and collapsed, managing to send the text minutes before blacking out. My mind filled with the images of her on the ground, waiting for me to find her. *Oh God.*

I took the stairs of our building, making it to the fourth floor in under a minute, and burst through the door.

"Stephanie?" I yelled and searched every room in our apartment. I came up empty. "Fuck!" I exclaimed, heading back out onto the street. I called the office asking if anyone there had seen her; the last ray of hope in my heart dying as I heard the word no.

The only other place left to check was the one place I prayed she wouldn't go; despite every instinct telling me she would. I hailed a cab and gave the driver the address to Cleo's apartment in Brooklyn.

I checked the time on my phone. I'd spent hours running all over New York, and it was already seven p.m. I opened my email, ready to explain my tardiness—or, as was looking more likely—my absence, when my battery died.

"Shit," I cursed.

It took nearly two hours to get through traffic, giving me nothing to do but fret and worry. I lay my head on the window, watching as the gray skies outside darkened to a starless black. It was the longest car ride of my entire life. A spring in the seat poked me in the ass, and the odor of a blueberry-ish scented car freshener assaulted my senses. The music on the radio was so upbeat, it set my teeth on edge. I absentmindedly drummed the beats against my leg as my heart raced and nausea crept up my throat.

"Can you turn that off?" I bit at the cab driver with a snarl. The man, whose dark eyes shot daggers at me in the rearview mirror, twisted the dial and plunged the car into silence as we made it across the Brooklyn Bridge.

The last two miles seemed to take the longest, but at last, the cab rolled to a stop outside the tall, gray-bricked building that housed the devil spawn who put my best friend through hell.

Possibly throwing more cash than the fare demanded, I bolted from the cab and rounded the corner to find Stephanie, still in her hospital gown, curled-up in a ball on the cold stoop with her knees to her chest and tears streaming down her face. "She won't let me in. She won't even talk to me."

I didn't know how long she'd been there, begging, but her body was shivering and tinged blue. With a relieved breath, I removed my jacket and wrapped it around her, tugging her softly to her feet and taking her in my arms, squeezing her tight as she cried. Pulling back, I guided her away from the building, my stomach turning as she thrashed, trying to fight her way back to the door. I gripped her shoulders and kept her in place until she tired herself out.

"It wouldn't matter if you stayed there all night, Steph. She's not going to answer."

"You don't know that!" Her voice broke.

But I *did* know. I'd seen it happen the first time Cleo hit Stephanie. They had been feeding ducks at the park when a random guy asked Steph on a date. Upon learning Cleo and Stephanie were together, the guy apologized. That hadn't mattered to Cleo, who was convinced Steph gave the guy signals with her eyes.

It made no sense in the real world, but to Cleo, it warranted fracturing Steph's right shoulder.

The second time, it was the same story in a different setting. During Pride week, New York went wild with LGBTQ+ pride, and it was a marvelous time to be had. As an ally, I'd been to many parties with Stephanie, and occasionally Cleo, over the years. Last year, however, I'd been too swamped with work to have any play time… at least, that's what I'd told Steph.

The truth: I didn't want to be anywhere near Cleo. I made the mistake of leaving Stephanie to go with her, alone, and that was something I'd never stop feeling guilty about.

A girl approached Steph and gave her a hug. Her name? Steph didn't know. Her face? She'd never seen it before, or since. It was a passing act of solidarity between members of the same community. Innocent.

But Cleo saw it as something else. She'd taken a hop, skip, and a jump to the wrong conclusion. Before long, Cleo built up a list of possible histories between the two in her head. *An illicit affair behind her back Steph was trying to cover up, a plan to leave her in the dust and run off with the girl, a romance before Cleo showed up in New York that Steph would crave once more.* And that's when she'd snapped.

Stephanie come home with injuries so severe; they made her current wounds look like a scratch. It was always the same thing that set it off, and it was always the same after: Complete and utter silence as a method of emotional torture. And worse than watching Stephanie writhe in pain was watching her sob because the woman who claimed to love her refused to talk to her.

But then, a miracle would happen: Steph would heal and accept that it was over. That was around the time Cleo would show up at the door with everything warped in her head and convince Stephanie she was the bad guy with the words, "*It's okay. I know you didn't mean to upset me.*"

I seethed, shaking my head, and wished for the power to change the outcome this time. Alas, I could control the decisions of a thirty-year-old woman as much as I could control the weather. It's not like I could lock her away until she quit Cleo cold turkey.

Finally, Stephanie stopped beating my chest and settled into my arms long enough for me to get her into a cab. The clock on the cab dashboard read close to ten p.m. now. I sighed as we entered lower-Manhattan, traffic moving an inch a minute. Cars stalled bumper-to-bumper—it was going to be at least two hours before we got home.

"It'll be faster if we walk," Stephanie muttered, her voice low.

"Can you walk?" I asked.

She nodded, and I paid the driver. Getting out, I wrapped my arm around her waist, lifting her up, and allowed her to put most of her weight on me. As we made our way down a cold back alley near Tenth Avenue, I wondered if Liana was already in one of the clubs around us. I bet she was, and she was most likely calling me an asshole for standing her up.

We walked for twenty-five minutes, emerging at the intersection of Broadway and East 14th Street before Stephanie grew tired, her legs wobbling. We were ahead of the traffic now, I realized. Hailing yet another cab, I lowered Stephanie in the back, making sure she was comfortable before I climbed in beside her.

She fell asleep instantly, her head propped up against the window. She slept all the way home and stayed sleeping as the car rolled to a stop. I smiled, glad she was getting some rest, and decided against waking her. Instead, I opened the car door slowly, and gathered her sleeping body in my arms. I carried her from the lobby, into the elevator, and into our apartment where I placed her gently on the sofa. She groaned, snuggling into the pillow from last night.

I huffed out a long breath, pouring myself a small glass of Jameson, and reached in my pocket for my phone. Plugging it in, I found three unread text messages, ten missed calls, an unread email, and two voicemails.

Deciding I'd deal with them in the morning, I turned my phone on vibrate and shut it in my desk drawer to charge. The email to Liana explaining my absence remained in my drafts, the task of finishing it too daunting for my tired mind.

My body screamed to lie down, my eyelids heavy. I refused, knowing the events of the past two nights would trigger my brain to conjure the demons of my past. Looking over at Stephanie, I thought it was no wonder I wasn't rushing head-first into immersing myself in love.

Love was dangerous, and brutal. It wasn't beautiful or miraculous—it was a barely survivable tumor that riddled its way through a person until they were nothing but a shell of who they once were. Liana would disagree, but she'd been brought up on the notion that love could change the world. To get through the turmoil of her parents' divorce, she'd gorged on rom-coms and romance novels, and believed every line.

To her, love was a beacon of light in this dark world.

My brow furrowed as I imagined her as a young girl, crying

in her room because her mom was sad. How crushingly depressing that must've seemed for her—like the world imploding; nothing worse going on outside her bedroom window.

But on a scale of her childhood to mine, I'd take hers in a heartbeat. She had siblings, parents, money...

She grew up in a home where affection was rare, but at least it existed.

My only examples of functioning relationships were hard, volatile, and violent. And no matter how many books I read, or how many movies I sat through; my vision of love was tainted. Every relationship I'd ever seen went bad around a month into it.

Depression wormed its way into my mind, as it so often did, and suddenly, I realized I couldn't do it anymore. The anxiety, the panic, the images of Stephanie dead on the floor causing my chest to constrict. No longer was I able to stand by and watch Stephanie destroy herself by staying with Cleo. In my office, she'd said she wasn't like my mom, but the more time went on, the more familiar the situation seemed, and I refused to live through that again. I wouldn't survive.

My skin prickled at the thought of giving her the ultimatum, terrified of how she'd react to it. The dread I'd endured running around trying to find her, was something I never wanted to feel again for as long as I lived. It was no longer healthy for my mind, or my heart, to watch the person I cared about most be so mistreated. It wasn't fair...

I tipped my head back, taking the rest of my whiskey down like a shot. As the glass emptied, and the burning in my throat subsided, it was time to wake Stephanie...

"Could you repeat that?" Steph blinked back the tears in her eyes.

I sat across from her, on the edge of our glass coffee table, with my shoulders tensed and my hands clasped. Swallowing down the lump in my throat, I repeated myself. "I said I can't live here unless you let Cleo go. I can't watch another person I love die at the hands of an abusive relationship."

"I'm not your mom, Kade."

"Not yet. But you'll end up like her if you don't walk away from Cleo, right now."

"It was nothing," she swore. "If anything, it was my fault."

"It's never been your fault, Stephanie!" I didn't mean for my voice to raise, but I couldn't fathom how she could ever believe, after everything, that Cleo was blameless. If I ever did choose to become a serial killer, I know who my first victim would be. I even know where I'd bury the bitch. They'd be finding bits of her in different states up and down the East Coast. They'd be searching for fucking weeks.

"I love her, Kade," Steph whispered.

"Why? What is so good about her? Name one thing she's ever done for you." I stood up and stalked backwards and forwards. "God, Steph. Why do you let her do it?"

Stephanie scoffed. "You of all people know you don't *let* it happen, Kade! Nobody lines up for the person they love to hurt them like it's a goddamn free day at the spa."

My eyes closed, hearing what I'd said play back in my ears. "I'm sorry. I didn't mean—"

"You think I don't know how messed up my relationship is?" Stephanie cried. "Of course, I do... But one day, Cleo and I are going to look back at this and think about how stupid we were, and we'll be okay. Someday, she'll change."

"You're wrong. She will *never* change." I sat back across from her and took her hand in mine.

"You don't get it." She shook her head, and the tears broke free. "It was *my* fault! We were at the bar and there was this guy. He was gorgeous, tall... Cleo said he was flirty, and that I was flirting back. I don't know, maybe I did?"

"You would know if you were," I said. "And even so, that does *not* justify what she did."

Steph sighed and, again, shook her head. "I was drinking. You know how I get when I've been drinking. I'd flirt with a streetlight. I don't blame Cleo for getting upset. I called her a jealous bitch, Kade. I had no right to call her that. And I have a girlfriend; no man or woman should be able to catch my eye, even for a second, right?"

"Unless you're not happy."

She gave an exasperated humph and her eyes rolled. "What *is* happy? Are *you* happy?"

"No," I said. "I'm a miserable bastard with an issue list so long I trip over it every time I do so much as take a piss. One of which is the fact I've mentally pinpointed and dug an unmarked grave to toss your girlfriend into." I snorted, hoping to lighten the mood but not even a slight smirk passed Stephanie's lips. I exhaled. "Maybe we're both fucked up, Steph. But I know who I am. I'm unapologetically an asshole, and I accept that about me because it's who I've been my whole life. *But you*? You were once a vibrant, confident person."

A stream of tears rolled down her face. She wiped them away. "Cleo took us in when we had nothing. We *both* owe her a lot."

"I don't owe her shit!" Derision laced my words. "And you don't owe her your life."

Steph sobbed so hard, she hiccoughed. "So, what are you saying? It's you or her?"

I nodded because I couldn't bring myself to say the words

out loud. Getting up, I poured her a drink and handed it over. She sighed at the ceiling and took it down like a shot.

"I can't leave her. I already left her once, remember? We both did."

If I heard that version of the events one more time, I was going to lose it. "We didn't leave her. It's not our fault we were out making something of our lives, and she was getting high and selling to junkies."

"What did I make of my life?" Steph spat, ripping her hand from mine. "I get the coffee..."

My mouth dropped open. "Don't act like we didn't have a *partnership*. Then Cleo showed up and all of a sudden you're happy as an assistant? What the fuck? In the beginning, we were both hungry for it. Jennings *and* Taylor, remember? What happened to that girl?"

She bit her lip to stop the tears. "I'm so fucking tired, Kade. I can't always be sunshine and sarcasm when my entire life is falling apart."

I reached for her hand again and my chest ached as she pulled away from me. "I think I need to sleep." She wiped her eyes with the back of her hand.

"Okay. Do you want to stay out here?"

Stephanie shook her head. Grabbing her pillow, she limped to her bedroom and shut the door.

Like that, I was on my own. Left to go over the conversation in my head and wonder how I could have softened the blow or pleaded my case better. The guilt eating me away, so immense it threatened to swallow me whole, pushed me to apologize and take it back; swearing to be by her side forever no matter what she chose. But the fact remained, my life was becoming stagnant and excruciating to deal with—too terrified to sleep, lonely, empty, and anxious.

And now that sex was off-limits, I could no longer ignore my inability to cope.

To preoccupy my head, I sat in front of my laptop hoping to get some work done, but somehow ended up making a Power-Point of pros and cons for dating Cleo in hopes of swaying Steph when she woke up.

So far, I had only cons. It became more of a smear campaign if I was being honest.

I sighed as a low vibration caught my attention and searched for the source. Remembering my phone in the desk drawer, I slid it open to find Liana's face grinning up at me on screen.

With another sigh, I answered it. "I'm sorry for not showing up, sweetheart, but it's not a great—"

I was cut off by a tirade of talking so fast, I couldn't keep up. My eyebrows furrowed as I caught the last syllable of each word and tried to string them together in a sentence that made sense. The corners of my mouth twitched, amused. "Miss Dawson, are you drunk?"

"Well fucking clearly," was her reply.

I bit my lip to stop from laughing and moved from my desk to sink down on my sofa. Resting my head on the back, I stared up at the ceiling and realized I was in for another long night.

She was muttering about girls, back alleys, *Jubilee*, drinking, dancing, guys, and sex. I didn't understand all of what she was saying, but I found the whole thing rather entertaining, until I heard her say, "...and I'm going home with him."

And my heart skipped a beat. "Wait, Liana—" The line went dead. "*Shit!*"

Fuck. I should have been happy she was out doing exactly what I'd told her to do, but I hadn't told her to get so fucking zonked before she did it.

On my feet in seconds, I grabbed my jacket and keys, and headed out the door. Taking the stairs, I jumped down them two at a time until I reached the lobby and zoomed out of the apartment building. Outside, I tried to hail a cab, but saw none driving by. Pulling up a car service app on my phone, I discovered all drivers were busy.

"Shit, shit, shit," I cursed and took off in another brisk jog—my second of the day, and probably third or fourth of the decade—in the direction of a private parking garage on East 94th Street that housed the red Maserati GranTurismo I'd bought on a whim and swore I'd never drive.

I got halfway before I stopped for breath, bent over clasping my knees and panting like a dog, unable to believe I was about to go and stop someone from having sex on a Friday night. Who was I but a disgrace to my former self? Kade from a month ago would roll his eyes.

And maybe Liana would tell me to fuck off and let her enjoy her first one night stand when I found her, but I couldn't let it happen when she wasn't in the right frame of mind to give informed consent. That was why I was so resolute in finding her. It had nothing to do with the fact that earlier in the day, her legs were wrapped around my torso and every part of me wanted to be back on that couch with her. I didn't.

So why was I replaying the moment with a happier ending in my head?

A cramp in my leg made me stop again, and a stitch in my chest made it hard to breathe. I wheezed, taking a huge gulp of air, and started running again until I reached my car. I hopped in the driver seat and wasted no time in pumping the gas and speeding down the street.

And I didn't stop until I saw the bright pink lights of *Jubilee*.

CHAPTER 19

KADE

arking a block away, I ran until I reached *Jubilee*, stopping in my tracks outside the doors. I questioned my plan of action. I had no right to waltz inside and snatch Liana off the lap of some guy and carry her home. For a start, she was nothing to me other than a woman who I'd been on one *bad* date with and shared a mutual business arrangement.

Secondly, it was her choice what she wanted to do. If she wanted to go home with the dude, I couldn't stop her. All I could do was make sure she was in a state where she was able to make the right choice for her.

Deciding I would go in to check on her, I bypassed the line and slipped the bouncer a hundred before heading through the windowless metal doors, plugging my nose to the rancid smell of spilled beers festering on the hallway carpet. Inside, the building was jam-packed with people, making it difficult to spot the unique red of Liana's gorgeous hair.

I checked the bar first, lifting my hand to get the bartenders attention. "You see this girl in here tonight?" I asked, pulling up a picture of Liana up on her Instagram. The guy stopped to look and placed his tongue between his teeth. His face scrunched in careful ponderance.

"Yeah. She left about twenty minutes ago."

I sighed. "Did she look okay?"

"You mean was she wasted?" he asked, and I nodded. "Yeah, she was pretty drunk. She left with this big dude. And I mean *big*. Dude was about your size, but with bigger muscles."

My nose wrinkled and my teeth clenched. What were muscles in the grand scheme of things when I had a face like mine? I scoffed, then remembered that wasn't the point. The issue was that Liana left with the guy, and she was drunk. *Focus.*

I headed out, the frustration in me building. The cold air whipped around me as I wrapped my mind around the situation. Liana was drunk, about to be invaded by a 'big dude', and it was all my fault. I was the one who'd told her she was depriving herself, I was the one who'd suggested getting her laid, I was the one who'd left her high and dry on her first go-round, and I was the one who'd told her she needed to get out of her own head and try new things.

It occurred to me that just because *I* liked random sex, it didn't mean everybody else did. And maybe Liana would hate it. Maybe she'd hate me for pushing her into it.

"Fuck!" I yelled, kicking my car before climbing into it. If she did hate me, or god forbid, the guy she went home with was a creep, I'd hate myself even more than I already did. I called her to find her phone was off.

Resting my head back against the leather headrest, I took a deep breath. My eyes slid to the time on my dashboard. One a.m. Too late to show up pounding at her door. I was stuck, the weight of everything crushing on my brain, aching like a boot stomping on my head.

In an attempt to clear my mind, I went for a drive. Unclenching my jaw, I put the car into drive and turned the radio up. The station played pop songs from varying generations, one after another.

The streets were less packed than they were earlier in the night. I drove around the city, and into Brooklyn with the top down and the wind beating on me. With every song played, my smile widened and dropped depending on the beat and the overall feel. Apparently, being made numb by a night of heavy emotions meant I was easily susceptible to allowing music to control my mood. And, as the song changed to "Freedom '90" by George Michael, my body flooded with adrenaline and my mouth moved into a full grin.

At the height of its popularity, I hadn't appreciated how fun the song was. In fact, I'd found it teeth-gratingly annoying. Now, I really liked it. I drummed my fingers on the steering wheel and gave a small laugh. It wasn't lost on me how quickly my entire vibe changed. It didn't bode well for my sanity. I'd gone from upset to annoyed to panicked to wanting to dance the night away—all inside an hour.

I didn't think I had a destination in mind, but as I turned the corner into the street where Cleo's building was, I thought perhaps this is where I was headed all along. The sight of the gray bricks and the stoop where I'd found Stephanie was enough to make my smile drop and allow the rage to take hold again. But as my eyes skirted the building, and I caught sight of Cleo's apartment window, I was no longer angry...

I was fucking infuriated.

Right there, in the window of the third-floor apartment, was Cleo—her lips all over a blond girl with pale skin covered in tattoos. Slamming the breaks, I watched for a moment to make sure my assumptions were correct. But every second that ticked by, I realized the truth was worse.

The girl thrust her hands into Cleo's black hair as the two made out, and when they broke apart, smiling, I spotted the unmistakable shape of a needle in Cleo's hand. The girl looked apprehensive, shaking her head in refusal. But as Cleo kissed her again, whispering something in her ear, her head nodded, and she relented.

"Like hell," I snarled. My phone in hand, I snapped a quick video of the scene and turned the radio to full volume as I got out of the car. In the next few minutes of my life, I would learn the definition of 'autopilot' in real time. Letting the music take me over, I danced my way to the trunk of my car, popped it open and grabbed the only thing in it: a silver baseball bat that was already in there when I bought it.

All but skipping over to her building like a seasoned psycho, I searched the street until my eyes landed on the Sriracha-colored Mustang Cleo owned for as long as I'd known her.

Fitting color since it belonged to the devil.

It was parked out front in an obscene attempt at parallel. Half of her back bumper was hanging out of the spot, and in my professional opinion, it'd been parked while under the influence—adding fuel to my fury.

Looking up, I realized she'd be able to see me from her window—if I made enough of a scene to grab her drug-addled attention, that is. *Good!* That way, I could destroy something *she* loved in front of her very eyes and see how she liked it.

Choking up on the bat with both hands, I raised it above my head and brought it down as hard as I could on the bonnet of the car. The sirens wailed in protest, and the headlights lights flashed wildly as I smashed away. They were the next thing to go after the bonnet was successfully fucked up beyond repair, and finally: I swung like Babe Ruth and shattered the side windows and cracked the windscreen.

It wasn't enough.

Unable to stop, I tossed the bat aside and climbed up on the wrecked bumper, realizing my body weight could do even more damage. I jumped like King Kong, bringing my feet down like strikes of thunder.

"Fuck!" *Jump.* "Abusive!" *Jump.* "Bitches!" *Jump.* "And!" *Jump.* "Fuck!" *Jump.* "Big!" *Jump.* "Ass!" *Jump.* "Dudes!"

Booting the already cracked windscreen, it exploded under my foot as the wipers dropped to the ground. With one final attack, the sirens became a soft cry before dying out completely —the Mustang's way of letting me know it had enough. It was dead, and I'd killed it.

"What the hell?" I heard Cleo's venomous voice spew as she hung out of her window, her hazel eyes narrowed into slits. "Kade!"

I stopped jumping and looked up.

"Oh. Hey, Cleo," I greeted, offering a wide smile. "It's been a while, hasn't it? So, how you been?"

"Are you fucking serious?" she spat through paper-thin lips. "You destroyed my car!"

Well, she had a point. I scratched the back of my head and let out a low whistle, observing my damage. "Yeah, I guess I did, huh? Sorry about that."

"*Sorry*?" she shrieked.

"Oh. I forgot you didn't know the word. 'Sorry' is an adjective. When you say it, it means you feel regret, which, actually, I guess I don't." I laughed, holding up my middle fingers. "I retract my sorry. Fuck you, you twisted bitch."

Cleo's face went red. "You're a fucking psycho!"

I bowed my head, my smile turning to a full-blown grin. "You're probably right about that."

Hopping to the ground, I collected my bat, calmly, and balanced it over my left shoulder. With my free hand, I picked up the remnants of the windscreen wiper from the ground and positioned it back into place with care.

With a smile, I looked back up to the window where Cleo looked at me with the venom of a thousand snakes searing in her beady eyes. "Get a fucking therapist." My sights landed on the girl behind her. "Maybe then you could stop beating your girlfriend so hard you break her nose and fracture three of her ribs to feel better about the fact you're a lowdown junkie and she's out of your league."

The blond girl put a hand over her mouth and turned away. I hoped it was to collect her stuff and get out, but I didn't stay long enough to find out. I turned my back on the building and bounced back to my car, as merry as a kid on Christmas, sliding in as the song ended.

I waited for the next song—Diana Ross' *"I'm Coming Out."* to start before pressing the gas. With a huge smile, I burst into laughter and shook my head, replaying what I'd done like a scene from a movie. I laughed harder.

"Yeah-p! That's definitely thirty ticks in the fucking deranged column," I said aloud, adding one tick for each time I'd hit her car. Nodding along to the music, I thought about the events of the day. Stephanie was broken, Liana was with a guy, and I'd strained my relationship with my best friend and committed a crime.

What a fucking shit-show.

The dashboard read 3:15 in the morning, and by the time I got home, it'd be close to five. If Stephanie was awake, she would hear me open the door. Oh, God. She'd demand to know where I'd been. I'd have to show her the photos. I'd have to tell her what I'd done.

She'd be heartbroken and pissed all at the same time. I imagined she'd cry... and then she'd kill me.

With a raised fist, I pounded on the door, loudly. It was nearing four a.m., and I had no business being so loud, but I needed to talk.

Listening for any signs of life, I heard the shuffling of feet on carpet and a giggle. She was moving slow, but she was coming, and she was awake. *Not having sex.* I stopped knocking.

Finally, Liana opened the door. Her hair was curly and looked so soft to the touch. My hand itched to reach out and twirl a piece of her around my finger. The smile on her lips moved into a surprised line.

I was too chicken to go home, I admit it. But it wasn't the only reason for my visit to Liana's apartment. I breathed a sigh of relief seeing she was lot less drunk than she had been and still in her club clothes.

Holy fuck. My eyes moved down to the dress she wore. A slender black, skin-tight dress that outlined every curve she had. *Wow.* My mouth hung open and a jolt shot through me, zinging below my waist and back up again, panging in my chest.

"Kade? What're you—"

"You look amazing," I said.

"Uh, thanks. Are you okay?" She asked.

I nodded. "Sorry for showing up so late, or early as it were. You sounded drunk on the phone, so I wanted to check on you. Can I come in?" Looking past her, I saw a tall Italian guy who looked like he'd stepped off the set of a movie where he simultaneously played the body double for The Rock, and the face double for the actor who played the lead guy in that movie Stephanie made me watch. *John-Whatever-Must-Get-Murdered,* or some shit like that.

"Never mind, I see you already have company." I forced a smile. "I guess I should go..." I feigned moving away from her door, but only got two steps before she called me back and invited me in.

I crossed the threshold with an innocent smirk, stepping into my new role of cockblocker like I was born for it.

"I'm Kade," I introduced himself with a strong handshake.

"Luka."

Luka, it seemed, was already feeling the tension of my presence. I couldn't blame him. Objectively speaking, I was just as tall, but looks-wise, I was ahead by a marginal portion. The only thing Luka had on me were his biceps, which—in my opinion—were an obvious overcompensation for smaller things. I didn't have that issue.

"Is there something wrong, Kade?" Liana asked me.

"What? No. I needed to see you. There's, uh, things we need to talk about... *in private.*"

Liana nodded and motioned for me to follow her as Luka took a seat on the couch and began drumming his legs with his palms, humming the rhythm of *Eye Of The Tiger.*

"Fucking weirdo," I murmured under my breath.

Liana's room was different than I expected it would be. For one thing, it was a hell of a lot neater. Even from our brief interactions, I knew a lot about Liana, and from what I could tell, she was disorganized and easy-going. On my first visit to her apartment, her work area was abstract art. Books scattered all around, pens in disarray, and notebook paper crinkled into small balls that had missed or fallen off the overflowing trashcan where her feet would be. So walking into a room where everything was neatly tucked away in designated spaces, and nary a speck of dust blew through the air, was shocking.

"This room doesn't suit you," I said without thinking.

"It's Kit's." That made more sense. "So what's up with—"

"Who's that guy?" I interrupted, pointing back through the ajar door when Luka was on his second verse of the song.

"Luka is complicated." She sighed and I raised my eyebrows as a sign for her to continue. "Okay, so in high school..."

She told me the story of what had to be the worst senior prom night imaginable as my mouth propped open. Zoe and Luka left Liana and Zoe's soon-to-be ex-husband looking for them while they committed a heinous violation on the bleachers where Liana found them, naked, at the end of the night. And if that wasn't bad enough, Liana finished her story with Zoe doing the same thing over again in the club.

"You got a picture of this sister?" I asked, and she snorted.

"*That's* your response to my story?"

"Humor me." I said, curious what could be so special about this *Zoe* person.

She did and pushed her phone into my hand, open on Zoe's social media account. I scoffed. Luka was stupid, blind, or both. "You are *way* more beautiful, and the fact you were willing to give her the benefit of the doubt after everything she's done is astounding. You're a ten across the board, Liana Dawson."

Liana smiled, a blush creeping up her neck. "You think so?"

"I do," I replied. "So, I have to wonder why the guy who broke your heart is sitting on your couch right now when he's not worth pissing on if he was on fire?"

She sighed. "I don't know. I ran into him after Zoe stole my guy of the night, and... I guess I wanted him to be here when she gets home."

Oh, he was a pawn in her petty plan. I felt better. "So you're not going to sleep with him?"

Liana smirked and shook her head. "Don't get me wrong, he's *so* hot—"

"I'm hotter."

"But..." She pretended not to hear me. "I realized tonight, I'm no good on the prowl. Maybe it's something that comes with practice. But I don't think it's for me."

I tried not to look too relieved. "That's okay. Do what makes you feel comfortable." I smiled. "Maybe we should go with your original idea. I'll be your sounding board and help you write beta responses until you feel confident enough to go at it alone."

Liana nodded and took a seat on the edge of Kit's bed, patting a spot beside her as an invitation for me to sit as well.

"So, what really brought you to my apartment at an inappropriate time in the morning?" She asked. "You look like you've had a rough night, and there's a shard of glass on your jacket."

I looked down to see she was right. A thin sliver of window glass was imbedded in the fabric of my clothes. Liana flicked an eyebrow, silently asking how it got there. "*Rough* is an understatement." I admitted, and then wondered, "How bad would it be if I, *hypothetically*, committed a Class D felony?"

Her eyes widened. "I'm gonna need a little more than that."

I winced and told her the definition I'd found online of what my charges would be if Cleo called the cops. "Intentional destruction of property wherein the damages amount to around fifteen thousand dollars."

Her mouth opened and shut twice before she finally found her voice. "Start at the beginning, and don't leave anything out."

Chapter 20

Liana

Kade was gorgeous, fearless, strong, and fascinating as all hell.

He was also ten shades of batshit crazy.

He'd taken a baseball bat to a Mustang. It wasn't a healthy response to any situation, and he definitely had issues he needed worked out, but I would be lying if I said I didn't find his reaction vindicated.

I'd never met Cleo, but after five minutes of hearing Kade talk about her, even *I* wanted to go to her apartment and smash more things that belonged to her. *Her TV, her phone... her jaw.* But fighting violence with violence would make me as bad as she was, and that wasn't something I ever wanted to be.

"Do you want me to talk to Stephanie?" I asked. "Maybe I could help her, woman to woman."

"I don't think it'd work." Kade covered his mouth with his hand. I could feel his pain and frustration like they were my own. Reaching out, I squeezed his arm, wishing there was some way I could make things better for him. His eyes flicked to my hand on his arm, and he swallowed, letting out a quaking breath. His other hand covered mine, burning my skin with his body heat, sending currents through me.

Silence. Neither of us spoke as our eyes flittered to each other's lips and back again, staying locked on each other. The aching in his eyes made my hand drop. He needed advice, not me fantasizing about his thick, soft lips on mine. He needed a friend...

"Liana, I—" The door to my apartment flew open and shrieks of girlish laughter sounded from the other room. Kade sighed. "To be continued..."

I didn't want us to be continued, I wanted him to tell me about every thought in his beautiful head, even the bad ones.

"Go." He forced a smile. "You have a sister to make jealous, remember?"

I snapped back to reality, seeing Luka sitting on the sofa through a crack in the door and remembered why I brought him home in the first place, though after seeing Kade's pain, my plan to piss Zoe off seemed even pettier than I thought it was. I stalled.

Kade nudged me forward, telling me to go for it.

The plan was to be sitting on Luka's knee by the time Zoe came home, but I couldn't do it. Not with Kade watching me. Instead, I moved into the living room and sat beside Luka on the sofa, leaving a modicum of space between us. He grinned, shuffling in closer, and wrapped his arm around my waist like he did anytime we were close in high school. My surprise was short-lived before I was taken in by the familiar hug. It was as though no time passed at all. My breath hitched in my throat as the warm skin of his hands landed on my bare thigh. I didn't want to feel hot, but unfortunately, the nerve endings in my body didn't ask permission before they decided to light up like a Christmas tree.

Zoe's eyes landed on us, and her face changed. Her smile dropped to a scowl and whatever she'd found so funny died a tragic death. Behind her trailed Gregg the fireman and Jana. I let out a scoff and my eyes narrowed into slits. Zoe knowing

Andy was wavering on their divorce and bringing a guy back to sleep with was low, even for her.

Without missing a beat, Zoe's mouth twisted into a sickly-sweet smile. "We couldn't find you in the club, so I brought Gregg back for you..." Lifting a hand, she moved her fingers in a flirty wave. "Hi, Luka."

"Zoe." Luka greeted her, but his eyes... they stayed on me.

Gregg and Jana stood by the door, unsure of their role in the dynamic. One thing I knew for certain: he wasn't there for me. It was evident in the way he scowled at Zoe in disbelief that she'd offered him up on a platter.

Not one for subtlety, Kade leaned on the wall and smirked. "Well, this is awkward."

All eyes pulled to him.

"Who are you?" Zoe's eyes finally left Luka and landed on Kade. She flattened her hair, put a hand on her hip and wiggled her fingers in the same flirty wave she'd given Luka. "I'm Zoe."

"I don't care," Kade said, and I smirked. His eyes moved to me and offered a wink that sucked all the breath from my body and rendered Luka's touch cold.

"What is your problem, Zoe?" I asked, finding my voice. "It's like you have a compulsion to hit on any guy I'm with."

Luka's hand left my leg. "You're with this guy?"

"What? *No!*" I hurried out.

"No," Kade said at the same time.

Zoe sneered. "Well how am I supposed to know which guys are yours? Three guys are here to see you. Maybe you should make up your mind and pick *one*."

The way she said it, with such snark, made her intention clear. She wanted to make out like me being involved with three guys was typical. A classic attempt of slut-shaming—for Luka's benefit, I was sure.

"How dare you?" I barked, standing to face her. "Kade is a business acquaintance, Gregg is a random guy whose tongue was so far down *your* throat in the club, it could have poked out of your asshole, and Luka is..." I trailed off, unsure what to say.

All of a sudden, I was an animal at the zoo. The entire room watched me, awaiting my response. Jana stood idly in the back, observing the scene like a daytime drama.

"I better go," Kade filled the silence for me. "Liana, it's been a pleasure, as always." He walked over and planted a sweet kiss on my cheek that made my skin tingle. "I'll see myself out."

Luka's hand found mine, grasping it hard, and tried to pull me back down beside him. I jerked, staying on my feet; my hand clasped in his. Frozen in disbelief, I stilled long enough for Kade to get out the door before my body caught up with my mind.

"Wait..." I pulled my hand from Luka's like he was on fire and chased after Kade. He was by the elevator by the time I caught up. I reached out, grasping his arm, and spun him around. Kade looked confused as I stared up at him. Without thought, I launched at him, looping my arms around his neck, and rested my head on his shoulder. My senses were over-whelmed with the smell of his cologne—sandalwood and oakmoss with spicy undertones—and I let out a soft, intoxi-cated moan.

His body tensed for a moment, before he leaned into the hug, burrowing his nose into the crook of my neck, and wound his arms around my body. I giggled, ticklish in the spot where he was. He grinned against my skin, burying deeper until I squirmed.

His teeth nibbled the skin and I belly-laughed, pulling back. He smiled, the same boyish smile that touched his eyes I'd only seen once. My stomach burst into flutters. I bit my lip, reaching up on my tiptoes, and placed a gentle kiss on Kade's cheek.

"What was that for?" he asked, softly.

"For caring enough to come check up on me," I said with a

small upturn of my lips. "Jeez, it's a circus in there. I wish we could be alone. I want to hear more about Stephanie, and I'd like to meet her. Why don't we do lunch tomorrow? All of us. If she's feeling up to it, I mean."

"I'll ask her." Kade smiled as the elevator doors dinged open. Stepping on, he clicked the down button, grimacing as the doors began to close. "I think you're still carrying a torch for Luka. Be careful."

As much as I wanted him to be, Kade wasn't wrong. I *was* hot for Luka. The second his skin touched mine, I remembered what it was like when we were kids. Though, this time when he touched me, there was something else there. The way his fingertips brushed my skin like I was delicate... every inch of me vibrated.

It was a bad idea to bring him back. And, as I walked back into the awkward mess of my own creation, I realized *how* bad. Luka had taken off his jacket and shoes and stretched out on the sofa like he belonged there. He smiled, and my heart went pitter-pat. I scolded myself on the inside and forced a smile—until I heard a derision-filled scoff beside me. My smile dropped as I turned to Zoe.

"Look, Zoe," I started. "Take Gregg into your bedroom and accept that your marriage is over because you're a vapid bitch and be done with it. I accept that about you, now. You should accept it, too."

Zoe's mouth hung open. "At least I don't keep it in the family!"

My mouth dropped, and I stumbled back in shock. Of course she brought up Ronnie. Nothing was over-the-line for her. I clenched teeth so tight, my back molars crunched together.

"Yikes," Jana muttered. "I feel like I should leave, but I need to know what happens."

I narrowed my eyes at Jana who ducked my glare. My eyes

landed on Luka, his jaw so on edge he looked like Johnny Bravo. But to my surprise, he let out the breath he was holding, stood up, and smiled. "The past is the past. I slept with her sister, and she… dated my brother. The way I see it, we're on even playing field."

Walking forward, he wrapped his well-muscled arms around my waist and pulled me to him. His cologne, peppermint and generic in contrast to Kade's, made my nose itch. As his fingers played at my hips, a fire in his eyes told me he wanted to kiss me. I shook my head and gave him a look that told him not to try.

His hands stayed above my waist, and his face stayed at arm's length.

"I didn't want to do this with an audience," he whispered. "I fucked up in high school, Lee… but it was always you I loved. And I don't want to put you on the spot, but if you want to go on a date with me, I'd be ecstatic."

The flicker of memories dancing in my mind's eye screamed to say yes, but something was missing. The burst of butterflies I expected to take me off my feet lay dormant. My tongue refused to utter an answer either way.

Instead, I said, "What about Ronnie?"

Luka stepped back, dropping his hands. Eyebrows furrowed, he scoffed. "I thought you were over him?"

"I am. But there's a history to be considered. You two are so close… I refuse to be the Elena Gilbert in this situation." I said, referencing the love triangle on *The Vampire Diaries* that almost broke two brothers apart. "Won't he be mad?"

Luka shook his head. "Ronnie knows I never got over you. He told me to get in touch with you a year ago, but I chickened out. I thought I had no right to invade your life after what I did. I guess fate knew better, huh?"

The two sides of my brain were at war, which wasn't helped by the spectators. Jana might as well have been eating a bowl of popcorn and slurping Coke through a straw, and Zoe was so red in the face, she could pass for Clifford the Dog. Only Clifford smiled more and screwed less people over.

When I opened my mouth, a squeak came out. All the years I'd spent in my room monogramming notepads and binders in pathetic '*I heart Luka*' stickers, or worse '*Mrs. Liana DiMaggio*' seemed a world away, and now I was left with two over-whelming questions: Was I stalling because my love for Luka was nothing but a teenage crush? Or was I simply scared of feeling for him again?

"At least say you'll think about it?" Luka asked, lacing our fingers together.

It wasn't an unreasonable request. I nodded and a small smile spread across Luka's face. He started to say something else but, thankfully, was cut off by the sound of the door opening again.

Kit tossed her keys on the side and took in the scene. Her face, puffy and pink. To the rest of the room, it may have seemed like she'd gotten a case of rosy cheeks after being caught in the cold, but I knew better. It was the unmistakable rarity of a tear-stained Kit.

"What's going on here?" Kit asked. "*Luka DiMaggio*? And who the hell are all of you people?"

"They're all leaving," I decided, jumping at the chance to clear the place out.

"We are?" Jana and Gregg asked simultaneously.

"*I* am?" Luka asked. "I thought we'd have one of our infamous sleepovers."

The thought was tempting, but the roaring fire in his eyes made me unsure I could trust him—or myself—to share a bed and sleep.

"Sorry. I have to work all day tomorrow," I lied. "But I'll call you."

Luka took my decision with little argument and headed for

the door with Jana after him, mouthing to call her with updates. Gregg the fireman, however... the only door he filed through was the one leading to Zoe's bed.

"Bitch," I muttered as the door closed. Staring down at my phone, I pulled up the video I'd taken in the club of Zoe all over Gregg.

"What's that?' Kit asked, removing her jacket and scarf, hanging them on the hook by the door.

I handed my phone over for her to get a better look. "I'm sending it to Andy."

"*What*?" Kit shook her head, handing the phone back. "Liana, that's messed up."

"Nu-uh. You're not talking me out of this the same way you talked me out of telling him everything the night of prom."

Kit's mouth moved into a thin line. "This isn't high school anymore. This is a marriage."

It annoyed me Kit thought I hadn't considered Andy in my decision. Of course I had. But I had to go with my gut, and it screamed I was doing the right thing. I knew the damage cheating did to a person, and worse: the damage it does to a child watching their parents fight, argue, and hurt each other over and over again. For sure, Kit, Dylan, and I would've been better off if our parents divorced when we were kids. At least then, we'd know where our mom was, or if she was alive, even. Maybe we'd have a relationship with our father that didn't hinge on resentment and hatred if he did the right thing and left my mom when we were kids.

At the core, my decision seemed almost like a gift to Andy. He could get out before they had kids.

I shook my head. "The ring is still on her finger, and she's in there getting naked with another guy. She has no consideration for her husband, but I do. And why don't we admit the truth? Zoe only wants Andy because *daddy's* money comes with conditions and Andy's doesn't. She can't get away with that!" I clicked Andy's contact information and loaded the video, ready to send.

"I hear you," Kit said. "But nine times out of ten, the messenger gets shot in these situations."

"Lucky I have health insurance," I clicked the send button and watched as the message receipt turned from one tick to two.

Andy knew, and my job was done.

"Now," I turned my attention to Kit. "Are you going to tell me why you're so upset?"

Kit's eyes looked everywhere but at mine. "Who said I'm upset?"

I gestured to her cheeks, painted in tear streaks coated with the remnants of her mascara, and pink from the temperature of her pain.

"It's cold out." Kit shrugged. "My eyes watered."

Bullshit. This had something to do with her *bossfriend*, Jacob. I raised my eyebrow at her. She folded her arms as more tears welled in her eyes and her bottom lip began to quiver.

"Okay, so maybe I am upset. But I don't want to talk about it."

Kit turned her back on me and raced to her room. I reached out, grasping her arm, but she shrugged me off as her tears began to fall. I moved after her, hoping she'd let me in, but as her bedroom door slammed in my face and her cries became muffled, I was deterred. And as my body ached, I left her door and climbed into bed.

I lay tossing and turning—the voice in my head telling me that the redness in Kit's eyes wasn't the result of an argument, but something serious. Accepting I wasn't getting an easy sleep, I reached for the T.V. remote on my bedside table to play the abundance of classic rom-coms I had on standby, but my hand stopped midway as I caught sight of my phone screen lighting up with an incoming email from Kade. It said Stephanie wouldn't be joining us at lunch.

I frowned. The email told me everything it needed to, but an ominous stabbing in my stomach believed there was more to the story, and Kade needed a friend. I shot off an email back, asking if he was okay and locked my phone, not expecting him to message back right away—or at all, knowing Kade.

I moved to put it back on the table and jumped in surprise as vibrations tickled my skin. Kade's face lit up my screen, the photo he'd taken that day in the café as Casper. His staple half-smirk and mess-of-color eyes glazed, so beautiful I almost missed his call by staring at him.

Biting my lip, I took a deep breath and clicked the green button.

"Hey," I said, worry worming its way through me. "Is everything alright?"

CHAPTER 21

KADE

I got home a little after six a.m. and sure enough, Stephanie sat on the sofa waiting for me. Heading for the minibar, I poured a whiskey over ice, and waited for her to speak.

"Where've you been?" She asked, her face puffy as though she'd been crying. "I thought you'd left."

"I did leave," I said. "I went out."

Stephanie hiccoughed, and then scoffed. "No. I thought you'd *left*. Never to return, left. You can't do that, okay? I need a thirty-day notice, minimum."

"Don't be stupid." I smirked, swirling the drink in my hand. "I'd never leave my whiskey collection behind."

Taking a seat on the edge of the glass table across from her, I clasped my hands together and leaned forward with my elbows on my knees. "Have you given any thought to my—to what I said?"

She nodded. "I've made my decision."

I sat back, swallowing my nerves. "And?"

Stephanie took a deep breath, her eyes flitting to the floor. "I don't want to lose you; you're my best friend and I love you. But Cleo... needs me."

My stomach pricked like the stingers of a million wasps descended on it. "Really?" I dug my phone out of my pocket and slipped it onto the sofa beside her. "Does this look like she needs you?" I watched as she clicked play on the video, her eyes filling with tears.

"And I didn't even shoot the good part." I drank my glass down in one. "Still feel like defending her?"

Stephanie threw my phone away from her. It bounced off the opposite sofa and landed on the floor. Tears rolling down her cheeks, she shook her head. "If she's using again then, it's not her fault. She needs me more than ever now."

What? I scoffed.

"Wake up, Stephanie!" I didn't mean to shout, and flinched hearing it in my ears. The guilt of seeing her wince made me sick. I lowered my voice to a whisper. "I can't do this anymore."

"So what're you saying?"

"I'm saying you can count this as my official thirty-day notice. You can keep the apartment. I'll start looking for somewhere new in the morning. Goodnight." My breath shook, unsteady. It was times like this I missed the sweet release of crying. I hadn't cried in so long; I wasn't sure I remembered how.

The urge to head to a bar and fuck the first woman who wanted it overwhelmed me. Liana had taken away the only thing that made me hurt less. I stood, unable to look at Stephanie anymore, and grabbed my phone from the floor behind heading for my bedroom.

"So we're not friends anymore?" she asked, her voice small and quivering.

I stopped, keeping my sights on my bedroom door so she wouldn't see the heartache in my eyes. "I'll always be your friend, Stephanie. And when you realize your worth, give me a call. I'll be there."

I shut the door behind me and did my best to ignore the

wretched sounds of her cries as my chest panged with guilt. I never wanted this, but every night that passed in nightmares and fear gave me no other choice.

I opened a fresh email to Liana and told her Stephanie wouldn't be at lunch. Outlining word for word what was said and describing how I sat alone in my bedroom, I explained my inability to cry, and the urge for casual sex.

'No crying, no sex, and I left the whiskey bottle in the living room. It would be awkward to go back out there to get it, right? I need something to take the edge of. Perhaps if I masturbate enough, I'll pass out. But odds are, my dick will end up looking like a limp noodle before that happens.

I'm so tired, Liana. Tired, and sad. Perhaps you won't see this until the morning. Perhaps you're dealing with Zoe. I don't know. All I know is, emailing you seems to be the only time I feel anything other than an empty black hole.

Sincerely, Kade.'

I didn't expect to hear back from her, but she was online it seemed because no sooner had I clicked send, she emailed back.

'I'm sorry, Kade. I wish Stephanie could see sense, but she's blinded by Cleo. Abusive people have a knack at leaving their victims with tunnel vision, as though looking through a kaleidoscope. Every-thing around Stephanie is a jumble of overwhelming swirls and shapes she can't make out... The only thing she can see clearly is Cleo, standing at the end of the tunnel like a warm bright light, unaware she's an oncoming train in disguise.

Is there anything I can do or say to make things better? I hope you're okay.

Love, Liana.'

My breath hitched in my throat. For years, I'd wondered what it was that made Stephanie stay with Cleo, and I could never make sense of it. Until now. The way Liana worded her email made everything crystal clear.

I started another email, but I was unable to put my appreciation into words. Instead, I brought up her contact information on my phone, and clicked call.

"Hey," her sweet voice answered after a long moment.

It was only then, when her voice was disconnected from her body, did I realize how much I liked it. It was soft, melodic, and feminine, and held an underlying tone of genuine concern. The spot on my cheek where her lips had been burned hot, and a warm feeling settled in my chest.

What the hell did that mean?

"Do you think I was selfish to give her the ultimatum?" I asked.

There was a beat, and a breath, before she answered. "I think you have to do what's best for you. You can't be around something that's pushing you back into your past. Whatever happened back then, it seems bad."

I sighed. Deciding to get changed, I unzipped my trousers and let them pool at my ankles before kicking them away. "It wasn't fucking good, that's for sure. I am who I am because of my past, but I want to move forward. But I..." I stopped, swallowing the lump in my throat, the next words hard to admit. "I've been getting nightmares. Not very manly to wake up in a fit of sweat and tears, I know. But it's been getting worse lately. I think a large part of that is because of Stephanie. Domestic abuse is—" I coughed, clearing my throat. "There's a history..."

Another beat, as though she was deciding whether or not to prod. I hoped she wouldn't.

"Nightmares aren't anything to be embarrassed about. We all get them. But if they're impacting you, maybe you need some help," she said.

Taking a seat on my bed, I lay my head back against the wall and smirked. "That's why I have you."

"Well, I'm flattered." She gave a little laugh. "But I only studied psychology to be an advice columnist. Kade, I think you need—"

With one hand, I got to work unbuttoning my shirt and let it fall open as her words registered with me. "Oh. Fuck me!" I hung my head with an exasperated sigh. "You think I need a therapist."

"Well, obviously." Liana snorted. "I've known you two weeks, and I could have told you that thirteen days ago."

I put my tongue between my teeth and smiled. "The last two weeks are the tip of the iceberg, believe me."

"I doubt that."

"I'm serious." I stretched my legs out and got comfortable. "Even as a kid I was a little nuts."

Liana stayed silent for a second. I could hear the sound of her bedsprings squeaking as she readjusted and cursed the lust that shot through me. I wondered what she was wearing.

"I assumed the crazy amounted as you grew up," she teased with another small laugh.

"*Nah.*" I laughed. "It got more pronounced as I got older and stopped giving a fuck, but I've got stories you wouldn't believe..."

Liana laughed. "Oh, yeah? Tell me some."

I smiled, recalling the only tales from my childhood where I was happy.

"When I was twelve, I was living inside of a slide at a play-ground in Chicago," I told her, unable to believe I was about to tell a story I'd never told another soul before. "Across the street, there was this animal shelter. One day, I was home during the day when I heard two guys say a Pitbull puppy named Lucky was going to be put down the next day because nobody wanted him. That night, I crawled through a small back window they left open, and I stole the dog."

"You did not!" Liana gasped on the other end, laughing. "What else?"

I grinned, launching into another story. And then another. And another. Liana listened, laughing, and urged me on for the next tidbit from what she now called 'The Kade Chronicles.'

Every story I told her was met with the same disbelieving exclamation.

"I swear I did, gorgeous," I said, reliving the first time I was arrested at fifteen "It was Halloween of '04, and I was a jackass the entire night."

"I can't believe it," she repeated. "You really egged a police officer?"

I nodded as though she could see me. "In my defense, he was an off-duty officer dressed as a pig. It wasn't until he pulled out his badge I realized his costume was on-the-nose. A whole night in jail for one egg. But hey, at least Lucky and I had a bed for the night."

Liana snorted. "Thank God for silver linings. Speaking of Halloween, it's two days away. Any plans?"

"Yup. I have thirty days before I need to move out, so I'll be dressing up as a ghost and going apartment *haunting*."

"A ghost?" She asked, her voice laced with sarcasm. "Which one? Wait, let me guess... *Casper*?"

"Oh, I trundled right into that one, didn't I? Touché." I laughed. "I could use some help if you're free. Maybe you could be my Wendy?"

"Actually," her voice said, turning low and breathy, "I was thinking of wearing that cupid's outfit I emailed you about."

I hardened, recalling her offer to dress up as Cupid. "I never did get those photos." My throat dried as Liana's breathing slowed on the other end. "If I didn't know better, Liana, I'd say you were flirting with me."

"Maybe I am," she giggled. It was a glorious sound. "Maybe I'm trying to make you feel better, give you something good to think about. Maybe you should take advantage."

A sensitive tingle shot through the tip of my penis, demanding my attention. Doing as she suggested, I reached beneath the waistband of my shorts and took myself in hand, letting a groan rip from my throat.

"This costume of yours... describe it to me," I demanded.

"It's not something I can wear outside," she started, her voice sultry and enchanting. The sound of her covers ruffling as she slipped a hand between her thighs. "I'd be put in handcuffs for sure."

Liana in handcuffs, tied to my bed. I moaned, pumping my hand up and down as she continued.

"I would be completely naked, except for my wings," she said, a soft sigh at her lips. "My wild hair grazing my hard nipples... *Oh, God, I wish you were here.*"

"I do too, gorgeous," I growled, envisioning her the way she described. *The curve of her hips, the softness of her thighs, her beautiful breasts heaving.* My hand worked faster. "What else?"

"Of course I'd have my bow," she breathed out, moaning as her fingers worked her core. The most magnificent sound I ever heard.

"Of course. And where would I be in this scenario?" I silently begged for her to tell me what she wanted me to do to her—all I needed to push myself over the edge, the sweet release of an orgasm only moments away. "Tell me."

"You'd be showing me how you use your arrow!" She yelled out, and the call descended into dead silence.

I paused. She paused.

Sucking my lip into my mouth, I bit down to stop the chortle in my throat but as a small snigger broke free, I couldn't help myself. I laughed. So hard. I tried to pull it back, worried

I'd embarrass her, but as a sweet fit of giggles blessed my ear, I snorted.

"I regretted that line the second I said it," she said, her voice less sultry.

I shrugged, letting go of my manhood. "What is phone sex without a little comedy?"

"Awkward?" she offered, with a sigh. "I feel stupid now. You must think I'm the most boring phone sex partner ever."

"Not at all." I frowned, hating that she'd ever feel embarrassed with me. "Though I am sad I didn't get to hear you reach orgasm." I succumbed to the urge to let her know how wild she drove me. Clearing my throat, I took on a sultry voice of my own. "Not knowing how you sound when you come is killing me. I have to hear you."

Liana gasped, her breathing becoming shallow once more. "What do you want me to do?"

I growled, my thumb flicking over the tip of my penis before I took it in my hand again. "Take your clothes off."

"But you didn't say please," she teased.

"Liana," I scolded. "Do as I say."

"I will," she promised. "As soon as I hear the magic word."

I smirked. "Liana Dawson, please remove every item of clothing covering your incredibly sexy body."

The sounds of her bed creaking as she disrobed sent me wild. *How I wanted to be in that bed, touching her.*

"My body is bare of anything but my black lace thong. Shall I keep that on?" Her voice held an amused glint. "I can take it off if you like."

"Don't you dare!" I bit back a groan. *Liana handcuffed to my bed in nothing but a thong.* What a sight. My strokes became vigorous. Hearing her so emboldened was the most turned on I had ever been, even with a naked woman in my bed.

"Are you lying down?" I asked.

"I am."

A smirk played at my lips. Slowing my strokes, I took a moment to calm down, so I didn't arrive soon. If I could, I would make this moment last forever. "I want you to get on top of your covers and spread your legs." I listened as the covers were tossed aside in a swift motion. Liana moaned. "Feel the cool air on your hot body? How does it feel?"

Her sharp intake of breath made me close my eyes. I licked my lip, the soft moans of Liana exploring her body becoming too much for me to handle.

"Good." I pumped my hand and groaned. "Now, I want you to tell me exactly what you want me to do to you..."

~··~··~

I heard her climax. *Jesus Christ.* Liana moaning my name as she came down from an orgasm was a sound I would never stop hearing as long as I lived. Every time her cry of release resounded in my head; my manhood engorged again. Five times I rubbed myself raw to the echo of her sweet dulcet moans before I fell into the most relaxed sleep I'd had in as long as I could remember.

And yet, I awoke hard as a pole.

I pushed myself into an upright position, my back pressed against the headrest of my bed as my body screaming in protest. But if I didn't get up now, I would be late for our lunch date.

We agreed to meet at an Italian restaurant at noon, but I wasn't sure if I should go now for two reasons. Number one: *How was I meant to go to lunch after hearing her orgasm?* Christ, I'd be rock solid before the complimentary bread was served. And that was unacceptable.

You could be hard while eating a club sandwich, or even a

steak melt. You could be hard with a burger in your hand, or some kind of kebab. But it was an absolute travesty and insult to think about sex while eating Italian food.

And number two: What if Liana didn't show? She was notoriously shy when it came to sex. It would kill me to find out she regretted our dalliance. I wondered if we *should* regret it? We'd put our professional relationship in jeopardy for sure. But the only thing I regretted was that it hadn't been my hands that felt her shudder as she came.

My phone beeped with a reminder that my date with Nikki was in twenty-four hours. I bit back an expletive. To go on the date with Nikki, I would need Liana's advice on how to behave, and asking for it was going to be awkward as ass now.

Sighing, I swung my legs off my bed, the crack of metaphorical eggshells sticking my skin as I stood up. *Better get used to them*, I thought seeing as how I'd be walking on them for a while.

Making my way to the kitchen, I slipped two slices of bread into the toaster and made a pot of coffee. As the toaster dinged, I coated the golden-brown bread in a thick layer of butter and slipped them onto a tray along with a cup of coffee. Placing the tray in front of Stephanie's door, I knocked twice and walked away.

Like a mouse out of its cubby-hole, she peeked her head out of the door and dragged the tray inside. Her eyes met mine and my gut wrenched, seeing them so puffy and hurt. She shut the door.

I poured a cup for myself and blew out my cheeks, almost choking on the atmosphere. Part of me wanting to apologize and take everything back—if only to alleviate the tension. But doing that wouldn't change a thing.

I realized, between masturbation sessions, that thirty days' notice was our way of clinging to each other as long as we could, her hoping that, in time, I would go back on my word. And she was right, I would. The longer I stayed, the more I would waver.

Which is why I decided I wouldn't be staying past the week.

Separate from Stephanie, I realized I'd lived in New York for over ten years, pissing money away on a rented apartment. With no plans to leave Manhattan in the next decade, and nearing thirty, I thought it was perhaps time I spent some of the cash I squirreled away and bought a forever home.

It made coping easier to think this could be the start of something, rather than the end.

Finishing my coffee, I checked my email with a smile. As I knew there would be, an email from Liana sat in my inbox. The timestamp: twenty minutes after we'd hung up the phone. The curious side of me demanded to know what it said, the logical side already knew—she would insist I pretend it never happened, and never mention it again—but the wicked side of me? I *wanted* to talk about it. In person. Over Italian food.

I wanted to see the pink in her cheeks as she admitted what we'd done. I wanted to hear her trip over her glorious tongue as she rushed to dissuade me from mentioning it. But I would not be dissuaded. It was the closest we would ever be to having sex, and I refused to brush it under the rug like it was nothing.

I'd been celibate for a whole week, and in those seven days, I had been in a sexual situation only twice—and both times, it was with Liana, the one woman entirely off-limits to me.

Fuck.

I got dressed in an Armani navy-blue button down and black jeans, adjusting myself in such a way that if Liana incited a biological response, my erection would get no detection, and headed out the door at one p.m.

Our date was at two, but as someone who'd been late and a little bit unhinged at our first meet-up, and technical no-show to our last—unless showing up at her door in the a.m. counted —I decided to get to Georginio's café half an hour early.

It was cold out, but all the indoor tables were taken, so I grabbed a table for two in the outdoor patio and waited. I couldn't wait to see her face when she saw me waiting for her for a change. Maybe I'd even play a joke.

"Where have you been, Liana? We agreed to meet at one!" I practiced in my most stern voice, an amused smile twitching at my lips. "Perfect."

With nothing to do, my head offered me an array of conversational topics and I began to outline a plan.

But it wasn't normal to plan, I was reminded. So, rejecting every natural impulse I had, I focused on the world around me to occupy. When Liana arrived, I would go by the fly of my seat —a concept that sparked my anxiety.

I tapped out the rhythm of my favorite song on my legs then stopped, remembering how I'd called Luka a weirdo for doing the same thing.

'You over plan so you won't be caught unprepared. It's a mechanism to avoid your own anxiety rather than treating it.'

I heard the voice of Dr. Jesionowski, the first therapist I ever saw, in my head. Back then, I had been so convinced she was talking out of her ass. Now, I wasn't sure. Maybe she was right. But if that were true, then Dr. Yuri and Dr. Tran were right, too —and I point blank refused to believe that because they were dicks.

The anxiety in my chest spiked again when I realized planning would do no good with Liana anyway. I never knew what response I'd get from her. So, really, it wasn't my rejection of natural urges that demanded I wing it; it was Liana.

I'd never felt anxiety this way. My palms turned clammy, and my heart pounded at the thought of her. I was perspiring like nobody's business, and a fluttering attacked my chest. I took a deep breath, my mind reliving our conversations, and started to feel like I couldn't breathe.

And as my eye caught sight of a mane of red hair styled perfectly around the most beautiful face, all breath left me completely.

Chapter 22

Liana

I sat at my desk, yawning, and tried to get some work done. But my brain was busy and loud—like Times Square in peak tourist season. I got maybe two hours' worth of sleep before indecision and shame jolted me awake.

What started as a check-up email an hour after Kade left turned into a two-hour-and-thirty-seven-minute phone call with him in the early hours of the morning that ended in a much more confusing way than it started. A way I hadn't been able to stop thinking about since...

A way that had given me the most intense orgasm of my entire life.

The sound of the pipes churning as a shower turned on in Kit's bathroom pulled me out of my thoughts, and I was grateful. One more minute of reliving last night, I would've been on my bed with my vibrator between my legs, calling out Kade's name and delving deeper into an idealistic fantasy.

I shot off an email commanding him not to mention out tryst at lunch, as I listened for the water to shut off. When it did, I ran to the kitchen where I waited for Kit under the guise of making coffee. She exited her bedroom in her robe with a towel wrapped around her hair and groaned, seeing me standing with my back against the countertop. I flicked an eyebrow.

"Good morning," I said. "Want some coffee?"

"Yeah—uh—" She stalled. "On second thought, do we have decaf?"

I snorted. "Decaf? *You*?" I nearly crumbled to the floor in the shock. The thought of anyone—especially Kit—drinking coffee solely for the flavor was unfathomable. I blinked at her, but all she did was shrug and stand back at the other side of the kitchen, her face the epitome of nonchalant.

"I'm weaning myself off caffeine."

Weaning herself, my ass. Kit's ability to lie to me was nonexistent. Something about being the older sister gave me a *Spidey-sense*, and it was tingling powerfully at the base of my skull.

Replacing the filter, I filled it with decaf coffee beans and closed the lid. As the beans churned into liquid, I leaned back against the countertops with my arms crossed and faced Kit, inquisitive. "What brought on the sudden need to be deprived of energy?"

"I realized I feel better without it."

Another snort ripped from my throat. "Nobody feels better without coffee."

Kit forced a half-laugh as the pot filled. Pouring herself a cup, she matched my stance and sipped at her pointless coffee in silence. We were playing a game of emotional chess. All I needed was a hint—one wrong move on her behalf—to latch onto. My eyes narrowed, considering a change of tactic.

"Can you believe Zoe?" I scoffed, inching my knight forward. "It's bad enough she went after a guy I liked, *again*, but to go behind Andy's back like that, *again*?" I shook my head.

"Well, her marriage is over now. So she got hers, right?"

"I guess." I squinted my eyes. Kit's mouth turned pensive, and my hackles rose. She looked more than sympathetic to

Zoe's cause. She looked pissed and judging—*me*. "But if you ask me, she deserves much worse."

"God, Liana, people make mistakes!" Her outburst scattered her pieces all over the board for the taking. But I wasn't in the position to check her King just yet.

"Mistakes are one thing, but this? I just hope she used protection."

Kit's eyes flamed and her nostrils flared like an angry bull. She threw her cup, missing me by inches, and I watched the ceramic crash into the sink and clatter into six or seven pieces —the sweltering hot liquid pouring down the drain.

"What the hell?" I barked. "You almost hit me."

"Lay off!" she raged, and I couldn't understand why until she said, "Just because you're a sexless shut-in who's never forgotten a condom, doesn't mean everybody else is as goddamn perfect!"

Through the hurt in my chest at being called a sexless shut-in, panic and pity surged. And like that, it clicked. *Checkmate.*

"Kit... are you pregnant?"

She stilled, her hands fisting her hair as her eyes glazed over in tears. "God, this is the worst time for this. My career is taking off... my life is good again."

I didn't know what to say. A rare moment when I had no advice to give. All I could think to say was a generic: "Whatever happens, I'll support you."

She nodded, taking a deep breath. "I know. Zoe said the same thing."

A sharp pain in my chest made me wince, like my heart had been stabbed through with a Samurai sword and sliced down to my stomach. And suddenly, it all lined up in my head. Zoe in my room, tickling my curiosity with Kit's late nights at work *just* enough so I would go snooping—a master manipulator behind the scenes, pulling the strings unnoticed... and I let it happen.

"You *told* Zoe?" I asked.

Kit's jaw inched forward past her nose, pointed and sharp. Her arms crossed her chest like an elementary school teacher who caught a kid with chewing gum in class. "Why should I have told you? You haven't been a great sister lately. Last night, you torpedoed Zoe's life like you were baking a cake..."

I bit down on the inside of my cheek so hard, I could taste blood. "Zoe had it coming." A ball formed at the back of my throat. I blinked away the familiar sting of tears in my eyes. "I knew this would happen. You let her in here and she got between us."

Kit rolled her eyes like I was being dramatic, and maybe I was. But it didn't feel like an overreaction. I trusted my sister enough to tell her anything, and it hurt that she didn't trust me the same. *Zoe?* Of all people, that snarky bitch was the person Kit told? My chest hurt again.

"Maybe Zoe isn't the problem. You're acting like a crazy person. What happened to giving me advice, *Love, Liana*?" she spat.

My lip curled, and I could no longer stand in front of her without bursting into tears. I stormed past her, grabbing my purse off the hook on my way.

"Lee..." I reached for the doorhandle and stopped as she said my name. Turning to face Kit again, I waited for an apology. Instead, I got a slap to the face. "While we're putting everything out on the table, you should know I'm going back to work for—"

I left before she could finish, making sure to slam the door with such rage, it jittered. I was so angry, I got halfway down the street before I realized I was in my nightwear. Technically it *was* an outfit—leggings and an old T-shirt. But the leggings had holes above the knee, and the T-shirt was a failed attempt at tie-dye from 08'. My mass of curly hair was thrown into a bun at the top of my head, and my face was bare and lacking moisturizer.

I had four hours before my lunch-*not*-date with Kade at the restaurant, and with that brought a whole other mess of emotions. It was stupid of me to allow myself to be swept up in the moment with him on the phone.

Now, I heard the symphony of him groaning my name on repeat. *A symphony consisting of only grunts and breathing, but a symphony no less.* The fact it was me who did that to him—I was a damn goddess.

It was the second time I let my willpower slip around him. But it wouldn't happen again. An epiphany struck as I came down from my pleasure moment and hung up the phone. *Kade would never be the guy I ended up with.*

He wanted me because he couldn't have me, and I wanted him because he was unattainable and going for someone I could see a real future with, like Luka, would make me vulnerable again.

I couldn't be hurt by something I knew was doomed from the start.

At lunch, I resounded to tell him that the flame (more like goddamn inferno) between us had to be smothered by a pillow before it burned our house down. But I couldn't go looking the way I did. I would pass-out on the spot if he asked about my outfit—the same clothes I'd discarded to the floor when he'd told me to. For one thing, it would take all the illusion of me being a scantily clad Porn Star out of the fun. For another, I already felt like crap without having the added blow to my self-esteem of sitting across from a hunk like Kade, in clothes I wouldn't dress a dog in.

Whispers from my purse beckoned me to the black card tucked away in the crevice of my wallet. A last-ditch attempt of bribery from Eric Dawson. I bit my lip in indecision. I should have cut it up the day he handed it over. I almost did. Scissors in-hand, I placed the card in between the blades ready to clamp down, but I couldn't go through with it; some pathetic part of me convinced I would need it at some point.

A back-up plan, only for emergencies, I swore.

But as I gawked at myself in a store window, I failed to see how this didn't qualify as one. I looked like I'd been dragged by my hair through a hedge, dipped in six different paints, and thrown into a woodchipper.

It also didn't help that the tears in my eyes had broken free.

I hadn't noticed until the distinct sensation of wetness coated my cheeks, but they were coming thick and fast, and stuck the free hairs to my face. Taking a deep breath, I wiped them away, desperate to steady my emotions.

Kit and Liana. Liana and Kit.

I hiccoughed, choking on a sob. I needed to focus on something else, or I would never stop crying. Forcing my mind onto my blog in an effort to comfort myself, I was shocked to find it made me feel nauseous. The looming deadline added to the weight in my chest until I couldn't breathe—my lungs crushed under the stress. Weeks flew by and I hadn't made any real progress on the new section. *Love, Liana* was all about romance, and it showed on the page. The pretty pastel colors, the floaty writing, the fact my tabs were clouds with tiny cherubs on them —it was all light and so cute it bordered on sickeningly sweet.

The sex section needed to be *a pop-up porno,* according to Jana. Like scrolling through a seemingly wholesome site and being sucked down an X-rated rabbit hole. I handed the reins to Jana and hoped what I got back would be tasteful and sexy. That meant my only job was to deliver the advice—and, so far, I was blowing it. If I could go back, I would have told the fans no way, or, at least, given myself a realistic deadline. Two months? *Stupid!*

The sound of a hair dryer pulled me out of my stupor enough to see a salon. My hand wound up into my hair, pinching a dry strand between my index finger and thumb. The ends were all snapped, half-way up the hair. Suddenly, my head hurt under the weight of a mane that took too much time to tame.

A stylist with beautiful, blond hair emerged from the door with a vape pen in hand. She took a long drag and blew it out. Her green eyes met mine and offered a smile, like a beacon of shining light beckoning me to her.

"Excuse me," I said. "Do you take walk-ins?"

～……～…

When I got in the chair, the stylist—aptly named Sally—asked what I wanted. But I had no idea. *A blowout or a big change?* I looked to Sally for advice. She suggested cutting my hair to an inch below my shoulders and taking my red tones to fire-truck levels, but that felt like too much at once. Instead, we decided to cut it to my breasts and make the most of my natural color; ramping it up a few levels with gleaming low and highlights that made it soft and playful.

While she worked, I talked. I off-loaded to her, a complete stranger, about everything. Kit, my blog, Zoe, Luka, even my situation with Kade and our lunch non-date. By the time I looped back around to Kit, I was crying again. I was so pitiful that Sally sweetly offered to do my make-up for no extra charge. Nothing too flashy, but enough concealer and eyeliner to cover the fact my eyes were swollen.

I left feeling better. My head was floating, it was so light. I wasn't used to it being so light.

Or so red.

I passed a store window and couldn't help but check myself out. It was nice to feel a little confidence boost. I searched out a clothing store. Walking down Fifth, my eye caught sight of an old toy store and my heart panged as memories danced in my mind's eye, replaying the shopping trips my mom used to take us on.

She once told me the change was instant. Once Eric made his name, that was it. Gone were the days of living happily in their one-bedroom. They upgraded, replacing happiness with expense, and moved into a huge apartment overlooking Central Park, where nine years later I would be born, and Kit almost two years after me. Somewhere between us two, Eric began his tirade of affairs, and broke mom's heart time and time again without a care.

That was the man Kit chose to crawl back to? It still hadn't sunk in.

Heading for the first store I could find, I picked up the first two things I spotted to make an outfit—a bandeau, gray, cotton jumper-dress that hemmed mid-thigh, and a pair of ankle boots—and wore them out.

I shoved the card back into the holder and swore I'd cut it up when I got home.

Taking a slow stroll, hoping it would help the ache in my chest, I headed for *Georginio's* around the corner where I found Kade at a table outside. Seeing me, he inched forward in his seat and his breathing slowed. My heartrate double-timed.

I took a seat across from him, determined to keep us on neutral ground. "So, I did some research this morning and found a therapist for you. Her name is Dr. Jesionowski."

"Oh, shit." Kade sighed. "I saw her a couple times, and kind of burned that bridge..."

I shrugged. "So, apologize. She'll probably take you back as long as you weren't too *Kade* about your last exit."

At this, he perked up. I stilled as he arched his eyebrow and smirked. "What's wrong with being too like me?" he asked. "You seemed to enjoy it last night."

My heart stopped.

I wanted to run away. My eyes turned wide, my mouth was

an 'O' and my cheeks blushed cherry-red. Kade was an asshole, smirking at me as though the entertainment he got from seeing me squirm was too appetizing to pass up.

I hid my face with my hands. How I could be so brazen over the phone, yet have trouble breathing after one small comment? It was unfathomable.

"So," he continued his torture. "Are we planning another late-night phone call? I could—"

"How's the situation with Stephanie?" I promptly changed the conversation and rearranged my cutlery, so I had something to do with my hands. His smile inched up further watching me fidget.

"I don't want to talk about Stephanie, I want to talk about how you sound when you're moaning out my name."

My eyes near popped out of their sockets, searching around us in case anybody heard. I sat forward and lowered my voice. "Stop it."

He held up his hands and feigned backing off. "That's a nice dress. Is it new?" he asked.

My shoulders relaxed and I released the breath I held. "It is."

He smirked. "It suits you. Though, perhaps not as much as wings and a thong..."

My cheeks flamed red once more. Taking sips of my complimentary water, I fanned my face. "Did you not get my email?"

His mouth curved up. "I decided not to read it."

"Why not?"

Kade shrugged. "Because I already knew what it would say. You want me to pretend it never happened. The problem with that is it happens to have been the most stimulating experience of my life."

The sip of water caught in my throat and sputtered out with a cough as he continued.

"I've never been as hard as I was last night. Many times, in fact. It had a lasting effect. My cock, and the palm of my hand, are virtually skinless."

I bit my lip and his glorious eyes landed on my mouth. I silently begged for him to stop because it was driving me crazy.

"God, the things I want to do to you when you bite your lip."

My breath hitched and my hand flew to my chest, my fingertips grazing beneath my collarbone. I licked my bottom lip, rolling it into my mouth and bit down stifling the beginnings of a moan. My blood burned hot, coursing through my body, the urge to beg him to take me on the table screamed in my veins.

I cleared my throat and guided us back to business before I lost all control. "I need you to step up your side of our deal…"

"I thought I did that last night?" He winked, and my eyes darted in every direction. He laughed. "You're so reserved. If you're doing it, you should be able to talk about it with pride."

"I'm not *that* reserved," I argued.

"You can't even say the words," he teased, and I narrowed my eyes; psyching myself up to meet his challenge. "Go ahead, say it. Last night, you and I engaged in phone sex until we each reached gratification." He kept his voice even, deadpan, to show how natural it was. But every syllable out of his mouth rendered me flustered.

"Jeez, Liana, that was factual." He sighed. "It's not like I said we talked dirty while we each rubbed one out until we came."

A shadow cast over our table as I looked up to find the waiter standing there, his pen dropping to the ground. He scrambled to pick it up and scurried away without taking our orders. *Oh my god.*

I turned to Kade, embarrassment burning my face. My eyes wide and irritated, I scoffed. "Now look what you did, *Mr. Grey*! You chased off the guy who gets us food."

"I admit that was a mistake." He exhaled, opening his menu. "Oh, well. Nobody's perfect."

Chapter 23

Liana

Kade and I settled in front of my open laptop as I wrote a blog post requesting sex questions. I put a pause on all romantic questions for two hours so we could focus on the *sextion*.

"How many questions should we take?"

"Four," he suggested.

"That works." I clicked post. I set a restriction for a maximum of ten questions—first come, first served—and watched as they poured in. When the ten spots were filled, we flicked through them, and I let Kade pick his favorites.

"That one." He scrolled and highlighted the questions on my blog. "And those three."

"Seriously?" I quirked an eyebrow. "Even the last one?"

"*Definitely* the last one. He deserves a response for having the brass balls it takes to admit something like that."

I twisted my neck to look at him, deadpan. "Did you write this when you went to the bathroom?"

"Sweetheart, I wish I were that creative." He laughed. "I may be good at what I do, but what I do isn't *that*. Jesus."

I shivered. "I feel dirty just reading it."

"That's why I chose it," he admitted. "You need to get

comfortable answering the tough ones." He nudged me. "Are you ready?"

No. But what choice did I have? I clicked the first email and read the contents out loud. "Dear, Liana... I had my first—*Oh my God!*"

Kade burst out laughing. "Move over, amateur. Dear Liana, I had my first *orgy* last night. My husband won't look me in the eye. I love my husband. Boring sex and all. I never wanted to make him uncomfortable. Now, I don't know how to fix it. Please help. Signed, *Kinky123.*"

"This one is all you because I have no idea what goes down in an orgy."

"Neither do I." Kade said, and I gaped in shock. "I'm not a fan of splitting my time and attention. When I fuck a woman, I like to spend as much time as I want teasing her, getting to know her likes and dislikes, finding out what drives her crazy..."

When he said *fuck*, my core quivered. I bet he could sense it too, because while I could hide my vagina sending out a penis-shaped bat signal, the pink on my cheeks shouted it loud and clear.

"Feeling a little hot?"

I sputtered, almost swallowing my tongue in a rush to deny it, but it was hopeless. Instead, I decided to be the boldest I'd ever been in person and told him the truth. "I was just thinking how great it'd be to *fuck* you." I slid my hand above his knee, letting my fingertips brush the underside of his thigh. As he took in a sharp breath, I ripped my hand away and sat back with a smirk playing on my lips.

For the second time, I shocked him. His jaw slackened, his eyes moved to my mouth, and when he breathed, it was shallow. I liked it. *Even if nothing could come of it...*

Kade cleared his throat, heat rising on his neck. I tingled everywhere, feeling a sick amount of accomplishment at making him flustered. *Strangely exciting to watch the stoic squirm,* as sang by Alanis Morrisette.

He moved in, and suddenly I was the one in dire need of an oxygen tank. The air between us shifted as his tongue swiped across his bottom lip, making it glisten. So inviting. I moved in too, until we were inches from each other's mouths; so close I could feel every breath he took, when—

—he pulled away, smirking.

"So, about Suburban Sally..."

That bastard.

⁓⁓⁓

"You're never going to build a *sextion* if you call your clients weirdos," Kade said, *again.*

A scoff ripped from my throat. "Even when they like to dress as leather dogs and be electrocuted in the junk with a taser? One malfunction and his sausage is fried."

"He sets it to low voltage." Kade laughed. "It's a sex section of an online blog, Liana... there's going to be freaky-deaky people with freaky-deaky sex lives."

He was right, but it didn't make my job any easier. I was so far out of my comfort zone. I sighed, running my hands through my hair. He pushed my laptop in front of me.

"Time to dive in at the deep end. You can do it. Write whatever comes to mind and, if it needs edits, I'll help."

Edits? I almost laughed. It would need far more than slight touch-ups; it would need full rewrites and a hell of a lot of sexual know-how. "I need a drink."

"Coming up," Kade said. As he stood up, his chair scraped against the hardwood floors Kit installed. I internally winced, but then I thought... *good.* I hoped he scuffed the floors. In fact, I hoped he chipped them beyond salvation. No doubt, Kit would freak if he had, but *so what*? What was she going to do? Never talk to me again?

Who gave a damn? I sure as hell didn't. Okay, so maybe that was a lie, but it hurt less to believe it. Kade returned with a bottle of vodka and two shot glasses. I smiled. Him being around dulled the ache in my chest.

"Fastest way to loosen up." He grinned.

"You and I loosened up alone. Is that a good idea?" I asked, my nerves descending into chaos. I shifted in my seat, trying to calm the urge to scream. Kade and I alone... drunk. *Holy shit.*

"The best one I've had all week." He smirked. "I can control myself if you can."

I bit my lip and nodded that I could, but I wasn't convinced. My core was already vibrating, burning, begging... I needed to diffuse the tension, move to a safe topic. And I knew one that was sure to put us on ice. "When is your date with Nadia?"

"Nikki," he corrected.

"Right." I took down a shot, ignoring the way it burned in my throat. "When is that?"

"Tomorrow." He sighed. "I wanted your advice, but I didn't know if you'd be comfortable."

I forced my shoulders to shrug. So nonchalant... *not.* "Why wouldn't I be?"

Kade breathed out a sigh that sounded a little too much like relief to not hurt my feelings. *Ouch.*

I hid my face by taking another shot. I should have been glad the mention of Nikki turned the heat between us stone-cold. Instead, I felt a little used. Which was fair; I used him too. But I never expected I would crave to do it again.

"What do you need advice on?" I took a shot.

He took one too. "Dating. To me, dates are a courtesy precursor to the sex."

I took another. My whole body shook, I stuck out my tongue and scrunched my face. Shooting vodka was like drinking gasoline. *Blergh.* "You've never been on a single date that didn't end with the girl in your bed?" I shuddered again.

"Of course I have!" His eyes turned playful. "I dated you."

I rolled my eyes, clinking my glass down on my desk.

He let out a chuckle. "Actually, our date was the most nervous I've ever been. I guess between Caspergate and you wanting to be fucked like a porn star, it was the first time in my life I've ever been truly unprepared. It didn't help that you're sexy as hell."

Oh My. If I wore pearls, I would have clutched them. The cool Nikki vibe disappeared the second he called me sexy, replaced by the need to squeeze my thighs together. Fluttering attacked my chest and stomach and moved down to my clitoris, sending me wild. Nobody—not even Luka or Ronnie—ever called me sexy. I was always sweet, pretty, angel-faced... but never sexy.

My body hummed, and suddenly I was drawn to him. I moved in, knowing this time neither of us would pull away. I could feel the heat of his breath fanning my face and when his lips puckered, they brushed against mine. A single movement would close the gap between us. All I had to do was—

My phone blared with an incoming call, blasting out my favorite song that I now hated it with a fiery passion.

"Saved by the bell," he whispered, but neither of us moved away. Only when his eyes slid down to my phone screen did he sigh and leave me cold. "You should probably get that."

I looked down and sucked my bottom lip into my mouth. "Oh."

Luka's name and an old picture of us shone on the screen. It was taken in the quad of our school. We were huddled together, tight, and looked like a perfect couple. I used to stare at it for hours and pretend we were. Luka's arms were wrapped around me, pulling me close, and my eyes gleamed as I looked up at him. I clicked the green button and lifted the phone to my ear. "Hello?"

"Hey, Lee. I was wondering if you had any plans for tomorrow night?" Luka's voice echoed and I wished I'd turned my volume down. Kade's jaw shifted like he was chewing gum, and his brows hunched forward.

"Tomorrow night?" I paused, the pressure bearing down on me. One part of me wanted to hang up and slide onto Kade's lap, colliding my lips with his. The other was ecstatic for being asked out by Luka. But neither feeling was smart. "I, uh... I'll get back to you when I have a chance to check my plans." I hung up before he could say anything else and placed my phone, silent, face down on the desk.

"Hot date?" Kade asked.

I shrugged. "Depends on if I have a lapse in judgement at any point in the next twenty-four hours."

"You almost just did." He winked.

I forced a smile, moving my attention back to my blog and doing my best to stay casual. "Kade, kissing you wouldn't be a lapse in judgement, It would be discarding all judgement entirely."

Chapter 24

Liana

"You did an awesome job responding to the pervert." Kade commended, stretching out. "It's like you've been doing it your whole life. I don't think you have anything to worry about."

I wasn't too sure on that. The only reason the advice was so dead-on was because of his edits.

"I should get going." He stood from the chair and stretched out. "Back to the apartment where the floor is made of eggshells."

I made a face of pity. The thought of him being sad and alone made my stomach tinge with a need to make it better for him. "You could—" I shook my head, realizing my idea was more than stupid, it was downright self-destructive. "Never mind."

"What?" He stopped.

"Nothing. It's not a good idea."

"Since when has that ever stopped me?" he asked. "Tell me what you're thinking."

My feet tingled and I fidgeted on the spot, unable to keep still. "If you don't want to go back home and deal with Stephanie, you could... stay the night."

"That's not a bad idea; it's a fucking disaster waiting to happen." He smirked, but he didn't say no. "Would I be in your bed?"

I hadn't thought about it, but I guessed he would be. I nodded.

"I'm in."

My stomach exploded with nerves, and *excitement*. He was staying over. A man. In *my* bed for the first time since I moved in. Not just a man—*Kade Jennings*.

"No sex." It had to be established before he slid between my sheets and tried to slide between my thighs. "I might be a glutton for torment, having you there and not doing anything about it. But I think it's for the best."

He nodded, but the twinkle in his eye was dangerous. It was the twinkle of a man thinking *whatever happens, happens*. "Of course, if you change your mind, I won't be too disappointed."

"Not gonna," I swore—more to myself than him—but it would take all of my willpower to stick to it.

He chuckled. "Fine. But I assume you won't mind me sleeping in my underwear?"

I swallowed. Hard.

He was trying to get to me, and God was it working. But after a night spent responding to some particularly dirty confessions online, and more than a couple shots of straight vodka, my shame level seemed to be nonexistent, and I rose to his challenge.

I shrugged. "Why bother with the underwear? Feel free to sleep nude. I'm going to."

Turning my back on him, I whipped my t-shirt over my head and discarded it to the floor, parading my naked back for him. My reward: a short, sharp intake of breath that sent electric currents through my body. My skin tingled, all the way down to my center. I was sans bra, and my freshly-cut hair grazed the bare skin between my shoulder blades. My senses were so heightened, I could feel every strand. I wound my left hand up my neck and swept the hair over to my one side, giving him full view of the nape of my neck as well as a short glimpse of the side of my left breast. He whimpered.

It was like music to my ears.

I never thought I'd have the balls to strip in front of him, but there I was. Everything about Kade challenged me, like playing a game of dares I so desperately wanted to win. I loved the look on his face when I managed to shock him, and the more I saw it, the more I wanted to see it again.

He followed me to my bedroom and shut the door behind him with a click. He leaned his back against the wood and watched me turn slowly, giving him a full view of my breasts. His eyes travelled down my body, and his mouth lay open in a silent moan. I brushed my right hand against the soft skin of my collarbone, and moved it down, grazing the curves of my breast. My left hand started at my navel and travelled to the edge of my abdomen between my stomach and my most intimate part, which begged for attention. Kade's eyes followed everywhere my hand moved. I smirked, letting my fingers play with the waistband of my jeans. And boy, was I glad the shop assistant talked me into a new lingerie set. I unzipped my jeans and let them fall to the ground. I kicked them to the side and stood in nothing but my black lace panties. Kade's eyes met mine and I raised a challenging eyebrow, telling him to catch up.

First thing to go was his suit jacket. And then his socks. I whimpered as he purposely drew out the striptease to torture me—all the while taking in every inch of my near-naked figure like I was something made of pure gold. I fought the urge to squirm under his stare and kept my feet planted firmly to the ground, despite every fiber of me pulsing.

Finally, his fingers worked the buttons of his shirt—one by one—until his naked chest was exposed. It was glorious, decorated with a light patch of hair, and better than any chest I'd seen in my life, including those of Channing Tatum and Zac Efron.

My desire was made all the more intense by the neon sign above his head flashing the word 'forbidden.' Wetness pooled between my legs, my core aching to touch him and to be touched by him. I was bubbling over the edge, about ready to pop, when he unzipped his trousers and dropped them to the floor, kicking them away.

There we stood—him in his Calvins and me hiding extraordinarily little of Victoria's secret.

A stand-off. *Who would be the first to cave?*

His fingers played with the waistband of his shorts, inching them down slowly until the full glory of his hips were on show. He waited for me to make the next move, but my hands stilled, frozen by indecision. Sucking my lip into my mouth, I shook my head, deciding I wouldn't show him all of my parts at once. I smirked and made my way around the bed where I grabbed a crop top from my bedside drawer. I pulled it over my naked breasts and covered half of my stomach.

Kade groaned. "What happened to sleeping naked?"

"This is my version of it." I slid between the sheets of my bed and did my best to ignore the wild buzzing between my legs. I chickened out, and I cursed myself for it, but deep down I knew it was the smart thing to do. If I let Kade see me, and if I saw him in return, I would cave on my no-sex rule. I was already teetering on the edge of giving in, but as much as I wanted to let Kade ravish me, the question remained: What would happen after? It's not like I'd wake up in his arms and have myself a boyfriend. Odds were, I'd wake up alone and never hear from him again.

I eyed Kade, waiting for him to join me in the bed and pick a movie—something Disney and lacking sex scenes—but he stayed standing at the edge of my bed. When my eyes met his, he smirked. That dangerous half-smile that was so sexy, I could have died.

"Well, sweetheart, my version of sleeping naked is this—"

Yanking his boxers down, he stood in all of his naked glory. My mouth gaped as my eyes trailed down his body. There was not a dot or blemish anywhere on him that couldn't be considered sculpted by gods. He was a picture-perfect Adonis. The pinnacle of male physique, in my opinion. He wasn't ripped—missing four of the eight-pack—and he had love-handles I wanted to grab tight and never let go. He was fit, but not gym-rat fit. More like, 'I lift occasionally and like to do cardio'-fit.

I hadn't realized until that moment, but he was my perfect type. It shocked me because I'd always assumed I was attracted to the Hollywood standard of 'muscles equal hot'. The big guns, the 'V' shape, and the contoured ab muscles every leading man in the movies inevitably sported under their pressed suits and t-shirts two sizes too small for their machine gun arms.

No, sir.

This is what I liked. Kade was toned enough to have the shadow of a 'V,' but with spectacular curves. An ass I could bounce a quarter off, heavy arms I craved wrapped around me, and his cock—well, he hadn't been exaggerating his size as a lot of men do. But for a man with his size ego, I was surprised he hadn't mentioned his impressive girth along with his length.

I blushed, unable to take my eyes off him.

He hardened under my stare—which did nothing to turn me off—and moved toward the bed. The urge to get on my knees and take him in my mouth was so strong, I had to grip my bedsheets with my toes to stay still.

Climbing atop the covers, he kneeled inches from my face. "Are you sure you don't want to throw the rulebook out of the window for a night?"

Rules are made to be broken. But more often than not, breaking them had some dire consequences, and I didn't want to deal with those. I swallowed down the lump in my throat and clenched my knees together. I didn't trust opening my mouth in case I moaned, so I shook my head.

He smirked. "Your loss."

Lifting the covers, he slid under and turned on his side to look at me. I could barely breathe—the lust between us was suffocating.

If someone told me a month ago that I would be in bed half-naked with a god-like man lying beside me, and *not* touching him, I would have said they were crazy. My clit went wild with desire. Tingling, pulsating, longing to be touched...

His eyes stayed on me, which did nothing to assuage my thirst for him. My breathing because shallow, and my nipples hardened under my shirt. I couldn't take it anymore. I was faced with two choices: get out or give in.

"I need to go to the bathroom," I rushed out, jumping from the bed as though it caught fire. "And I might take a cold shower, so if you happen to hear the shower head running, that's why. No other reason."

He bit his lip with a small smile, his eyes on my mound. His tongue licked at his lips, slowly, and every word he said was punctuated with desire. "If you need to touch yourself, why not do it here?"

My heart jumped. I could feel the heat rise on my cheeks. The thumping in my chest was so loud I could hear it in my ears, deafening me to the point I wasn't sure I'd heard him right. All of the blood in my body migrated to my brain, leaving me faint. "Excuse me?"

Stepping from the bed, Kade closed the space between us

with two strides. So close, I could feel his heartbeat and lick the salt off his skin. He raised an eyebrow, asking permission before he took my right hand in his and placed it at the edge of my navel. Torturing me, he took control of my fingers and lightly brushed my skin, moving down—teasing and tickling me with my own hand—until I could barely contain myself.

Closing my eyes, I gave him full rein and threw my head back in a silent moan.

Drawing circles with my fingertips, I basked in the anticipation of him moving my hand closer to my intended target. With a gasp of pleasure, I *finally* grazed the fabric covering my mound. Kade pressed in, brushing my hand over my clit, and a soft moan escaped my lips.

He moved closer, allowing me more freedom but not dropping my hand, and lay a trail of kisses starting with the nook of my neck. I moaned again, touching myself over my panties as he sucked on the sweet spot on the underside of my jaw, and then moved between my breasts. I stumbled back against a hard wall as his body covered mine, his hardness pressed into my leg. He groaned, hoisting my top up, and took my left nipple into his mouth.

"Is this okay?" he asked, and I cried out an enthusiastic *yes* as he moved his attention to my right breast, kneading my left with his free hand.

Obeying my cries, he took full control of my hand once more and sped up my circular motions. I bit my lip on the verge of orgasm.

"Please," I whispered, and Kade's mouth again moved to my neck. Smirking against my skin, he dropped my hand and took over, caressing my bare thigh with *his* fingertips. I shivered. Achingly slow, he moved them up until they played at the hem of my panties with the promise of ripping them to one side and giving me the touch I so badly craved.

And that's when my mind slammed back into place.

"We need to stop." I tried to sound authoritative, but the breathy moan in my voice gave me away, I wanted nothing less than to stop. I wanted him to throw me onto the bed and fuck me all night long, but Kade didn't need to be told twice. He stopped kissing my neck and dropped his hand. Taking a comforting step back, he swallowed his lust and nodded.

"I'm sorry if I overstepped a boundary," he said, and I almost snorted. *A boundary, singular*? Oh, we'd overstepped a million, but that was as much my choice as his.

"We're good," I assured him. "We let ourselves go too far is all."

And if we went any further, I wouldn't have been able to stop, I neglected to add. The façade of our working relationship would have crumbled to dust, and I would have been magnificently fucked—in more ways than one. "I'm going to the bathroom, and when I get out, you need to be wearing boxers, *at least*."

He nodded.

"Good. And then you can use the bathroom. Clean up when you're done."

With that, I turned my back and closed the door. Staring at myself in the mirror, I looked like a sex kitten. My face was flushed pink, and I was shocked to see a look in my eyes I'd never seen before: *Pure, unrestrained hunger.*

Taking a deep breath in, I let it out slowly and fanned my face until I was normal temperature again. My entire body was *on*. Buzzing. *Begging*. I needed release. And if I couldn't get it from Kade, I went with the next best thing: the pulsating showerhead in my bathtub.

Sinking down into the cold, ceramic oval, I found the right pressure and melted into the relaxed pleasure, building my orgasm slowly before I increased the pressure again and again until my body writhed and shook. I opened my mouth, letting out a soft sigh as I pushed myself over the edge. I screamed out, wave after wave of pleasure making my body stutter and thrash as the most intense orgasm wracked my body, spurred on by thoughts of Kade.

"*Kade!*" I cried out, coming back down to earth, and prayed he heard me.

CHAPTER 25

KADE

Jesus Christ.

I stiffened; the soft whimpers of Liana getting herself off fluttering through the small crack in her bathroom door sending tremors through my cock. Her moans, for the most part, were like hearing angels sing—melodic and divine, almost whispering. I could have listened to it for days.

Every so often, she'd cry out, the showerhead between her legs edging her closer to orgasm. I groaned, the pulsing in my groin begging for my attention, and prayed she'd come to thoughts of me.

If I thought hearing her over the phone was something special, this was... *damn.*

The fact I could hear her at all was a miracle; one I knew she afforded me as a method of torture. And it worked like a charm. The throbbing ached so bad, I feared it would cause a heart attack, but I didn't care. I would die happily by the virtue of her pleasure.

With one final, lasting outcry, Liana reached the edge of pure bliss. I closed my eyes and imagined how magnificent she looked, her body writhing in the bathtub as she rode out the wave. Maybe it was because she was off-limits to me, but never had I yearned for a woman the way I did for Liana.

Every move she made seemed deliberate to drive me fucking insane.

Even her hair turned me on. I wanted to count every strand on her strawberry-blonde head. I wanted to feel it run through my fingers. I wanted to thrust my hands into it and grip tightly while giving her the more earth-moving kiss of her entire life.

It was crazy that we hadn't kissed.

I'd kissed her neck, touched her breasts, controlled her hand while she touched herself, and even took her nipple in my mouth. But I was yet to kiss her. *And fuck, did I want to...*

I craved to kiss every inch of her, starting with her plump and beautiful lips. But I needed to stay focused and remember why I reached out in the first place. I desired to learn about love, not lust. Lust I had down to a science.

Sighing, I cursed my weak brain for entertaining thoughts of Liana when my focus should have been on my upcoming date with Nikki. She was the one I had a shot with, and she seemed the perfect type of woman I needed in my life—witty, funny, not easily offended.

So why, every time I tried to think of Nikki, could I no longer remember her face? Why, when I shut my eyes, did I only see wild red hair instead?

Liana emerged from her bathroom in only a towel, and I near perished—my heart rate flatlining. Her hair was damp, and when she moved past me, the smell of lemon caressed my senses. I shuddered.

Before her, lemon wasn't a smell I cared much about. Now, it was my favorite smell in the whole world, and every time I caught a whiff of it, the image of Liana's smile would force its way into my mind.

"All yours." She shot off a finger gun, then winced, looking like she really, *really* regretted it.

I cleared my throat and nodded, heading for the shower. The second the water started spurting from the holes in the head, I wrapped my hand around my shaft and relieved myself to mental images of everything, A to Z, I wanted to do to, and with, Liana Dawson.

⁓⸳⁓⸳⁓

Liana was sitting cross-legged on her bed, in a pair of cotton bottoms and a long, blue t-shirt with the words, *'Smile, sun, sleep...'* written on the front as I exited her bathroom. Her hair, in a loose bun atop of her head, was messy with strands that fell around her bare face, her skin so soft it appeared freshly-moisturized.

"You look comfy," I commented.

"I was comfier before, but I thought it would be better if we didn't tempt ourselves," she sighed.

She made a good point, which is why I rolled my boxers back over my legs and pulled them up, using the towel around my waist as a cover.

"I can sleep on the couch if you want me to. I don't want to make you hot. I mean, if you usually sleep nude, I wouldn't mind." I grimaced. "Everything I'm saying is coming out sexual, isn't it?"

"Only because we can't stop thinking about sex," she huffed, flicking through movie options, and avoiding my eyes. "The couch is comfy to sit on, but I slept on there once after an all-night writing session and woke up with a kink in my neck. I'm good if you are?"

"I'm *fine*." I forced a smile, the atmosphere thick in the air around us as Liana and I skated around each other like the morning after a bad one-night stand. Honestly, it would have been less awkward if I went home, slept on Stephanie's floor, and begged her to stay with me. "So," I said, attempting to apply a cool solace on the heat between us. "About this date tomorrow. Got any advice?"

Her shoulders relaxed, a small smile spreading across her face. "No creating fake facts about yourself. You're not a bad guy to be around, so show that off. Oh, and stay away from the hard-hitting topics. The date won't go well if you get pissy and leave before the appetizers arrive."

Right. "No mom, no childhood, no homelessness. Got it." I nodded. "But what if she brings up those things?"

"Deflect." Liana cleared her throat, taking on a deeper voice. *"No offense, Natalie, but maybe we should save that stuff for the second or third date."*

"Nikki," I corrected, *again.* "Why can't you remember her name? I remember Luka's."

Liana scoffed. "On average, I answer thirty-six emails a day. Sometimes names are interchangeable to me. I'm sorry if I offended the love of your life, *Cameron.*" She smirked. "See? I even do it with your name."

"Whatever, Linda," I retorted.

She giggled, rolling her eyes, and pressed play on an old 80's rom-com. Lifting the covers, she got into bed and hunkered down as the opening credits sang out. Climbing in beside her, I realized she'd retrieved an extra sheet from the storage closet so we would be sleeping on two separate levels of the bed. It made sense. We couldn't touch each other if we weren't under the same sheet, right?

Wrong.

As Liana fell into a comfortable sleep, her head made its way over to my chest and her sheet-clad leg curled around my body. I froze and contemplated rolling her over to her side, but as she gave a contented hum, I smiled and surrendered to her. The thought of waking her felt sinful. She was too cute for me to resist hunkering down into her mattress and pulling her closer. Curving my body into hers until we fit like two puzzle pieces, I basked in the aroma of her shampoo and watched a small smile tug at the corners of her mouth. I wondered what she was dreaming of. I hoped it was something wonderful.

Ripping my eyes away from her face, I turned my attention to the movie. It wasn't something I'd ever pick because it was all about romance, but Harry and Sally were such interesting characters, they drew me in with their banter and chemistry. And, by the end of the movie, even *I* found myself rooting for them to *finally* get together. Again, my eyes slid back to Liana sleeping soundly, and a pang of jealousy twinged my stomach. I was wide awake, my mind overstimulated as the next movie on a list called 'All-Time Favorites' played of its own accord. Another Meg Ryan flick I couldn't tear my eyes away from. Kathleen and Joe weren't as compelling as Harry and Sally, in my opinion, but they had an interesting way of meeting—over email. I gave a small laugh, thinking about where I was... in the bed of an amazing woman I'd met over email.

A strange warmth burst in my chest.

I didn't have time to analyze the feeling before another movie started, and then another... And before I knew what happened, I'd watched all night. By the time the sun shone through the shades of Liana's window, I'd watched *Notting Hill*, *Sleepless in Seattle*, *Pretty Woman*, and lastly, *Bridget Jones' Diary*.

No wonder Liana was so obsessed with love, I thought. When it was laid out like that, I could definitely see the appeal. Love changed everything for the characters on screen. Their lives before were a mess, but by the final kiss, they became better people with well-rounded emotions. It reminded of why I sought Liana's help to begin with: because I wanted to be better. I looked down at Liana, pouting in her sleep, and smiled again. Her movie list allowed me to discover she was a big fan of the slow-burn romance. Turns out, to my unending surprise, I was, too.

My eyes drifted closed, finally tired. Snuggling down into

bed, I nuzzled my head into hers and sighed, letting sleep take over.

My body groaned, it felt like I'd been asleep only minutes before Liana nudged me awake. "Kade, go shut the curtains. But also, don't move because I'm comfortable."

As an avid believer of a late morning, especially after a night spent watching chick flicks, I groaned. "You shut the curtains. I'm a guest in your bed. Be courteous."

"Hmm," she breathed out and snuggled deeper into me. "*Please!*"

A twitch pulled near my leg, I let out a little moan. "I like hearing you beg."

Liana's leg flew out, kicking me in the shin. I started to laugh. She gave another hum, and I was powerless to argue with her. Tossing the blanket off my body, I hurried as fast as I could from her bed and swooped the curtains closed, plunging the room into a relaxed darkness. Taking advantage of her being half-asleep, I slid back into the same position and wrapped my arms around her before she had the chance for her consciousness to seep in and remind her we weren't supposed to be touching. Liana sighed, a content smile on her face, and curled into me once more. It was so relaxed, so easy, so *terrifying*. I had never cuddled with a woman—especially one I had never seen naked. It felt wrong, and *right*, and everything in between.

Which is why I slid back out of the sheets and collected my pants from the ground. I slipped them over my legs.

"Where'd you go?" Liana whined.

"It's morning." I jumped into my pants and zipped them up. "And it's a big day, remember? Dates all-around."

Liana grumbled, pushing herself into an upright position and hugging her legs. "No. *You* have a date. I have a Luka. It's *not* a date."

I snorted. "You're going to a restaurant, coming back here

and fucking." I almost growled at the idea of Luka in her bed. "What's not a date about that?"

"Who said we're going to have sex?" she scoffed. "Who said I'm even going to the restaurant?"

I forced a smile. "Liana, you've been itching for some for weeks, and you have a history with this guy. If not him, and you won't touch me, then who?" I know I made a valid point because her face twisted.

"But what if I don't want him anymore?" Her eyes slid over to mine and she bit her lip.

My breath hitched in my throat. *Did she mean...?* "What do you want?" I asked.

Her eyes travelled my body, from the top of my head to the tip of my toes and back again, landing on my lower region. I bit back a groan, hardening under her stare. Liana sighed, throwing the comforter away from her body. "We should prepare for your date with Nikki. Unless you decided not to go?"

What? I didn't understand. It wasn't my choice to go out with Nikki. It was Liana's exercise. I wouldn't bail on something she asked me to do. "Of course I'm going."

She nodded. Pulling her knees closer to her chin, she rested her head on them. "Do you want to go over some conversation topics before you go?"

I almost rolled my eyes, my lips tugging into a smirk. "No thanks, mom. I think I've got it covered. Gee, I hope her Dad doesn't answer the door. Golly, that might be awkward." I even added a peppy 'aw, shucks' arm gesture to my sarcasm.

Liana's eyes narrowed. "I hope you crash and burn."

I smirked like she was funny, but inside I hoped the same. I didn't want Nikki. Sure, she was hot, feisty, and everything a woman could hope to be, but suddenly, I became very aware of one single fact: *Nikki wasn't Liana.* And if I wasn't going to have sex with a woman, I wanted that woman to be Liana Dawson.

What the fuck did that mean?

"Breakfast?" Liana offered. "I can make you French toast?"

I started to say no, but as my stomach gave an almighty growl, and my mouth filled with drool, I couldn't resist. With an emphatic yes, I followed Liana out to her kitchen, only to find Liana's definition of making French toast was me doing the brunt of the work while she sat at her desk and scrolled through the admiration pouring in on her blog.

"We make a great team." She grinned. "They love the new section! And Jana sent over a mock design. Come look."

I flipped the French toast in the pan twice and served it up with maple syrup. Putting a plate in front of Liana, I took my seat beside her at her desk and looked over her shoulder as she took a bite. The theme was a complete one-eighty to the rest of her blog. Unlike her romance tab, which was a pretty picture of clouds and happiness, the sex section had an edge to it in the form of a red background, and a tastefully provocative, black and white photograph of a shirtless man kissing a woman in black lingerie—perhaps a little *too* hot to be comfortable.

"Nice," I said, not wanting to rain on her parade.

"*Nice?*"

"What do you want me to say, sweetheart? I don't get hard over web design." I shrugged, and then sighed as her eyebrows lifted like she was awaiting a detailed opinion. I tried to keep mine at bay, but the niggling in my throat demanded I spit it out. "That being said, as a fan of your blog, I think it's a harsh switch from tabs made of clouds to red backgrounds and half-nude photos."

Her lips flattened into a line. "I think I agree. Less is more in this case, right?" She asked and I nodded, taking a deep bite of breakfast. *So fluffy, so good.* I moaned and she laughed, sucking a drop of syrup from her thumb. *God, did she know what that did to me?* "So, what are your plans for the day."

I sighed. I hadn't thought about plans beyond the hour.

"Maybe I'll go into work at some point. I've been slacking lately."

Liana nodded. Turning to her side, she stretched out her legs and rested them on my lap. I took a sharp intake of breath, my heart pounding in my chest. This woman would be the death of me, and she didn't seem to notice.

"Join the club," she said, continuing the conversation as though she wasn't driving me wild. "But now, I've got Kit to worry about, so my attention is split."

The mention of Kit's name somehow materialized her in the room. She glided past Liana and I like we were ghosts and headed to the kitchen.

"Is it me, or did it get cold in here?" I murmured.

"It's not you." Liana sighed. "We had a fight yesterday when I found out she told Zoe she was pregnant before she told me."

I winced. "*Rough.* I thought you two were close?"

Liana scoffed. "So did I. But apparently, she and Zoe are closer. It hurts to think—"

She didn't get to finish her thought before Kit burst into the room like a bulldozer, yelling so loud the birds outside of the apartment windows took flight at the high-pitched sound. "If you're going to talk behind my back to a guy you barely know, then why should I tell you anything? Clearly Zoe isn't the two-faced one!" She spat, her hands on her hips.

Liana blinked. "I'm not talking about you behind your back. I'm talking to my—*to Kade*—about how *I* feel."

"About *my* life!" Kit seethed, flicking her hair over her shoulder. It stuck midway on her navy blue blazer. "And since when are you two friends? Right around the time you slept with him, perhaps? Sleeping with clients, Liana? *Really?* Dad's right, you are going to run your blog into the ground."

A silence settled over the apartment as Liana's jaw dropped. "You talked to Dad about me?"

Kit's eyes widened, her mouth closing.

Liana's legs dropped from mine as she jumped from her chair, her face as red as a tomato screamed her anger; but her eyes, glazed in tears, said she was hurt. "You tell Zoe before me you're pregnant, and now you're bad-mouthing my ability to do my job to our father?"

It was all very personal to be aired in front of me, a stranger to Kit. I let out a low whistle, deciding it was time to leave. "This is none of my business. I should go. I'll call you later, Liana."

Her eyes met mine, wide as though she forgot I was there at all. They were noted in heartache, and my gut clenched. "I can stay if you need me to," I offered. I don't know why I offered, but I did. Liana shook her head, seeing me to the door and smiled when I asked if she'd be okay.

She leaned on her tiptoes and pecked my cheek. "Good luck tonight."

I waited for her to close the door before I made my way down to the lobby and out of her building. Standing out on the cold street, I realized I had nowhere to go. With yesterday's clothes on, I couldn't go to work—I'd never looked disheveled in front of my employees before, and I wasn't starting now—and having already eaten breakfast, a café would only work for the length of time it takes to drink a cup of coffee. It was too early to go to a bar, and I wasn't dressed to go anywhere active.

Which only left one option: I had to bite the bullet and head home.

I hailed a cab and rehearsed a couple of small talk conversations I could bring up with Stephanie in the back. Starting with the weather, I planned to move to the latest on those rich women she loved to watch, and then maybe round it out with: 'Hey, did you see the news?' Or 'How about them Knicks?' And then, I'd rotate them as many days as it took to find a new apartment.

As the cab rolled to a stop, I realized how much I would miss my building. Though it never felt like home, it was the

237

best one in Carnegie Hill as far as I was concerned. When I moved, it would be out of area. Maybe I'd give the Upper West a chance. Maybe I'd find an apartment near Liana's building.

My thoughts were silenced as I stepped off the elevator on my floor and I was hit by the all-too-familiar mix of cinnamon and violet. Steph was burning her candles again. It was a tradition of hers the night before Halloween and, once upon a time, it would've filled me with a fuzzy feeling—like being back for the first time after a long vacation—but, when I opened the door to my apartment, a sharp throbbing burned my stomach like someone had driven me through with a sword and the devil was dancing on my balls in six-inch heels made of spikes.

"You've gotta be fucking kidding me," I spat and blinked five times to be sure I wasn't hallucinating. I hoped I was. It was the only thing that would make sense of what my eyes were showing me—my worst nightmare come to life.

I rubbed at my eyes, sure I was tripping balls. I fucking had to be...

Because, to my utter shock and vehemence, Cleo was sitting on my couch.

And boxes of her stuff were stacked all around me.

Chapter 26

Liana

K it and I had been going at each other's throats over an hour when Zoe came home, bringing the pungent odor of self-importance spritzed with Chanel No.5 with her, and sneered, crossing the room to stand at Kit's side.

"Guess I don't have to ask whose team you're on." I scoffed.

"What'd you expect? You sent a video to my husband of me—"

"*Whoring it up?*" I offered, and then felt bad for having taken the cheap shot.

Zoe stepped forward, baring her teeth like a rabid dog. Kit put an arm out to stop her.

"Lee, I'm taking Dad's offer to head up his PR department." Kit sighed, stepping in front of me. "Maybe you should reconsider his bid to buy the blog. It's not a bad sum of money. You could invest it into your next great idea, and we could all work together. You, me, Dylan, we could be a family again."

My mouth dropped open, hearing her describe such an insult with the optimistic inflection of a Disney fairytale.

Kit was stupid.

It wasn't something I ever thought of her before, but now it was all that was going through my head on repeat. *She was fucking idiotic.*

Dylan, Zoe, our father—three of the most manipulative people I'd ever met, and Kit was ready to jump into their bullshit with both feet tied and a blindfold on. Worse, she wanted to drag me down with her.

And suddenly, it all made sense. Zoe was a plant from the beginning; dedicated to breaking us down, until one, or both of us were lonely enough to beg for his help. I'd bet she'd been updating Eric for weeks; bragging about the seeds of discontent she'd sown, buzzing like a bee over Kit's unexpected news and how desperate she was, and especially happy about how it would leave me alone.

And it worked. The closest person in my life chose to crawl back to an empire that treated me like dirt, was now best friends with my worst enemy, and was in cahoots with our father—who, the last I spoke to him, was rooting for me to fail. I'd never felt so isolated in my entire life.

Tears pricked in my eyes, stinging my corneas like acid drops. Made worse by the fact I couldn't blink because if I did, they would fall, and I refused to look pathetic in front of Zoe.

I wished I had someone to talk to, but I was lacking in personal relationships in favor of a career. It wasn't something I'd ever regretted until I looked around and found my side empty; a singular captain on a team of nobody. I didn't have a boyfriend or any other people in my life, except Kade and maybe Jana. And my blog, though growing every week, wasn't pulling in enough traction to cover her living costs, but it demanded too much attention for me to get a side job.

My whole life was a tower of Jenga blocks ready to topple over. All it needed was that last foundation removed, and Kit removed it swiftly.

"And," Kit sighed. I shut my eyes, waiting for the final, fatal twist of the knife in my back. "If I am pregnant, I want to live on the Fifth like we did when we were kids. Zo and I are going apartment hunting later. We want you to move with us."

The last part was said with less enthusiasm, which made it clear: In Kit's eyes, I was to blame for the animosity in the apartment. I was a problem she wanted to leave behind but felt too guilty to admit it. Not that I would have jumped at the opportunity even if she offered it covered in sunshine and daisies, and with a rainbow shining out of her ass. How stupid did she think I was? An apartment on Fifth, even on Kit's impressive wage, was an impossibility. How low she'd sank to live in a place with Eric Dawson's name on the deed. I scoffed. My heart panged, and my blood boiled. My fists clenched at my side, digging my nails into the skin of my palm, hoping the pain would distract me enough to not cry.

I was hurt and annoyed, but a smile played at my lips, followed by a laugh, and then I couldn't stop. I snorted like a pig and wondered if I should set up my own therapy appointment, because as much as I ached inside, I couldn't stop laughing.

Something snapped inside, and my tears dried up. I laughed harder.

"Are you okay?" Kit asked.

I nodded, lifting my hands up like a white flag. With a final bark of laughter, I conceded defeat and turned my back on them, heading for my room. Zoe won. I was done. When it all blew up in Kit's face, I wouldn't be there.

Landing on my bed, I dragged my laptop over and logged onto *Love, Liana*. I hoped a deep dive into the other people's problems would distract me from mine. One thing that could be said of my career: *it was a hell of a distraction.*

Well, usually. Not this time though. The second I clicked reply on the first question in my inbox, Kit slammed right back into my mind and the anger flared up again. It didn't help the person asking the question was having family troubles. I began an answer that turned into a tirade of me complaining about my problems. My professionalism was at an all-time low. I grunted and deleted the paragraph before closing my laptop.

With a sigh, I spread out on my sheets and looked up at the ceiling. I turned my head to stare out of my window and caught whiff of something sweet and intoxicating. I buried my nose into the sheets, the scent of Kade strong and glorious.

Without thinking, I reached for my phone and scrolled through my contacts until I landed on Kade. My finger hovered over the call button, ready to press down, when I remembered he wasn't free for the night. He had his date with Lyla, or whatever.

Okay, so it was nowhere near to Nikki, but I was rapidly running out of 'N' names to use for her.

It was petty, and bitchy, and so below my usual standards. But, for some reason, the thought of Kade going on a date with a woman he'd already slept with the night after being in my bed... *ugh*. It bothered me.

The image of him between her legs, his lips on her plump mouth, his hands in her perfect straight hair... I couldn't lie, it made me jealous.

Now that I'd seen him naked, I couldn't stop thinking about how he'd feel with his body on top of mine—his hands exploring every part of me, and his—

A knock at the door pulled me out of my fantasy. I ground my back molars and hissed. "What?"

"I know you're pissed, but I'm ordering Chinese food. Are you staying in for dinner?"

Grumbling, I bit my lip. I wanted Chinese food. The debate between hunger and pettiness ended with my stomach giving an almighty growl. I relented. It's not like I had any other option... *except*—

"No," I yelled back. "I have a date."

It would kill Kit to hear me say that and not give her all of the juicy details, which made it all the sweeter. Scrolling down, I moved past Jana's info and down to the L's. Clicking call, I waited with bated breath until it connected.

"Lee!" He answered, excitedly.

"Hey, Luka. Is the offer for that date still on the table?"

⁓⁓⁓

Luka offered to pick me up, but I didn't want to subject him to the atmosphere. Instead, I chose a Chinese restaurant six blocks away, and told him to meet me there in an hour. I hung up and rolled off my bed toward my bathroom. After a quick shower, I stood in front of my wardrobe and realized I didn't have many date outfit options, which seemed accurate since I didn't have many dates. I wanted to look sexy but classy, but no matter how long I stared into the abyss of boring clothes, they weren't getting any more exciting under my scrutiny. I sighed and decided on a high-waisted black skirt that hemmed mid-thigh, and a white blouse with a black crop top underneath. I grabbed a random pair of ankle boots from my pile and left my room with minimal make-up, red lipstick, and wild hair.

Zoe's eyes raked over me with an intense glower. "You look like a hooker."

A grin spread across my face. I ruffled my hair and shrugged. "Damn. I was going high-class sugar baby. Oh well..."

I left my apartment without sparing a second glance at either Zoe or Kit and took the elevator down to the lobby. It was windy outside, I realized as I pushed the glass doors open and my hair blew in every direction, and in my mouth. I gagged and spat it out. I planned on walking to the restaurant but decided on hailing a cab before my curls became a little *too* crazy.

Luka was waiting outside as I arrived. His broad torso

donning a button down and a tie and looking way fancier than I did.

"You could've told me you were planning to dress-up, Mr. Suave." I closed the cab door and made my way to him.

His head turned at the sound of my voice and he cracked a smile. "I thought you were worth dressing up for." I reached him and stood awkwardly. Sixteen-year-old Liana would have hugged him and kissed his lips, but we weren't those two inseparable kids anymore. So I simply smiled. Luka, however, had no problem acting like no time passed. Leaning in, he pecked my cheek and lingered by my ear. "You look beautiful."

I shivered, my cold skin turning warm where his lips had been.

Slipping his hand in mine, he guided me through the restaurant to a table and pulled my chair out like a gentleman. Sitting down, I smiled, despite the fact the chair was a mile away from the table and I had to scoot in anyways, the wooden chair legs scraping against the tiled floor so loud people stared. The gesture was appreciated.

Luka grinned over his drink menu, and I grinned back, but then my smile died. I couldn't fake it with him; the leftover urge to tell him everything going on in my life never died.

"What's going on in that gorgeous head of yours, Lee?" he asked.

"Nothing," I said, not wanting to dampen the mood. Luka stared blankly like he didn't believe me. I sighed. "I had a fight with Kit over some stuff."

He shrugged. "Sisters fight, right? It's not a big deal."

"It was this time, we—"

"I'm sure it'll be fine. You guys are solid. Kit and Liana, Liana and Kit. One in the same, right? As far as sisters go, you two are practically interchangeable."

Interchangeable. Is that what he thought when he was screwing Zoe behind my back?

I flinched, my guard forcing itself up. Luka's eyed my tense shoulders and sighed.

"I need you to know how bad I feel about prom. I think about it constantly, the image of your face when you caught us. I can't get it out of my mind. I wish there was a profound excuse, but there isn't one outside being an asshole who picked sex over love. But I hope, in time, you'll learn to trust me again. Because, more than any other dream I have for us, I miss my best friend."

I blinked because that's all I could do. I cleared my throat and let out a breath I didn't realize I was holding. We descended into silence until the waiter arrived. After ordering, we fell into an easy conversation and my wall began to shrink, low enough for him to peek over the top.

And, as the night leapt on, it wasn't long before it crumbled completely and we were us again, sharing hilarious stories from our childhood and catching up on the details since.

"Married," I gasped. "Wow."

"For six months." Luka stifled a laugh. "It was a whirlwind shitshow. Very fast-spark-short-fuse. You are looking at a divorced man."

I couldn't help but snort. "Sorry. It's just, if I had to choose one person in my life who would get married and divorced inside a year, it would be you." Actually, it would have been Kade. But bringing him up would invite questions. I wondered how his date with Nancy was going.

Fine, Nikki. Whatever.

"Did I lose you somewhere?" Luka asked.

Snapping back into focus, I lied. "I was imagining you as a husband."

He grinned. "I'd say I was rather good. A ten out of ten for the short time I was hitched. But to be accurate, more data would need to be collected." He reached across the table and slipped his hand into my open palm.

"Are you asking me to marry you, Luka DiMaggio?"

"One day..."

My heart stopped, and then pounded like a drum in my chest. Luka lifted in his seat and moved forward like he was leaning in to kiss me. My eyes widened as his shut. *Our first kiss.* Or at least, the first one that would count.

Did I want to kiss him? Yes.

I wanted to know what it would be like to kiss Luka again after five years. But I was terrified that it wouldn't live up to my expectations—that it would be a regular kiss, and not the earth-stopping, fireworks, leg-popping experience I'd built it up to be in my head.

He was inches away from me when my phone vibrated in my purse. His eyes snapped open, and he pulled back. The moment was gone.

"Sorry," I apologized, fishing my phone out to find a text from Kade.

'Update: Nikki is as awesome as I remembered.
Are you sure I can't sleep with her?
P.S. You would not believe what happened when I got home. Should we meet for ice-cream after my date? (Since you took all other sweet treats off the menu.)'

I smirked.

"Who's that?" Luka asked.

"Hmm?" I looked up. "Oh, nobody. Kade texting me an update. He's on a date tonight, too." I wasn't going to lie about it. Kade had become such an ingrained part of my day-to-day life, and I'd grown to like it that way. He was an untapped barrel of excitement in a sea of never-ending stress and boredom. Somehow, along the way, he'd become a friend. If anything was going to progress with Luka, he had to be okay with that.

"Kade's the guy I met at your apartment, right?"

I nodded, waiting for the next obvious question.

Luka's shoulders squared. "Are you two—"

"Friends..." *Who sleep together in the same bed, have phone sex, and have seen more than a few parts of each other,* I neglected to add.

Luka accepted my answer at face value. His shoulders relaxed and his confidence slammed back into place.

"Okay," he said. "But, if at any point that changes, will you let me know?"

That seemed fair. I nodded. "It won't, but sure."

With Luka sated, the conversation carried on as our food arrived. The smell of the salt and pepper chicken made my mouth water as we strolled down memory lane, stopped off in anecdotes from our years apart, and even moved past my relationship with Ronnie with minimal awkwardness.

"He's getting married? Wow. Little Ronnie is a Ronald now."

Luka gagged. "If he ever heard you call him Ronald, he would have a fit."

I laughed. The conversation was flowing so easily, but in the back of my mind, all I wanted to do was say yes to ice cream before Kade caved on his celibacy pact.

"Bathroom break." Luka pointed toward the men's room.

"Awesome! Yes." I breathed out relief, my fingers itching to text Kade, and cringed at how excited I sounded about him going to the bathroom. "I mean, have fun."

Not better.

Luka smiled and went on his way. I watched the bathroom door shut behind him before I pulled out my phone.

'Update: I went out with Luka. I forgot how great of a guy he is when he isn't fucking my sister. I guess I should let that go, huh? He seems perfect for me... But I won't sleep with him. Not tonight, at least. Glad your date with Naomi is going good.
P.S. You would not believe what was said when you left.

Ice cream sounds perfect. Meet you by the fountain at ten to divulge?'

He read it instantly, as though my chat had been left open, waiting for my reply. But it was more likely he'd forgot to lock his phone before sliding it back into his pocket.

My phone vibrated again, and my heart leaped. He had been waiting.

'You know it's Nikki. Ten sounds perfect. See you then, sweetheart.'

The clock on my phone read nine-fifteen. I had been with Luka for two hours, and it was great. But I needed to wrap it up for three reasons: I had to get out in time to meet Kade, I was worried that if we spent any more time together it would all go wrong, and—the third and main reason—the type of trust Luka dashed would take longer than two hours to build back.

He got back from the bathroom as the waiter cleared our dishes from the table.

"Dessert?" the waiter asked.

"No," I said, as Luka nodded. He turned to me with narrowed eyes.

"Since when do you say no to ice cream?" he asked.

I didn't, that was the problem. "Sorry, I'm full." I turned to the waiter and smiled. "The check, please."

The waiter left and came back with the check as asked. I reached into my purse where I dug out some spare bills at the bottom, but Luka insisted it was covered. I thanked him as we made our way out of the restaurant.

"Back to your place?" Luka held the door open. My head whipped toward him, and I opened my mouth to tell him no when he held up his hands. "To talk, obviously."

I smiled. "I don't think so, Luke. Right now, things at my place are tense. And I promised Kade I'd meet him in the park to discuss his date."

"You're blowing me off to hang out with another guy?"

Essentially, yes. "But Kade's not another guy. Think of him as a girl. I'm meeting my girlfriend in the park to discuss her date."

He didn't look convinced but nodded his head, anyway. I hailed a cab.

"This is me." I leaned in to give him a hug goodbye and say something lame like 'we should do it again sometime' when his lips grazed my cheek again. I pulled back and my breath hitched in my throat. Luka's eyes bore into mine. My stomach flipped and swirled as he moved in again, this time aiming for my lips.

Part of me prayed for another distraction. It didn't feel like the right moment. The cold wind whipped me in the face, people rushed past us, the cabbie huffed with impatience, and the bulb in the overhead streetlight flickered like it was running out of juice. But no distraction came in time. His lips touched mine, softly at first, and then with more passion.

It was... nothing. No fireworks. No leg popping. No cartoon heart beating out of my chest, or hearts erupting from my eyes.

I kissed him harder, demanding to feel something. I tried to sink into it and feel the earth move around me, I pulled him closer and deepened the kiss, I even wrapped my arms around his neck and allowed his tongue access when he nibbled my bottom lip. But the whole thing seemed... wrong.

It wasn't a *bad* kiss. Quite the opposite. It was an expertly done kiss. But after all the build-up, it didn't measure up to the hype. And that sucked. As quickly as it begun, it was over, and the first thing I thought of when my eyes opened again was Kade waiting for me in the park. *Shit!*

"That was everything I thought it would be," Luka whispered.

I forced a smile. "Good night."

Luka waved and turned his back. I watched him walk away

before climbing in the back of the cab. He really did have a nice ass... though not as great as Kade's.

Ugh. There I was again, comparing the two.

It wasn't only their physical attributes—which was bad enough—but every little thing Luka did, I wondered how Kade would do it. The answer: he would do it better. Hotter.

More.

Kade would do everything with more finesse and style than Luka ever could. Which left me with a big, gaping confession: *if I had to choose between Kade and Luka based on attraction alone, Kade would win. No contest.*

But based on who I was more familiar with, Luka took the lead. And so, the comparison roundabout went on.

Who made me laugh more? *Kade.*

Who did I have more history with? *Luka.*

Who would I rather fall into bed with? *Kade,* but only by a small margin. Okay, so maybe a medium-sized margin. *Fine, a huge one.*

But who could I see a real future with? *Luka.*

I slid down in my seat and scolded myself for being so idiotic to think comparing them had a point in the first place. It didn't. The only thing I needed to compare was what each man wanted from me.

Luka wanted to date me.

Kade wanted to fuck me.

And there was nothing I could do to change that, even if I wanted to.

CHAPTER 27

KADE

Liana looked beautiful as she crossed the park to meet me by the fountain. *Dammit!*

I hoped she'd somehow become unsightly since I last saw her twelve hours ago. Hell, I was *still* hoping an ancient curse to turn her into a hideous beast by nightfall would take hold any moment. Maybe then I could give Nikki a real shot. Probably not, though. Because, whether I liked it or not—and I didn't—it wasn't Liana's mess of red hair, gorgeous eyes or curvy body that captivated me; it was her laugh, the way she talked, the advice she gave, and everything that made her so... *Liana.*

I looked down at the same suit I'd worn for two days and winced at how disheveled I looked in comparison to how stunning she was.

Even her texts made me smile, and I *hated* texting. All those delightful words shortened and replaced by emojis. I would rather write longhand and employ a carrier pigeon. The thought of emojis made me shudder, and that was the first hint Nikki wasn't the one for me. On my way to the restaurant, we were texting each other updates, and twice she'd used those dreadful yellow faces. One was winking, the second was smiling.

The second hint came when I realized I wasn't interested in getting to know her, at all. All through dinner, I barely listened to a word she said—half of it revolving around that guy, Simon. I was too preoccupied with checking my phone every few minutes to see if Liana texted back. And worse, Nikki picked up on my lack of interest.

"Are you waiting for a call?" she scowled. "Or are you a dick?"

I couldn't help the snort that ripped free from my nose. I *was* being a dick. "Both. I'm waiting for a text from Liana. I should apologize. I'm being rude. It's a pitfall of mine."

"You like her." Nikki smirked. "I knew it the day I saw you two in the park. The way you two scampered off together, smiling. Associates become friends so fast you barely realize, right? And friends have a way of becoming more than..." Her eyes dazed, filling with her thoughts. "But sometimes, it doesn't work out. Sometimes, his thick-eyebrow-having ass is engaged to the wrong girl and doesn't even notice you."

Nikki was right. Not about me liking Liana, but about the fact she'd become my friend so fast I barely noticed. I couldn't imagine not knowing her now. She was part of my everyday life, whether it was over email, text, calls, or me sleeping in her bed. I'd seen her most days since we met and—Stephanie troubles aside—I was the most unburdened I'd been in a long time. And her thick eyebrow—*wait, what*? I blinked. Again, Nikki was lost in her own thoughts. I went back to mine.

"I think Liana and I are friends, but I doubt we'll ever be more than," I said, feeling a weight in my chest.

"But you *want* to be?"

Nikki stumped me. My mouth hung open. *Did* I like Liana? No. It wasn't possible. I wanted to sleep with her... and wake up with her. And give her sweet kisses. And hug her whenever I wanted. And make her breakfast. And—*Oh, God.*

The panic in my throat solidified into a hard lump I choked down.

"I'll take that as a yes." Nikki laughed. "Well, I guess this has been a lovely waste of both of our times. Let's not do it again."

I grimaced, feeling bad for dragging her out on the date. "I'm sorry. But I've never liked anyone before, how was I supposed to know?"

"Beats me." She shrugged. "You just *know.*"

And know, I did. It was hard to pinpoint when I'd gotten the rush of new feeling that settled in my stomach, but I knew it was there. As far back as I remembered, it was there—since the day I met her in the café. Maybe even at Minnie's. Or maybe it was when I poured through her site like a teenage girl, reading her responses to people I didn't know, and getting to know what kind of person she was through her words. Words could say so much about a person—their intellectuality, their personality, their heart... their soul.

I knew Liana's like the back of my hand. And I was dazzled by it.

Now, as I watched her walk across the concrete of Central Park, with not even the faintest idea of what I would say to her, I was screwed. She had me. My heart hammered in my chest, and then panged remembering where she'd come from: her date with *Puke-a* (If she could be childish about names, so could I) and I knew telling her was out of the question. Her text said they had a great time. And though I'd seen it work in the movies, rushing over to her and slamming my lips to hers seemed much more likely to earn me a slap than a girlfriend.

Girlfriend? Where had that thought come from? I wasn't even officially her friend. *Fuck.*

How did people do this in books? My agency represented a

plethora of romance books. Maybe I should've fucking read one.

Oh, shit, she was getting closer. I wondered if I could read a few chapters of something before she got to me, but it was doubtful. With those glorious long legs sticking out from under her skirt, Liana took a mile like a step. My God, she had nice legs. Wait, what was I thinking about? I forgot, mesmerized by her kneecaps.

Of all things, I really liked her knees. It was weird, and probably warranted another tick in the *definitely deranged* column, but it was true. Her legs were quickly becoming my third favorite thing about her. The first being her hair, and the second being... *her*.

The problem with Liana was that she threw out the book on everything I thought I knew. Or, rather, she made *me* want to throw it out. If anybody else recommended a therapist, I would've told them *they* needed therapy for being crazy enough to even suggest it. Then, I would have hung up on them, ground my phone to dust, and never contacted them again.

But when Liana said it, I realized how right she was.

After walking out on Steph and Cleo without saying a word, I called Dr. Jesionowski and apologized for my last session. Apparently, it wasn't an uncommon thing in her field, and my apology wasn't warranted. It helped knowing that door was open, and I made a standing appointment for every Thursday afternoon for the foreseeable future. *I wouldn't miss a single one.*

"I'm surprised you're not half-undressed in Nelly's bed by now," Liana joked, reaching me. "Nice to know you can stick to rules."

"I thought I'd spend the night in your bed, instead." I smirked, not even bothering to correct her anymore. "If that's okay with you?"

Liana seemed to falter, but she regained her smile so fast I couldn't be sure if I imagined it.

"I can get a hotel for the night if you'd prefer. Maybe now you're dating *Puke-a*, I shouldn't be in your room."

"A hotel?" Her eyebrows wrinkled. "I know things are awkward with Steph right now but *paying* to get away from her seems a touch extreme."

My eyes moved down to the floor, and I gave a sigh remembering the smug look on Cleo's face as she told me she was moving in, and I was no longer welcome in *her* home. The anger that took hold of me was pierced by the knife to my heart that was Stephanie's silence.

Liana's eyes widened, and her hand reached out to squeeze my arm. "What happened?"

"Stephanie moved Cleo in last night while I was out." The pang was so fresh, I had to take a breath to get the words out without cussing, breaking something, or potentially shedding my first tears in over a decade. "I got home today to find boxes everywhere, and Cleo sitting on my couch looking proud of herself."

"What did Steph say?"

"Nothing, so I grabbed a bag, stuffed it with clothes and anything expensive within grabbing distance, said I'd be back for the rest at some point, and left."

Liana scoffed, her face turning red and flustered as we began to walk. "How can people move other people into your apartment without even consulting you first? Don't they care about you at all? It's a joke. A sick fucking joke."

The corners of my lips twitched into a small smirk. "Projecting, much?"

Liana took a breath. "Maybe a little. Kit and I had it out this afternoon, and standing in her corner like a ferocious chihuahua, was Zoe, who shouldn't even be in my vicinity much less *my* apartment."

I could feel her frustrations like they were my own. Perhaps they were. "Maybe ice cream is too timid tonight. How about a drink before I book into my hotel?"

A smile crossed Liana's face. "How about we *both* book into a hotel tonight?"

Oh, that seemed intimate. Too tired and awkward to go home was one thing, but purposely paying to share a bed was another. My smirk became a grin. I had to stop myself busting out something resembling an Irish jig as the small, niggling voice in my head reminded me that I couldn't have her—*in any way, shape, or form.*

"Same bed?" I asked, delicately.

"Adjoining rooms." She smiled. "I know it doesn't make a whole lot of sense since we've crossed that line already, but out of respect to Luka—and Nikki, if you decide to see her again. But mostly, so we don't have to torture ourselves."

"Being near you does that just fine." The words were out before I could stop them. It was so cheesy, if I could've kicked myself in the nuts and call myself a loser, I would have.

"Yeah, I know." Liana bit her lip. "Even knowing there's a door that leads from my room to yours is going to be hell."

My head danced like I was on a cocktail of unicorns and valium. I grinned wider. "Should we hit a bar first or take advantage of the minibar in our rooms?"

She gave a sound of mocking. "Are you kidding? We're not millionaires."

I agreed. The minibar of a hotel room was *way* overpriced. Smaller bottles for three times the price? Crazy talk. And even I wasn't *that* whacked.

"Although..." A fire lit in her eyes as a dastardly smirk spread on her face. "If we stop by a liquor store, we can refill them with some cheap stuff and not be charged."

"A true mastermind," I commended. Liana curtsied, and then looked like she wished she hadn't. She cringed.

"Was that as dorky as I'm picturing in my head?"

"Dorkier," I said. "But, somehow, dorky looks hot on you."

L aying on a queen-sized bed with lavishly soft, cream sheets in a room as extravagant as it could be without being called a penthouse, I stretched out with my feet on the wall at the head of the bed, and my head meeting Liana's in the middle as her feet dangled off the end. Our room was immense. It had a grand living room we were yet to use, two bedrooms, two bathrooms, and a fully functioning kitchen. The walls were a light, fresh gray, and the floors a white, sparkling tile. A full wall of bricks made of mirrors made the bathrooms downright livable, and the chandelier in the hallway bathed the place in a white-toned light. I sniffed, inhaling the scent of what smelled strangely like money.

The door to our separate bedrooms had been open since we got there. A chilled playlist of 80's rock ballads Liana found on YouTube hummed lowly on the smart TV, drifting from her room to mine.

She downed another mini bottle of tequila and giggled, which made me giggle along with her. I couldn't deny we were hammered. Turns out, the bottles were small but powerful, and we'd drank a lot of them. There was no way Liana's plan would work now; especially since the cheap stuff we'd bought tasted like gasoline, and we had to call room service to get more bottles.

"I forgot what it's like to not have to dread going home," she cooed.

"Me too." I nodded. "Not that I have a home anymore. I'm once again homeless. Oh, that feels weird to say again after all this time. Don't recommend it. Oof, the feelings... do we have any whiskey left?"

Her giggles died. Turning her head, she was so close I could feel her breathe. "Should we start apartment hunting? Or *haunting*, like you said, since it's Halloween."

I stilled, my eyes moving down to her lips and back up to her eyes. "Right, Halloween... I almost forgot." Images of her in her cupid's outfit once again occupied my brain. "Didn't you say something about dressing up?"

Liana pushed on my arm and reached for her phone. "We could look online."

"For costumes?"

She rolled her eyes. "For apartments."

"Okay." I smirked, jumping to my feet. "You do that, and *I'll* get the costumes."

Liana laughed like I wasn't serious, until her body bounced as I pulled the sheet from under her ass, and off the bed.

"What're you doing?" She got to her feet, watching in amazement as I did the same with her bed and rooted around for some scissors. It was a nice hotel; there had to be scissors somewhere.

I found some small ones in a kit in the bathroom and grinned, cutting two holes in each sheet. Passing one sheet to Liana, I pulled the other over my head.

"I'm Casper." I laughed.

Liana shook her head, giggling. She pulled her sheet over her head and winked through her eyehole. "Are we both Casper? Too bad the sheets weren't red; I could've been your Wendy."

Seeking out a pen from my jacket pocket, I made my way over to her. "Spoiler alert: Wendy died and became a ghost to join Casper in the afterlife." I pressed the pen to the space above her eyes. "Stay still."

She did and I wrote on her head, in block letters: I am Wendy. Stepping back to admire my work, I chuckled. "There. Now people know who you are."

Liana moved to the mirror on the wall and laughed. "What people? You, me, and the furniture?"

"You're right." I said, the rush of an idea demanding I bounce on the pads of my feet. "We should go out."

"In *bed sheets*?"

"I've been seen in worse." I shrugged. "But first, more drinks..."

"And dancing!" Liana added, turning the music up. "Oh, I love this song!"

Robert Palmer's "Addicted To Love" blared through the room as I watched Liana dance like nobody was watching—torn between being delighted with how comfortable she was around me, and hoping she'd blush a little... something to indicate any kind of feeling toward me other than friendship. Grabbing my arm, she pulled me into the middle of the room, and we danced together but apart. With me on one side, jumping from one foot to the other and playing a bad air guitar, and her on the other side, bouncing along to the beat with her hips swaying.

She spun, laughing, and sang along. Jumping up onto my bed, she grinned and pointed at me. "*Whoa, you like to think that you're immune to the stuff, oh yeah. It's closer to the truth to say you can't get enough. You know you're gonna have to face it, you're addicted to love!*"

I stilled, my heart rate doubling in speed. *Was I addicted to love?* I'd smoke Liana like a crack-pipe if I could—did that count?

My head spun. I wouldn't say I was in love, but the fluttering in my stomach told me I was deeply in like. Admitting it to myself was nausea-inducing, but it was also exciting. I wanted to take a running leap off the bed and fly through the air like Peter Pan.

Peter Pan—the boy who never grew up.

I had the opposite problem. I never understood Peter's fascination with wanting to stay young, my own childhood years were the worst of my life; but being around Liana was like being a teenager again. I wanted to go to a park and climb on the jungle gym, or BMX down a mud hill. But what really made me fly, was knowing no matter how juvenile my ideas, Liana would do it. Because that's who she was—she was insane.

And I *liked* that about her.

Chapter 28

Liana

Perfect, crazy, hilarious, amazing Kade.

How far he'd come. He smiled more, seemed less burdened, and he'd gone on a date. It was step one in his mission of falling in love.

Kade in love.

Even the thought of it made me smile. But then the image ended with him and another girl. My stomach twisted. Kade would be in love with someone else, not me. Probably Nancy or whatever. (*Fine, Nikki. Ugh.*)

He seemed to like her.

But I didn't care... *right?* Of course, I did. But why? I had Luka, *kind of.*

Hot, funny, sweet Luka—my childhood love. And I loved him... *ish.*

Okay, not really.

Our date was a colossal failure. On the surface, I'd had a good time. He'd made me smile, and I was reminded of why I'd fallen for him in the first place. But on the inside, I'd felt only the remnants of leftover feelings.

Mostly, my mind stayed on Kade.

The revelation that I was into him wasn't one I welcomed, but there was no other explanation for the way my heart went pitter pat around him. I couldn't deny it. The tingles vibrating over my body because he was squeezing my hand, the way my stomach fluttered when I smelled his cologne, or when he looked at me. The way my whole body vibrated when I thought about sleeping with him, and the way my heart ached when he was sad.

I liked him.

And it was stupid of me.

He was the definition of unattainable, and I wasn't the main character of a rom-com. I wasn't all-confident and brazen like Nikki. The only thing I had going for me was my blog—especially now Kit wasn't on my side anymore—and even that wasn't perfect.

I would never be the woman who made Kade Jennings fall in love. *Ouch.*

Burying my feelings, I forced the grin that'd been on my face all night to stay there against its will as we headed into the club. Jubilee was better this time round—better music, better drinks, better atmosphere—and everyone was dressed in awesome costumes. But my eyes never left Kade.

He was the most relaxed I'd seen him. The removal of the ever-present hunch between his brows made him look young and handsome, but his shoulders stayed tensed with worry. He hadn't said it, but now that Stephanie chose Cleo, Kade was left in a suspended state of wonder, and it was killing him inside.

His hands pulled me to him, and it didn't take long to realize I wanted to share his bed again, which wasn't great. It was pretty much despicable for me to consider sleeping with a client.

Then again, for all I knew, every guy in New York could be an anonymous client of *Love, Liana.* I couldn't stay single forever. Well, I could... but I didn't want to.

Pulling Kade closer, I pressed my body to his, ready to take the risk. To dive headfirst into falling in love myself for once. I stopped dancing, aware Kade and falling in love were becoming synonymous in my mind.

Oh boy, I really was a glutton for punishment.

"I need another drink." I pushed my way through the crowds and away from Kade as fast as I could, but he was fast behind me, never letting my hand drop from his. He grinned as I lead him to the bar.

"Are you having fun, *Wendy*?"

I couldn't help but giggle. "I am. And you, *Casper*?"

"I always do when I'm around you."

Big flutters. Big yikes.

I was screwed, standing at the edge of the canyon with two options: step back from the ledge, or freefall and hope for the best. I downed my drink and laced my fingers through his. "Do you want to get out of here?"

Falling it was…

⁓

We poured through the door—more like stumbled, really—and spent the next hour on the hallway floor, drinking. A bottle of something fruity I'd found at the convenience store for me, and Kade had his whiskey (*always whiskey*) from the top shelf of the hotel bar.

We decided not to risk sharing a bed, the sexual charge between us buzzing like a hive of bees, but we also didn't want to be alone. Thus, the idea of the hallway fort was born. It wasn't so much of a fort as it was blankets and pillows set up as makeshift beds in the space between our rooms.

Being in the hotel with Kade felt different than being at home. Like somehow, we were different people. It made asking him things easier. I started out slow, skirting around the edges of topics that weren't deep, but personal enough to nudge him into the harder stuff.

We came up with a question-for-question game where anything off-limits could be skipped, but soon enough we added the clause of 'pass means drink' and upgraded to a drinking game.

We blew through the trivial stuff like our favorite colors (*his: purple, mine: blue*), our favorite songs (*his: "Coming Back To Life" by Pink Floyd, mine: "Seven Wonders" by Fleetwood Mac*), and finally, our favorite movies. Mine was *Sleepless in Seattle*, and shockingly, his was the same.

"Really?" I snorted. "I wouldn't have thought you'd seen it."

"I hadn't until you left your damn movie playlist on all night. I'm now addicted to chick flicks. Sign me up for my monthly period."

I shook my head. "I think a lot of movies go underrated because men have the mindset that romance is feminine. I know you disagree, but love makes life worth living, and it's not only women who're alive. Men need love too."

"It *was* good," he said with a small smile. "And I don't completely disagree."

"Oh? Since when?" It was total bait on a hook, said with hope his answer would be since he'd met me.

"Since my date with Nikki," he said.

Ouch.

I forced a fake grin. "That's great! So, when are you going out again?"

Kade scratched his neck and cleared his throat. "I, uh, I don't know. When are you and *Puke-a* next seeing each other?"

I rolled my eyes at the name. "I'm calling him tomorrow," I said to save face.

"Yeah, I'll call Nikki tomorrow too." He shrugged.

Kade licked at his bottom lip and blew out a breath, his eyes alight with his thoughts. His mouth opened, the words in his head on the tip of his tongue, but then he repelled them and grinned. "I want ice-cream..."

He was on his feet and sprinting to the kitchen area before I opened my mouth, muttering a sing-song about the ice cream we'd bought at the store on our way back to the hotel. I'd forgotten all about it but, apparently, he hadn't.

"Mint chip or Vanilla?"

It was like a switch flipped and he wasn't *Kade* anymore. He was scared and evading. My heart panged in my chest, begging to know what he was thinking.

"Vanilla. Mint chip is disgusting." I laughed, saying the first thing that popped into my head to start a conversation.

He scoffed. "Mint chip ice cream is perfect. It's refreshing, it's cool, it's a palate cleanser, it—"

"Tastes like toothpaste?" I offered.

Kade snorted. "I think you haven't tried the correct brand of mint chip. Some brands can be truly awful, but this,"—he scooped a fair amount onto a spoon—"is like heaven."

Rounding the island, he stood in front of me. I parted my legs, allowing him to slide between my thighs, so close to me, I could hear every breath he took. He guided the spoon to my mouth.

I wrapped my lips around the edge. "Mm..." I moaned and genuinely meant it. He'd been right. Mint ice cream was always more ice than cream, but this time, it was so velvety and rich, it slid down my throat like water.

"I told you."

"*I told you,*" I mimicked, sticking out my tongue.

Kade laughed, pulling the spoon back and flinging it like a slingshot. It hit me square in the forehead, so cold, and dripped down my nose. My jaw dropped as the remnants of mint chip trickled down my face, invading my mouth. I licked my lips and grinned so wide, my eyes crinkled in the corners and my cheeks dimpled.

"I can't believe you did that!" I lunged out to punch his arm playfully and lost my balance, almost falling off my chair. Kade laughed, catching my hands, and pulled me to him. Finding the ticklish part below my rib, he dug his fingers in and I jumped, throwing my head back in giggles.

"You're so cute when you do that." He dug his fingers in a little more before giving me reprieve.

My whole body vibrated and danced. Kade looked at me with such an intense stare, it made me squirm. Something in his eyes, the way the array of colors lit up inside the solid black ring, told me he was deep in thought, and it killed me that I couldn't hear his inner monologue. The sides of his mouth lifted into a small smile as he moved in closer, but despite every instinct in me telling me, I refused to believe he wanted to kiss me... even as his nose brushed against mine.

Inch by inch, the distance between us lessened and I was close to passing out as my breath stuck in my throat. The adrenaline and the fluttering proved too much to handle. I couldn't breathe, and if he kissed me now, I might die. He moved slowly, seeking permission and I did nothing to dissuade him. My head nodded and my arms instinctively wrapped around his neck, giving the go-ahead without the approval of my brain. which shouted how bad of an idea it was, on repeat.

Once again, I prayed silently for another phone call, or for a bellboy to knock on our door for some reason, but then I remembered we'd asked not to be disturbed and we'd turned our phones off for the night. No Luka, Kit, Steph, or Nikki was going to stop us this time.

My spine tingled.

Kade's lips brushed mine softly and my breath hitched. He smiled, getting ready to close the gap completely. I had to stop him, or I'd be waking up on the floor. My heart pounded wildly, and my head spun. Kade's impact on me was so strong, it was hard to believe I'd only known him five short weeks. He already knew all of my deepest secrets—stuff even Kit knew nothing about.

The desperation for him begged me to ignore the voice in my head and crash my lips to his, but I wasn't ready for the image I'd built up in my head to be dashed and replaced with anything less than perfect like it had been with Luka.

I couldn't handle that from Kade.

"My nose is cold," was the only thing I could think to say to break the tension between us. His shoulders vibrated under my touch as he chuckled.

"Let me get that for you." His lips moved to my cheek and lay a small kiss—the beginning of a trail of soft and tickling kisses he left from the side of my mouth, all the way around my nose and back again. His laugh was glorious to my ears as he bent down and lay a final kiss on the tip of my nose. Lifting his sleeve, he wiped down the rest of the residue and smiled. "There. You're perfect."

I froze, unable to move, unable to speak. My heart raced and everything around me seemed to slow, awaiting our first kiss with as much anticipation as I was.

Never had I felt so much excitement, tension, desire, or arousal.

It didn't matter how many lists I made comparing Luka and Kade; there was no competition. Kade stole my breath, made me weak at the knees, and fascinated me to no end. It was a feeling I'd never experienced before.

And that's when it all clicked.

Luka was familiar, but nothing more than an old crush. It was startling to realize I was never in love with him. I allowed infatuation and delusion to break my heart.

With Kade's face so close, his forehead pressed against

mine, I knew what I was feeling for the haunted, mysterious man in front of me went way beyond a crush. I was with him. Passion, lust, teasing, playful bouts of annoyance...

There was only one thing for it: I was falling for him.

I couldn't say I loved him yet, but it crept up on me so silently, I couldn't turn back. *He had me.*

"I'm sorry if that was inappropriate. You know I have issues recognizing when I should and shouldn't do something. I guess it's part of being broken. But you make me want to be different," he whispered. "Can I be different with you?"

I wanted to tell him he could be anything he wanted to be—that he was amazing and incredible—but the words got stuck in my throat. Instead, I closed my eyes and tightened my grip, pulling him to me.

His hands travelled down my body and cupped my ass, lifting me in the air like I weighed nothing. My legs wrapped around his waist as he placed me gently on the island, and thrust a hand into my hair, holding me in place as his lips pressed to my neck.

I moaned as he nibbled and kissed on the sweet spot near my right shoulder, and then up my throat toward my lips. He stilled before his mouth reached mine.

"Nobody's stopping us this time," I whispered. "Do you want to stop?"

He went silent. I took that as a sign he wasn't interested and began to pull away, but I didn't get a chance. I got half a skootch back before his strong arms locked firmly around my waist.

"What're you doing?" I asked, my eyes flicking to his mouth and back again.

Kade's eyes landed on my mouth and my breathing became shallow, my heart hammering in my chest. My god, I never thought I'd ever feel this way. I was so deeply fucked, drowning in every detail of Kade. His smell, his eyes, the way his mouth twitched in the corners...

"You're not broken," I said, unable to believe he thought so little of himself. "You're a little bit cracked, but so am I. That's what makes us human... it's what's making me fall for you."

Kade's eyes widened, and I was sure he would pull away and run. But he didn't.

Perhaps it was a character flaw that I thought real-life romance couldn't measure up against the movies. I'd locked myself away, substituting my chance at a love story for stories about love, convinced the real thing would pale in comparison. Boy, was I wrong. In movies, moments so intense were accompanied by a soft orchestra playing a piano-heavy instrumental in the background. But the stillness that settled between us surpassed every moment I'd ever watched with flutters in my stomach, telling myself a love so deep couldn't exist beyond the screen.

The build-up, achingly slow, almost killed me. Our foreheads bumped together as his hand slid up my back and into my hair. My breathing labored, and his followed suit. I was so used to Kade being forward and taking charge, I'd expected him to ravage me like a hungry animal. But this, the slow and patient man touching me with delicate fingers, a cute smile playing at his lips... he was so beautiful, and the way he held me, like I was made of glass, said more than his words ever could.

He was scared. And his fear stopped him from taking the plunge.

I licked my lips and decided to take it for him. Closing the gap between us, I let my lips brush against his and suppressed a quiver. I tried, so desperately, to tease him. But for the life of me, I couldn't. I'd waited weeks to kiss him and every second I wasn't, was a second too long.

"Is this okay?" I asked. He nodded as decision landed in his eyes, and he took over. Cupping my ass again, he picked me up and parted my legs, so I straddled his waist. Moving his head down, he started by leaving a trail of soft kisses on my neck, ending at my jawline.

He pulled back, his hands grazing the inside of my thigh. And only as a breathy moan escaped me did his lips finally press to mine.

He kissed me, slow, and my whole body hummed as we got used to one another. Our lips parted as I opened my eyes to find Kade's staring back at me. My stomach swirled, like the moments spent being stalled at the peak of a rollercoaster, waiting to plunge into the vast abyss. Kade's eyes turned hesitant, as though he was afraid of the drop.

"I want you," I said. "No matter what happens next, I won't regret this." Even if Kade and I lasted only a night, I'd count myself a lucky woman for being so close to him, for his kisses, for his friendship, for his hands on my body. There was nothing about tonight I would regret.

All hesitation vanished as his mouth crashed to mine once more, deepening the kiss. One of his hands rested in the small of my back as the other thrust up into my hair. Taken by the adrenaline, every nerve-ending in my body electrified, my senses kicking into overdrive as the kiss became so passionate, I almost forgot my own name.

The world spun as I reveled in the feel of his skin, the way his hair tickled my fingers, the sound of his muffled breathing through his nose as my mouth covered his, the way he tasted of whiskey and mint chip, and smelled of sandalwood and oakmoss.

Kissing Kade was intoxicating... addictive. *He* was addictive.

His lips refusing to part from mine for more than the time it took to take a breath as he carried me to his bedroom. My legs wrapped around his waist, my arms around his neck, and my head was in the clouds.

Kade's body covered mine as we sank into the sheets. Our

lips met again as our hands worked to undress each other, ripping clothes off without a care if they tore. The touch of his bare arms made me dizzy and, as his hands crept lower, sliding between my legs, my world was more than spinning—it was completely off its axis.

CHAPTER 29

KADE

K issing Liana was beyond description.

Beyond Italian food. Beyond whiskey. Beyond sex.

Every vice in my life; I'd trade them all for the moment to last forever.

The only time our kiss broke was as we undressed each other. I pulled Liana's shirt over her head, and once again, she was sans bra. It irked me a little that her beautifully pert breasts were without their extra layer of protection when she was on her date with Luka, but that didn't matter now. It wouldn't even matter if she'd kissed Luka, or more... She was in bed with *me*. She was *falling* for *me*.

I was so light I could float.

She was blindingly amazing. *So* fucking special, it made me wonder where I'd be if I'd met her sooner... but the past was the past and wallowing in it already robbed me of so many good things. Yet I found myself unable to complain. If I hadn't spent the last two decades trapped in an isolated nightmare, I never would've reached out to Liana. And that didn't bear thinking about.

It wouldn't have been my first choice to have our first time in a hotel, but I thanked the Gods above we'd sprung for the more expensive room. Liana deserved the absolute best. Which is why, on our way over the threshold to the bedroom, I grabbed the remote and clicked blindly until a random music mix played on the smart TV. I braced myself, waiting for the music to start. For all I knew, I'd clicked play on a death metal mix.

The strumming of an acoustic guitar, slow and romantic, blessed my ears and relief washed through me. I opened an eye to find I'd thankfully chosen a mix of soft rock/indie ballads.

My kisses left her lips, moving their attention to her breasts. Kneading her left breast my hand, I flicked her right nipple with my tongue. She twitched, moaning, and a pulse shot through me. Fire burned in my stomach as she hissed, throwing her head back. I moved onto her left nipple, swirling my tongue until she shuddered. Lowering my head, I kissed my way down her body—so goddamn sexy—and stopped at her navel.

I parted her thighs with my hand and brushed the edges of my fingertips against her creamy, soft skin while nibbling the edge her stomach with my teeth. Liana laughed, and squirmed, and then moaned as my fingers crept closer to her core.

"Please," she whimpered as I pushed her panties aside to find she was ready for me. But I wasn't done playing yet. Demanding more access, I ripped her panties—black booty shorts that were somehow sexier than the thong she teased me with—over her knees and basked. *Finally*, I was able to see her in all her glory. I'd envisioned her for so long, I wasn't sure the real thing could measure up to the perfect image my brain created. I was wrong. *Dead wrong.*

Burying my head between the thighs I'd dreamed about for so long, I flicked her bud with my tongue and smiled as her body convulsed. I flicked her again, this time slowly, and swirled my tongue in small circles. Liana cried out, gripping my hair, and held me in place.

"I'm close," she said through shallow breaths. But I wasn't ready to let her get off so easily. I wanted to work for it. I wanted to earn the merit badge. Forcing my head back above her navel, I kissed and gnawed, tasting the salt on skin, until he was eye-to-eye with her again. "You couldn't let me have it, could you?" she sulked. "I was so close."

"Too easy," I said. "I want to feel what I do to you. I want you to build so much you can't take it, until you—"

She cut me off by crashing her lips to mine. I groaned against her mouth as her naked core ground against me, my shaft lining up with her opening as she moved. One more move and—she stopped, flicking an eyebrow. Apparently, two could torment. With a growl, I made my way back down her body and decided to take things painfully slow. Starting at her ankles, I kissed and nibbled upward, every part of me craving to be back between her legs, but the memory of how she'd teased me demanded satisfaction.

Swirling my tongue on the inside of her kneecaps, I reached up and entered her with my fingers. Liana let out a breath, pleading for more. My mouth upturned, hearing her pleas, and finally made its way back to her thighs. As I lay deliberate kisses around her entrance, she shivered, craving my tongue where she ached the most. Her hands gripped my hair as I delivered another slow strike of my tongue against her bud before pulling away. But only when she cried out, begging me, did I give into my urges. Her thighs, so soft and toned, tightened around my head, holding me in place as I delivered wave after wave of pleasure. Her breathing labored as her orgasm built. Reaching under with my fingers, I helped it along until she was on the edge of the abyss. With one final swirl of my tongue, she trembled, pushed over the edge as her core tightened and pulsed.

I'd heard symphonies. I'd been to operas. I'd seen Broadway musicals.

Nothing compared to the sound of her moans. It was one thing to hear her getting herself off, but to know I was the one giving her the pleasure she so desperately craved...

Wow. *Holy fuck-balls of wow.*

Her thighs tightened more as she bucked against my hand, riding it out. My head felt like it was being crushed, but even if it popped like a balloon, I refused to move until she was finished. Even if she suffocated me with those thighs, I would die a happy man.

She eased up, letting her legs drop open and allowing me to move up her body and press my lips to hers. Pulling back, I drank her in with one clear mission in mind—give the girl who deserved the world her first toe-curling experience—but beneath the lust pounding in my ears, her words echoed.

It's what's making me fall for you.

She was falling in love with me. And I was terrified. The fear of hurting her was almost paralyzing. Perhaps I wasn't the type of man who could fall in love and dedicate building his entire life around one person. It was uncharted waters, and I was afraid I'd drown in the riptide and pull Liana down with me.

Liana's hands gripped at my back as I steadied myself above her.

Despite the look in her eyes screaming for me to devour her with the cascade of flavors sure to condemn us both to the pits of hell, I decided to stick with vanilla for the night, easing into it as we got to know each other's bodies. Gliding between her legs, I kissed her lips and heard her sweet breathlessness as I slid inside of her. I stilled, wishing to savor the moment forever.

It was an admirable goal... *while it lasted.*

The second Liana's nails dug into my back and her teeth nipped the skin on my shoulder, all bets were off. I kicked it into a higher gear as her legs wrapped around me, pulling me in deeper. She was amazing. *The best sex I ever had.* The thought almost stopped me dead. A plethora of sex with a parade of experienced women—nothing ever came close to the feeling Liana gave.

It made no sense, until she breathed out my name as her second wave of pure white-hot pleasure hit her, and suddenly, it was crystal clear. It didn't matter if I risked drowning. I would welcome the suffocation of the waves, so long as I made her happy before I went under.

I would do anything to make her happy... *because I was falling for her, too.*

O utside of our hotel room, the rain pelted the concrete streets, splattering against the windows as Liana came down from her high, so beautiful and serene. The music played low, a slow song about finding love where you least expect it.

My fingers brushed the soft curls sticking to the light sheen of sweat on her face. I gazed down at her, and my body vibrated with the need to take those glorious lips. I leaned down, placing a soft kiss on her mouth, letting my tongue glide against hers. Her mouth twitched into a smile against mine as she gave a content hum that burst in my chest.

"Again already?" She draped her leg over me. "Not that I'm objecting."

"Hmm. I would love to." My fingers brushed her arm. "But maybe we could do something out of *my* comfort zone and talk."

"Need time to build up some more stamina?" she teased, poking me in the chest.

I scoffed. *The most ridiculous thing I ever heard.* "If you want to go, I will go right now. And this time, I won't hold back."

"You were holding back?" Her mouth dropped open.

"You have no idea." I pressed my lips to hers once more before pulling away. "But first, talk..."

Liana propped her head up on her hand and bit her lip. I could see the wheels turning in her beautiful eyes as she sought out a topic. I already had one in mind, but I didn't know how to approach it. My eyes moved down.

She slid her fingers through mine and sighed. "The day my mom left was my ninth birthday. I went to work with my dad so that he could buy me presents on the way back, and my mom was supposed to take care of the party while we were out. But when we got home, there was no party, and no mom. Just a note that said she was done. I haven't celebrated a birthday since."

It was like she knew I was ready and gave me the perfect opening. My breath hitched in my throat, and my eyes stung. Suddenly, my cheeks were wet, and a sob built at the back of my throat.

The song ended, replaced by one I'd heard before. Coldplay, "The Scientist". My chest ached, recalling the first time I heard it on the day I found my mom's body. It had played in a café where I sat, numb, reliving the heartbreak after I was done with the police.

"Tell me," Liana urged, lifting my hand to her mouth. She pressed a kiss to my palm.

My mouth opened, and the wall made of bricks in my mind crumbled like glass, letting free every childhood memory I repressed—some good, some bad, but all of them a separate dagger in my chest.

"I haven't celebrated a birthday since I was seven. My mom took me to Lincoln Park Zoo. It was the best day we ever had, but if I could go back, I would have begged to stay home because that was the day she met Garret."

My eyes closed as I took a deep breath. Liana stayed quiet, making sure to squeeze my hand every so often.

"They started dating, and after a while, I thought we were a family." I laughed, cold. How stupid I'd been. "Garret had an endless stream of cash, and he bought me anything I wanted. I loved it. I mean, what kid wouldn't love toys every day? By the time I realized he was a dealer, it was too late. My mom was gone."

My voice cracked, a sharp intake of breath sticking in my throat as I lifted my eyes to look at her. I wasn't prepared for the genuine concern that shone for me in her beautiful eyes. My head bowed as the tears fell and the sob broke free. "Six months in, she was hooked on his cocaine and then, when the high wasn't high enough, Garret brought out the big guns. He stuck a needle of heroin in her hand and said, 'Go ahead, baby. You'll like it.' I never saw my mom again after that, just her shell."

Liana's hands lifted my head to look at her again. "I'm sorry."

I swallowed the lump at the back of my throat and let out a slow breath. "After a while, he got violent toward both of us. I never knew what I'd be walking into at home, so I stayed out. Sometimes for days." I scoffed. "Can you believe that? A nine-year-old walking the streets of Chicago on his own all night? Nobody looking for him, nobody caring."

I let out a small laugh. It seemed insane, even now, that nobody noticed me. "When I was eleven, I started to collect change off the ground, hoping I could save enough for a month in rehab. I thought if I could get her into the program, she'd become the mom I—" My voice gave out as a small hiccough escaped. "Then, one weekend Garret went out of town and left her without a fix. He left her shaking, vomiting, climbing the walls for a momentary high... Anything she could get her hands on. She ransacked the apartment looking for loose change, or anything valuable she could sell or trade for a hit. She found my savings."

I blew out a breath as the tears came fast and hard.

"I begged her not to take it. I even told her what I was saving for. She didn't care. But I did. I fought with her, scrambling to the floor to grasp as much of the money as I could."

I blew out another breath, my heart aching. "The first time she looked at me in two years, she slapped me so hard the room spun, and I hated her *so much*. I was so angry, the angriest I've ever been in my life. I pushed her and she hit her head on my bedroom door. It didn't seem to faze her, but as luck would have it, in walked Garret."

Liana winced and swallowed down a shaky breath.

"He didn't even blink before he was on me, punching me. I couldn't breathe, couldn't run… I was numb. And then, he pulled his fist back again and my mom lunged for him. I was so happy. But she wasn't trying to save me; she was looking for a fix." I scoffed, shaking my head. "Either way, it was the distraction I needed. I ducked out of his hold and ran for the door, and the last time I heard my mother's voice, she told me to leave and never come back. I was officially a homeless eleven-year-old with cracked ribs and a beat-up face."

Liana's eyes welled up, leaking tears as she sucked in a breath.

"It's okay." I lifted my hand to caress her cheek.

"It's not okay!" Her head landed on my chest as her body enveloped mine like a warm blanket. Her breath stumbled over soft cries as her hand grazed my chest. I kissed her head. She let out a sigh, and I knew the question on the tip of her tongue.

"Go ahead," I said. "Ask."

Lifting her head, Liana looked deep into my eyes and softly asked, "What happened to your mom?"

I closed my eyes, recalling the worst day of my life. "I used to walk by the brownstone hoping to catch a glimpse of her.

Then, on my sixteenth birthday, there were police cars and an ambulance outside the door..." I breathed out, the ache in my chest like a concrete block. "I ran into the house and took the steps three at a time to get to her faster, but when I rounded the corner into her bedroom, she was gone; motionless on the ground."

Liana's breath hitched. "Did she OD?"

I gave a short, curt laugh. "You would think so, but no. Garret shot her up, then beat her, shot her up some more, and beat her again until..." A strangled sob ripped raw from my throat. "Her heart gave out."

Liana's body curled into mine, holding me so tightly, I was afraid she'd break a bone in my chest. I leaned down, burying my nose in her hair; the smell of lavender and lemon the only thing reminding me I wasn't back there.

Her hand reached up, wiping the tears from my cheeks as her mouth pressed softly against mine. The weight that had been in my mind for over ten years finally eased, having gotten it off my chest. I purposely kept it short—she didn't need to know the details—but bearing the worst parts of me to another person was freeing and sparked the courage to know I could work through the trauma with Dr. Jesionowski without crumbling.

"Thank you, Liana," I whispered.

She smiled. "For what?"

"For doing more for me than a surplus of therapists ever could."

A smirk played at her lips. "And you didn't even have to pay me."

"Well I could." I moved in to lay a kiss at the edge of her mouth. "But then this becomes a *very* different situation." Nuzzling my nose against hers, I sighed—a question on the edge of my tongue.

"What?" Liana asked. "What are you thinking?"

I clasped her hand in mine. "I'm wondering, after everything you've been through, seeing Eric be a hound and having your mom walk out on you... How can you believe in love the way you do?"

Her fingers brushed against the palm of my hand before sliding through mine. She sighed. "I used to read manuscripts for Eric. It gave me an escape into a world nobody else knew yet. Just me, and the writer. I loved it." Her free hand lifted to brush her hair out of her face. "For years, I read anything that crossed his desk. Each story so vastly different than the last, they had nothing in common... except *one* thing. There was always love. By the end of senior year, I must've read a thousand manuscripts. And no matter what I saw around me, I guess I thought a thousand people couldn't be wrong."

I was in awe of how her brain worked, how she thought, how she believed... "I wish I could see the world through your eyes."

Her throat bobbed. "It's not as glorious as it seems."

"But you see the bright in the world. All I see is despair. Or, at least, that's all I saw." I pressed my forehead against hers and let our lips brush.

"What do you see now?" She asked, breathing slow.

"Now, I see you. And believe me, Liana Dawson... You're a hell of a sight."

Her cheeks blushed pink. "What do I look like? In painstakingly emotional detail if you please."

Fuck. I couldn't find the words. My throat turned dry and scratchy, and my brain deafened me with an indistinguishable cacophony of music from six different Broadway shows, and a Mariachi band—but not enough coherent words to form a full sentence.

Liana's fingertips broke through the sound barrier, caressing strands of my hair. "Kade, it's okay. It's not like I need to hear a list of things that make me so wonderful."

My mouth opened, desperate to tell her how my heart thumped like a bass drum whenever I was around her, how my hands burned to touch her, and how I liked her so damn much, it drove me crazy.

Instead, I let my lips twitch into an amused grin and said, "Just so you know, gorgeous, I don't usually cry after sex."

Chapter 30

Liana

The morning sun crept through the crack in the curtains. I woke to find Kade staring, counting the freckles on my face with his index finger. My breath hitched, the pallet of colors in his eyes belonged on a canvas in a goddamn museum. Every fleck an amazing work of art.

"Jesus," he said. "I think a lady lives in my brain now."

Not what I expected his first words the morning after we had sex to be. I blinked at him. "Are you drunk?"

"Not currently, but I am having some very romantic thoughts. It's weird." He moved in to kiss me good morning when a loud ding sounded from his phone before our lips could touch. He grumbled, reaching over to the bedside table, and grabbed his cell. I did the same thing, realizing it was time to pop the bubble on our little getaway. It was on only a second before fifteen consecutive dings sounded. "Everything okay?"

I nodded, reading the onslaught of text messages from Kit freaking out about me not coming home last night. I hit reply with two words: *I'm good.* "Yours?"

I turned to find Kade, his jaw hard as a rock and his nostrils flaring. "No, it's not..."

"What's wrong?"

He sighed, letting out a small whimper, and my soaring heart crashed to the earth's crust. "It's an email from HR." He blew out a deep breath. "With Stephanie's resignation letter."

I winced. "Are you okay?"

"No." He threw his phone clear across the room and watched as it hit the doorframe and damn near obliterated. "I can't believe this. I mean, I knew it'd happen eventually, but when I walked out of the apartment, I at least thought I could talk to her at work. I thought I could change her mind, but now Cleo has her completely isolated. No job, no friends... *Fuck!*"

"I'm sorry." I scooted behind him and wrapped myself around his body. His hands covered mine as I kissed his shoulder and snuggled my head into the skin of his back.

"Me too. And on top of that, I now have to find a new assistant..."

I perked up at the prospect of being able to help him. I bounced off the bed to look him in the face. "I can find you someone. I used to interview people for Eric all the time. I have a list of names of great people he rejected for this-or-that reason."

"Oh, great," he scoffed. "An assistant your father deemed not good enough to be his?"

I rolled my eyes. "Oh, please. You know his standards are ridiculously high. He even rejected my résumé, and I was practically already working the job! I just wasn't being paid."

"That's because he's an ass," he spat and then raised an eyebrow. "You worked as an assistant?"

"Junior agent, actually. Six years." I scrolled through the names on my phone. "I have three people who I think would be perfect to work with you. Very go-with-the-flow and not easily offended. Do you want me to set up interviews?"

"I don't know what my schedule's like," he said. "And now

my phone is smashed. I should bring up my lack of impulse control with Dr. Jesionowski."

"Definitely." I passed him my phone. "Log into your server. I'll cross-check your schedule against what works for them and set up lunch dates."

He did, and I moved back to my side, pulling my glasses out of my bag. "Okay… So, you have an afternoon free tomorrow, but I've scheduled a different kind of date for then." I winked. "You can do a morning interview on Wednesday, and then two lunches back-to-back on Thursday, and have a new assistant by Friday morning, giving you the afternoon off to let your penis interview my—" I stopped talking and cringed. "That's not sexy, is it?"

Kade laughed. "No, but for the record it worked. If only we had time. I have to go into the office today. The work has mounted up."

"Crazy how that happens when you don't do it," I teased, but my heart gave a pang as I realized I needed to start looking for a side job. If Kit and Zoe were moving out, I needed a new place. Somewhere I could afford—though it killed me to have to give up my apartment.

"Won't that interfere with your blog?" Kade asked when I told him my thoughts.

I sighed. "Big time. But what else can I do? It's not even walking on eggshells at this point. More like shards of glass."

A smirk spread across his face, the wheels in his head turning. I narrowed my eyes at him, wishing I had the ability to read minds so I could figure out his thoughts.

"Why don't you come to my office with me for the day?" he asked. "At least then, you don't have to go home."

It was an offer to good to pass up—mainly because it meant avoiding Kit for a few extra hours.

"Okay," I said.

G oing into Kade's office hand in hand with him was... an experience. Apparently, seeing the boss walk *in* with a woman on his arm was an unusual occurrence. The heads of his employees turned to gawp in our direction. Kade gave them a stern look back, one that told them to get back to work.

I smiled seeing his office. It was very *Kade*. The walls were white and mostly bare, decorated only by black floating bookshelves, proudly displaying the books of the authors he represented. In the air was a smell of paper and pencil shavings. My nose tipped up, inhaling it. It was a smell I hadn't realized I'd missed.

Kade pulled me along with him toward his office. But outside the double doors, he stalled—his face twisting and falling.

I followed his eyeline and sighed. Perched outside his office was a big, empty desk. And empty didn't pertain only to the seat behind it. The whole area was bare. *Cleared out.*

Stephanie had been around to collect her things. As though breaking his heart wasn't bad enough, she was kicking him while he was down. It was cruel. And as far as I was aware, cruel wasn't a word in her vocabulary.

But it was in Cleo's.

We bypassed the sad space and locked ourselves in Kade's office. My core burned as the door clicked shut and Kade twisted the lock. I was ready to be taken on his desk, and the bulge in his pants said he was ready to take me. Unfortunately for our libidos, the eroticism of Kade popping his top button and slackening his tie was dampened by the mountain of manuscripts awaiting him on his desk.

"Sorry, sweetheart. Looks like it's all work and no play..." He sighed, taking a seat behind his desk.

"Wow, that's a lot of mail-ins," I commented. "I thought most people sent their manuscripts via email these days?"

Kade smiled. "They do, but I print them out. Not a great friend to the environment, I know, but I can't seem to get immersed in a book unless I have it in my hands. Don't worry, I plant a tree for every book I print."

I grinned, warmed by our similarity. I'd tried Kindles and audiobooks, but they couldn't seem to keep my attention. The thought of swiping to the next page as opposed to feeling the paper rub between my index finger and my thumb as I flicked it over—*shudder.*

"Can I help?" I asked with the enthusiasm of a child on Christmas morning.

"Are you sure? I know it's not exactly what we had in mind when I invited you into my office."

I snorted. "Are you kidding? This is like foreplay for me."

He shook his head and tossed me a pile of various genres. "Read until you get bored and write notes for me."

"Got it." I grinned, digging in. "I am so turned on right now."

He muttered something under his breath that sounded uncannily like 'weirdo.' I stuck my tongue out and held up a middle finger. Kade laughed.

Opening the first manuscript on the pile, I got to work. It had been so long since I'd read a raw book, unpublished. I was floating. I got so engrossed; I couldn't put it down. Even when Kade offered to go get lunch, I wordlessly waved him away, and curled up on the chair. I'd forgotten how much I loved to read. After I quit working for Eric, I managed to convince myself I was relieved, but it was a lie. Nothing beats the feeling of being the first set of eyes on a brand new world. And as my chest fluttered and my stomach burst with each turn of the page, I realized it was something I craved.

Two hours later, I was halfway through the book when a hankering for caffeine hit. If I was to be Kade's stand-in assistant, I supposed it was my job to fetch the nectar. Though it behooved me to put down a novel in the middle of unresolved turmoil, I sighed and placed it on the desk, committing an act of book blasphemy by ear-marking the page.

Looking up, I saw Kade with hunkered brows. He was adorable at work, all serious and focused. I smirked and turned away, but not looking at him didn't help. Every time he gave a content hum, I would smile wider. If I didn't stop grinning soon, my face would stick.

"Coffee?" I asked. He nodded without looking up. "Black, two shots with extra whipped cream and sprinkles, right?"

"The finer things," he muttered with a smile.

I bit my lip to stop a laugh. How far we'd come since our meet-not-so-cute in the café. "I was thinking while I was out, I'd swing by my apartment and get a couple things so I might be a while. Is that okay, or are you a strict boss?"

Kade finally looked up, his eyes glinting. In them, I could almost see his mind pumping out visions of us roleplaying a strict boss and an unruly employee. His eyes trailed my body, burning my skin.

"I don't mind," he said. "But before you go, I do want to talk about this whole assistant situation."

As if on cue, my phone vibrated in my pocket. "Speaking of, that was an email back from Racheal Skene. She's efficient, and I think you'll like working with her. I also have—"

Kade rounded his desk and put his index finger to my lips. I pursed my mouth to quiet the urge of wrapping my tongue around it, a rush of arousal taking me over. "I don't want anybody else, Liana. I want *you*."

I blinked. "You want me to work for you?"

"It's hardly work. It'll be helping me, and Steph when she comes to her senses, while doing something you love and getting paid for it. And with a lot of downtime at your desk to work on your blog. I get your expertise, and you get to keep your passion alive. It's a win-win."

I scoffed. "Sure, except for the part where I'm working as an underling for my boyfriend." I cringed, unable to believe I'd used that word. My eyes wide, I shrank away from him, and turned my back. "I mean a boy who is my friend... *with benefits*?"

Kade placed his hands on my shoulders and turned me back around, pulling me to his body. "You wouldn't be working *for* me. You'd be working *with* me. We'd take turns going for coffee runs and lunch orders. No boss-employee relationship. Just my... girlfriend," he said the word like he had trouble pronouncing it, "helping me out around the office and getting enough money to move."

My embarrassment gave way to euphoria. I launched myself into his arms and crashed my lips to his.

"So, is that a yes?" Kade pulled back with a smile.

"To being your girlfriend? Or to working with you?"

"I guess both."

"Yes." I grinned, the word barely out of my mouth before we sealed the deal with another kiss.

I wrapped my arms around his neck and deepened the kiss, Kade's want for more pressing against my hipbone, but the pile of work on his desk was only a fraction smaller than when we started, and now, I was on the clock. And I had to go home first.

I broke the kiss and grabbed my purse. "Wish me luck," I said, suddenly nervous at the prospect of seeing Kit.

"Good luck, and don't forget my sprinkles." He winked.

I rolled my eyes and headed out. Again, the office turned their heads to look at me as I passed, whispering in hushed tones. Lifting a hand, I waved on my way to the elevator. Swiftly, all heads turned away and only braved another look as the doors closed.

The air outside was cruel, whipping my hair into my eyes and mouth as I hailed a cab. I had to start remembering to tie it up. The taxi driver was nice enough to have the heating blasting as I climbed in the back. The address rolled off my tongue so easily, but it no longer felt like going home. My nerves played up as though I was visiting a stranger instead of my own sister. As the cab rolled to a stop outside my building, I found myself praying she'd be working late, and Zoe would be being tortured somewhere.

I only got part of my wish. The apartment was in dead silence with Kit nowhere to be found, but Zoe—sitting on the couch in her grandiose vintage nightgown, with a fashion magazine and a killer pout like she owned the place—looked far too comfortable in my apartment for my liking. She snarled as I shut the door behind me, adding an extra layer of ice to the atmosphere.

"If it gets any colder in here, the ceiling will start snowing," I muttered under my breath, tossing my keys on the side table, and headed for my bedroom.

"Out all night with Luka?" Zoe spat, following me. I ignored her snarky jibe and kept my mouth closed. "You really do love my sloppy seconds, huh?"

I wouldn't give her the satisfaction of knowing I had no feelings for Luka. She didn't deserve to know. I rolled my eyes, grabbing the duffel from the hallway closet, and filled it with my laptop and as much clothing as I could fit so I could stay away from the apartment as long as possible.

"You're an idiot, Zoe." Zipping up the duffel, I walked out of the apartment and past Kit, coming home from work. "Don't wait up. My keys are on the table. I'm not coming back."

And I meant it. They could keep my once-perfect apartment for themselves until they moved. I'd rather live in a hole than share space with an evil, blond hobbit, and her new side-kick. And with my bank account, a hole was looking like a very real possibility.

I was in the elevator with the doors closing before Kit got a chance to say anything. And, as if the universe decided to chime in with some well-timed irony, my phone dinged with a text from Luka.

'Missed you last night, Lee.
Maybe next time we can have one of our infamous sleepovers like we used too... but with less clothes.
Text me when you're next available.'

Once upon a time, a text like that would've made me blush. Now, it made me feel like an asshole. I'd promised Luka only twenty-four hours ago that Kade and I were friends, and now I was on my way back to him with an official title. I was Kade Jennings' girlfriend.

I slipped my phone back in my pocket and headed back to Kade's office. I got the cab to drop me off at the café where we met and picked up the same drinks we had that day. Mine, a frappé, and Kade's delightful mix of manly adult and playful child. Coffee in hand, I walked the two blocks back to work. When I stepped into Kade's office, his head popped up like a grinning meerkat. "Sprinkles?"

"Sprinkles," I said, a laugh at my lips. I placed the cup down in front of him and dropped my duffle by my chair. Grabbing my half-finished manuscript, I sipped my melted frappé and dove back in. Kade and I worked in silence, but every so often I would look up to steal glances at his chiseled face and find him staring back at me over the pages.

My cheeks burned. Biting my lip, I tore my eyes from his and continued reading. The skies outside Kade's windows moved through the spectrum of blue, into gray, and by the time we were done, it was dark out.

"Back to our hotel room?" He stretched out in his chair and yawned.

My heart skipped a beat.

Our hotel room. A room that was *ours*. Mine and Kade's...

Together.

Chapter 31

Liana

I got out of the shower to find Kade naked, holding chocolate sauce in one hand and whipped cream in the other. "Ready to sweeten things up?" He waggled his eyebrows.

My eyes slid down to his manhood, semi-hard and... wearing a banana peel as a hat.

"What the fuck?"

Kade smirked, squirting two small mountains of whipped cream where his hips met his penis, and dripped a small amount of chocolate sauce on his chest. "I made you dessert."

I burst into laughter, unable to believe my eyes.

He gave a teasing grin, moving toward me. "I figured we could move through all the flavor groups. Tomorrow night: Sour candy."

I put my tongue between my teeth and arched an eyebrow, staring at his perfect ass. "*Where?*"

Kade laughed. His mast seemed to engorge with every step, and by the time his fingertips played with the hem of my shirt, he was fully hard. My shirt was pulled over my head and discarded to the floor. With a smile, I brushed the naked skin of his taut, muscular arms and then moved down.

My hands travelled down, unable to stop myself from cupping his ass. It was too much of a great opportunity to pass up. It was *right there.*

He giggled as I gave it a firm squeeze. "Isn't it me who's supposed to be grabbing your ass?"

"Are you kidding? With a butt like yours?" I leaned in and lay kisses at the sweet spot on his neck, nibbling the skin. "You're going to have to pry me away."

"Why on earth would I ever do that? Roam away, Liana Dawson."

And roam, I did. My hands explored every inch from his butt to... *not-his-butt.* He hissed, throwing his head back and closing his eyes as I discarded the peel and took him in hand.

His lips collided with mine and I melted into him. It was nice, being so close to another person. I understood why sex was such a big deal, now. Being around him was enough to light my fuse and knowing I could write a list of things I was curious about and he wouldn't judge me for them, made me brazen in exploring sexual boundaries.

Taking the chocolate sauce from him, I uncapped the bottle and dripped a generous amount down his abdomen until his manhood looked like a novelty edible bought from a sex shop.

And suddenly, I had a craving for chocolate...

⁓

Twenty-three days into my new job, I found a small apartment in Brooklyn. It was by no means fancy, but it worked well enough as storage to keep all of my stuff safe until I could take my apartment back.

I was making good money working for Kade—better money than I'd made in my first three years at Liberty. I'd worked out, so long as I was frugal and squirreled enough away from my job with Kade, along with monthly dues from my blog, I could afford to live there alone within a couple months—providing it was still available.

The Brooklyn apartment was snug and vintage—a far cry from my modern home, but comfy. Yes, technically, the kitchen and the bedroom were in the same place and the 'walls' were curtain-dividers. But it was cheap and wouldn't suck up my savings in rent.

I spent my days off there, working out of the apartment like an office, but my nights... those were spent in the arms of Kade wrapped up in the sheets of our hotel room.

It was hard somedays to remember we weren't living *together*; that Kade being yet to find his own place was the only reason we cohabited at the hotel. I dreaded the day he found somewhere new, and I would be in Brooklyn full-time, alone. Which was why, as I sat on the gleaming, freshly-waxed, hardwood floors of a spacious third-floor apartment on the Upper West Side, I pouted like a petulant toddler.

"I don't know if it's *you*," I said. "It's nice enough, I guess."

"Nice *enough*?" He snorted. "This place is a palace."

"But worth the price tag?"

"Yes."

I shrugged. "If you're into that kind of life, I guess."

Again, Kade snorted. Taking a seat behind me on the floor, he wrapped his arms and legs around my body and placed his chin on my shoulder. "What's going on?"

"Nothing... I don't see why you're rushing into buying a place is all."

"I can't keep the hotel room for another month," he told me, again. "It's eating my savings."

"You could stay with me in Brooklyn?" I offered.

"Or," Kade pressed his lips to my ear. "*You* could stay with *me*?"

It was my turn to snort. "Yeah, sure. I don't have two spare nickels to rub together, but I'm going to live *here* rent-free?"

"Who said anything about rent-free? There are other ways to pay. Or maybe I could pay you," he teased, and I punched him playfully. *Pretty Woman* was a great movie, but I wasn't into living the life of Vivienne and Edward.

Kade smiled. "You have an apartment, remember? Think of it like staying with your boyfriend while your place is fumigated for termites. Which in Zoe's case..."

"Accurate."

He laughed. "You could keep the place in Brooklyn for all of your stuff and spend your nights here." His smile widened. He was smiling more often than not these days. And he had reason to be.

We were coming up on a month of being boyfriend-girlfriend, and he was working closely with Detective Hart. Cleo was being watched, and they were building enough evidence to bust her for dealing—though not enough to indict yet.

"Okay," I agreed, craning my neck to look at him. "I'll live here with you until I can go back to my apartment or afford a smaller place in my building."

A look crossed Kade's face, and his eyes lit up with an idea. "What?"

"I like your building," he said. "Are they all for lease?"

"There's a couple with the option to buy, I think."

Pulling out his phone, he dialed his estate agent. "Is it okay with you if I take a look? If not, I can take this place..."

"No, it's fine." I gave a teasing grin. "If we break up, you can move."

I expected him to roll his eyes or scoff, but he didn't. Instead, he caressed my face and pressed a soft kiss to my mouth. Looking deep into my eyes, he nuzzled my nose. "We're not breaking up."

Gulp.

He was inches of kissing me again when my phone beeped.

He sighed. "We have *got* to get rid of technology."

"It's Jana. I'm a week away from the launch, and she's suggesting some kind of special *Love, Liana* event."

"Seven days? That went by fast."

"I know." I sighed. "I've been doing the beta rounds on my own for a couple weeks, and they've gone... well. But I don't know if I'm ready to up my workload to assistant, love guru, and sex sage all at the same time. I barely have enough time to answer the love section. But, according to the pre-stats, the new section could double my readership. Popularity like that is a quick-fire way to getting a book deal."

"There're faster ways. Damn, if only you were sleeping with an agent." He winked.

I rolled my eyes. "It's the logical next step in my career, but it all seems overwhelming. And weird timing. Who launches *anything* on a random day in November? If it were up to me, I'd delay the launch until midnight on the last day of the year. As the New Year ushers in, so does the new era of *Love, Liana*..."

Kade's eyebrows pulled forward. "That's not a bad idea. Start a new Instagram dedicated to the website to promote your event and hit launch on the sextion as the ball-drops. You might be onto something."

"A new Instagram?" I groaned.

"I know you hate it but in this day and age, it's all about the social media, sweetheart."

I gave him the same argument I gave when Jana originally suggested Instagram. "Nobody wants to see me, tatty-haired and syrup-covered, with pancake batter on my face, after an all-nighter and six cups of coffee."

"I would."

I ignored the tingles in my tummy. "Okay, fine. But it's not up to me. I gave a date. They're expecting the section in a week."

Kade shrugged. "Things get pushed back all the time. You don't want to half-ass something because you're not ready for it.

Besides, who launches anything on a random day in November?"

I shook my head, amused. And then something occurred to me. "Why're we sitting here if you're not moving in?"

His phone vibrated. "You're right. We should go look at the two available in your building instead." Pushing himself up, he held out a hand and pulled me from the ground.

I hoped I wouldn't run into the two witches of the Upper West side as we walked the four blocks to my building. My tummy rumbled as we stepped onto the elevator and was doing backflips by the time we got off. Apparently, the first available apartment was a two-bedroom... right next door to my apartment.

"Have you heard from Kit at all?" Kade asked as we stepped off onto my floor.

I shook my head. "I don't even know if she's pregnant or not." I peeked my head around the corner, listening for any signs of movement behind my door. "Clear."

Kade hummed the theme tune to *Mission Impossible* as I skimmed the wall, ready to freeze at any given moment.

"Keys," I demanded, holding out my hand. Kade looked at me like I was insane and tossed them overhead. I caught them midair and scrambled to unlock the door, so focused on getting inside without Kit seeing me, I flitted through a crack in the door and slammed it closed behind me before I remembered Kade on the other side.

Shit. I opened the door again.

"Move your ass." I grabbed a fistful of his shirt and yanked him inside. As I slammed the door a second time, Kade blew out a low whistle.

"This place is nice."

I looked around, my eyes widening. "Better than nice. It's like my apartment's more attractive sibling." Like my apartment, it was open plan. But unlike mine, the lack of a third bedroom gave more space for the hallways, and an extra two feet of dining area.

"I'm not sure about the two-bed situation," he said. "Someday, I may need a third room."

"An office?"

Kade smiled. "Sure... or a nursery."

My breath stuck in my throat. I must've blacked out for a second and gone into a dream world. Did he say nursery? Or did I need a doctor?

"Relax, I'm not ready to be a father. But if I buy an apartment, I want it to be a permanent place, so I'm thinking ahead."

I pressed a hand to my hip. "If you ever do have kids, none of them will call me mommy, *right*?" I said, reiterating his words from the night of our failed date.

He smirked. "Touché."

I blew out an unsteady laugh to relieve the tension, but my brain was in overdrive. He was thinking ahead... *way* ahead. The thought of seeing Kade carrying a baby on his hip and singing lullabies was almost too much to bear. My knees quivered, the romance autopilot in my brain imagining the baby would be ours.

"Well," I cleared my throat. "Someday, if I figure out a way to make *Love, Liana* global, maybe I could buy mine and we could knock the wall down to make one huge apartment with space for an office, *and* a nursery."

"*We*?"

I bit my lip and moved through the apartment. "This place is great. Good fixtures, amazing décor, furniture included... a girlfriend next door. What's not to love?"

"The last detail really sold it. I'm putting an offer in." *Swoon.*

We moved into the master bedroom. It was roughly the same size as mine when I first moved in—until I gave it up to Kit and took the smaller room, since she was paying the lion's share of the rent—except Kade's had a lot of extra storage space and a hidden room on the other side of the en-suite that could make an amazing library/reading nook.

"I love this place." I grinned so wide; it reached my eyes. "I could really see you living here." I could really see *myself* living there. But admitting it aloud seemed like too much.

The last thing I wanted was to freak Kade out when we were so happy.

I was so happy...

CHAPTER 32

KADE

I signed the contract for my new apartment with Liana by my side. It was a good day.

Hell, it was a good life.

It was a strange thing to be looking to the future for the first time in... ever. But I liked it. Sure, I planned boring shit like business meetings ahead of time, but before I met Liana and started my weekly trips to therapy, I couldn't have cared less about anything that didn't bring immediate pleasure. Now, I was a normal person... *Almost,* anyway.

I still gave less than a single fuck about the average person or their opinion, but I had real feelings. And though I would carry the scars of my childhood forever, I was healing with the help of Dr. Jesionowski, and my girlfriend. The tools therapy taught me, coupled with Liana's support, were making all the difference—I hadn't broken anything in almost a month, since I smashed my phone in the hotel.

Everything in my life was going great. Well, almost everything. I thought about Stephanie every single day, and more so after I bought my apartment. Maybe it was because doing so changed the address on my license; or maybe it was the therapy session after I signed the lease, but she would not leave my head.

It killed me not knowing if she was okay. Once every hour I considered going back to the apartment to see if I could spot her from a distance and make sure she was alright. But when Dr. Jesionowski informed me watching from a distance was the same thing I did with my mom, I realized I'd made a mistake leaving her to fend for herself. I thought doing so would stop history repeating itself, but now I saw it already was.

But this time, I had the foresight to change it.

Stepping off the elevator after a month of not being in the building was a weird experience. Again, I could smell the mixture of incense Stephanie burned on the run up to holidays. This time it was gingerbread and butterscotch to usher in December. I inhaled the scent as a small smile pulled at the edges of my mouth.

I raised my fist and knocked on the door with trepidation, hoping Stephanie would be alone. When the hardwood pulled back, I released a breath I hadn't realized I was holding. She was okay, and her face was near back to normal; but there were fresh bruises on her neck and arms. I winced, the guilt punching a hole in my stomach.

Her eyes widened, seeing me there, and then glazed over in floods of tears. They streamed down her face like a waterfall as she crashed into my arms and held me tight.

"I'm so sorry, Kade," she cried against my shirt. "I knew I made a mistake the second you left. I didn't invite Cleo to move in, you need to know that. She didn't give me an option, and now I feel like I'm stuck. And I'm so scared. Scared that if I try to leave, she might hurt herself, or me. I don't know what to do."

I swallowed the hard lump in my throat and wrapped my arms around her, so tight, I was afraid I'd crush her. Pulling back, I kissed her forehead, her words taking a moment to catch in my ear. "Do you want to leave?" I asked. "Because we can, right now."

"No... maybe. I don't know." Stephanie shrugged, wiping away her tears and wincing as she lifted her arm. I cursed under my breath. "I'm not in love with her anymore, but I have love for her. I'm terrified of what she'll do. And there's history to be considered. I owe her a lot."

That damn argument. I hated it.

"No. If Cleo got her way, you'd be in a Chicago crack den right now, addicted to heroin. And that's only if you hadn't over-dosed already. *Stephanie*," I took her face in my hands. "You owe *yourself* the chance to walk away. *You* said no to drugs. *You* came to New York. *You* helped me build something great. You had dreams before her, she stopped you reaching them. You don't owe her anything."

A sob retched from her throat as she buried her face in her hands.

"Leave with me," I whispered. "We can pack everything and go before she gets back. You don't have to even see her."

Her hands dropped and she shook her head. "It's not that I don't want to, but it won't do any good. Cleo will never stop. She'll keep finding me, calling me, getting in my head until I agree to come back. If I ever have a chance at getting out, I need to know she can't come after me."

Fuck, I thought, wracking my head for a way, and then it hit me. I slipped my hand into my jacket pocket; the same one I wore that day in the hospital and found a card with a cellphone number on it.

Detective Hart.

Reaching for my cell, I called the number on the card and asked the detective to meet us at the café where Liana and I first met face to face.

"Let's go." I reached for Stephanie's hand. She nodded, but then held up a finger and told me to wait at the door. Inside, she rushed around, snatching-up small bits and pieces, and throwing them into a bag. Grabbing her jacket off the hook by the door, she locked the door behind her and left her keys on the mat.

We hurried out the building, in case Cleo came back, and hailed a cab. An hour later, we were sat across from Detective Hart, discussing protective custody in exchange for Stephanie's testimony. To my surprise, Steph pulled the bag onto the table and from it emerged files of evidence, documenting Cleo's eight years of cruelty—videos of her attacks from the first to the last, photographs of injuries...

And even better, she had voice notes, ledgers, and copies of bank statements that were more than enough to send Cleo to prison for a long time.

"To be sure, we would like some concrete evidence of her dealing." Detective Hart said. "To give Cleo a chance to bury herself, we have set up an undercover officer who she agreed to meet with tonight. All we need is the final nail in her coffin, and then we'll make the arrest."

"How long could she be looking at?" I asked.

Detective Hart sat forward. "Hard to say for sure, but our prosecutor wants to make an example out of her. If she gets her way, Cleo Kilmer could be in prison for upwards of a decade."

Stephanie expelled a breath at hearing those words. Her shoulders dropped and tears pricked in her eyes, whether of relief or pity for the woman she'd loved, I wasn't sure. Me, I was fucking ecstatic.

A whole ten years. I grinned. I couldn't help it. I'd been rooting for Cleo's downfall for years—plotting it like a comic book villain. Or antihero, as the case could be made. I had even idly surfed the net for a vat of toxic waste to drop her in, but as all the comic books and movies foretell, it wouldn't kill her as much as give her cool superpowers. And Cleo didn't deserve superpowers.

"How soon can we indict?"

"Once our officer makes the drop and we know exactly what she's dealing, we can move in." Detective Hart smiled. "Our UC is making the call tonight. She should be in cuffs by tomorrow morning."

"Tomorrow..." Suddenly the *Annie* song was playing in my head. Liana made me watch it, and now I understood the hype about tomorrow. *It was only a day away.* "Brilliant. Thank you, Detective Hart."

"Call me Julie." She smiled. Her eyes slid over to Stephanie. "The hope is for her to be incarcerated until the hearing, but in case she makes bail, I want you in protective custody until the end of the trial. Starting now." Behind us, two uniformed officers stood, waiting to take Steph away.

She stood up to greet them, and then turned to me with a smile drawing at the corners of her mouth and tears rolling down each cheek.

"Thank you," she whispered, reaching for my hand. I took hers and gave it a squeeze, pulling her in for a long hug.

"I'll see you soon, okay?" I kissed her on the edge of her hairline. Stephanie squeezed my hand one last time before leaving with the officers to go I didn't know where. I sat back down, relief washing over me. Stephanie was safe, for the first time in eight years, and I was on top of the world.

※

I t was eight a.m. when I got the call. Cleo had been arrested, and the arraignment hearing would take place in the afternoon.

"Thank you, Detective." I hung up as Liana's body began to stir.

"What's going on?" She gave the content hum she gave

every time she woke up. It was fucking adorable and made my heart thump in my chest. I smiled. "Cleo's in jail."

Liana bolted awake, breathing a sigh of relief. "That means Stephanie can come home soon, right?"

I nodded, laying back down. The weight lifted off my shoulders, giving me momentary reprieve before another crushing load of anxiety took its place. I scowled, my eyebrows wrinkling, and pulled Liana into my arms. Her head found its way to my chest as I strummed strands of her wild hair through my fingers. "Should we take the day off?"

Liana's leg lifted, settling on my hip. "I'd have to ask my boss."

"I think he needs a day to lie around naked and process everything. I have an appointment with Dr. Jesionowski tomorrow, and with all the changes lately, I feel like I need to decompress."

"Then we'll stay in bed." She angled her head back to look at me. "Movies?"

"Hm. And popcorn." I titled my chin to kiss her, the weight in my chest expanding. I pulled away from her and stepped from the bed under the guise of brushing my teeth. Truth is, I needed some air. I couldn't breathe.

I found my toothbrush in the holder next to Liana's, and the toothpaste on the side of the basin in the shape of a peanut because she squeezed from the middle instead of the bottom. My heart thumped twice as a smile crossed my face and I squeezed some peppermint toothpaste onto my brush, evening out the tube before putting it back into the medicine cabinet where it belonged. As I brushed, I thought of Liana.

Essentially, we were living together. My chest became so heavy, I doubled-over, gripping the sides of the basin until the strain lessened. When it did, I was left with a nauseous sinking in my stomach. *What was that about*? I closed my eyes and found myself imagining the apartment without her.

There would be one toothbrush in the holder, the tooth-paste would stay where it was, in its true form, only half of the closet space would be used—though she kept most of her clothes on what she called a *floordrobe*—there'd be no tiny balls of paper littering the floors, and there would be bare space in the corner of my bedroom where her huge mountain of shoes lived.

But the lonely silence I once craved so much would seem deafening without Liana's innermost thoughts being blurted out randomly every few minutes. Or one of her vices keeping the apartment alive—whether it was a movie or her Spotify playlist with music from every generation, the coffee maker being overworked every hour, or her relentless typing and sighs of frustration when she couldn't think of the perfect word.

The weight eased a little. I smiled, craning my neck to stare at her. Her body spread out like a starfish, and her head nuzzled into her pillow as she drifted in and out of sleep. Rinsing my mouth out with spearmint wash, I spat it out and made my way back into the bedroom. Perching myself on the edge of the bed, I leaned down and kissed Liana's forehead.

She gave a moan of serenity as her eyes fluttered open.

I smiled. "I remembered we're out of popcorn for our movie day."

Sitting up, Liana yawned, and threw the comforter off her body. "I'll go to the store." She stripped down, and I hardened as she pulled a pair of gray sweatpants over her legs and pushed her arms and head through a black tank-top hoodie. Digging into her pile of shoes, she produced a pair of salmon pink vans and slipped them on.

"Do you want me to come with?" I asked.

"Nah." She leaned down to kiss my lips. "I'll be back soon."

Off she went, her red hair unbrushed, her face unmade, and in an outfit that would be looked down upon by most of

Manhattan, and I could honestly say, I'd never met a more beautiful woman in my entire life.

My eyes slid back over to the unorganized pile of shoes. I smiled. Even her annoying habits were things I loved about her.

Love.

My smile dropped as a heat crept up my neck. Too hot. I couldn't breathe. Suddenly, the weight seemed crushing. A shooting pain fired through my chest. Doubling over, I gasped for air, unable to take any in as I stared down at little balls of paper on the bedroom floor, then to her hairbrush on the side table, the wallpaper she'd helped me pick out at the store, her clothes everywhere.

Her Liana-isms were all over my apartment.

I gripped my chest, willing the pain to stop as mass amounts of panic spread through me.

Fuck.

Chapter 33

Liana

I locked the door behind me and set off down the hallway. A flutter of muffled laughter drew my eye to the door of my old apartment, and sadness ached in my stomach. The last I had heard from Kit was a week after Kade and I moved into the hotel room, a two-word text message: *False alarm.*

That's it. No apology or mention of making amends. She didn't ask where I was or who I was living with. For all she knew, I was homeless. And, to rub salt in my already stinging wounds, I knew they were looking for a new apartment because the building manager had contacted me, since it was my name on the lease, to confirm I wanted out.

But I didn't.

Jana had crunched the reports and analytics. *Love, Liana* was on course to become the biggest advice blog online; the last three beta rounds got gleaming feedback, the blog was pulling in more and more people every day, and once the sex section was launched, the world was my oyster. I'd be able to afford my apartment alone.

Next door to my scathingly hot boyfriend.

With a smirk, I hit the button for the lobby and watched as

the doors closed. Kit wasn't *Kit* anymore, but another of Eric Dawson's mindless automatons, and we would never be the way we were. With that knowledge came acceptance, and a weight lifted from my shoulders. I was lighter, happier... free of my family, once and for all.

Outside, the world looked different. I hadn't realized how jaded I'd been. The crushing hurt had stopped me appreciating the changes New York went through in the beginning of winter. It was my favorite part of the year. The streets were lined grit to melt the oncoming black ice, brown leaves I could kick aside as I walked, and the remnant of rain drops in the air filled my chest with a warm excitement.

Pretty soon, snow would fall, and Christmas would come. My first with Kade.

My mind moved back to the blog.

The fans took the date pushback with little grievance, and some even agreed New Year was a better fit. A couple were even calling for an 'Ask Liana' channel on YouTube.

It wasn't a bad idea, but the thought of updating an Instagram account regularly was enough to make me sweat. The idea of being on livestream answering sex-based questions with my face on camera—big yikes. I wasn't there yet, but maybe someday.

I headed into the store and dumped their whole supply of popcorn and ice cream into my cart. The cashier at the store took my money with a curious smile, eyeing up my purchases. I'd bought enough popcorn to last us a long winter, in theory. But Kade *loved* popcorn, so in reality, it would last a night.

"Having a party?" She handed over my change.

"Not quite," I said as the dollar bills and some quarters slipped into my palm. "Thank you."

Grabbing my bags, I headed back home.

Home. It was nice to call living with Kade home. Being able to touch him, kiss him, make love to him any time I wanted. *It was heaven.*

"Liana..."

I was lost in my own little world of me and Kade, but the voice was enough to burst my bubble. It was a voice I'd recognize anywhere, and it sent spikes up my spine.

"Luka." I acknowledged him with a head tilt and kept walking, the guilt of ghosting him pooling in my stomach.

"*Woah.* Wait a second." He stepped in front of me, blocking my path. "What happened? We went out and then nothing."

"I don't know what to tell you. I'm sorry." I rushed past him.

Catching up to me, he fell in step and matched my strides. "Look, if I did something on our date to offend you—"

"It's not you, it's me." *Cliché. Contrived. Pathetic.* I winced and huffed out a breath. Luka stopped walking and once again blocked my path, his eyebrow raised. "I fell in love with someone else."

His mouth hung open, the start of a scoff emitting in stutters, but halfway, it turned to a laugh. "You're kidding? That Kade guy?" He laughed again, and I braced myself for the backlash. "Why didn't you just tell me that? I've been in hell thinking I'd done something to mess up our friendship *again*."

My shoulders relaxed, seeing Luka smile. "You're okay with that?"

He shrugged. "Can't say it doesn't sting, but what can I do? I missed my chance to be your guy, that doesn't mean I don't want to be your friend."

My mouth inched up into a smile as relief poured through me.

Luka opened his arms for a hug, and I fell into them, my chest warm at the thought of us being able to hangout as the us we were as kids. *Just* friends. He walked with me back home, taking another trip down memory lane. We laughed and fell into the rhythm of being *Luke and Lee* again, so easy, it was hard to believe so much time had passed without my best friend. He left me at the building door with a promise of a coffee date.

I could not stop grinning as I stepped off the elevator. Luka was in my life again, and my Adonis boyfriend was waiting in our bed to do a movie day of all the wholesome rom-coms he'd become addicted to. The popcorn rustled in my bags as I all but ran down the hallway to get to him faster.

Opening the apartment door, I hoped to find him naked under the sheets. Instead, I found him sitting stoic on his white, leather sofa wearing a formal suit complete with a tie. My eyebrows furrowed, and dread settled in my chest.

In an instant, I knew...

Hoping I was wrong, I placed the bags on the kitchen counter and faced him. His sloping shoulders and the crease of frustration between his eyebrows were like reading a book I didn't want to read. "I-uh... I got vanilla ice cream. They were all out of mint chip."

"That's fine," he said, but his gritted jaw told a different story.

My eyebrows hunkered down again, and I let out a breath; unable to ignore the truth on his face. "Something is bothering you..."

He looked to the ground and let out a sigh. "We need to talk. Liana, I—" Without warning, he stood from the sofa and headed into the bedroom. "I can't do this."

"Do what?" I was fast on his heels. "It's okay. Talk to me."

He groaned, sitting on the edge of our bed, his breathing rapid and out of rhythm. "It's not okay. I'm an asshole. It hit me that we're living together, and now it feels like there's a fucking bus parked on my chest. Liana, I—"

I held up a hand, cutting him off before he could say it. I didn't need to hear what came after. *I already knew.*

I dropped to seated position beside him, static ringing in

my ears. My chest ached, and tears pricked in my eyes. "You're
breaking up with me."

~~~~

I n his bedroom, I packed my clothes into two small
suitcases, thankful I hadn't moved all my stuff in, as Kade
sat on the couch in the living room with his head buried
in his hands. Zipping up the suitcases, I stood them up and
rolled them out of the room.

"I'm such a dick." I heard him say.

I didn't want to disagree with him, but he'd come leaps and
bounds since I'd met him, and I feared calling him a dick
would undo some of the progress he'd made in therapy.

"Yeah, you are." It slipped out anyway.

A slight laugh escaped his lips, but then his eyes moved
down, and guilt set in. I took it back.

"You're not a dick. I should've seen this coming." I sighed,
fighting back the urge to cry. I took a seat beside him on the
sofa. Oh, how I would miss his sofa, and his bed, and the duck
feather comforter. Mine was held hostage next door.

"Why do you think you freaked out?"

"I don't know. I have all of these thoughts and feelings
and I have no way of deciphering which fucking feeling
caused the anxiety. It's like I know in the back of my mind,
but I can't get to it. I don't know how to talk about it." His
head fell into his hands again, and he grasped at his hair. "It
won't go away. It started when I saw your toothbrush next to
mine, and then I looked around and your shit is fucking
everywhere! Even my goddamn pillows smell more like you
than they do me. You made this place a home, *your* home. It
was too much. Too much, I can't fucking breathe." He
grabbed at his chest, clawing, and sighed. "I can't do this. Us.
The last month has been indescribable, and I've felt things I

313

never thought I could feel. But learning about love and being in a committed relationship are two different things. You called yourself my girlfriend and then everything between us happened so fast."

I called *myself* his girlfriend? "Don't you dare put this all on me! You pursued us just as much as I did, remember? I can't believe how easy it is for you to throw me away. What was I? A challenging lay that got too deep?"

I didn't believe that, and logically, I could understand his actions. But that side of my brain was switched off, taken over by raw, hurt emotions. Nothing would process but the fact I was being dumped. "Are you saying this is my fault?"

"No... maybe." Kade crinkled his brow, his voice low. "I don't know. All I know is it feels like I'm having a heart attack. My chest is a fucking wrecking ball. We got so close so fast. I can't —I'm sorry. Maybe I should have kept it to myself and hoped it would pass, but Dr. Jesionowski says I have to be honest about my feelings."

I laughed, cold, tears welling in my eyes. His reasoning for breaking me—*us*—was because we were too close. It was stupid! *So fucking stupid.* "Well, I appreciate your honesty, but also... *fuck you, Kade!*" I shook my head, frustration bubbling under the surface. Pushing myself to my feet, I paced back and forth. "I'm such a goddamn idiot. I took a job working with you, and I moved into your apartment. Both *your* ideas by the way. But I use one word, and I'm the one who moved too fast?"

He hung his head. *Good.* He *should* be ashamed.

"And now, I'm fucked. *You've* fucked me. I have no job, no boyfriend, no family."

Kade stood, stopping me mid-pace. He kissed my forehead and pulled me in his arms. I pushed him away.

"I'm sorry. I just think, maybe we both need some space. I mean, come on, Liana... you can't want *this*? You knew what you were getting into when you signed up for my shitshow! This was bound to happen. Don't you get it? You need someone more stable who can fall for you the way you deserve."

"Do not tell *me* what *I* deserve!" I scoffed and fought to keep my tears at bay. "And don't act like you're doing me some grand chivalrous favor, sparing my feelings in the long run. *You* need space. I was fine an hour ago." A small sob broke free.

Kade's eyes softened, but then he pushed out a scoff, and they became harder than I'd ever seen them. His jaw locked and he squared his shoulders, forcing his eyebrows into a scowl. He laughed. "I thought you were smart, but I guess not. If you were, you would have run from me the second we met. A lapse in fucking judgement, that's for damn sure." I stumbled back, hit by his words, but I wasn't convinced he meant them. They were all for my benefit, to make it easier on me. *Like anything would...* My mouth opened to argue with him when he held up a hand, silencing me. "What part of this do I have to spell out for you? I'm. A. Fucking. Prick!"

But he wasn't. Not really. He was Kade, the guy with a plethora of issues, a beautiful soul, and a huge heart he didn't know how to trust. The first of my tears fell and I rushed back into his arms, inhaling as much sandalwood and oakmoss as I could in case I never smelled it again.

Kade buried his face in my hair and his arms locked around me. His shoulders relaxed as he let out a sigh, followed by a hushed cry. "I wish I knew how to be normal," he whispered, his voice breaking.

My heart constricted, squeezed in an ironclad vice, and tightening with every word. I shrugged. "It's a process."

"Why can't I skip a couple steps?"

My shoulders wracked before my sobs broke free, punching my chest—loud and unbroken, they ripped my throat apart. I was unable to take in a breath; but I couldn't help the small, gruff laugh that escaped as tears rolled down my cheeks. "What would Dr. Jesionowski say to that?"

He stood back and sighed, wiping the tears from my face. His cheeks were wet too. "She'd say things take time and rushing it won't make it easier."

Why the fuck did I ever suggest therapy?

Because I loved him, and I wanted him to be healthy. *Oh, right... Fuck me for caring, I guess.*

"We should trust the woman with the degree, right? Even if it means we can't be together." My stomach dropped, another sob wrenching from my throat as I realized someday Kade might fall for someone new, someone he could overcome his panic for.

I wasn't enough. A steel dagger dipped in alcohol and set ablaze stabbed me in the chest, puncturing my lungs. I burned, third degree, on the verge of suffocating.

Kade stayed silent, looking down at his feet. It was time for me to go, but his arms refused to let me go. He was unable to make the final move. I let out a slow breath and took it for him. I slid my fingers into his hair to remember the softness of his waves and traced the contours of his face. Tears pricked in his eyes, and it made it easier to know it was killing him as much as me.

"With my issues, this was never going to be easy, was it?" He asked, a single tear rolling down each cheek.

"Nothing worth having ever is." I pressed my forehead against his.

He tried to smile, but barely managed a crooked upturn before his mouth dropped again.

"It's not okay. We're not okay," I cried, another dagger in my heart as he let out a whimper. I nuzzled my nose against his, swallowing down the urge to apologize. The last thing I wanted was to hurt him, but this—

This was all Kade. My brain screamed to tell him to go to hell, my heart pined to kiss him, my soul refused to let me believe it was over for good, despite knowing better.

"Think of it as another experiment of ours. We won't text, won't call, won't email... And maybe with some distance, you'll realize what you want." Hope was a double-edged sword, cutting me up inside. But it was all I could cling to, and I was clinging on for dear life.

"And what if you're the one who realizes you don't want me?" he asked.

"What if the world was made of pink elephants and unicorns?" I retorted. Kade blinked, his eyebrows pulling down. He took a look around, as though imaging his apartment in such a world. I giggled. "See how stupid that question sounded?"

"Fucking moronic." Kade's mouth twitched up into a sad smile. Lifting my chin, I closed my eyes as his lips brushed against mine, long and sweet before deepening into something new. It wasn't passion, or lust... No, Kade kissed me as though he feared he'd never get another chance. His left hand wound up into my hair and his right hand cupped my face.

I was the one who broke the kiss before I sank too far into it, knowing if I didn't, I would happily die by his kiss if it meant I could stay with him. But as I caught glimpse of his eyes, relief hiding behind the tears and hurt, I sucked my lips into my mouth so I couldn't press them to his once more.

I sniffled, forcing the sob at the back of my throat to stay where it was. "It's not okay," I whispered, my thumbs tracing the edge of his mouth... and then, we said goodbye.

CHAPTER 34

KADE

I couldn't stand the silence. For two weeks, it had been unwavering stillness.

The second Liana left, I drowned my sorrows in whiskey, reminded of why I'd emailed her in the first place. The aching loneliness that came from being with my own thoughts was paralyzing. But in the midst of my inner turmoil lay a revelation: I had been using Liana as a crutch because I was scared of being alone.

It wasn't right of me. Liana deserved the world. She deserved the earth-stopping kiss, the background orchestra, the emotion, the intensity; the love she so badly craved. And though it would kill me, I knew that she'd have better luck finding it without me. So, I let her go, and I let her stay gone.

Every inch of me begged to call her, to go to her apartment in Brooklyn and plead her forgiveness. I regretted letting her leave as soon as the panic attack—Dr. Jesionowski's official diagnosis—subsided. But how was I supposed to ask her to come back when another attack could hit at any moment? Only for me to ask her to leave again. That wasn't fair to her.

Three-quarters of the way through self-analyzing, and a bottle of whiskey, a knock sounded at the door.

My heart leapt in my chest. "Liana?" I rushed for the door so fast I almost lost a leg as I tripped over my foot. I ripped back the hardwood and the aching pang in my chest lessened slightly, edged out by warmth. My hope to see Liana standing there died, replaced by relief and delight. I smiled—not a full grin, but a small one.

"Stephanie."

"Hey, brother," she beamed. It was my first time seeing her since the trial. Her face was bare and smiling; young and radiant. The bruising on her arms was almost completely gone, and for the first time in as long as I could remember, she didn't look on the verge of tears. "Got a cup of coffee for an old friend?"

I opened my arms and she fell into them, squeezing me tightly with the arm not holding her duffle bag. My nose landed in her hair, inhaling the scents of coconut and blueberry conditioner. Letting her go, I stepped aside and let her cross the threshold.

"Don't worry. I won't be here more than the night. I'm thinking I need a fresh start. I found an apartment I'm interested in, and I'm waiting on a confirmation. After that, I'll leave you and Liana to your bliss. Where *is* Liana?" She dropped her duffle by the door.

So many ways to say it landed in my head.

Liana moved out because we needed space.

I decided it would be best if we took some time apart and she agreed.

Liana and I decided we moved too fast.

All acceptable answers and all somewhat true. But when I opened my mouth, I couldn't repel the truth anymore. "I fucked up, Stephanie. I really fucked up."

Steph sighed, taking a seat at my kitchen island. "Tell me what happened."

I lay my arms on the marble countertop, cold on my skin, and reached for a bottle of whiskey. Stephanie's hand blocked mine. "It won't help, and you don't need it." She took it from the table and twisted the lid back on. "Talk."

I hung my head. "I had a panic attack and broke up with her." It sounded harsh when I said it that way, but it was true. I ran my hands through my hair and sighed. "I'm such a stupid asshole."

"Why would you do that?"

"Because she's the first woman I've ever loved, and it terrifies me." Steph's eyes widened. "I love her so much."

"Have you told her?"

Oh, sure, because that's something I would do. "Why wouldn't I have told her? I'm a normal person, so open with my feelings. I don't have a panic attack every single time the word edges closer to the tip of my tongue. It was easy for me to tell my first ever girlfriend all about being so in love with her, I can't breathe when I think about her." I scoffed, my jaw hardening. "Of course I haven't fucking told her..."

Stephanie didn't blink. I was being a dick, and she barely reacted. Oh, how I'd missed her.

"When did you realize you loved her?"

"Right around the time I saw her shoes piled mountain-style in the corner of my bedroom and realized I wanted it to stay there forever." The corner looked so bare without them, now.

"You freaked because you realized you had a live-in girlfriend?"

"No." I gulped down the lump in my throat and forced the truth to come out of my mouth. "I panicked when I realized I *wasn't* freaking out. I know it makes no sense, but Liana living here was like sunshine and daisies, sing-along musicals in my brain every day, *Sleepless in Seattle*, When Harry met goddamn Sally... My life was finally good. I was finally happy. I was a goddamn Disney princess."

"So, what happened?"

I sighed. "The niggling voice at the back of my head whispered that I don't deserve her. And it's right. I don't. Because I'm a horrendous prick who spent the better part of a decade slamming my way through New York's female population to stave off the nightmare in my head. I used so many good women to avoid dealing with my own shit." The shame rose in me, lurching acid into my throat. "Why should I get to be with someone as good as Liana? She should be dating the kindest, most well-mannered, most amazing man in the world. Instead, she's stuck with me and my back catalogue of trauma and shitty attitude because I *chose* to get her involved in my trainwreck of a life. How is that fair to her?" By the time I got out the last syllable, the tears welled my eyes. I pushed them back, blowing out my cheeks.

"You're a fucking idiot." Stephanie scoffed, hopping down from her chair. She stalked back and forward, muttering under her breath, and glaring.

"What?" I asked.

"Your lack of self-awareness is astounding," she spat. "Christ, Kade, you're the reason I'm standing here fighting to regain control of my life. You're the reason Liana is confident enough to go through with her expansion. And nobody is kinder than you are. Sure, you're brash and a dick, but you're the most amazing person I've ever met!" She said, so vehemently I almost believed her. "And if it wasn't for you, I never would've made it to New York. I might have caved to the pressure and died by the needle or worse. But you made sure I didn't give in. You made sure I stayed fighting. And I refuse to let you shit all over yourself because... you saved my life, you asshat!"

I took a breath, my eyes softening. "Steph..."

"No! If you want to tell someone how unworthy you are, it's not gonna be me. Or Liana, because I guarantee that girl loves you. And she's never once thought she was too good for you."

"But she is too good!" I yelled.

Stephanie smirked, crossing her arms across her chest. "If you think so highly of her, then ask yourself: would someone like her, who is so smart, beautiful, and kind, think so little of herself she'd slum it with some 'prick' who doesn't deserve her?" She flicked an eyebrow, as though she'd made a great point. She hadn't.

"Some of the best people in this world have been with people who don't deserve them. You were..."

She took a step back, her mouth hanging open. Scowling, she narrowed her eyes. "By saying that, you put yourself on the same level as Cleo. Are you the same as my abusive ex-girlfriend, Kade?" I opened my mouth to argue, and then closed it again. "I didn't think so." Her voice grew softer. "You have to get it out of your head that you're somebody who doesn't deserve to be loved."

Her words hit me like a bus. But it was too late now...

"I fucked up, Stephanie," I repeated.

"So, fix it..."

⁓‿⌒‿⸳

S tephanie and I settled in front of the TV and watched some of the trash shows she liked. I stopped myself rolling my eyes every five seconds, or every time I heard the word '*bible*' in place of 'I swear.' It was mind numbing but I suffered through them for her. She grinned, laughing at every stupid joke—so unburdened and relaxed, eating the popcorn Liana bought for our movie night... *until I messed it up.* God, would the ache in my chest ever go away?

A beeping on Stephanie's phone drew her attention, and mine. I looked over to find her grinning, her butt wiggling in her seat like she was dancing. My brow crinkled as she caught me staring.

"Oh, it's nothing." She pushed her phone back into her pocket.

It didn't seem like nothing, but I let it go.

For dinner, we ordered Chinese food and played poker with a set I found in the back of my closet, left over from the previous owners of my apartment. We sat on the floor in the middle of my spacious living room with a pile of chips between us, the full-moon high in the sky outside.

"Do you think the moon is this big and bright in Chicago?" she asked, a sigh at her lips.

What? "Probably," I said. "I don't know shit about the moon. Why?"

She shrugged, laying down her hand. Two pairs, not bad. I had a straight. Stephanie sighed.

"We're not playing for actual money, right? Because I'm fresh out." She sat back, leaning on her hands. "I can write you a check that will definitely bounce."

My hands paused, mid-shuffle. I eyed her curiously as she fidgeted under my stare. I frowned, crinkling my eyebrows. "What happened to your savings?"

My biggest fear was Cleo having blown through them. In hindsight, that would have hurt less.

Stephanie bit her lip. "There's something I need to tell you."

I winced. Nothing good ever came after those words. I stayed quiet, waiting for her to spit it out. She sighed, pulling her knees to her chin, and avoided my eyes.

"I bought an apartment," she said, almost in a whisper, looking at her feet. I was at a loss as to why that would be a bad thing, until she said, "In Chicago."

Excuse me? Did I hear that right? "I think I'm having an aneurysm, because there's no way you said what I think you said."

"Kade," She breathed out. "I can't stay in New York. There are too many bad memories here. Cleo is in prison at Rikers, thirty minutes away. I feel like I'm tethered to her. Plus, my grandma is sick, and I miss home."

But what about me? "What about our partnership?" I asked, instead.

"We live in the age of Facetime," she said. "I can work from Chicago. And I can fly back and forth when you need me." She finally looked at me and pushed as much optimism into her voice as she could. "Nothing is going to change. Families live in different states all the time. Doesn't mean you're not my brother."

If she was trying to convince me her moving was a good idea with her words, it wasn't working. What did work, was the look in her eye.

"This is what you want?" I asked. "You think you could be happy in Chicago?"

She nodded. "I do."

"Okay." I hung my head and let out a low breath. As much as I hoped she would stay with me, the last thing I wanted was to be the reason she was unhappy. "I don't know what I'm going to do without you, but *okay*."

Stephanie grinned. "Maybe you should come home with me for a couple weeks?"

I appreciated the sentiment, but the thought of being back in Chicago—walking by the brownstone where my mom died, or the park where I lived, knowing Garret was in prison there— it caused the acid in my stomach to swirl and revolt up my throat. I shook my head.

Sighing, I finished shuffling the deck of cards and dealt us a hand each. "At least we get to have Christmas together before you go." I grimaced seeing her face change. "You won't be here for Christmas, will you?"

Again, her eyes moved everywhere other than on me.

I swallowed the urge to whine like a child and forced myself to ask the question. "When do you go?"

Stephanie flinched, her cheeks turning red. "I leave for the airport in three hours."

"*What*?" I demanded. My jaw set. "Why didn't you tell me? Buying an apartment takes time, so you've known about this for what? Two weeks? You didn't think I deserved the courtesy of knowing?"

She shrugged, her eyes glazing in tears as a sad smile pulled at her lips. "I didn't want our last night to be filled with a depressed stroll down memory lane and painful goodbyes," she cried. "And I didn't want to give you enough time to talk me out of it."

"But I wouldn't have." I was surprised as she was by the idea of accepting her going away. "As long as you're happy, Steph, I don't care where you are."

Was that a healthy response? I think it was. Note to self: send Dr. Jesionowski a fruit-basket. Liana deserved diamonds.

"You mean that?" Her mouth lifted up into a wide grin.

I smiled, nodding my head. "Of course, I do."

Once again Stephanie launched herself into my arms, squeezing me tight. I squeezed back as hard, but I refused to cry, knowing it would make leaving harder for her if I did. Instead, we ate our Chinese food and played poker all the way up until it was time for her to leave. We didn't say goodbye or act like it was permanent, rather like she was going on a long trip, and I would see her soon.

When it was time, I walked her out to the street and hailed a cab. Sliding in the back with her, I held her hand from my building until the wheels of the car rolled to a stop outside JFK. I carried her duffel bag for her, noting how light it was. She'd packed extraordinarily little from her life in New York.

A fresh start, indeed.

I managed to keep my composure as Stephanie checked in, I kept it as the overhead voice called for her to board, I even kept it as I said *see you soon* to my best friend with a smile on my face, knowing I wouldn't see her soon. I watched her wander, apprehensively, through the gate; turning back to take one last look. Her eyes were filled with tears, but her mouth was turned up at the edges and spread so wide, it took up half her face—the excitement of a new life beckoning her. I gave an encouraging nod of the head as she finally turned the corner out of sight.

And that's when I unraveled. The water flooding my eyes was kept at bay by sheer willpower alone. Inside, I was a mess. Stephanie was the only family I had, and the thought of her not being in New York was a new and strange desolation—one engulfed in joy. It made no sense that the two emotions could go hand in hand. How could I be happy about being sad?

I held it together until my feet trudged through the snow outside of the airport. And then... I let the tears fall. They came down thick and fast, the lump in my throat so big, I could drown on my tears before I managed a breath. I reached up, using the sleeve of my cotton gray overcoat to soak the emotions up. I smiled. "This will be good for her," I said to myself, and prayed it would be true.

It had to be.

The universe owed Stephanie Taylor a happy life, and if that was in Chicago, then I hoped she never came back.

Chapter 35

Liana

Christmas day was quiet. Lonely. Spent with eggnog, movies, and other broken hearts on the internet. They asked for my help, I gave them all the raw emotion I had, hoping my own hurt would give them some insight into their own.

Kade hadn't reached out beyond manuscripts sent back and forth. In the first two weeks, I hadn't expected him to, but we were nearing a month with no personal contact. The good news was that I could think about him without crying. The bad news was that I hadn't managed to stop thinking about him, even for a minute.

I wrapped myself in a crazy big green blanket that doubled as a hoodie and sat at the rickety thing I called a dining table, tapping the keyboard of my laptop as gentle as I could for fear the rusted metal would collapse if I typed too hard. Adding cinnamon to a mug of half-eggnog, half-Irish coffee, I drank it down as I finished the requests in my inbox and announced the end of beta rounds.

The sextion was finally ready.

All that was left was to approve the designs and advertise

the launch. Jana called me early in the morning to wish me a merry Christmas, and to tell me she was sending the final designs over—rectified with my suggestions of toning them down—along with her marketing plan.

I sucked down the remnants from the bottom of the mug and waited for my laptop to beep. When it did, I jumped at it— the most pathetic part of me hoping to see Kade's name in my inbox, even if it was only another job for me to do. His sign off, *Sincerely, Kade,* was worth the ache of his words being cold and professional. My hopes dashed seeing Jana's name at the top of my emails. I sighed and double-clicked.

'MERRY CHRISTMAS!

Here are the final designs. I feel like everybody thinks of sex and chooses a black background. But this isn't a porn site, it's a safe space for curiosity, so I chose a fuchsia pink conceptual pattern on a gunmetal gray background. It's neutral, it's sexy, and it goes with the black-and-white header I chose. I already have ads out on Instagram promoting the launch. See attached for details on the event I planned for you.

I hope you love my genius as much as I do! So excited and proud...

Love, J.'

I scrolled down to see the header was an image of a sultry woman who looked eerily like me, winking with a finger to her lips. Beside it, a tagline read, *Ask me your questions, tell me your secrets...*

The design wasn't over-the-top sexy, just the right amount of hot. It was perfect. Jana's 'genius' event was me answering questions from both sections in real time on New Year's Eve before the launch. It was a great idea and allowed me to interact with fans, but I was yet to feel excited. As far as I was concerned, New Year's Eve was but another night I'd spend without Kade.

My gut punched; I took a look around my apartment and the gnawing emptiness expanded in my stomach. It was around this time that Kit and I used to watch movies and attack piles of junk food like we'd never seen chocolate before. At the very least I could keep that tradition alive, even if I did it alone.

With an armful of snacks, I carried my laptop into the corner I'd carved out as a living area and sunk down into one of the two beanbag chairs bought at a clearance sale. My movie playlist loaded, I scrolled through. It felt wrong to pick a movie without an argument and a million veto's first.

I pressed play on *The Holiday* and cried alongside Iris as she found out her asshole ex-boyfriend announced his engagement to someone else. The thought of Kade getting married someday was like a dagger to the chest. I hiccoughed and sniffled. As far as Christmas movies go, this one was on the lighter side, but there I was sobbing as though I was watching a Nicholas Sparks marathon. I cried from credits to credits. My faced burned as I rubbed at my eyes until they were puffy and pink.

The sound of a fist pounding on my sliding door echoed through the room, making me jump. My breath hitched and my stomach burst with butterflies and hope that it was Kade coming to declare his love the same way Amanda did for Graham in the movie.

Placing my laptop on the floor, I fought to get out of my beanbag. Fuck, I forgot how much suction the damn beans held. My only option was to roll out of it. I threw myself to the side, landing on the hard floor, face down before scrambling to my feet and launching myself at the door. I twisted the lock and ripped it open, my hope dying a violent death as I found the abominable snowman on the other side—or rather, Luka covered head-to-toe in snow, with a suitcase at his side.

"Hey," I answered, dejected.

"Nice to see you, too," he laughed on the other side of the threshold. Holding up a bottle of vodka, he sighed. "I just got dumped on Christmas. As the only other single and sad person I know, I thought you'd be in the mood to wallow with me?"

"God yes." I grabbed the bottle and moved aside to welcome him in as I went to the only cupboard in my kitchen, in search of plastic cups. Luka closed the door behind him and surveyed my outfit.

"Wow, Lee, you look..." he started, grimacing at my ensemble of sweatpants and blanket hoodie, fluffy socks, and Crocs. "...like you've escaped from a locked ward somewhere."

I laughed, filling each cup halfway and topping them off with pineapple juice, the only mixer in the fridge.

"Funny, that's how I feel, too." I handed him a glass. "What's with the suitcase?"

Luka sighed at the ceiling. "Well, my boss wants to send me to Rome tonight, and before my now ex-girlfriend delivered her brutal dumping, I was going to surprise her with tickets for a romantic getaway. I only have to work for two days, but the room was booked to stay over the New Year."

I winced. "Oof, that blows. What are you going to do?"

He shrugged. "I told my boss what happened. He's trying to get one of the married partners and their spouse to take my place, but it's all up in the air. I'm waiting on his call. Until then, I'm all yours. What do you want to do?"

The edges of my mouth twisted into a playful smirk. "When was the last time you watched *Bridget Jones*?"

Luka grinned, hanging his head. "My birthday, junior year."

"Pull up a beanbag and grab a snack, DiMaggio. It's movie time."

He laughed and tugged on the back of my hoodie-blanket as I passed him on my way back to the living. "What is this? And why do I want to wear it?"

I snorted. "It's an Oodie, and I have another in pink if you're interested. It's on my bed."

He didn't need to be told twice. Pulling back the divider to my bedroom, he emerged in a flamingo pink hoodie. "It should be illegal to be this comfy." He flopped back onto the beanbag beside me as I pressed play.

Having Luka over was nice. It didn't replace the hole in my heart left by Kade, or Kit, but it helped to know I wasn't the only person in the world hurting. High school Luka and Liana would be so happy to see us hanging out like this, neither of us harboring any grudges or an unspoken crush. We were back to the way we'd been when we were ten, before hormones and feelings got in the way.

For the first time in a month, a flicker of happiness flitted through me. Which was why, when his phone rang halfway through the movie, I hoped he wouldn't have to go on his business trip.

"Hello," he answered, and then his face contorted into a deep scowl. "Yes, sir. I'll head to the airport now. I understand. Thank you for trying."

I pouted. "If it means anything, I wish you didn't have to go," I said, and then realized how stupid I sounded. An all-expenses paid vacation in Rome sounded like heaven. "Actually, if I'm wishing for things, I wish *I* could go."

Luka's beamed, his eyes alight with an idea. "Why don't you? I have two tickets, and we're both miserable in Manhattan. Maybe a best friend trip to Rome is exactly what we need! It's perfect because they say misery loves company, and there is no one else I'd rather be miserable with. Flight leaves from JFK in two hours. What do you say?"

I didn't know what to say. My mouth propped open as I pondered his proposal.

Rome, my favorite place in the entire world. At least there I wouldn't be sat staring at the same four walls, getting drunk on eggnog and Irish coffee, feeling like I could burst into tears at any given moment. Even if a trip to Italy didn't help, it couldn't hurt. It's not like I would be more miserable surrounded by succulent carbohydrates and the world's best gelato. And launching my new section from Rome was a power move.

As far as I could see, going to Italy with Luka was all pros and no cons.

"Okay, I'm in." I closed my laptop and wrapped it up with its charger, ready to chuck it into my suitcase. "I should probably change first."

"Don't you dare. If you don't wear an Oodie in first class, I'll look stupid. And I refuse to take this off ever again."

With a snort, I grabbed enough clothes for five days and stuffed them, unfolded, on top of my laptop in my suitcase. Next, I packed the essentials. Underwear, two sets of pajamas, a toothbrush, toothpaste, and a hairbrush later, I was fully packed and ready to go in the space of five minutes.

Luka ordered a cab service as I switched out my Crocs for boots. As it arrived, we ran out of the door to meet our driver on the street and heaved our suitcases into the back with us, neither of us caring how cramped we were.

Everything was happening so fast. An hour ago, I was steadfast in drinking and crying alone. Now, I was en route to the airport with Luka, Italy-bound. Absurd, I thought, and then I belly laughed for the first time since Kade dumped me, and I didn't stop until the car wheels stopped spinning at JFK.

By the time we went through security and got checked in, the flight was near-boarding. We made our way to the first class lounge where we ordered two bottles of beer and took a seat at the bar.

"Who would have thought two people as hot as we are would be drowning our sorrows on Christmas?" Luka offered a pitying smile. "Speaking of heartache, do you want to talk about him?"

I shook my head, my eyes welling up again.

Luka's mouth drew into a pensive line, only perking up when he got an idea. "Why don't we take a picture?"

His phone was out before I could intervene. He held it out at arm's length to get us both in the frame and held up our plane tickets with his spare hand. I put my head on his shoulder and forced a smile, throwing up a peace sign and hoping the bags under my tired, cried-out eyes wouldn't be *too* visible.

"I need a witty caption," he said. "Is *When In Rome* too cliché?"

I nodded. "How about *Rome-ing the world*?"

He grinned, typing it out on screen. "*Rome-ing the world with the beautiful and brilliant, @LianaDawson.* Perfect." He tagged me in the photo and slipped his phone back into his pocket as the overhead voice announced it was time to board.

Luka offered me his hand. "You ready?"

"To go to the other side of the world?" I hesitated. Would I still think about Kade with that much distance between us? Probably, but maybe the time away would help me heal and move on. It had to, because if I couldn't, if my heart stayed broken, I wasn't sure how long I'd be able to keep from drowning.

Four thousand two hundred and seventy-nine miles away from New York, four thousand two hundred and seventy-nine miles away from Kade. *Would it be far enough?*

I slipped my hand into Luka's, letting him wrap his arm around me as we boarded the plane, and took my seat beside him in first class, my mind flooded with thoughts of Kade as I stared out of the window at the tarmac below us. Somewhere in the city, he was celebrating Christmas. Was he alone? Or had he reverted back to his life of endless one-night stands?

Both hurt in different ways, but the thought of another woman in the bed we used to share was like acid burning a hole in my stomach. My heart ached, crushed under the weight of not knowing, and I bit back the tears threatening to spring free from my eyes. Sinking back in my seat, I closed my eyes and prayed.

Please, God, let it be far enough...

CHAPTER 36

KADE

F uck Christmas.

CHAPTER 37

KADE

O*of, my head felt like it had been run over by a goddamn dump truck.*

Through cracked eyes, I lifted it from the pillow to see it was light outside. Why was I on the floor? This was hangover behavior, but I hadn't drunk a single whiskey—not even when I woke up on Christmas morning, alone and Liana-less. What a swell time to make a bullshit promise to Dr. Jesionowski that I would cut back.

Fuck.

I couldn't fathom why I had concrete blocks in my eyes and a jackhammer piercing my brain. But then, I looked up to find Liana's movie playlist displayed on my TV, and I realized my migraine came from sitting on the floor, crying to movies all night like a fucking teenage girl, and hugging the pillow she left until I passed out. It smelled like lemons and lavender. *God, it hurt.* My chest constricted like a python had wrapped itself around me, intending to squeeze me to death.

Was this heartbreak? I think it was. I was heartbroken. *'Tis the season, my ass.* I'd cried for three days, and only now did I feel like my eyes were empty. I wasn't worried, though. They would fill back up in time to sob like a newborn as the ball dropped on the New Year in sixteen hours.

Stephanie found a place in Chicago, under her grandmother's maiden name, and gave me a virtual tour on Christmas day before she grilled my ass on Liana. It was a nice place. She seemed happy there, happier than she ever was in New York. I tried not to let that sting, but it did anyway.

"Have you talked to Liana yet?" she had asked, for the millionth time in two weeks. And my answer was the same every time:

"I'm building up to it."

Her response was to roll her eyes and start another pain in the ass tirade on how I needed to make my move, grumbling with daggers shooting at me through the phone screen. *Yikes,* she was scary when she was pissed. But I held the ultimate Uno reverse card now—the best part of having a best friend over Facetime; the ability to hang up on her, which I had, many times since she left. And every time, I received the same text after:

'*Asshole.*'

I last spoke to Steph five days ago. Not through lack of trying on her part, but because I was preoccupied spending my time wallowing in self-pity to answer her calls. The profanity that snowballed in her texts was extensive, even for me.

I chuckled for a moment, but then the gaping ache swallowed me again.

It's not that I didn't want to reach out to Liana. I did. In fact, I was halfway out the door in nothing but my boxers—ala *Bridget Jones*—ready to run to Brooklyn in the snow if that's what it took. But then I saw the photo of her and Luka, in matching Oodies, on their way to Rome for a romantic trip, and stopped dead.

The caption he posted made me nauseous. '*... with the beautiful and brilliant, @LianaDawson.*'

He wasn't wrong. She was beautiful, and brilliant, and far too good for that prick.

Okay, maybe he wasn't a prick. Maybe I was jealous.

I was definitely jealous.

But how else was I supposed to feel when the girl of my dreams jetted off with the guy she thought of as the love of her life, and it was all my fault? It should have been me in a flamingo pink Oodie with my arm wrapped around Liana.

My eyes stung, but no tears came. Dried out, like I said. I sighed, hanging my head. I sat back on my sofa, my open laptop staring me in the face with that goddamn picture of the happy couple on Instagram. I slammed the lid shut and threw myself back, groaning.

Worse than feeling like I let my one chance at happiness to slip through my fingers was the peace I held inside knowing Liana was loved. Luka loved her. He could give her everything she wanted. He was the guy she shared the epic love story with.

And I had watched enough chick flicks to know now that I was the side character in their love story. The guy she almost ended up with, only to tell her grandchildren of her lucky escape one day. I harrumphed, resolving to stay away from her and let her live her life without any more interference from the goddamn plot device.

It stung like a million papercuts dipped in salt, but I was okay. I would always be okay, so long as she was happy.

Her playlist updated on my TV screen, and I furrowed my brows. Huh. If she was so happy, why was she watching *The Notebook*? Stephanie always said that was a movie to watch when nursing a broken heart.

Was she heartbroken too? It was mid-afternoon in Rome. She should have been out gallivanting and making memories with her boyfriend. *Unless...*

I launched myself from the couch like a cannonball and scrambled for my remote on the floor. My knees collided with the oakwood, and I winced, letting out a low hiss. Pushing myself back onto the sofa, I clicked play and watched alongside her.

Noah and Allie were an explosive couple. They argued a lot —bickered more than they talked, actually. But they shared a deep connection neither of them could shake. One that withstood the death of a parent, Noah's depression, and Allie falling in love with someone else.

My heartbeat broke every bone in my chest as I watched the credits roll, tears in my eyes. Liana was hurting. She had to be.

I burned all over.

Inspired, I sniffled, and pulled my laptop onto my knee. Opening a blank document to start my first of what would become a year's worth of emails, I grinned and then stopped.

What was I thinking? I didn't have a year. She was in one of the most romantic cities in the world with her ex-(possibly-not-ex)-boyfriend.

Fucking moron.

I needed to think fast and act faster. After a month spent watching rom-coms, I had to have something up my sleeve by now—some big declaration I could make to let her know I was in love with her. I sighed, the niggling in my head once again told me to leave her alone. But the rest of me, the parts on fire when I thought of her, said I would regret it if I didn't try.

And before I knew what I was doing, I took a page out of a million classic romances. I bought a last-minute cancellation ticket for Rome that left in less than an hour. I ran from my apartment with nothing but my phone, my passport, and my wallet. I didn't even grab a jacket to throw over my sweatpants and week-old black T-shirt; shivering in the snow outside as I hailed a cab. Catching my reflection in the window before I climbed in the back, I winced. Christ, the bags under my puffy eyes were bad, and my unbrushed hair was sticking in a hundred different directions. Like a college stoner was not how

I imagined I would look when I saw Liana again, but beggars can't be choosers. It was now or never.

"JFK," I yelled to the driver. "As fast as you can..."

T he skies were black outside of the windows as we touched down on the tarmac in Rome, Italy. I basked in the knowledge Liana was somewhere in this beautiful city and sighed when I realized I had no idea *where*. I really hadn't thought this through.

I checked both her and Luka's Instagram's on my way through the airport, hoping for a sign somewhere—a landmark or a hotel detail, anything to give me the general vicinity.

I checked the time on my phone. Eleven fifteen p.m. *Would she kiss Luka at midnight and realize he was the one she loved?*

I groaned, making my legs work faster. I ran through the terminal, coming out at the front of Roma Urbe Airport, my knees swollen, sore and bruised under my sweatpants. According to Liana's Instagram, she'd stayed at three hotels in Rome, and I intended to check them all until I found her.

My heart thumping, I slid into the backseat of a taxi and gave the man the first address by showing him my phone. He nodded, waving his thumb as we set off. The first hotel was huge, a white bricked building in the shape of a semi-circle. Keeping the driver waiting, I rushed inside and thrust the photo of Liana and Luka into the face of the receptionist. All I got was a head shake as a response.

Shit! One down, two to go and only twenty-five minutes to midnight. If I didn't find her before she kissed Luka, I could lose her forever. It was always the final kiss that counted in the movies. That one moment cemented the ending couple. If it was Liana and Luka, I feared I would never recover.

The second hotel, only a few *strides* away, was a smaller

place with lights above and below every window. I imagined that would get annoying through the night, and Liana must have thought so, too, because she was nowhere to be found.

Dammit! Dammit! Dammit!

Fuck. My knees throbbed like someone hit me with a sledgehammer as I ran back to the cab and gave the driver the final address.

The third place on her Instagram was more akin to a hostel than a hotel. A small, one story place with boarded up windows and people smoking and drinking outside. I didn't bother going in to check. No way Luka would be caught dead staying there. Though it made sense that Liana had. Each trip, her accommodation worsened. From her father's credit card to her salary at Liberty, to her last trip a week after she quit her job.

I got back in the taxi, dejected, and muttered the first words that came to mind when I thought of Rome.

"Trevi Fountain, *per favore.*"

I figured it was as good a place as any to look. Liana's Instagram was ninety percent her trips around Italy, but nowhere had she taken more photos than the fountain. Fireworks burst in the sky above the taxi, and I realized it would be easier to find a needle in a haystack. There were crowds of people everywhere, waiting for midnight.

The driver slammed on the breaks as we rolled up to the hordes congregating around the fountain. He shook his head and held out his hand, which I took to mean he couldn't get through the people and expected his fare. I winced, remembering I only had dollars.

"*Scusami.*" I apologized, throwing my entire wallets worth of dollars at him. I jumped out of his car as he yelled something out of my understanding. I assumed he called me an asshole.

I didn't mind. *I was used to it.*

I ran through the crowds as another firework popped overhead. Italian music played loudly through a speaker by the fountain, and families were out in force to dance and sing. I pushed past them as carefully as I could, searching for that gorgeous head of red hair.

Truthfully, I didn't expect to find her. Which is why when I spotted her perched on the side of the fountain, working on her laptop, I realized...

I had no fucking clue what to say to her.

Her head popped up like an adorable meerkat, looking around. I froze, it was almost as if she could feel me. The cruel tricks of my mind convinced me the longing on her face was for me. But it was impossible. As far as she was concerned, I was in Manhattan.

I checked my time on my phone again. *Eleven fifty-eight.* Again, her head popped up, probably in search of Luka. The thought hurt, but I wouldn't let it stop me. Even if she chose him, at least I would never be left with dreaded what-ifs.

Eleven- fifty-nine... One minute to go. No time like the present.

My breath hitched, a fuzzy feeling bursting in my chest as I pushed through the crowds to get to her. Or limped, as it was; both of my knees almost giving out at the sight of her.

"Liana," I yelled, but she didn't hear me. I tried again. "Liana!"

Her eyes searched the crowds before colliding with mine, and my heart stopped completely. Her mouth popped open, and her eyes filled with tears. I froze, breathless, unable to move a muscle while she looked at me with those perfect lake-green eyes, alight with glistening affection. Her mouth curved into a grin as the first tear rolled down her cheek.

I couldn't believe I ever let her go. I was an idiot—a stupid, reckless moron. How did I ever think I could live without her gazing at me that way?

Never again.

I would go to therapy for the rest of my life to be sure I wouldn't fuck this up.

Battling through the crowds, I moved toward her as fast at lightning speed as a multitude of fireworks took to the sky, bursting in patterns of blue, greens, pinks and white. Bells rang in the distance and a chorus of "Valzer Delle Candele" sang out to the tune of "Auld Lang Syne" as I reached her. My mind was oblivious to the words I would use.

"Kade," she gasped as I snaked my arms around her body, pulling her to me. Her arms wound up into my hair. "What are you—"

Who the fuck needs words?

I cut her off by crashing my lips to hers as my hands gripped tight on her waist. I broke the kiss, nuzzling my nose against hers, and I couldn't keep it in any longer. "I love you," I whispered, my breath fanning her face. "I'm sorry I didn't tell you. I'm sorry I let you leave. I'm sorry—"

It was her turn to cut me off. She pressed her finger to my lips, the fire in her eyes dancing. "Say that again," she commanded. My eyes collided with hers and her breath hitched. "Say it…"

"I love you, Liana Dawson. With every fiber in my body, I love you… *I love you, I love you, I love you…*"

Tears stung in my eyes as I kissed her again. "I should have come after you the night you left," I said. "I was scared, and stupid."

"It's okay," she whispered, wiping my tears away. "You're worth the wait…"

Chapter 38

Liana

"I don't understand." I clicked refresh and watched the traffic on my site explode through the roof. "How do this many people know about the launch?"

It was close to six a.m. in Rome but nearing midnight in New York. The three of us were in a giant hotel room, paid for by Luka's boss, watching the ball drop online. The walls were a soft gold, the floors a hard marble, and works of art donned every single wall.

Luka poured three flutes full of champagne, handing one to me, one to Kade, and keeping one for himself.

"I don't know." He shrugged. "Didn't Jana say she would post an ad or something?"

"She did." But the ads were pay-per-view, which meant *this* amount of people would cost some coin I didn't have. "There was a budget limit."

"Perhaps it's word-of-mouth." Kade sipped his bubbly and sat down beside me. He spied my count over my shoulder, his eyes wide. "Perhaps people really like to talk."

I shook my head, my mouth dropping to my chest as I refreshed again, and the number hit half a million.

"Jesus Christ," Kade exclaimed. Luka joined my other side

with the same exclamation. I almost laughed, my two favorite guys in the world; the love of my life and my best friend, sat beside me on a long, emerald green chaise lounge, and they were civil. In fact, more than civil. Since Luka finished work and joined us in the room, he and Kade acted like long-lost friends.

"I don't understand," I repeated.

Luka pulled his phone from his pocket. His eyebrows narrowing, he gasped. "Maybe this has something to do with it."

I ripped the phone from him, my hand flying to my mouth. "Holy shit."

There were ads everywhere, but they weren't Jana's. I knew because of the photo used. A candid of me wearing my glasses and chewing on the edge of a pen. Somehow, I looked insightful, sexy, smart, and gorgeous. The picture was set against the sensual gunmetal gray background. Sprawled across it in near neon pink writing were the words: '*Love, Liana. Here for you when you need her.*' The caption wasn't written impeccably, but it did the job. It told people where they could find advice and mentioned the launch date for the sextion. It was enticing, and clearly, it worked.

It wasn't lost on me that the ad matched the aesthetic of the new section, and I wondered how much Kit's hand helped design it.

"Double holy shit," Kade said, scrolling through his own Instagram. Again, my mouth dropped.

Celebrities were posting about me. Authors, actors, singers— either reposting or endorsing my blog. I was on Stories, in the feed, a top trending topic on Twitter. It seemed Kit had hit up everyone on Eric Dawson's client list, resulting in nearly a million people flooding through my blog, leaving new comments on old advice.

How am I only now finding this blog?

Where was Liana when a month ago when I needed her! Subscribed!

Insightful and helpful. Liana has a talent...

I can tell what my new obsession is going to be! I already love this blog. Bring on the steamy responses.

Thousands of comments posting every minute. I gawped. Not all of them were complimentary, of course, there were a few trolls in the mix.

"This one says I look like a mix between a shaggy dog and rat," I snorted, and then grinned.

My heart leapt in my chest. Kit would suffer the consequences of this stunt for months from our father, already tweeting like crazy to disparage his client's posts, but she did it anyway. It wasn't a resignation handed in to Eric Dawson, or an eviction notice to Zoe, but it lit a spark of hope in my stomach —an olive branch that offered promise our sisterhood wasn't dead.

"The balls dropping." Luka jumped to his feet with a kazoo in his mouth ready to blow.

My nerves shot through the roof, watching the seconds tick by on the screen.

"Are you ready?" Kade lay his lips to my cheek, and I shivered. "Relax, sweetheart. I trained you well."

I smacked his chest, laughing. "Well, I trained you too."

Kade's smile stretched from ear-to-ear, so glorious to look at. "You did. And I am so thankful."

I grinned, wrapping my arms around his neck. He pulled me close and locked his hands on my waist as the countdown began.

"I love you," he said, and my heart burst hearing those words come from that beautiful mouth.

My body inundated with adrenaline. "I love you, too."

Ten, nine, eight, seven...

I fidgeted and stretched out my fingers, preparing to type as fast as I could for the live Q&A event Jana set up. My goal was to answer forty questions with advice, but with over a million people watching me, I decided I'd strive for at least a hundred before I went to sleep.

Six, five, four, three, two, one...

The vibrating, low-pitched kazoo in Luka's mouth rang out with a chorus of "Happy New Year" from the crowds in Times Square. I pressed the launch button as I crashed my lips to Kade's and melted into his kiss, only breaking it as my laptop gave an almighty ding, and then another, and another, and then I put it on mute as question after question poured in from both sections.

"Go become a sensation, Liana Dawson," he said. "And when you're done, come to me." Standing up, Kade kissed my forehead and headed for our bed on the left side of the room.

Luka smirked. "I guess he's not a *terrible* guy."

"Oh, yeah?" I chuckled. "You think you guys could be friends at some point?"

His face turned serious, his mouth pushing into a line as he looked me in the eyes and said, deadpan, "Liana, we have tickets to the next *Hamilton* show, and we're going to a Knicks game when we get back to Manhattan. Or maybe it was dinner and a movie when we got back and the Knicks game next month."

Oh, great. My boyfriend got a boyfriend. That was something new for Kade. But maybe it would do him good to have someone else to hang out with now that Stephanie lived in Chicago. Speaking of, my phone dinged beside me with an incoming message from her, congratulating me on my successful launch. We'd been texting back and forth since the trial ended, though most of it was her talking about Kade and I being as stubborn as each other.

As I moved to put my phone down, it dinged again in my hand.

'Congratulations, Lee. Nobody deserves it more. I love you, always. – Kit.'

"I'm going to bed." Luka headed for his room. "Have fun becoming a superstar."

As his door clicked shut, I let out an excited squeal and launched myself back on the chair and watched as the number grew and grew. Thousands of comments showed up each minute. Some thanked me for listening to my fans, others asked for another section soon. I ignored those, realizing I had been forced into the expansion, and while I was grateful to have so many people wanting my help, I decided I would be moving at my own pace from now on.

Picking a question from the bunch, I got to work on answering as many as I could. It hit three a.m., New York time, before I was too tired to carry on. With the widest smile on my face, I crawled into bed beside Kade and wrapped myself around him, laying kisses on the nape of his neck. He sighed, happily, as I pressed against him and nuzzled my nose into his back. It was hard to believe he was the same brash man who catfished me in a café using the alias of a little ghost boy. The one who feared himself a sociopath and confessed to never having experienced love. He was so different now. Not his attitude—that would never change—but the way he felt things. Once the dam broke, he flooded with so much emotion, he was delicate.

He turned to face me and puckered his lips. My stomach

fluttered as I pressed mine against his for a long, sweet kiss. He pulled back, letting out a gentle moan.

"I'm so proud of you," he whispered.

The corners of my mouth pulled higher. I was proud of him, too.

I watched him drift into a deep sleep. He was so beautiful and kind, happy and sad, fractured yet whole. A compelling enigma, Kade Jennings. And he was mine.

Forever...

Epilogue

Liana

Two years later

"Unfortunately, that's all we have time for today. As always, I will keep a record of all unanswered questions for next week. Until then, this has been *Ask Liana: Live*, episode twenty-two. Have a great day! *Love, Liana*..." I smiled. Talking into a camera was a weird experience, and I hadn't quite gotten the hang of reading the next question on the live chat while answering the last, but my newest venture was—so far—a success.

I ended the livestream in time to hear Kade snickering through the crack in his office door about a piece of advice I'd given. "Flatpack furniture leading to orgasms. I wonder where you got that from," he yelled, and I rolled my eyes; reminded of the night we set up his desk and shelves.

"Hmm. Well, when you go through three hours of pure hell with your fiancé because he decided he could put furniture together without any prior experience whatsoever, it sticks with you." I shuddered making my way over to the doorway of what used to be my old bedroom before we knocked down the walls between our two apartments. Now, it was Kade's office. His eyes lifted from his novel to roam my body.

"But you have to admit, it was satisfying when it was over."

I quivered, recalling the way he'd lifted me onto the completed desk, and we took all of our frustration out on each other's bodies.

"Speaking of…" I lifted my bare leg from under my skirt and straddled the doorframe, biting my lip, seductively. "I've finished my work for the day. How is your book coming?"

Kade groaned. "I'm begging you, stop biting you lip like that. I'm not doing well enough to take a break, and now I'm hard *and* on the verge of tears." He scoffed. "I can't cry with a fucking hard-on, Liana. It's not the natural way." Burying his head in his hands, he sighed. "I forgot how torturous writing is. It's like… Now the only analogy I can think of is flatpacks. I don't think I have the imagination to be a writer."

"Yes, you do." I moved to sit on the edge of his desk. "Your imagination isn't the problem, Kade. Writing the story of your life, seeing the words on the screen, it's got to be hard."

"It is." He nodded. "But therapeutic. Writing it all down, I get to remember the way my mom was before. Details of her are coming back to me as I go. Memories I didn't know I had. Happy ones. I get to show her for the woman she was. But then I want to delete everything after my seventh birthday and keep her character pure forever."

"Kade—"

"I know, I can't. If I start warping things to fit my ideal Disney childhood, I might as well start writing children's books…"

A terrifying thought. "The children would be scarred." I laughed as he stuck up his middle finger. "Ever the gentleman. Do you want some coffee?"

He moaned. "Say that again slowly, and preferably naked."

I winked. "Maybe you need something to motivate you," I lifted my shirt to flash him, a sneak peek. His mouth dropped open, almost drooling.

"I suppose I could take a small break."

I giggled, my eye colliding with the mahogany clock on the wall behind his head. I was already late to meet Kit. "If you finish two chapters by the time I get back, you can do whatever you want to me." I rounded the desk, pressing my mouth to his for a long, sultry kiss. "*Anything.*"

Kade groaned as I brushed his manhood with the back of my hand. "What do I get if I have three done?"

I smirked. "Write them and find out."

I brewed a pot of coffee, placing a mug on his desk before I left.

"Tell Kit I said hi," he yelled as the door closed. "And make sure you get lots of stretching in while you're out. You're going to need it."

I moaned, the imagery of what he would do pooled between my legs. I wanted to cave in, go back to his office and lie back on his desk as he ravaged me. But I already promised Kit I would help her unpack and set up in her new place while her new husband was hard at work on their newest venture. Of course, I would be the one doing the brunt of the unpacking. Ever since her infamous —not to mention *viral*—exit from The Dawson Talent Agency, blowing out the door like a tornado and taking Zoe down on her way, she'd been on a mission to take the publicist world by storm. So, the thought of her doing menial work with me, without having an input on every single aspect of their business, was laughable.

And I was right.

We'd barely unpacked a single box before Kit was in the office of her apartment with a list of ideas. I had to laugh as I heard my brother-in-law groan as she came up with five more on the spot.

In a way, I was glad Kit's attention wasn't on me because I didn't feel like hearing the words she said every time we hung out since I'd gotten engaged. *When are you guys going to set a date already? It's been two years!*

I sighed. Truthfully, I was starting to wonder if Kade and I would ever take that step. It was a huge thing for him to commit to an engagement, and I was happy (enough) to be known as his Kade Jennings' fiancée and introduce him as mine. But hearing Kit say *'my husband'* when she had been a relationship half the time I had... stung.

My eyes collided with a picture of Kit and her husband on their wedding day, smiling wide in the grandest hall of the plaza. A summer wedding, as she'd always wanted.

Me, I wanted a December wedding with a winter wonderland theme in that same hall. But as two Decembers passed, a third coming up, with Kade talking about our wedding as a distant future event, I decided to accept my role as a perpetual fiancée.

I finished the last box of Kit's stuff and headed out unnoticed. The air turned crisp and cold, signaling the end of November and the beginning of the Christmas season. I got giddy at the thought of hosting a packed apartment over the holidays. Stephanie would fly in from Chicago with her girlfriend; Luka, his fiancée, and their one-year-old twins would drive back to the city from the suburbs; and Kit and I would argue over movies while everyone else rolled their eyes.

Our own, dysfunctional family.

I t was dark out by the time I stepped off the elevator on my floor and opened our apartment door to find my fiancé naked and waiting for me with a can of whipped cream in one hand, a bowl of mint chip ice cream in the other, and standing next to a—

"Is that a swing?"

Kade grinned. "Same-day delivery, and this time I *swung* for a professional to put it together." He winked. "Isn't it great? I think we should have one of these in our honeymoon suite."

I stuttered a laugh. With the rate we were going, I doubt I'd be using a sex swing at eighty-five. Ignoring the punch in my gut, my eyebrow quirked. "Did you finish your three chapters?"

He nodded, pulling his bottom lip between his teeth. "You're quite the muse. I even decided how I was going to end the book."

I gawked at him, excitement worming its way through me. "Kade, that's amazing! How?"

A smirk twitching at the corners of his mouth, he set the bowl of ice cream on the table. Emerging with his phone from God knows where, Kade clicked play on a voicemail, his eyes alight with mischief.

"Hi, Mr. Jennings, I am calling to reconfirm your booking of the grand ballroom for December 31st of next year. If you could, please let us know you are still interested in having the Jennings-Dawson wedding at our hotel. Thank you."

What? My eyes were wide with tears welling in them as the words dawned. *I was getting married in a year.*

Tears pricked in my eyes. Kade made his way over to me, brushing the wetness from my cheeks. His mouth covered mine as my arms wound up, gripping his hair. Kade's eyes bore into mine, his hand grazing my cheek.

He whispered, "I was thinking it would end with a long-overdue wedding."

I couldn't breathe, couldn't speak. All I could do was nod and crash my lips to his, hard and fast. Kade's tongue moved against mine as he pressed me against the wall of our living room. His hands pinning my arms above my head, he broke the kiss, a dastardly smirk on his lips. His eyebrows waggled.

We were getting married. He'd surprised me with a winter wedding set at the Plaza. It was the most romantic thing he'd ever done, including following me to Italy to declare his undying love.

He nuzzled his nose against mine and my breath hitched as he kissed me again, soft, and sweet, his body vibrating as he pulled away. My heart fluttered, ready to hear a sonnet of how in love we were emit from his open mouth.

In typical Kade fashion, he looked me in the eye and said...

"Now, about this swing..."

If you enjoyed Liana and Kade's story, please consider leaving a review on Amazon and Goodreads.

ACKNOWLEDGMENTS

To start, I would like to thank my close friend, Brittany, for believing in this book—long before I did—and putting up with the relentless amount of editing and late-night discussions of what comes next. Without you, this book would not exist the way it is. You made me a better writer and stuck by me through meltdowns and sixty-thousand rewrites... *And then the final rewrites.* I can't thank you enough for the time and effort you've put into being there for me, and I'm so glad that one tweet brought you into my life.

Luz, my spirit twin. You were my first ever author friend, and the first person to ever set sights on the crazy story of Liana and Kade. You loved them in their first draft and are largely responsible for keeping them going until the end. You wouldn't let me give up on myself, and for you I will be eternally grateful. It's incredible to me that a single comment on a message board could become three years of amazing friendship. Here's to more!

Beth, you were the first person who ever told me I should be a writer, way back in college when we met. You've read everything I've ever written, including first chapters of bad ideas that will never see the light of day. Thank you for always supporting me, and for reading every single updated version of this book—and loving it more each time. Your feedback was invaluable.

Racheal and Kamara, my sisters, thank you for being excited to read this book. It makes me so anxious that it is now out in the world, and I can no longer stop you. Ha! I'm going to be on edge until I know every thought you have. Preferably texted to me at the end of each chapter...

Mam, thank you for listening to my incessant back-and-forth on this crazy dream of mine. For being there through the rejections and celebrating each yes. You're my best friend and I love you so much.

To my Dad, Nana, Nanny, and Grandads—If you're reading this, it should only be because I've showed you this *one* page. I will melt down and die on the spot if any of you ever read this book. Thank you for always supporting me.

Miss Robson, thank you for awakening me to the lovely world of words. I once told you that wherever I ended up, it would be because of you. Well, here we are...

My fellow authors, and the team at Lake Country Press & Reviews. Thank you for reading, for loving, for making my dream come true, and for believing in me. You have made my first foray into the world of publishing an absolute BLAST. I've had so much fun at every stage and loved being part of an awesome group of people.

And finally, to the readers. I appreciate every single one of you. Thank you for joining me on this wild ride.

ABOUT THE AUTHOR

Allie Doherty spends more time watching romantic comedies and reading than should be humanly possible and has a slow-building vinyl collection she hopes will be enviable one day. After trying her hand at many things, she found nothing more fulfilling than writing her first novel. When she's not writing, she is usually found drinking too much coffee, talking incessantly about *Buffy The Vampire Slayer* and *One Tree Hill*, or planning her next tattoo. Nothing is more important to her than friends and family, which includes Staffie pups, Monty and Mitzi. She is a sucker for romance in all of its forms, across all genres, age-groups, and tropes. Whether YA, NA, or Adult, she will devour anything so long as it has a swoon worthy couple to root for, and a happily ever after when all is said and done— even if it takes six books, a hundred-and-one break-ups, and a rollercoaster of emotions. Other than writing, she is a big fan of movies and TV shows. In the near future, she hopes to make a community of friends on YouTube and Patreon who love diving into all forms of media and obsessing over every little detail as much she does.

Lightning Source UK Ltd.
Milton Keynes UK
UKHW041343270123
416070UK00004B/295

9 798986 07480